#1 *New York Times* **Bestselling Author**

DEBBIE MACOMBER

ALMOST PARADISE

D0047018

**HARLEQUIN
BESTSELLING
AUTHOR
COLLECTION**

**HARLEQUIN®
BESTSELLING
AUTHOR
COLLECTION**

Recycling programs
for this product may
not exist in your area.

ISBN-13: 978-1-335-23084-3

Almost Paradise
First published in 1988. This edition published in 2021.
Copyright © 1988 by Debbie Macomber

The Soldier's Redemption
First published in 2018. This edition published in 2021.
Copyright © 2018 by Lee Tobin McClain

Second Chance on the Chesapeake
Copyright © 2021 by Lee Tobin McClain

This edition published by arrangement with Harlequin Books S.A.

For questions and comments about the quality of this book, please contact us at CustomerService@Harlequin.com.

Harlequin Enterprises ULC
22 Adelaide St. West, 40th Floor
Toronto, Ontario M5H 4E3, Canada
www.Harlequin.com

Printed in U.S.A.

**Praise for #1 *New York Times* bestselling author
Debbie Macomber**

"As always, Macomber draws rich, engaging
characters."

—*Publishers Weekly*

"I've never met a Macomber book I didn't love!"
—#1 *New York Times* bestselling author
Linda Lael Miller

"Debbie Macomber tells women's stories in a way
no one else does."

—*BookPage*

**Praise for *USA TODAY* bestselling author
Lee Tobin McClain**

"Lee Tobin McClain dazzles with unforgettable
characters, fabulous small-town settings and a big
dose of heart."
—#1 *New York Times* bestselling author Susan Mallery

"[An] enthralling tale of learning to trust…. This
enjoyable contemporary romance will appeal to
readers looking for twinges of suspense before
happily ever after."

—*Publishers Weekly* on *Low Country Hero*

Debbie Macomber is a #1 *New York Times* bestselling author and a leading voice in women's fiction worldwide. Her work has appeared on every major bestseller list, with more than 170 million copies in print, and she is a multiple award winner. Hallmark Channel based a television series on Debbie's popular Cedar Cove books. For more information, visit her website, www.debbiemacomber.com.

USA TODAY bestselling author **Lee Tobin McClain** read *Gone with the Wind* in the third grade and has been an incurable romantic ever since. When she's not writing angst-filled love stories with happy endings, she's probably Snapchatting with her college-student daughter, mediating battles between her goofy goldendoodle and her rescue cat, or teaching aspiring writers in Seton Hill University's MFA program. She is probably not cleaning her house. For more about Lee, visit her website at www.leetobinmcclain.com.

CONTENTS

Also by Debbie Macomber

MIRA

Blossom Street

The Shop on Blossom Street
A Good Yarn
Susannah's Garden
Back on Blossom Street
Twenty Wishes
Summer on Blossom Street
Hannah's List
"The Twenty-First Wish" (in *The Knitting Diaries*)
A Turn in the Road

Heart of Texas

Texas Skies (*Lonesome Cowboy* and *Texas Two-Step*)
Texas Nights (*Caroline's Child* and *Dr. Texas*)
Texas Home (*Nell's Cowboy* and *Lone Star Baby*)
Promise, Texas
Return to Promise

Visit her Author Profile page on Harlequin.com,
or debbiemacomber.com, for more titles!

ALMOST PARADISE

Debbie Macomber

Chapter 1

"Mirror, mirror on the wall—who's the fairest of us all?" Sherry White propped one eye open and gazed into the small bathroom mirror. She grimaced and quickly squeezed both eyes shut. "Not me," she answered and blindly reached for her toothbrush.

Morning had never been her favorite time of day. She agreed with the old adage claiming that if God had intended people to see the sun rise, He would have caused it to happen later in the day. Unfortunately, Jeff Roarke, the director of Camp Gitche Gumee, didn't agree. He demanded his staff meet early each morning. No excuses. No reprieves. No pardons.

Fine, Sherry mused. Then he'd have to take what he got, and heaven knew she wasn't her best at this ungodly hour.

After running a brush through her long, dark curls,

Sherry wrapped a scarf around her head to keep the hair away from her face and returned to her room where she reached for a sweater to ward off a chill. Then she hurried across the lush green grass of the campgrounds to the staff meeting room. Once there, a hasty glance around told her she was already late.

"Good morning, Miss White," Jeff Roarke called, when she took the last available seat.

"Morning," she mumbled under her breath, crossing her arms to disguise her embarrassment. He'd purposely called attention to her, letting the others know she was tardy.

His sober gaze had followed her as she'd maneuvered herself between the narrow row of chairs. Now his intense eyes remained on her until her heart hammered and indignation caused heat to color her cheeks. She experienced a perverse desire to shatter Jeff Roarke's pompous attitude, but the feeling died a quiet death as she raised her gaze to meet his. It almost seemed that she saw a hint of amusement lurking there. At any rate, he was regarding her with a speculative gleam that was distinctly unsettling. Evidently satisfied that he'd unnerved her, he began to speak again.

Although she knew she should be taking notes, Sherry was having trouble tearing her gaze away from the camp director, now that his attention was off her. Jeff Roarke was tall, easily over six feet, and superbly fit. His jaw was lean and well defined—okay, he was absurdly good-looking, she'd grant him that. But to Sherry's way of thinking he was arrogant, uncompromising and pompous. She'd known a month earlier when she'd met Mr. Almighty Roarke for the job interview that they weren't going to get along. She'd flown to Sacramento from Seattle for a meeting in his office, praying she hadn't made the long trip in vain. She'd wanted this job so badly…and then she'd blown it.

"I think it's a marvelous idea to name the camp after a cute children's song," she'd said cheerfully.

Roarke looked shocked. "Song? What song? The camp's name is taken from the poem 'Song of Hiawatha' by Henry Wadsworth Longfellow."

"Oh—uh, I mean, of course," Sherry said, her face flaming.

From there the interview seemed shaky, and Sherry was convinced she'd ruined her chances as Roarke continued to ask what seemed like a hundred unrelated questions. Although he didn't appear overly impressed with her qualifications, he handed her several forms to complete.

"You mean I'm hired?" she asked, confused. "I… I have the job?"

"I'd hardly have you fill out the paperwork if you weren't," he returned.

"Right." Sherry's heart had raced with excitement. She was going to escape her wacky stepmother, Phyliss. For one glorious summer no one need know where she was. But as Sherry began to complete the myriad forms her enthusiasm for her plan dwindled. She couldn't possibly put down references—anyone she'd list would be someone who'd have contact with her father and stepmother. The instant her family discovered where Sherry was hiding, it would be over.

Roarke seemed to note Sherry's hesitancy as she studied the forms. "Is there something you disagree with, Miss White?"

"No," she said, hurriedly filling out the names and

addresses of family friends and former employers, but doing her best to make them unreadable, running the letters together and transposing numbers.

Nibbling anxiously on her bottom lip, Sherry finished and handed over the completed paperwork.

From that first meeting with Jeff Roarke, things had gone swiftly downhill. Sherry found him...she searched for the right word. Dictatorial, she decided. He'd let it be known as director of Camp Gitche Gumee that he expected her to abide by all the rules and regulations—which was only fair—but then he'd proceeded to give her a Michener-length manual of rules and regulations, with the understanding that she would have it read by the time camp opened. Good grief! She'd been hired as a counselor for seven little girls, not as a brain surgeon.

"Are there any questions?"

Jeff Roarke's words to the early-morning assembly broke into her consciousness, startling Sherry into the present. Worried, she glanced around her, hoping no one had noticed that she'd casually slipped into her memories.

"Most of the children will arrive today," Roarke was saying.

He'd gotten her up at this time of day to tell her that? They'd have to be a bunch of numskulls not to know when the children were coming. The entire staff had been working all week to prepare the cottages and campgrounds for the children's arrival. Sherry glared at him for all she was worth, then squirmed when he paused and stared back at her.

"Is there a problem, Miss White?"

Sherry froze as the others directed their attention to her. "N-no."

"Good—then I'll continue."

The man never smiled, Sherry mused. Not once in the past week had she seen him joke or laugh or kid around. He was like a man driven, but for what cause she could only speculate. The camp was important to him, that much she'd gleaned immediately, but why a university professor would find such purpose in a children's camp was beyond Sherry's understanding. There seemed to be an underlying sadness in Jeff Roarke, too, one that robbed his life of joy, stole the pleasure of simple things from his perception.

But none of the counselors seemed to think of Jeff Roarke the same way she did. Oh, the other female staff members certainly noticed him, Sherry admitted grudgingly. From the goo-goo eyes some of the women counselors were giving him, they too were impressed with his dark good looks. But he was so stiff, so dry, so serious that Sherry considered him a lost cause. And she had enough on her mind without complicating her life worrying about someone like the camp director.

Sherry expected to have fun this summer. She needed it. The last year of graduate school, living near home, had left her mentally drained and physically exhausted. School was only partly to blame for her condition. Phyliss was responsible for the rest. Phyliss and her father had married when Sherry was a college freshman and Phyliss, bless her heart, had never had children. Seeing Sherry as her one and only opportunity to be a mother, she'd attacked the project with such gusto that Sherry was still reeling from the effects three years later. Phyliss worried that Sherry wasn't eating well enough. Phyliss worried about the hours she kept. Phyliss worried that she studied too hard. To state the problem simply—Phyliss worried.

As a dedicated health nut, her stepmother made certain that Sherry ate correctly. There were days Sherry would have killed for a pizza or a hot dog, but Phyliss wouldn't hear of it. Then there was the matter of clothes. Phyliss loved bright colors—and so did Sherry, in moderation. Unfortunately, her stepmother considered it her duty to shop with Sherry and "help" her choose the proper clothes for college. As a result, her closet was full of purples, army greens, sunshine yellows and hot, sizzling pinks.

So Sherry planned this summer as an escape from her wonderful but wacky stepmother. Sherry wasn't exactly proud of the way she'd slipped away in the middle of the night, but she'd thought it best to avoid the multitude of questions Phyliss would ply her with had she known Sherry was leaving. She'd managed to escape with a text sent from the airport that stated in vague terms that she was going to camp for the summer. She hated to be so underhanded, but knowing Phyliss, the woman would arrive with a new wardrobe of coordinated shades of chartreuse—and order Sherry's meals catered when she learned that her beloved stepdaughter was eating camp food.

Sherry had chosen Camp Gitche Gumee because it had intrigued her. Being counselor to a group of intellectually gifted children in the heart of the majestic California redwoods sounded like the perfect escape. And Phyliss would never think to search California.

"Within the next few hours, fifty children will be

arriving from all around the country," Roarke continued.

Sherry childishly rolled her eyes toward the ceiling. He could just as well have given them this information at seven—the birds weren't even awake yet! Expecting her to retain vital information at this unreasonable hour was going beyond the call of duty.

"Each cottage will house seven children; Fred Spencer's cabin will house eight. Counselors, see me following the meeting for the names of your charges. Wherever possible, I've attempted to match the child with a friend in an effort to cut down on homesickness."

That made sense to Sherry, but little else did.

As Roarke continued speaking, Sherry's thoughts drifted again. In addition to Jeff Roarke, their fearless leader, Sherry knew she was going to have problems getting along with Fred Spencer, who was counselor for the nine-and ten-year-old boys. Fred had been a counselor at Camp Gitche Gumee for several summers and was solidly set in the way he handled his charges.

Sherry had come up with some ideas she'd wanted to talk over in the first few days following her arrival. Since Fred was the counselor for the same age group as hers, it had seemed natural to go to him. But Fred had found a reason to reject every suggestion. Five minutes with him and Sherry discovered that he didn't possess a creative bone in his body and frowned dutifully upon anyone who deviated from the norm.

More than disagreeing with her, Sherry had gotten the distinct impression that Fred highly disapproved of her and her ideas. She wasn't sure what she'd done to invoke his ire, but his resentment was strong enough to cause her to feel uneasy whenever they were in the room together.

With a sigh, Sherry forced her attention back to Roarke. He continued speaking for several minutes, but most of what he had to say was directed to the housekeepers, cooks and groundskeepers. The classroom teachers had been briefed the day before.

A half hour later the staff was dismissed for breakfast—and not a minute too soon, Sherry mused as she walked toward the large dining hall. Blindly she headed for the coffeepot. If Jeff Roarke was going to call staff meetings when the moon was still out, the least he could do was provide coffee.

"Miss White," Roarke called, stopping her.

Sherry glanced longingly toward the coffeepot. "Yes?"

"Could I speak to you a minute?"

"Sure." She headed toward the back of the dining hall, where he was waiting for her.

Roarke watched the newest staff member of Camp Gitche Gumee make her way toward him, walking between the long tables, and he smiled inwardly. That Sherry White wasn't a morning person was obvious. During the staff meeting, her eyes had drooped half-closed and she'd stifled more than one yawn. For part of that time her features had been frozen into a far-away look, as though she were caught in some day-dream.

Thinking about her, Roarke felt his brow crease into a slight frown. He'd hired her on impulse, something he rarely acted upon. He'd liked her smile and her spirit and had gotten a chuckle out of her misunderstanding about the name of the camp. He found her appealing, yet she made him nervous, too, in a way he couldn't explain even to himself. All he knew was that she'd shown up for the interview, and before he'd realized what he was doing, he'd hired her. In analyzing his actions later, Roarke had been astonished. Liking the way she smiled and the way her eyes softened when she spoke of children were not good enough reasons to hire her as a counselor. Yet he felt he hadn't made a bad choice. In spite of her apparent dislike of his methods, Roarke felt she would do an excellent job with the children, and more than a good personality match with him, the youngsters were what was most important.

"Yes?" Sherry asked, joining him. Her gaze remained a little too obviously on the coffeepot on the other side of the room.

Opening his briefcase, Roarke withdrew a camp reference sheet and handed it to her. "I'm sorry to bother you, but your application form must have gotten smeared across the top—I wasn't able to read the names of your references."

Sherry swallowed uncomfortably. She should have known scribbled letters and numbers wouldn't work.

"Could you fill this out and have it back to me later this afternoon?"

"Sure—no problem," she said, her smile forced.

"Good," he said, puzzled by the frown that worried her brow. "I'll see you later, then."

"Later," she agreed distractedly. Her gaze fell to the form. If worst came to worst she could always give him false telephone numbers and phony addresses. But that could lead to future problems. Of course if she didn't, it could lead to problems right now!

Depressed, Sherry folded the form, then made a beeline for the coffee. Claiming her seat, she propped her elbows on the table and held the thick ceramic mug with both hands, letting the aroma stir her senses to life. She might not function well in the mornings, but she'd manage for this one summer. She'd have to if Roarke intended to keep holding these merciless 5:00 a.m. staff meetings.

"Morning," Lynn Duffy called out as she approached. Lynn, who had been assigned as housekeeper to Sherry's cabin, claimed the chair next to Sherry's. She set her tray on the table and unloaded her plate, which was heaped with scrambled eggs, bacon and toast. "Aren't you eating?"

Sherry shook her head. "Not this morning."

"Hey, this camp has a reputation for wonderful food."

"I'm not hungry. Thanks anyway." Sherry rested her chin in her hands, worrying about the references and what she could put down that would satisfy Jeff Roarke. "I wonder what kind of stupid rule he's going to come up with next," she muttered, setting the paper beside her mug.

"Jeff Roarke?"

"Yes, Roarke." Somehow Sherry couldn't think of the camp director as "Jeff." She associated that name with someone who was kind and considerate, like Lassie's owner or an affectionate uncle.

"You have to admit he's got a grip on matters."

"Sure," Sherry admitted reluctantly. Roarke ran this camp with the efficiency of a Marine boot camp. "But I have yet to see a hint of originality. For instance, I can't imagine children's cottages named Cabin One, Cabin Two and so on."

"It's less confusing that way."

"These kids are supposed to be geniuses, I strongly suspect they could keep track of a real name as easily as a boring, unadorned number."

"Maybe so," Lynn said and shook her head. "No one's ever said anything before."

"But surely the other counselors have offered suggestions."

"Not that I've heard."

Sherry raised her eyebrows. "I'd have thought the staff would want something more creative than numbers for their cabins."

"I'm sure Mr. Roarke thought the kids would be more comfortable with numbers. Several of the children are said to be mathematical wizards."

"I suppose," Sherry agreed. Roarke was totally committed to the children and the camp—Sherry didn't question that—but to her way of thinking his intentions were misdirected. Every part of camp life was geared toward academia, with little emphasis, from what she could see, on fun and games.

Lynn's deep blue eyes took on a dreamy look. She shook her head. "I think the whole idea of a special camp like this is such a good one. From what I understand, Mr. Roarke is solely responsible for organizing it. He worked years setting up these summer sessions. For the past four summers, he hasn't taken a penny for his efforts. He does it for the kids."

The news surprised Sherry, and she found herself revising her opinion of the camp director once again. The man intrigued her, she had to admit. He angered and confused her, but he fascinated her, too. Sherry didn't know what to think anymore. If only he weren't such a stick-in-the-mud. She remembered that Lynn was one of those who had been making sheep's eyes at Roarke earlier. "I have the feeling you think Jeff Roarke is wonderful," she suggested.

Lynn nodded and released a heavy sigh. "Does it show that much?"

"Not really."

"He's so handsome," Lynn continued. "Surely you've noticed?"

Sherry took another sip of her coffee to delay answering. "I suppose."

"And so successful. Rumors flew around here last summer when Mr. Roarke became the head of the economics department for Cal Tech."

Again Sherry paid close attention to her coffee. "I'm impressed."

"From what I understand he's written a book."

A smile touched the corners of Sherry's mouth. She could well imagine what dry reading anything Roarke had written would be.

"Apparently his book caused quite a stir in Washington. The director of the Federal Reserve recommended it to the President."

"Wow!" Now Sherry really was impressed.

"And he's handsome to boot."

"That much is fairly obvious," Sherry allowed. All right, Jeff Roarke was lean and muscular with eyes that could make a woman go all soft inside, but she wasn't the only one to have noticed that, and she certainly wasn't interested in becoming a groupie.

"He really gets to me," Lynn said with a sigh.

"He does have nice eyes," Sherry admitted reluctantly.

Lynn nodded and continued. "They're so unusual. Yesterday when we were talking I would have sworn they were green, but when I first met him they were an incredible hazel color."

"I guess I hadn't noticed," Sherry commented. Okay, so she lied!

Carefully Lynn set her fork beside her plate, her look thoughtful. "You don't like him much, do you?"

"Oh, I like him—it's just that I figured a camp for children would be fun. This place is going to be about as lively as a prison. There are classes scheduled day and night. From the look of things, all the kids are going to do is study. There isn't any time left for fun."

Evidently Lynn found her observations humorous. A smile created twin dimples in her smooth cheeks. "Just wait until the kids get here. Then you'll be grateful for Mr. Roarke's high sense of order."

Maybe so, Sherry thought, but that remained to be seen. "You worked here last summer?"

Lynn nodded as she swallowed a mouthful of eggs. "I was a housekeeper then, too. Several of us are back for a second go-round, but Mr. Roarke's the real reason I came back." She hesitated. "How old do you think he is?"

"Roarke? I don't know. Close to thirty-five or -six, I'd guess."

"Oh dear, that's probably much too old for someone nineteen."

Lynn's look of abject misery caused Sherry to laugh outright. "I've heard of greater age differences."

"How old are you?"

"Twenty-three," Sherry answered.

Lynn wrinkled her nose, as though she envied Sherry those years. "Don't get me wrong. There's no chance of a romance developing between Mr. Roarke and me, or me and anyone else for that matter—at least not until camp is dismissed."

"Why not?"

"Mr. Roarke is death on camp romances," Lynn explained. "Last year two of the counselors fell in love, and when Mr. Roarke found them kissing he threatened to dismiss them both." Lynn sighed expressively and a dreamy look came over her. "You know what I think?"

Sherry could only speculate. "What?"

"I think Mr. Roarke's been burned. His tender heart was shattered by a careless affair that left him bleeding and raw. And now—years later—he's afraid to love again, afraid to offer his heart to another woman." Dramatically, Lynn placed her hand over her own heart as though to protect it from the fate of love turned sour. She gazed somberly into the distance.

The strains of a love ballad hummed softly in the distance, and it was all Sherry could do to swallow down a laugh. "You know this for a fact?"

"Heavens, no. That's just what I think must have happened to him. It makes sense, doesn't it?"

"Ah—I'm not sure." Sherry hedged.

"Mr. Roarke is really against camp romances. You should have been here last year. I don't think I've ever seen him more upset. He claimed romance and camp just don't mix."

"He's right about that." To find herself agreeing with Roarke was a surprise, but Sherry could see the pitfalls of a group of counselors more interested in one another than in their charges.

Lynn shrugged again. "I don't think there's anything wrong with a light flirtation, but Mr. Roarke has other ideas. There are even rules and regulations on how male and female counselors should behave in each other's company. But I suppose you've already read that."

When Sherry didn't respond, Lynn eyed her speculatively. "You did read the manual, didn't you?"

Sherry dropped her gaze to the tabletop. "Sort of."

"You'd better, because if he catches you going against the rules, your neck will be on the chopping block."

A lump developed in Sherry's throat as she remembered the problem with her references. She'd need to keep a low profile. And from the sound of things, she had best be a good little counselor and keep her opinions to herself. What Lynn had said about studying the manual made sense. Sherry vowed inwardly to read it all the way through and do her utmost to follow the rules, no matter what she thought.

"You'll do fine," Lynn said confidently. "And the kids are going to really like you."

"I hope so." Unexpected doubts were jumping up and down inside Sherry like youngsters on pogo sticks. She had thought she'd be a natural for this position. Her major was education, and with her flair for originality, she hoped to be a good teacher.

The kids she'd come here to counsel weren't everyday run-of-the-mill nine-and ten-year-olds, they were bona fide geniuses. Each child had an IQ in the ninety-eight percentile. She lifted her chin in sudden determination. She'd always appreciated a challenge. She'd been looking forward to this summer, and she wasn't about to let Jeff Roarke and his rules and regulations ruin it for her.

"The only time you need to worry is if Mr. Roarke calls you to his office after breakfast," Lynn said, interrupting Sherry's thoughts.

Sherry digested this information. "Why then?"

Lynn paused long enough to peel back the aluminum tab on a small container of strawberry jam. "The only time anyone is ever fired is in the morning. The couple I mentioned earlier, who fell in love last summer—their names were Sue and Mark—they talked to Mr. Roarke on three separate occasions. Each time in the afternoon. Every time Sue heard her name read from the daily bulletin she became a nervous wreck until she heard the time of the scheduled meeting. Mark didn't fare much better. They both expected to get the ax at any minute."

"Roarke didn't fire them?"

"No, but he threatened to. They weren't even allowed to hold hands."

"I bet they were miserable." Sherry could sympathize with both sides. She was young enough to appreciate the temptations of wanting to be with a boy at camp but old enough to recognize the pitfalls of such a romance.

"But worse than a camp romance, Mr. Roarke is a stickler for honesty. He won't tolerate anyone who so much as stretches the truth."

"Really?" Sherry murmured. Suddenly swallowing became difficult.

"Last year a guy came to camp who fibbed about

his age. He was one of three Mr. Roarke fired. It's true Danny had lied, but only by a few months. He was out of here so fast it made my head spin. Of course, he got called in to Roarke's office in the morning," she added.

"My goodness." Sherry's mouth had gone dry. If Roarke decided to check her references her days at Camp Gitche Gumee were surely numbered.

"Well, I'd best go plug in my vacuum."

"Yeah—" Sherry raised her hand "—I'll talk to you later."

The other girl stood and scooted her chair back into position. "Good luck."

Sherry watched the lanky teenager leave the mess hall, and for the first time she considered that maybe escaping Phyliss at summer camp hadn't been such a brilliant idea after all.

Chapter 2

Three hours later the first bus load of children pulled into Camp Gitche Gumee. The bus was from nearby Sacramento and the surrounding area, but Roarke had announced at their morning get-together that there were children traveling fromas far away as Maine and Vermont. The sum these parents paid for two months of camp had shocked Sherry, but who was she to quibble? She had a summer job, and in spite of her misgivings about the camp director, she was pleased to be here.

Standing inside her cabin, Sherry breathed in the clean scent of the forest and waited anxiously for her charges to be escorted to her cabin. When she chanced a peek out the door, she noted Peter Towne, the camp lifeguard, leading a forlorn-looking girl with long, dark braids toward her.

Sherry stepped onto the porch to meet the pair. She

tried to get the girl to meet her gaze so she could smile at her, but the youngster seemed determined to study the grass.

"Miss White, this is Pamela Reynolds."

"Hello, Pamela."

"Hi."

Peter handed Sherry Pamela's suitcase.

Thanking him with a smile, Sherry placed her free hand on the shy girl's shoulder and led her into the cabin.

The youngster's eyes narrowed suspiciously as she sat on the nearest bunk. "You're not scared of animals, are you?"

"Nope." That wasn't entirely true, but Sherry didn't consider it a good idea to let any of her charges know she wasn't especially fond of snakes. Not when the woods were ripe for the picking.

"Good."

"Good?" Sherry repeated suspiciously.

With a nervous movement, Pamela nodded, placed her suitcase on the thin mattress and opened it. From inside, she lifted a shoe box with holes punched in the top. "I brought along my hamster. I can keep him, can't I?" Blue eyes pleaded with her.

Sherry didn't know what to say. According to the camp manual, pets weren't allowed. But a hamster wasn't like a dog or a cat or a horse, for heaven's sake. Sherry hedged. "What's his name?"

"Ralph."

"That's a nice name." Her brain was frantically working.

"He won't make any noise and he barely eats anything and I couldn't leave him at home because my parents are going to Europe and I know we aren't supposed to bring along animals, but Ralph is the very best friend I have and I'd miss him too much if he had to stay with Mrs. Murphy like my little brother."

Appealing tears glistened in the little girl's eyes and Sherry felt herself weaken. It shouldn't be that difficult to keep one tiny hamster from Roarke's attention.

"But will Ralph be happy living in a cabin full of girls?"

"Oh, sure," Pam said, the words rushing out, "he likes girls, and he's really a wonderful hamster. Do you want to hold him?"

"No thanks," Sherry answered brightly. The manual might have a full page dedicated to pets, but it didn't say anything about adopting a mascot. "If the others agree, I feel we can keep Ralph as our mascot as long as we don't let any of the other cabins find out about him." Sherry cringed inwardly at the thought of Jeff Roarke's reaction to her decision. The thought of his finding a pet, even something as unobtrusive as a hamster, wasn't a pleasant one, but from the looks of it the little girl was strongly attached to the rodent. Housing Ralph seemed such a little thing to keep a child happy. Surely what Ironjaw didn't know wouldn't hurt him…

Three ten-year-olds, Sally, Wendy and Diane, were escorted to the cabin when the next busload arrived. Although they were different in looks and size, the three shared a serious, somber nature. Sherry had expected rambunctious children. Instead, she had been assigned miniature adults.

Sally had brought along her microscope and several specimens she planned to examine before dinner. Sherry didn't ask to see them, but from the contents of

the jars that lined Sally's headboard, she didn't want
to know what the child planned to study. Sherry's social circle didn't include many nine- and ten-year-olds,
but she wasn't acquainted with a single child who kept
pig embryos in jars of formaldehyde as companions.

Wendy, at least, appeared to be a halfway normal
preteen. She collected dolls and had brought along an
assortment of her prize Barbies and Kens, including
designer outfits for each. She arranged them across
the head of her bed and introduced Sherry to Barbie-
Samantha, Barbie-Jana and Barbie-Brenda. The Kens
were also distinguished with their own names, and
by the time Wendy had finished, Sherry's head was
swimming.

Sherry didn't know what to make of Diane. The ten-
year-old barely said a word. She chose her bunk, unpacked and then immediately started to read. Sherry
noted that Diane's suitcases contained a bare minimum
of clothes and were filled to capacity with books. Scanning the academic titles caused Sherry to grimace; she
didn't see a single Nancy Drew.

Twins Jan and Jill were the next to make their entrance. They were blond replicas of each other and
impossible to tell apart until they smiled. Jan was lacking both upper front teeth. Jill was lacking only one.
Sherry felt a little smug until she discovered Jill wig-
gling her lone front tooth back and forth in an effort
to extract it. Before the day was over, Sherry realized,
she would be at their mercy. Fine, she decided, the
two knew who they were—she'd let them sort it out.

The last child assigned to Cabin Four was Gretchen.
Sherry recognized the minute the ten-year-old showed
up that this child was trouble.

"This camp gets dumpier every summer," Gretchen grumbled, folding her arms around her middle as she surveyed the cabin. She paused and glanced at the last remaining cot. "I refuse to sleep near the window. I'll get a nosebleed and a headache if I'm near a breeze."

"Okay," Sherry said. "Is there anyone here who would like to trade with Gretchen?"

Pam suddenly found it necessary to feed Ralph.

Sally brought out her microscope.

Wendy twisted Barbie-Brenda into Ken-Brian's arms and placed them in a position Sherry preferred not to question. Soon, no fewer than three Barbies and an equal number of Kens were in a tangled mess of arms and legs.

Jan and Jill sat on the end of their bunks staring blindly into space while Jill worked furiously on extracting her front tooth.

Diane kept a book of mathematical brainteasers propped open in front of her face and didn't give any indication that she'd heard the request.

"It doesn't look like anyone wants to trade," Sherry told the youngster, whose mouth was twisted with a sour look. "Since you've been to camp before, you knew that the first to arrive claim the beds they want. I saw you lingering outside earlier this afternoon. You should have checked in here first."

"I refuse to sleep near the window," Gretchen announced for the second time.

"In that case, I'll place the mattress on the floor in my room and you can bunk there, although I feel you should know, I sometimes sleep with my window open."

"I sincerely hope you're teasing," Gretchen returned, eyes wide and incredulous. "There are things crawling around down there." She studiously pointed to the wood floor.

"Where?" Sally cried, immediately interested. Her hand curled around the base of her microscope.

"I believe she was speaking hypothetically," Sherry mumbled.

"Oh."

"All right, I'll sleep by the window and ignore the medical risk," Gretchen muttered. She carelessly tossed her suitcase on top of the mattress. "But I'm writing my mother and telling her about this. She's paying good money for me to attend this camp and she expects me to receive the very best of care. There's no excuse for me to be mistreated in this manner."

"Let's see how it goes, shall we?" Sherry suggested, biting her tongue. This kid was a medical risk all right, but the only thing in danger was Sherry's mental health. Already she could feel a pounding headache coming on. By sheer force of will, she managed to keep her fingers from massaging her temples. First Roarke and now Gretchen. No doubt they were related.

"My uncle is a congressman," Gretchen said, to no one in particular. "I may write him instead."

The entire cabin pretended not to hear, which only seemed to infuriate Gretchen. She paused smugly. "Is Mr. Roarke the camp director again this year?"

"Yes," Sherry answered cheerfully. She knew it! Roarke was most likely another of this pest's uncles. "Would you like me to make an appointment for you to speak to him?"

"Yes. I'll let him handle this unfortunate situation." Gretchen removed her suitcase from the bunk and gingerly set it aside, seemingly assured that the camp director would assign her a cot anywhere she wanted.

"I'll see if I can arrange it when you're in the computer class," Sherry said.

By afternoon Camp Gitche Gumee was in full swing. Cabins were filled to capacity and the clamor of children sounded throughout the compound.

After the girls had unpacked and stored their luggage, Sherry led them into the dining hall. Counselors were expected to eat their meals with their charges, but after lunch Sherry's time was basically free. On occasion she would be given the opportunity to schedule outdoor activities such as canoeing and hiking expeditions, but those were left for her to organize. Most of the camp was centered around challenging academic pursuits. Sessions were offered in biochemistry, computer skills and propositional calculus. Sherry wondered what ever happened to stringing beads and basket weaving!

When the girls were dismissed for their afternoon activities, Sherry made her way to the director's office, which was on the other side of the campgrounds, far from the madding crowd, she noted. It was all too apparent that Roarke liked his privacy.

Tall redwoods outlined the camp outskirts. Wildflowers grew in abundance. Goldthreads, red baneberry and the northern inside-out flower were just a few that Sherry recognized readily. She had a passion for wildflowers and could name those most common to the West Coast. Some flowers were unknown to her, but she had a sneaky suspicion that if she picked a few, either Sally or Diane would be able to tell her the species and Latin title.

When she could delay the inevitable no longer, Sherry approached Roarke's office. She knocked politely twice and waited.

"Come in," came the gruff voice.

Squaring her shoulders, preparing to face the lion in his den, Sherry entered the office. As she expected, his room was meticulously neat. Bookshelves lined the walls, and where there weren't books the space was covered with certificates. His desk was an oversize mahogany one that rested in the center of the large room. The leather high-backed chair was one Sherry would have expected to find a bank president using—not a camp director.

"Miss White."

"Mr. Roarke."

They greeted each other stiffly.

"Sit down." He motioned toward the two low-backed upholstered chairs.

Sherry sat and briefly studied the man behind the desk. He looked to be a young thirty-five although there were lines faintly etched around his eyes and on both sides of his mouth. But instead of detracting from his good looks, the lines added another dimension to his appeal. Lynn's words about Roarke suffering from a lost love played back in Sherry's mind. Like her friend she sensed an underlying sadness in him, but nothing that could readily be seen in the square, determined lines of his jaw. And again it was his piercing gaze that captured her.

"You brought back the reference sheet?" Roarke prompted.

"Yes." Sherry sat at the edge of her seat as though she expected to blurt out what she had to say and make a mad dash for the door. She'd reprinted the names and addresses more clearly this time, transposing the numbers and hoping that it would look unintentional when the responses were delayed.

"I have it with me," she answered, and set the form on his desk. "But there's something else I'd like to discuss. I've been assigned Gretchen Hamburg."

"Ah, yes, Gretchen."

Apparently the girl was known to him. "I'm afraid I'm having a small problem with her," Sherry said, carefully choosing her words. "It seems Gretchen prefers to sleep away from the window, but she dawdled around outside while the others chose bunks, and now she's complaining. She's asked that I make an appointment for her to plead her case with you. She...insinuated that you'd correct this unfortunate situation."

"I'm—"

Sherry didn't allow him to finish. "It's my opinion that giving in to Gretchen's demands would set a precedent that would cause problems among the other girls later."

His wide brow furrowed. "I can understand your concerns."

Sherry relaxed, scooting back in her chair.

"However, Gretchen's family is an influential one."

Sherry bolted forward. "That's favoritism."

"Won't any of the other girls trade with her?"

"I've already suggested that. But the others shouldn't be forced into giving up their beds simply because Gretchen Hamburg—"

"Have you sought a compromise?" he interrupted.

Sherry's hands were clenched in such tight fists that her punch would have challenged Muhammad

Ali's powerful right hand. "I suggested that we place the mattress on the floor in my room, but I did mention that I sometimes sleep with my window open."

"And?"

"And Gretchen insisted on speaking to you personally."

Roarke drummed his fingers on the desktop. "If you haven't already noticed, Gretchen is a complainer."

"No!" Sherry feigned wide-eyed shock.

Roarke studied the fiery flash in Sherry's dark brown eyes and again experienced an unfamiliar tug on his emotions. She made him want to laugh at the most inappropriate times. And when he wasn't amused by her, she infuriated him. There didn't seem to be any in-between in the emotions he felt. Sherry White could be a problem, Roarke mused, although he was convinced she'd be a terrific counselor. The trouble was within himself. He was attracted to her—strongly attracted. He would have been better off not to have hired her than to wage battle with his emotions all summer. He'd need to keep a cool head with her— keep his distance, avoid her whenever possible, bury whatever it was in her that he found appealing.

Sherry was convinced she saw a brief smile touch Roarke's mouth, so faint that it was gone before it completely registered with her. If only he'd really smile or joke or kid, she would find it infinitely more pleasant to meet with him. A lock of hair fell across his brow and he brushed it back only to have it immediately return to its former position. Sherry found her gaze mesmerized by that single lock. Except for those few strands of cocky hair Roarke was impeccable in every way. She sincerely doubted that as a child his jeans had ever been torn or grass stained.

"Well?" Sherry prompted. "Should I send Gretchen in to see you?"

"No."

"No?"

"That's what I said, Miss White. I can't be bothered with these minor details. Handle the situation as you see fit."

Using the arms of the chair for leverage, Sherry rose. She was pleased because she didn't want Ms. Miserable to use Roarke to manipulate her and the other girls in the cabin. Sherry was halfway out the door when Roarke spoke next.

"However, if this matter isn't settled promptly, I'll be forced to handle the situation myself. Dorothy Hamburg has been a faithful supporter of this camp for several years."

Well, she might as well jerk Pamela and Ralph from the center cot, Sherry thought irritably. One way or another Gretchen was bound to have her own way.

Chapter 3

Dressed in their pajamas, the seven preteens sat cross-legged on their cots, listening wide-eyed and intent as Sherry read.

"And they lived happily ever after," Sherry murmured, slowly closing the large book.

"You don't really believe that garbage, do you?" Gretchen demanded.

Sherry smiled softly. Gretchen found fault with everything, she'd discovered over the course of the first week of camp. Even when the girl enjoyed something, it was her nature to complain, quibble and frown. During the fairy tale, Gretchen had been the one most enraptured, yet she seemed to feel it was her duty to nitpick.

"How do you mean?" Sherry asked, deciding to play innocent. The proud tilt of Gretchen's chin tore at her heart.

"It's only a stupid fairy tale."

"But it was so lovely," Wendy chimed in softly.

"And the Prince…"

"…was so handsome," Jan and Jill added in unison.

"But none of it is true." Gretchen crossed her arms and pressed her lips tightly together. "My mother claims that she's suffering from the Cinderella syndrome, and here you are telling us the same goofy story and expecting us to believe it."

"Oh no," Sherry whispered, bending forward as though to share a special secret. "Fairy tales don't have to be true; but it's romantic to pretend. That's what makes them so special."

"But fairy tales couldn't possibly be real."

"All fiction is make-believe," Sherry softly assured her chronic complainer.

"I don't care if it's true or not, I like it when you read us stories," Diane volunteered. The child had set aside Proust in favor of listening to the bedtime story. Sherry felt a sense of pride that she'd been able to interest Diane in something beyond the heavy reading material she devoured at all hours of the night and day.

"Tell us another one," Wendy begged. Her Barbie and Ken dolls sat in a circle in front of her, their arms twisting around one another.

Sherry closed the book. "I will tomorrow night."

"Another fairy tale, okay?" Pamela insisted. "Even though he's a boy, Ralph liked it." She petted the hamster and reverently kissed him good-night before placing him back inside his shoe-box home.

Sherry had serious doubts about Ralph's environment, but Pamela had repeatedly assured her that the box was the only home Ralph had ever known and that he'd never run away. All the time the child spent grooming and training him lent Sherry confidence. But then, she hadn't known that many trick hamsters in her time.

"Will you read *Snow White and the Seven Dwarfs* next?" Sally wanted to know. She climbed into her cot and tucked the microscope underneath her pillow.

"Snow White it is."

"You're sort of like Snow White, aren't you?" Diane asked. "I mean, your name is White and you live in a cottage in the forest with seven dwarfs."

"Yeah!" Jan and Jill chimed together.

"I, for one, resent being referred to as a dwarf," Gretchen muttered.

"Wizards then," Wendy offered. "We're all smart."

"Snow White and the Seven Wizards," Sally commented, obviously pleased with herself. "Hey, we all live in Snow White's cottage."

"Right!" Jan and Jill said, with identical nods.

"But who's Prince Charming?"

"I don't think that this particular Snow White has a Prince Charming," Sherry said, feigning a sad sigh. "But—" she pointed her index finger toward the ceiling "—some day my prince will come."

"Mr. Roarke," Gretchen piped in excitedly. "He's the handsomest, noblest, nicest man I know. He'll be your prince."

Sherry nearly swallowed her tongue in her rush to disagree. Jeff Roarke! Impossible! He was more like the evil huntsman intent on doing away with the unsuspecting Snow White. If he ever checked her references, doing away with her would be exactly what happened! In the past week, Sherry had done her utmost to be the

most accommodating counselor at camp. She hadn't
given Roarke a single reason to notice or disapprove
of her. Other than an occasional gruff hello, she'd been
able to avoid speaking to him.

"Lights out everyone," Sherry said, determined to
kill the conversation before it got out of hand. The
less said about Roarke as Prince Charming, the better.

The girls were much too young to understand that to
be called princely a man must possess certain character traits. Sherry hesitated and drew in a shaky breath.
All right, she'd admit it—Jeff Roarke's character was
sterling. He was dedicated, hardworking and seemed
to genuinely love the children. And then there were
those incredible eyes of his. Sherry sharply shook herself back into reality. A single week with her charges
and already she was going bongos. Roarke was much
too dictatorial and inflexible to be a prince. At least
to be *her* Prince Charming.

With a flip of the switch the room went dark. The
only illumination was a shallow path of golden moonlight across the polished wood of the cabin floor.

Sherry moved into her own room and left the door
ajar in order to hear her seven wizards in case of bad
dreams or nighttime troubles. The girls never ceased
to surprise her. It was as though they didn't realize
they were children. When Sherry suggested reading
a fairy tale, they'd moaned and claimed that was *kids'*
stuff! Sherry had persisted, and now she was exceptionally pleased that she had. They'd loved *Cinderella*
and eaten up *Little Red Riding Hood*. Diane, the reader,
who had teethed on Ibsen, Maupassant and Emerson,
wasn't sure who the Brothers Grimm were. But she

sat night after night, her hands cupping her face as she listened to a different type of classic—and loved it.

Sally, at ten, knew more about biochemistry than Sherry ever hoped to understand in her lifetime. Yet Sally couldn't name a single record in the top ten and hadn't thought to bring a radio to camp. Her microscope was far more important!

These little geniuses were still children, and if no one else was going to remind them of that fact, Sherry was! If she could, she would have liked to remind Jeff Roarke of that. He had to realize there was more to life than academia; yet the entire camp seemed centered around challenging the mind and in her humble opinion, leaving the heart empty.

Sitting on the edge of her cot, Sherry's gaze fell on the seven girls in the room outside her own. She had been given charge of these little ones for the next two months, and by golly she was going to teach these children to have fun if it killed her!

"Ralph!"

The shrill cry pierced Sherry's peaceful slumber. She managed to open one eye and peek toward the clock radio. Four-thirteen. She had a full seventeen minutes before her alarm was set to ring.

"Miss White," Pamela cried, frantically stumbling into Sherry's room. "Ralph is gone!"

"What!" Holding a sheet to her breast, Sherry jerked upright, eyes wide. "Gone? What do you mean gone?"

"He's run away," the little girl sobbed. "I woke up and found the lid from the shoe box off-kilter, and when I looked he was…m-missing." She burst into tears and threw her arms around Sherry's neck, weeping pathetically.

"He didn't run away," Sherry said, thinking fast as she hugged the thin child.

"He didn't?" Pamela raised her tear-streaked face and battled down a fresh wave of emotion. "Then where is he?"

"He's exploring. Remember what I said about Ralph getting tired of his shoe-box home? He just went on an adventure into the woods to find some friends."

Pamela nodded, her dark braids bouncing.

"I suppose he woke up in the middle of the night and decided that he'd like to see who else was living around the cabin." The thought was a chilling one to Sherry. She squelched it quickly.

"But where is he?"

"I... I'm not exactly sure. He may need some guidance finding his way home."

"Then we should help him."

"Right." Stretching across the bed, Sherry turned on the bedside lamp. "Ralph," she called softly. "Allie, allie oxen free." It wouldn't be that easy, but it was worth a shot.

"There he is," Sally cried, sitting up in her cot. She pointed to the dresser on the far side of the outer room. "He ran under there."

"Get him," Pamela screamed and raced out of Sherry's quarters.

Soon all seven girls were crawling around the floor in their long flannel nightgowns looking for Ralph. He was still at large when Sherry's alarm clock buzzed.

"Damn," she muttered under her breath. She looked up to find seven pairs of eyes accusing her. "I mean darn," she muttered back. The search party returned to their rescue mission.

"I've got to get to the staff meeting," Sherry announced dejectedly five minutes later when Ginny, the high-school girl who was working in hopes of being hired as a counselor next summer, arrived to replace her. "Listen, don't say a word to anyone about Ralph. I'll be back as quickly as I can."

"Okay," Jan and Jill answered for the group.

Because she knew what Roarke would say once she asked him about the hamster, Sherry had yet to mention Ralph's presence in their happy little cabin. To be honest, she hadn't figured on doing so. However, having the entire cabin turned upside down in an effort to locate the Dr. Livingstone of the animal kingdom was another matter.

Dressing as quickly as possible, Sherry hopped around on one foot in an effort to tie her shoelace, then switched legs and continued hopping across her pine floor.

"That's working," Diane cried, glancing in Sherry's direction. "Keep doing it."

"I see him. I see him. Ralph, come home. Ralph, come home," Pamela begged, charging in the flannel nightgown over the cold floor.

A minute later, Sherry was out the door, leaving her charges to the mercy of one fickle-hearted hamster. By the time she reached the staff meeting she was panting and breathless. Roarke had already opened the meeting, and when Sherry entered, he paused and waited for her to take a seat.

"I'm pleased you saw fit to join us, Miss White," Roarke commented coolly.

"Sorry. I overslept," she mumbled as she claimed the last available chair in the front row. Rich color blossomed in her already flushed cheeks, reminding her once again why she'd come to dislike Jeff Roarke. The man went out of his way to cause her embarrassment—he actually seemed to thrive on it.

Roarke read the list of activities for the day, listing possible educational ventures for each cabin's nightly get-togethers. Then, by turn, he had the counselors tell the others how they'd chosen to close another camping day.

"We discussed how to split an atom," the first counselor, a college freshman, told the group.

This appeared to please Roarke. "Excellent," he said, nodding his head approvingly.

"We dissected a frog," the second counselor added.

As each spoke, Sherry grew more uncomfortable. The neckline of her thin sweater felt exceptionally tight, and when it was her turn, her voice came out sounding thin and low. "I read them the Cinderella story," she said.

"Excuse me." Roarke took a step closer. "Would you kindly repeat that?"

"Yes, of course." Sherry paused and cleared her throat. "I read my girls 'Cinderella.'"

A needle dropping against the floor would have sounded like a sonic boom in the thick silence that followed.

"'Cinderella,'" Roarke repeated, as though he was convinced he hadn't heard her correctly.

"That's right."

"Perhaps she could explain why anyone would

choose to read a useless fairy tale over a worthwhile learning experience?"

The voice behind Sherry was familiar. She turned to find Fred Spencer glaring at her with undisguised disapproval. Since their first disagreement over Sherry's ideas, they hadn't exchanged more than a few words.

Sherry turned her head around and tucked her hands under her thighs, shifting her weight back and forth over her knuckles. "I consider fairy tales a valuable learning tool."

"You do?" This time it was Roarke who questioned her.

From the way he was looking at her, Sherry could tell that he was having a difficult time accepting her reasoning.

"And what particular lesson did you hope to convey in the reading of this tale?"

"Hope."

"Hope?"

The other counselors were all still staring at her as though she was an apple in a barrel full of oranges. "You see, sometimes life can seem so bleak that we don't see all the good things around us. In addition, the story is a romantic, fun one."

Roarke couldn't believe what he was hearing. Sherry was making a mockery of the goals he'd set for this year's camp session. Romance! She wanted to teach her girls about some fickle female notion. The word alone was enough to make his blood run cold.

"Unfortunately, I disagree," Roarke said. "In the rational world there's no need for romantic nonsense." Although he tried to avoid looking at Sherry, his gaze refused to leave her. She looked flustered and embarrassed, and a fetching shade of pink had invaded her cheeks. Her gaze darted nervously to those around her, as if hoping to find someone who would agree with her. None would, Roarke could have told her that. His gaze fell to her lips, which were slightly moist and parted. Roarke's stomach muscles tightened and he hurriedly looked away. Love clouded the brain, he reminded himself sternly. The important things in life were found in education. Learning was the challenge. He should know. By age twelve, he'd been a college student, graduating with full honors three years later. There'd been no time or need for trivial romance.

Sherry had seen Roarke's lips compress at the mention of romance, as though he associated the word with sucking lemons. "People need love in their lives," Sherry asserted boldly, although she was shaking on the inside.

"I see," he said, when it was obvious that he didn't.

The meeting continued then, and the staff was dismissed fifteen minutes later. Sherry was the first one to vacate her chair, popping up like hot bread out of a toaster the second the meeting was adjourned. She had to get back to the cabin to see if Ralph had been caught and peace had once again been restored to the seven wizards' cabin.

"Miss White." Roarke stopped her.

"Yes." Sherry's heart bounded to her throat. She'd hoped to make a clean getaway.

"Would it be possible for you to drop by my office later this afternoon?" The references—she knew it; he'd discovered they'd been falsified.

Their eyes met. Sherry's own befuddled brown clashed with Roarke's tawny-hazel. His open challenge stared down her hint of defiance, and Sherry dropped her gaze first. "This afternoon? S-sure," she answered finally, with false cheerfulness. At least he'd said afternoon rather than morning, so if Lynn was right she didn't need to start packing her bags yet. She released a grateful sigh and smiled. "I'll be there directly after lunch."

"Good."

He turned and Sherry charged from the meeting room and sprinted across the grounds with the skill of an Olympic runner. Oh heavens, she prayed Ralph had returned to his home. Life wouldn't be so cruel as to break Pamela's heart—or would it?

Back at the cabin, Sherry discovered Pamela sitting on her bunk, crying softly.

"No Ralph?"

All seven children shook their heads simultaneously.

Sherry's heart constricted. "Please don't worry."

"I want Ralph," Pamela chanted, holding the pillow to her stomach and rocking back and forth. "Ralph's the only friend I ever had."

Sherry glanced around, hoping for a miracle. Where was Sherlock Holmes when she really needed him?

"He popped his head up between the floorboards a while ago," Sally explained, doubling over to peek underneath her bunk on the off chance he was there now.

"He's afraid of her microscope," Gretchen said accusingly. "I'm convinced that sweet hamster was worried sick that he'd end up in a jar like those…those pigs."

"He knows I wouldn't do that," Sally shouted, placing her hands defiantly on her hips, her eyes a scant inch from Gretchen's.

"Girls, please," Sherry pleaded. "We're due in the mess hall in five minutes."

A shriek arose as they scrambled for their clothes. Only Pamela remained on her bed, unmoved by the thought of being late for breakfast.

Sherry joined the little girl and folded her arm across the small shoulders. "We'll find him."

Tears glistened in the bright blue eyes. "Do you promise?"

Sherry didn't know what to say. She couldn't guarantee something like that. Pamela was a mathematical genius, so Sherry explained in terms the child would understand. "I can't make it a hundred percent. Let's say seventy-five/twenty-five." For heaven's sake, just how far could one hamster get? "Now, get dressed and go into the dining room with dry eyes."

Pamela nodded and climbed off her cot.

"Girls!" Sherry raised her hand to gain their attention. The loud chatter died to a low hum. "Remember, Ralph is our little secret!" The campers knew the rules better than Sherry. Each one was well aware that keeping Ralph was an infraction against camp policy.

"Our lips are sealed." Jan and Jill pantomimed zipping their mouths closed.

"After breakfast, when you've gone to your first class, I'll come back here and look for Ralph. In the meantime I think we'd best pretend nothing's unusual." Her questioning eyes met Pamela's, and Sherry gave her a reassuring hug.

With a gallant effort, Pamela sniffed and nodded. "I just want my Ralphie to come home."

After the frenzied search that had resulted from his disappearance, Sherry couldn't have agreed with the little girl more.

Before they left the cabin for the dining room, Sherry set the open shoe box in the middle of the cabin floor in the desperate hope that the runaway would find his own way home. She paused to close the door behind her charges and glanced over her shoulder with the fervent wish: *Ralph, please come home!*

In the dining hall, seated around the large circular table for eight, Sherry noted that none of her girls showed much of an appetite. French toast should have been a popular breakfast, but for all the interest her group showed, the cook could have served mush!

As the meal was wearing down, Mr. Roarke stepped forward.

"Isn't he handsome?" Gretchen said, looking toward Sherry. "My mother could really go for a man like him."

After what had happened that morning, Sherry was more than willing to let Gretchen's mother take Jeff Roarke. Good luck to her. With his views on romance she'd be lucky if she made it to first base.

"He does sort of look like a Prince Charming," Sally agreed.

"Mr. Roarke?" Sherry squinted, narrowing her gaze, wondering what kind of magic Roarke used on women. Young and old seemed to find him overwhelmingly attractive.

"Oh, yes," Sally repeated with a dreamy look clouding her eyes. "He's just like the prince you read about in the story last night."

Sherry squinted her eyes again in an effort to convince the girls she couldn't possibly be interested in him as a romantic lead in her life.

Standing in front of the room, his voice loud and clear without a microphone, Roarke made the announcements for the day. The highlight of the first week of camp was a special guest speaker who would be giving a talk on the subject of fungus and mold. Roarke was sure the campers would all enjoy hearing Dr. Waldorf speak. From the eager nods around the room, Sherry knew he was right.

Fungus? Mold? Sally looked as excited as if he'd announced a tour of a candy factory that would be handing out free samples. Maybe Sherry was wrong. Maybe her charges weren't really children. Perhaps they really were dwarfs. Because if they were children, they certainly didn't act like any she'd ever known.

Following breakfast, all fifty wizards emptied the dining room and headed for their assigned classes. Sherry wasted little time in returning to her cottage.

The shoe box stood forlornly in the middle of the room. Empty. No Ralph.

Kneeling beside the box, Sherry took a piece of squished French toast from her jeans pocket and ripped it into tiny pieces, piling them around the shoe box. "Ralph," she called out softly. "You love Pamela, don't you? Surely you don't want to break the sweet little girl's heart."

An eerie sensation ran down her spine, as though someone were watching her. Slowly Sherry turned to find a large calico cat sitting on the ledge of the open window. His almond eyes narrowed into thin slits as he surveyed the room.

A cat!

"Shoo!" Sherry screamed, shooting to her feet. She whipped out her hands in an effort to chase the monster away. She didn't know where in the devil he'd come from, but he certainly wasn't welcome around here. Not with Ralph on the loose. When the cat ran off, and with her heart pounding, Sherry shut and latched the window.

By noon, she was tired of looking for Ralph—tired of trying to find a hole or a crack large enough to hide a hamster. An expedition into the deepest, darkest jungles of Africa would have been preferable to this. She joined the girls in the dining room and sadly shook her head when seven pairs of hope-filled eyes silently questioned her on the fate of the hamster. Pamela's bottom lip trembled and tears brimmed in her clear blue eyes, but she didn't say anything.

The luncheon menu didn't fare much better than breakfast. The girls barely ate. Sherry knew she'd made a terrible mistake in allowing Pamela to keep the hamster. She'd gone against camp policy and now was paying the price. Rules were rules. She should have known better.

After lunch, the girls once again went their separate ways. With a heavy heart, Sherry headed for Roarke's office. He answered her knock and motioned for her to sit down. Sherry moistened her dry lips as the girls' comment about Roarke being a prince came to mind. At the time, she'd staunchly denied any attraction she felt for him. To the girls and to herself.

Now, alone with him in his office, Sherry's reaction to him was decidedly positive. If she were look-ing for someone to fill the role of Prince Charming in her life, only one man need apply. She found it amus-ing, even touching, that somehow even in glasses, this man was devastating. He apparently wore them for reading, but he hadn't allowed the staff to see him in them before now.

"Before I forget, how did you settle the problem with Gretchen Hamburg?"

"Ah yes, Gretchen." Proud of herself, Sherry leaned back in the chair and crossed her legs. "It was simple actually. I repositioned her cot away from the wall. That was all she really wanted."

"And she's satisfied with that?"

"Relatively. The mattress is too flat, the pillow's too soft and the blanket's too thin, but other than that, the bed is fine."

"You handled that well."

Sherry considered that high praise coming from her fearless director. He, too, leaned back in his chair. He hesitated and seemed to be considering his words as he rolled a pencil between his palms. "I feel that I may have misled you when you applied for the position at Camp Gitche Gumee," he said after a long pause.

"Oh?" Her heart was thundering at an alarming rate.

"We're not a Camp Fire Girl camp."

Sherry didn't breathe, fearing what was coming next. "I beg your pardon?"

"This isn't the usual summer camp."

Sherry couldn't argue with that—canoeing and hik-ing were offered, but there was little else in the way of fun camping experiences.

"Camp Gitche Gumee aspires to academic excellence," he explained, with a thoughtful frown. "We take the brightest young minds in this country and challenge them to excel in a wide variety of subjects. As you probably noted from the announcements made this morning, we strive toward bringing in top educators to lecture on stimulating subjects."

"Like *fungus and mold*?"

"Yes. Dr. Waldorf is a world-renowned lecturer. Fascinating subject." Roarke tried to ignore her sarcastic tone. From the way she was staring back at him, he realized she strongly disapproved, and he was surprised at how much her puckered frown affected him. Strangely he discovered the desire to please her, to draw the light of her smile back into her eyes, to be bathed in the glow of her approval. The thought froze him. Something was drastically wrong. With barely restrained irritation, he pushed his glasses up the bridge of his nose.

Her lack of appreciation for the goals he'd set for this summer put him in an uncomfortable position. She saw him as a stuffed shirt, that much was obvious, but he couldn't allow Sherry's feelings to cloud his better judgment. He didn't want to destroy her enthusiasm, but he found it necessary to guide it into the proper channels. He liked Sherry's spirit, even though she'd made it obvious she didn't agree with his methods. He hesitated once more. He didn't often talk about his youth, saw no reason to do so, but it was important to him that Sherry understand.

"I would have loved a camp such as this when I was ten," he said thoughtfully.

"You?"

"It might astonish you to know that I was once considered a child prodigy."

It didn't surprise her, now that she thought about it.

"I was attending high-school classes when most boys my age were trying out for Little League. I was in college at twelve and had my master's by the time I was sixteen."

Sherry didn't know how to comment. The stark loneliness in his voice said it all. He'd probably had few friends and little or no contact with other children like himself. The pressures on him would have crumpled anyone else. Jeff Roarke's empty childhood had led him to establish Camp Gitche Gumee. His own bleak experiences were what made the camp so important to him. A surge of compassion rose within Sherry and she gripped her hands together.

"Learning can be fun," she suggested softly, after a long moment. "What about an exploration into the forests in search of such exotic animals as the salamander and tree frog?"

"Yes, well, that is something to consider."

"And how about camp songs?"

"We sing."

"In Latin!"

"Languages are considered a worthy pursuit."

"Okay, games," Sherry challenged next. Her voice was slightly raised as she warmed to her subject. She knew she wouldn't be able to hold her tongue long. It was better to get her feelings into the open than to try to bury them. "And I don't mean Camp Gitche Gumee's afternoon quiz teams, either."

"There are plenty of scheduled free times."

"But not organized fun ones," Sherry cried. "As you said, these children are some of the brightest in the country, but they have one major problem." She was all the way to the edge of her cushion by now, liberally using her hands for emphasis. "They have never been allowed to be children."

Once again, Roarke shoved his glasses up the bridge of his nose, strangely unsettled by her comments. She did make a strong case, but there simply wasn't enough time in a day to do all that she suggested. "Learning in and of itself should offer plenty of fun."

"But—"

Sherry wasn't allowed to finish.

"But you consider fairy tales of value?" he asked, recalling the reason he'd called her into his office.

"You're darn right I do. The girls loved them. Do you know Diane Miller? She's read Milton and Wilde and hasn't a clue who Dr. Seuss is."

"Who?" He blinked.

"Dr. Seuss." It wasn't until then that Sherry realized that Roarke knew nothing of Horton and the Grinch. He'd probably never tasted green eggs with ham or known about Sam.

Roarke struggled to disguise his ignorance. "I'm convinced your intentions are excellent, Miss White, but these parents have paid good money for their children to attend this camp with the express understanding that the children would learn. Unfortunately, fairy tales weren't listed as an elective on our brochure."

"Maybe they should have been," Sherry said firmly. "From everything I've seen, this camp is so academically minded that the entire purpose of sending a child away for the summer has been lost."

Roarke's mouth compressed and his eyes glinted coldly. Sherry could see she'd overstepped her bounds.

"After one week you consider yourself an expert on the subject?"

"I know children."

His hands shuffled the papers on his desk. "It was my understanding that you were a graduate student."

"In education."

"And a minor in partying?"

"That's not true," Sherry cried, coming to her feet.

Roarke rose as well, planted his hands on the desktop, and leaned forward. "Fairy tales are out, Miss White. In the evening you will prepare a study plan and have it approved by me. Is that understood?"

Sherry could feel color filling her face. "Yes, sir," she responded crisply, and mocked him with a salute. If he was going to act like a marine sergeant then she'd respond like a lowly recruit.

"That was unnecessary!"

Sherry opened her mouth to argue with him when the calico cat she'd witnessed earlier in her cabin window suddenly appeared. A gasp rose in her throat at the tiny figure dangling from the cat's mouth.

"Ralph!" she cried, near hysteria.

Chapter 4

"Ralph?" Roarke demanded. "Who in the love of heaven is Ralph?"

"Pamela's hamster. For heaven's sake, do something!" Sherry cried. "He's still alive."

Slowly, Roarke advanced toward the cat. "Buttercup," he said softly. "Nice Buttercup. Put down…" He paused, twisting his head to look at Sherry.

"Ralph," Sherry supplied.

Roarke turned back to the cat. "I thought you said the name was Pamela."

"No, Ralph is Pamela's hamster."

"Right." He wiped a hand across his brow and momentarily closed his eyes. This just wasn't his day. Cautiously, he lowered himself to his knees.

Sherry followed suit, shaking with anxiety. Poor Ralph! Trapped in the jaws of death.

"Buttercup," Roarke encouraged softly. "Put down Ralph."

The absurdity of Roarke's naming a cat "Buttercup" unexpectedly struck Sherry, and a laugh oddly mingled with hysteria worked its way up her throat and escaped with the words, "The cat's name is Buttercup?"

This wasn't the time to explain that his mother had named the cat. "Buttercup isn't any more unusual than a hamster named Ralph!" Roarke said through gritted teeth.

Sherry snickered. "Wanna bet?"

Proud of her catch, Buttercup sat with the squirming rodent in her mouth, seeming to wait for the praise due her. Roarke, down on all fours, slowly advanced toward the feline.

"Will she eat him?" That was Sherry's worst fear. In her mind she could see herself as a helpless witness to the slaughter.

"I don't know what she'll do to him," Roarke whispered impatiently.

By now they were both down on all fours, in front of the sleek calico.

"I'll try to take him out of her mouth."

"What if she won't give him up?" Sherry was about an inch away from pressing the panic button.

Lifting his hand so slowly that it was difficult to tell that Roarke was moving, he gently patted the top of Buttercup's head.

"For heaven's sake, don't praise her," Sherry hissed. "That's Pamela's hamster your cat is torturing."

"Here, Buttercup," he said soothingly, "give me Ralph."

The cat didn't so much as blink.

"I see she's well trained." Sherry couldn't resist the remark.

Roarke flashed her an irritated glance.

Just then the phone rang. Startled, Sherry bolted upright and her hand slapped her heart. A gasp died on her lips as Buttercup dropped Ralph who immediately shot across the room. Roarke dived for the hamster, falling forward so that his elbow hit the floor with a solid thud. His glasses went flying.

"Got him," Roarke shouted triumphantly.

The phone pealed a second time.

"Here."

Without warning or option, Roarke handed Sherry the hamster. Her heart was hammering in her throat as the furry critter burrowed deep into her cupped hands. "Poor baby," she murmured, holding him against her chest.

"Camp Gitche Gumee," Roarke spoke crisply into the telephone receiver. "Just one moment and I'll transfer your call to the kitchen."

Sherry heard him punch a couple of buttons and hang up. In a sitting position on the floor, she released a long, ragged breath and slumped against the side of the desk, needing its support. At the rate her heart was pumping, she felt as if she had just completed the hundred-yard dash.

Roarke moved away from her and she saw him reach down and retrieve his eye-glasses.

"How is he?" he asked, concerned.

"Other than being frightened half to death, he appears to be unscathed."

Silence.

"I… I suppose I should get Ralph back to the cabin," she said, feeling self-conscious and silly.

"Here, let me help you up." He gave her his hand, firmly clasping her elbow, and hauled her to her feet. Sherry found his touch secure and warm. And surprisingly pleasant. Very pleasant. As she stood she discovered that they were separated by only a few inches. "Yes…well," she said and swallowed awkwardly. "Thank you for your help."

His eyes held hers. Lynn was right, Sherry noted. They weren't hazel but green, a deep cool shade of green that she associated with emeralds. Another surprise was how dark and expressive his eyes were. But the signals he was sending were strong and conflicting. Sherry read confusion and a touch of shock, as though she'd unexpectedly thrown him off balance.

Roarke's gaze dropped from her eyes to her mouth and Sherry's breath seemed to jam in her lungs.

She knew what Roarke wanted. The muscles of her stomach tightened and a sinking sensation attacked her with the knowledge that she would like it if he kissed her. The thought of his mouth fitting over hers was strongly appealing. His lips would be like his hand, warm and firm. Sherry pulled herself up short. She was flabbergasted to be entertaining such thoughts. Jeff Roarke. Dictator! Marine sergeant! Stuffed shirt!

"Thank you for your help," she muttered in a voice hardly like her own. Hurriedly, she took a step in retreat, unable to escape fast enough.

Roarke stood stunned as Sherry backed away from him. He was shaking from the inside out. He'd nearly kissed her! And in the process gone against his own policy, and worse, his better judgment. Fortunately, whatever had been happening to him hadn't seemed to affect her. She'd jumped away from him as though she'd been burned, as if the thought of them kissing was repugnant. Even then, it had taken all the strength of his will not to reach out and bring her into his arms.

Sherry watched as Roarke's mouth twisted into a mocking smile. "When you return to your cottage, Miss White, I suggest you read page 36 of the camp manual."

Without looking, Sherry already knew what it said: no pets! Well, anyone with half a brain in his head would recognize that Ralph wasn't a pet—he was a mascot. In her opinion every cabin should have one, but Sherry already knew what Roarke thought of her ideas.

"Miss White." He stopped her at the office door.

The softness in his accusing voice filled her with dread. "Yes?"

"I'd like to review your lesson plans for the evening sessions for the next week at your earliest convenience."

"I'll... I'll have them to you by tomorrow morning."

"Thank you."

"N-no," she stammered. "Thank you. I thought we'd lost Ralph for sure."

Sherry didn't remember walking across the campgrounds. The next thing she knew, she was inside the cabin and Ralph was safely tucked inside his shoebox home.

Her heart continued to pound frantically and she sank onto the closest available bunk, grateful that

Ralph had been found unscathed. And even more grateful that the issue of her application form and the references had been pushed to the side.

As much as she'd like to attribute her shaky knees and battering heart to Buttercup's merciless attack on Ralph, Sherry knew otherwise. It was Roarke. Like every other female in this camp, she had fallen under his magical spell. For one timeless moment she'd seen him as the others did. Attractive. Compelling. Dynamic. Jeff Roarke! There in his office, with Ralph in her hand, they'd gazed at each other and Sherry had been stunned into breathlessness. She wiped a hand over her eyes to shake the vivid image of the man from her mind. Her tongue moistened her lips as she imagined Roarke's mouth over hers. She felt herself melting inside and closed her eyes. It would have been good. Very, very good.

It took Sherry at least ten minutes to gather her composure, and she was grateful she'd kept her wits about her. It wasn't so unusual to be physically attracted to a man, she reassured herself. She had been plenty of times before; this wasn't really something new, and it was only an isolated incident. As a mature adult, she was surely capable of keeping her hormones under control. For the remainder of the summer she would respond to Roarke with cool politeness, she decided. If he were to guess her feelings, she would be at his mercy.

Somehow, Sherry got through the rest of the day. Peace reigned in the cabin, and when the evening session came, Sherry read her young charges the story of Snow White and the Seven Dwarfs. She'd promised them she would, and she wouldn't go back on her word. But to be on the safe side, she also decided to teach them a song.

"Okay, everyone stand," she instructed, when she'd finished the story.

Simultaneously, seven pajama-clad nine-and ten-year-olds rose to their feet.

"What are we going to do now?" Gretchen cried. "I want to talk about Snow White."

"We'll discuss the story later." Sherry put off the youngster, and extended her hands. "Okay, everyone, this is a fun song, so listen up."

When she had their attention, she swayed her hips and pointed to her feet, singing at the top of her lungs how the anklebone was connected to the legbone and the legbone was connected to the hipbone. Seven small hips did an imitation of Sherry's gyrating action. Then the girls dissolved into helpless giggles. Soon the entire cabin was filled with the sounds of joy and laughter.

To satisfy her young charges, Sherry was forced into repeating the silly song no less than three times. At least if she were asked to report tomorrow on their evening activity, Sherry would honestly be able to say that they'd studied the human skeleton. It felt good to have outsmarted Roarke.

"Five minutes until lights-out," Sherry called, making a show of checking her watch. From the corner of her eye, she saw the girls scurry across the room and back to their cots.

"I still want to talk about Snow White," Gretchen cried, above the chaos. "You told me we'd have time to discuss the story."

"I'm sorry," Sherry admitted contritely, sitting

on the edge of the young girl's mattress. "We really don't—not tonight."

"But when the lights go out, that doesn't mean we have to go to sleep."

"Yeah," another voice shouted out. Sherry thought it came from Diane, the reader.

"Someone—anyone, turn out the lights," Sally cried. "Then we can talk."

The room went dark.

Gretchen's bed was closest to the cabin entrance. The room felt stuffy, so Sherry opened the door to allow in the cool evening breeze. A soft ribbon of golden light from the full moon followed the whispering wind inside the cabin.

"Did any of you know that Camp Gitche Gumee is haunted?" Sherry whispered. The girls' attention was instant and rapt.

"There's no such thing as ghosts," Gretchen countered, but her tone lacked conviction.

"Oh, but there are," Sherry whispered, her own voice dipping to an eerie low. "The one who roams around here is named Longfellow."

"Oh, I get it," Diane said with a short laugh. "He was the author of the poem—"

"Shh." Sherry placed her index finger over her lips. Dramatically, she cupped her hands over her ears. "I think I hear him now."

The cabin went still.

"I hear something," Wendy whispered. In the moonlight, Sherry could see the ten-year-old had all ten of her Barbies and Kens in bed with her.

"You needn't worry." Sherry was quick to assure

the girls. "Longfellow is a friendly ghost. He only does fun, good things."

"What kind of things?"

"Hmm, let me think."

"I bet Longfellow brought Ralph back."

Sherry hadn't told Pamela how Buttercup had captured the hamster. Her pet's narrow escape from the jaws of death would only terrorize the softhearted little girl.

"Now that I think about it, Pamela, you're right. Longfellow must have had a hand in finding Ralph."

"What other kinds of things does Longfellow do?" Jan and Jill wanted to know. As always, they spoke in unison. Jill's front tooth was still intact, but it wouldn't last much longer with the furious way she worked at extracting it.

"He finds missing items like socks and hair clips. And sometimes, late at night when it's stone quiet, if you listen real, real hard, you can hear him sing."

"You can?"

"Actually, he whistles," Sherry improvised.

The still room went even quieter as seven pairs of ears strained to listen to the wind whisper through the forest of redwoods outside their door.

"I hear him," Diane said excitedly. "He's real close."

"When I was a little kid," Sally told the group excitedly, "I used to be afraid of ghosts, but Longfellow sounds like a good ghost."

"Oh, he is."

"Can you tell us another story?" Gretchen pleaded. "They're fun."

For the chronic grumbler to ask for a fairy tale and admit anything was fun was almost more than

Sherry could absorb. "I think one more story wouldn't hurt," she said. "But that has to be all." Remembering the conversation with Roarke earlier that afternoon, Sherry felt a fleeting sadness. After tonight, her stories would have to come from more acceptable classics. She thought her girls were missing a wonderful part of their heritage as children by skipping fairy tales. If she didn't want this job so badly, Sherry would have battled Roarke more strenuously.

Leaning back against the wall, she brought her knees up to her chin, sighed audibly while she chose the tale, and started. "Once upon a time in a land far, far away..."

By the time she announced that "they lived happily ever after" the cabin was filled with the even, measured breathing of sleeping children. If the girls weren't all asleep they were close to it.

Gretchen snored softly, and taking care not to wake the slumbering child, Sherry climbed off her cot and checked on the others. She pulled a blanket around Jan's and Jill's shoulders and removed inanimate objects from the cots, placing Sally's microscope on the headboard and rescuing the Barbies and Kens from being crushed during the night. Ralph was firmly secured in his weathered home, and Sherry gently slid the shoe box from underneath Pamela's arm.

"Sleep tight," she whispered to the much-loved rodent. "Or else I'll call Buttercup back."

As she moved to close the cabin door, Sherry was struck by how peaceful the evening was. Drawn outside, she sat on the top step of the large front porch and gazed at the stars. They were out in brilliant display this evening, scattered diamonds tossed on thick folds of black velvet. How close they seemed. Sparkling. Radiant.

Sherry's hands cupped her chin as she rested her elbows on her knees and studied the heavens.

"Good evening, Miss White." Roarke had heard their singing earlier, had come to investigate and had been amused by her efforts to outwit him.

The sound of Roarke's voice broke into Sherry's thoughts. "Good evening, Mr. Roarke," she responded crisply, and straightened. "What brings you out tonight?" Good grief, she hoped he hadn't been around to hear the last fairy tale, or worse, her mention of Longfellow.

He paused, braced one foot against the bottom step and looked over the grounds. "I like to give the camp a final check before turning in for the night."

"Oh." For the life of her, she couldn't think of a single thing more to say. Her reaction to him was immediate. Her heart pounded like a jackhammer and the blood shot through her veins. She'd like to fool herself into believing the cause was the unexpectedness of his arrival, but she knew better.

"How's Ralph?" Roarke questioned.

"Fully recovered. How's Buttercup?"

"Exceptionally proud." The soft laugh that followed was so pleasant sounding that it caused Sherry to smile just listening to him.

"You have a nice laugh." She hadn't meant to tell him that, but it slipped out before she could stop herself. As often was the case when she spoke to Jeff Roarke, the filter between her brain and her mouth malfunctioned and whatever she was thinking slid out without forethought.

"I was about to tell you how effervescent *your* laugh sounds."

Sherry couldn't remember a time she'd ever given him the opportunity to hear her laugh. The circumstances in which they were together prohibited it. Staff meetings were intensely serious. No one dared show any amusement.

"When—"

"Tonight. I suppose you plan to tell me that the legbone connected to the hipbone is a study of the human skeleton?"

Words ran together and tripped over the tip of her tongue. "Of course not...well, yes, but..."

He laughed again. "The girls thoroughly enjoyed it, didn't they?"

"Yes."

"That sort of education wasn't exactly what I had in mind, but anything is better than those blasted fairy tales."

Sherry was forced into sitting on her hands to keep from elbowing him. Fairy tales weren't silly or senseless. They served a purpose! But she managed to keep her thoughts to herself—with some effort.

Silence again.

"I have my lesson plan if you'd like to see it," she said, and started to get up, but his hand on her forearm stopped her.

"Tomorrow morning is soon enough."

He surprised her even more by climbing the three steps and taking a seat beside her. He paused and raised his eyes to the sky.

"Lovely, isn't it?" he asked.

"Yes." The one word seemed to strangle in her throat. Roarke was close enough to touch. All Sherry would have had to do was shift her weight for her shoulder to gently graze his. Less than an inch separated their thighs. Although she strove to keep from experiencing the physical impact of brushing against him, there was little she could do about the soft scent of the aftershave Roarke wore, which was so masculinely appealing. Every breath she drew in was more tantalizing than the one before. Spice and man—a lethal combination.

It was the night, Sherry decided, not the man. Oh, please, not the man, she begged. She didn't want to be so strongly attracted to Jeff Roarke. She didn't want to be like all the others. The two of them were so different. They couldn't agree on anything. Not him. Not her.

Neither spoke, but the silence wasn't a serene one. The darkness seemed charged with static electricity. Twice Sherry opened her mouth, ready to start some banal conversation simply to break the silence. Both times she found herself incapable of speaking. When she chanced a look in his direction she discovered his thick eyebrows arched bewilderedly over a storm cloud of sea-green eyes.

Naturally, neither one of them had the courage to introduce the phenomenon occurring between them into casual conversation. But Sherry was convinced Roarke felt the tug of physical attraction as strongly and powerfully as she did. And from the look of him, he was as baffled as she.

"Well, I suppose I should turn in," she said, after the longest minute of her life.

"I suppose I should, too."

But neither of them moved.

"It really is a lovely night," Sherry said, looking to the heavens, struck once again by the simple beauty of the starlit sky.

"Yes, lovely," Roarke repeated softly, but he wasn't gazing at the heavens, he was looking at Sherry. He'd believed everything he'd said to her about romance being nonsense, but now the words came back to haunt him. Right now, this moment with her seemed more important than life itself. He felt trapped in awareness. The sensations that churned inside him were lethal to his mental health and he wouldn't alter a one. This woman had completely thrown him off balance with the unexpected need he felt to hold her. Slipping his arm around her shoulders seemed the most natural act in the world…and strictly against his own camp policy. The urge to do so was so strong that he crossed his arms over his chest in an effort to keep them still. He was stunned at how close he'd come to giving in to temptation. Stunned and appalled.

Whatever caused Sherry to turn to meet his gaze, she didn't know. Fate, possibly. But she did rotate her head so that her eyes were caught by his as effectively as if trapped in a vise. Mesmerized, their gazes locked in the faint light of the glorious moon. It was as though Sherry were looking at him for the first time—through a love-struck teen's adoring eyes. He was devastatingly handsome. Dark, and compellingly masculine.

Unable to stop herself, she raised her hand, prepared to outline his thick eyebrows with her fingertips, and paused halfway to his face. His troubled eyes were a mirror of her own doubtful expression, Sherry realized. Yet his were charged with curiosity. He seemed to want to hold her in his arms as much as she yearned to let him. His mouth appeared to hunger for the taste of hers just as she longed to sample his. His shallow breath mingled with her labored one. Deep grooves formed at the sides of his mouth, and when his lips parted, Sherry noted that his breathing was hesitant.

Driven by something stronger than her own common sense, Sherry slowly, inch by inch, lowered her lashes, silently bending to his unspoken demand. Her own lips parted in welcome as her pulse fluttered wildly at the base of her throat.

Roarke lowered his mouth to a scant inch above hers.

Sherry was never sure what happened. A sound perhaps. A tree branch scraping against the roof of the cabin—perhaps an owl's screeching cry as it flew overhead. Whatever it was instantly brought her to her senses, and she was eternally grateful. She jerked her head back and willfully checked her watch.

"My goodness," she cried in a wobbly, weak voice, "will you look at the time?"

"Time?" he rasped.

"It's nearly eleven. I really must get inside." Already she was on her feet, rushing toward the front door as though being chased by a mad dog.

Not waiting for a response from Roarke, Sherry closed the door and weakly leaned against it. Her heart was thumping like a locomotive gone out of control.

Her mouth felt dry and scratchy. Filled with purpose, she walked over to the small sink and turned on the cold water faucet. She gulped down the first glass in huge swallows and automatically poured herself a second. In different circumstances, she would have taken her temperature. There was something in the air. Sherry almost wished it was a virus.

The next morning, Sherry was on time for the staff meeting. She hadn't slept well and was awake even before the alarm sounded. At least when she was a few minutes early she could choose her own seat. The back of the room all but invited her and she claimed a seat there.

Lynn Duffy scooted in beside her.

"Morning," Sherry greeted her.

"Hi. How's it going?"

Sherry pushed the cuticle back on her longest fingernail. "Just fine. The kids are great."

"You got Gretchen Hamburg—don't tell me everything's fine. I know better."

"She's a cute kid!"

"Gretchen?" Lynn grumbled. "You've got to be teasing. The kid's a royal pain in the rear end!"

Two days ago, Sherry would have agreed with her, but from the minute Gretchen had announced that fairy tales were "fun" she'd won Sherry's heart.

Roarke stepped to the podium, and the small gathering of staff went silent. Sherry noted that he took pains not to glance in her direction, which was fine by her. She preferred that he didn't. This morning the memory of those few stolen moments alone under the stars was nothing short of embarrassing. She'd rather forget the entire episode. Chalk it up to the decreased layer of ozone in outer space. Or the way the planets were aligned. The moon was in its seventh house. Aquarius and Mars. A fluke certainly. She could look at him this morning and feel nothing...well, that wasn't exactly true. The irritation was gone, replaced by a lingering fascination.

After only a minimum of announcements, the staff were dismissed. Sherry stood, eager to make her escape.

"Sherry," Lynn said, following her out of the meeting room, "do you have some free time later?"

"After breakfast."

Her friend looked a bit chagrined. "I have to run into town. Would you like to come along?"

"Sure, I'll come over to your cabin after I get my wizards off to their first class."

Lynn brightened. "I'll look for you around eight, then."

Her friend took off in the opposite direction and Sherry's gaze followed the younger girl. Now that she thought about it, Lynn didn't seem to be her normal, cheerful self. Sherry had the impression that this jaunt into town was an excuse to talk.

It was.

The minute Sherry got into Lynn's car she could feel the other girl's coiled tension. Sherry was uncertain. She didn't know if she should wait until Lynn mentioned what was troubling her, or if she should say something to start Lynn talking. She chose the latter.

"Are you enjoying the camp this summer?" Sherry asked.

Lynn shrugged. "It's different."

"How's that?"

Again her shoulders went up and down in a dismissive gesture. The long country road that led to the small city of Arrow Flats twisted and turned as it came down off the rugged hillside.

"Have you noticed Peter Towne?" Lynn said quietly.

"The lifeguard?"

"Yeah…it's his second year here, too. Last summer we were good friends. We even managed a few emails since then. I wished him a Merry Christmas, and he said hi at Easter and asked if I'd be coming back to camp. That sort of thing."

As Sherry recalled Peter was a handsome sun-bleached blond who patrolled the beaches during the afternoons and worked in the kitchen after dinner. "How old is he?"

"Nineteen—the same age as me."

Whatever was troubling Lynn obviously had to do with Peter. "He seems to be nice enough," Sherry prodded.

"Peter is more than nice," Lynn said dreamily. "He's wonderful."

Sherry wouldn't have gone quite that far to describe him. "So you two worked together last year?"

"Right."

The teenager focused her attention on the roadway, which was just as well since it looked treacherous enough to Sherry.

"What makes you bring up his name?" Sherry ventured.

"Peter's?"

"Yes, Peter's."

"Did I bring him up?"

"Lynn, honestly, you know you did."

The other girl bit the corner of her bottom lip. "Yeah, I suppose his name did casually pop into the conversation."

It seemed to Sherry that Lynn regretted having said anything so she let the matter drop. "I had my first run-in with ol' Ironjaw."

"You mean Mr. Roarke?"

"He and I had a difference of opinion about the evening sessions. He'd prefer for me to discuss the intricacies of U.S. foreign policy. I'd rather tell ghost stories. I imagine we'll agree on a subject somewhere in between."

"I saw you put something on the podium for him this morning."

"Lesson plans."

"He's making you do that?"

"As a precaution."

"Oh."

Lynn eased the car to a stop at the crossroads before turning onto the main thoroughfare. Arrow Flats was about ten miles north of the camp. Sherry noticed the way Lynn's hands tightened around the steering wheel at the intersection.

"Two nights ago, I couldn't sleep," she said in a strained, soft voice. "I decided to take a walk down to the lake. There was an old piece of driftwood there so I sat down. Peter…couldn't sleep, either. He happened to come by, and we sat and talked."

"From everything I've seen, Peter's got a good head on his shoulders."

"It was nearly one before we went back to camp. He kissed me, Sherry. I never wanted anyone to kiss me more than Peter that night in the moonlight. It was so romantic and... I don't know... I've never felt this strongly about any boy before."

Sherry could identify with that from her own surprising experience with Roarke, the night before on the porch. Maybe there really was something in the air, she thought hopefully.

"Now every time I look at Peter I see the same longing in his eyes. We want to be together. I... I think we might be falling in love."

Sherry thought it was wonderful that the friendship between the two had blossomed into something more, but she understood her friend's dilemma. The camp was no place for a romance.

"Oh, Sherry, what am I going to do?" Lynn cried. "If Mr. Roarke finds out, both Peter and I will be fired."

Chapter 5

"Good morning, Miss White."

Roarke's voice rose to greet her when Sherry slipped into the back row of chairs in the staff room. She muttered something appropriate, embarrassed once again to be caught coming in tardy for yet another early-morning session. On this particular day, her only excuse was laziness. The alarm had gone off and she simply hadn't been able to force herself out of bed.

As always, Roarke waited until she'd settled in her seat before continuing.

Sherry tried her best to listen to the day's announcements, but her mind drifted to Lynn and Peter and their predicament. It felt peculiar to side with Roarke, but Sherry agreed that a romance at camp could be a source of problems for the teenagers and everyone else. Lynn's attraction to Peter was a natural response for a nineteen-year-old girl, and Peter was a fine boy, but camp simply wasn't the place for their courtship. Sherry had advised her friend to "cool it" as much as possible. In a couple of months, once camp had been dismissed, the two could freely date each other.

Sherry's gaze skidded from the tall blond youth back to Lynn. They were doing their best to hide their growing affection for each other, but from the not-so-secret glances they shared, their feelings were all too obvious to Sherry. And if she could see how they felt, then it probably wouldn't be long before Roarke did, too.

A chill ran up Sherry's arms, and she bundled her sweater more tightly around her. She yawned and rubbed the sleep from her eyes, forcing herself to pay attention to what Roarke was saying.

The others were beginning to stand and move about before she realized that the session had come to a close. Still she didn't move. Standing, walking about, thinking, seemed almost more than she could manage, especially without coffee. What she needed was some kind soul to intravenously feed her coffee a half hour before the alarm went off.

"Is there a problem, Miss White?"

Sherry glanced up to find Roarke looming above her.

"No," she mumbled and shook her head for emphasis.

"Then shouldn't you be getting back to your cabin?"

She nodded, although that, too, required some effort. A giant yawn escaped, and she cupped her hand over her mouth. "I suppose."

"You really aren't a morning person, are you?"

Her smile was weak. "It just takes a while for my heart to start working."

Roarke straddled a seat in the row in front of her and looped his arm over the chair back as he studied her. She looked as though she could curl up right there and without much effort go back to sleep. The urge to wrap her in his arms and press her head against his shoulder was a powerful one. He could almost feel her softness yield against his muscled strength. Forcibly, he shook the image from his mind. His gaze softened as he studied her. "Did you hear anything of what I said?"

"A…little," she admitted sheepishly. He grinned at that, and she discovered that his smile completely disarmed her. Speaking of getting her heart revved up! One smile from Jeff Roarke worked wonders. No man had the right to look that good this early in the day. Her mind had come up with a list of concrete arguments for him to postpone these sessions to a more decent time of day, but one charming look shot them down like darts tossed at fat balloons. "I don't know what it is about mornings, but I think I may be allergic to them."

"Perhaps if you tried going to bed earlier."

"It doesn't work," she said, and yawned again. "I wish I could, but at about ten every night, I come alive. My best work is done then."

Roarke glanced at his watch, nodded and stood. "Your cabin is due in the mess hall in fifteen minutes."

Sherry groaned and dropped her feet. Her hand crisply touched her forehead. "Aye, aye, Commandant, we'll be there."

Roarke chuckled and returned her mock salute.

When Sherry entered the cabin, she discovered the girls in a frenzy. Pamela had climbed to the top of the dresser and was huddled into a tight ball clutching Ralph, her knees drawn up against her chest. Gretchen faced the open door, a broom raised above her head, prepared for attack, while Jan and Jill were nearby, holding their shoes in their fists like lethal weapons.

Ginny, the high-school girl who had been assigned to stay in the cabin while Sherry was at the morning meeting, was in as much of a tizzy as the girls.

"What happened?" Sherry demanded.

"He tried to kill Ralph," Pamela screamed hysterically.

"Who?"

"I read about things like this," Diane inserted calmly. "It's a natural instinct."

"What is?" Sherry cried, hurriedly glancing from girl to girl.

"The cat," Jan and Jill said together.

"Ralph was nearly eaten," Pamela cried.

Sherry sagged with relief. "That's only Buttercup."

"Buttercup!"

"He belongs to Mr. Roarke."

"Mr. Roarke has a cat named Buttercup?" Gretchen said, lowering her broom to the floor. A look of astonishment relaxed her mouth into a giant O.

"Apparently so."

"But he tried to get Ralph." Pamela opened her hands and the rodent squirmed his head out between two fingers and looked around anxiously.

"We need a cage," Sherry said decisively. "That shoe box is an open invitation to Buttercup."

"Can't Mr. Roarke keep his cat chained up or something?" Wendy suggested. The Barbies and Kens were scattered freely across the top of her mattress.

"I thought we weren't supposed to have pets," Gretchen complained. "I find Mr. Roarke's actions highly contradictory."

"Since we're keeping Ralph, mentioning Buttercup to Mr. Roarke wouldn't be wise," Sherry informed them all with a tight upper lip.

"But we've got to do something."

"Agreed." One glance at her watch confirmed that her troop was already late for breakfast. "Hurry now, girls. I'll take care of everything."

"Everything?" Pam's bold eyes studied her counselor.

"Everything," Sherry promised.

By the time Sherry and her cabin arrived at the mess hall, the meal was already half over. The stacks of pancakes had cooled and the butter wouldn't melt on them properly. Gretchen complained loudly enough for the cooks in the kitchen to hear.

In the middle of breakfast, Sally produced a huge tannish-gold hawk moth she'd trapped the night before and passed it around the table for the others to admire, momentarily distracting Sherry.

"Girls, manners. Please," she cried, when Wendy stuffed a whole pancake into her mouth. Sticky syrup oozed down the preteen's chin.

"But we have to hurry," Diane complained.

"You'll talk to Mr. Roarke about his cat, won't you?" Pam wanted to know as she climbed out of her chair, her meal untouched.

"I'll see what I can do."

When the last girl had left the dining room, rushing to her class, Sherry sighed with relief. She hadn't so much as had her first cup of coffee and already the morning was a disaster.

"Problems, Miss White?" Again Roarke joined her. He handed her a steaming mug of coffee.

She cupped it in her hands and savored the first sip. "Bless you."

Roarke pulled out a chair and sat down across the table from her.

"Buttercup paid us another visit," she said after a long moment.

"Ralph?"

"Is fine…"

His jaw tightened. "May I remind you, Miss White, that it is against camp policy to have a pet?"

"Ralph is a mascot, not a pet."

"He's a nuisance."

"You're a fine one to talk," she returned heatedly and took another sip of coffee in an effort to fortify her courage. "As for camp policy—what do you call Buttercup?"

"The camp cat."

"She's not a pet?"

"Definitely not."

"My foot!"

"If there are problems with Ralph, then the solution is simple—get rid of him."

"No way! Pamela's strongly attached to that animal." Surely Roarke wasn't heartless enough to take away a child's only friend. "This is the first time Pamela's spent more than a few days away from home and family. That hamster's helping her through the long separation from her brother and parents."

"If I allow Ralph to stay, then next year someone is likely to bring a boa constrictor and claim it's not a pet, either."

Sherry twisted her head from side to side, glancing around her. Lowering her voice, she leaned forward and whispered, "No one knows about Ralph. I'm not telling, the girls aren't telling. That only leaves you."

"Buttercup knows."

"She's the problem," Sherry gritted between clenched teeth.

"No," Roarke countered heatedly. "Ralph is."

From the hard set of the director's mouth, Sherry could see that discussing this matter would solve nothing. She held up both palms in a gesture of defeat. "Fine."

"Fine what? You'll get rid of Ralph?"

"No! I'll take care of the problem."

"How?" He eyed her dubiously.

"I haven't figured that out yet, but I will."

"That I don't doubt. Just make sure I don't know a thing about it."

"Right." Playfully, she winked at him, stood, reached for a small pancake, popped it into her mouth and left the dining hall. She understood Roarke's concerns, but occasional exceptions to rules had to be made. Life was filled with too many variables for him to be so hard-nosed and stringent. Ralph had to be kept a secret, and more than that, the rodent couldn't continue to rule the lives of her seven charges. A cage was one solution, but knowing Buttercup, that wouldn't be enough to distract the cat from her daily raids.

She found the answer in town. That night after the

evening meal, Sherry carried in the solution for the girls to examine.

"What's it for?" Sally wanted to know when Sherry held the weapon up for their inspection.

Bracing her feet like a trained commando, Sherry looped the strap over her shoulder and positioned the machine gun between her side and her elbow. "One shot from this and Buttercup won't be troubling Ralph again."

"You aren't going to…" Jan began.

"…shoot him?" Jill finished her twin's worried query.

The girls' eyes widened as Sherry's mouth twisted into a dark scowl. "You bet. I'm going to shoot him— right between the eyes."

A startled gasp rose.

"Miss White," Pamela pleaded, "I don't want you to hurt Buttercup."

Sherry relaxed and lowered the machine gun, grinning. "Oh, I wouldn't do that. This is a battery-operated water gun."

"Really?"

"A water gun?" Diane asked, lowering her book long enough to examine Sherry's weapon.

"I knew that all along," Gretchen said.

"I'll show you how it works." Sherry aimed it at her bedroom door and fingered the trigger. Instantly, a piercing blast of water slammed against the pine door ten feet away.

"Hey, not bad," Diane said excitedly.

"It's as accurate as a real gun," Sherry explained further. "After a shot or two from this beauty, Buttercup won't come within fifty feet of this cabin."

The spontaneous applause gladdened Sherry's heart. She accepted the praise of her charges with a deep bow and placed the weapon in her bedroom. Returning a moment later, she entered the room with a dark visor pulled down low over her eyes. She held out a deck of cards toward them.

"Okay, girls, gather 'round," she called. "Tonight's lesson is about statistics." Grinning, she playfully shuffled the cards from one hand to the other. "Anyone here ever played gin rummy?"

If Sherry had thought her charges enjoyed the fairy tales, they were even more ecstatic about cards. Their ability to pick up the rules and the theory behind the games astonished her. It shouldn't, she mused. After all they were real live wizards!

After she'd taught them the finer points of gin rummy, the seven had eagerly learned hearts and canasta. At nine-thirty, their scheduled bedtime, the girls didn't want to quit. Cards were fun, and there was precious little time for that commodity at Camp Gitche Gumee.

When the lights were out, Sherry lay in her own bed, wishing she could convince Jeff Roarke that camp, no matter what its specialty, was meant to be fun.

No longer did Sherry think of Roarke in negative terms. They still disagreed on most subjects, but the wall of annoyance and frustration she'd felt toward him had been a means of hiding the sensual awareness she experienced the minute he walked into the room. It pricked her pride to admit that she was like every other female over the age of ten at Camp Gitche

Gumee. Jeff Roarke was as sexy as the day was long. And since this was June, the days were lengthy enough to weave into the nights.

Sherry expelled her breath and sat upright in the darkened room. It wasn't only thoughts of Roarke that were keeping her awake. Guilt played a hand in her troubled musings. Her father and Phyliss were probably worried sick about her. Leaving the way she had hadn't been one of her most brilliant schemes. By this time, no doubt, her stepmother had hired a detective agency to track her down.

Contrite feelings about her evening sessions with the girls also played a role in her sleeplessness. She'd handed in the lesson plans to Roarke knowing that she'd misled him a little. It was stretching even her vivid imagination to link canasta and gin rummy with statistics.

This summer had been meant to be carefree and fun, and Sherry was discovering that it was neither. Tossing aside the blankets, she reached for her jeans. Because her cell was in a dead zone, she searched for a pay phone and found one situated on the campgrounds, directly across from her cabin. If she talked to her father, she'd feel better and so would he. There wasn't any need to let Phyliss know where she was, but it couldn't hurt to keep in touch.

Pulling her sweatshirt over her head, Sherry tiptoed between the bunks and quietly slipped out the front door. The night was filled with stars. A light breeze hummed across the treetops, their melody singing in the wind. Cotton-puff clouds roamed across the full moon, and the sweet scent of virgin forest filled the air. Tucking the tips of her fingers in her hip pockets, Sherry paused to examine the beauty of the world around her. It was lovely enough to take her breath away.

The pay phone was well lit, and Sherry slipped her quarters into the appropriate slot. Her father's groggy voice greeted her on the fourth ring.

"Hello?"

"Hi, Dad."

"Sherry?"

"How many other girls call you Dad?"

Virgil White chuckled. "You give me as much trouble as ten daughters."

"Honestly, Dad!"

"Sherry, where—"

Her father's voice was interrupted by a frenzied, eager one. "Oh, thank God," a female voice came over the line. "Sherry, darling, is that you?"

"Hello, Phyliss. Listen, I'm in a pay phone and I've only got a few quarters—"

"Virgil, do something… Sherry's nearly penniless."

"Phyliss, I've got money, it's just quarters I'm short of at the moment. Please listen, I wanted you to know I'm fine."

"Are you eating properly?"

"Three meals a day," Sherry assured her.

"Liver once a week? Fresh fruit and vegetables?"

"Every day, scout's honor."

The sound of her father's muffled laugh came over the wire. "You were never a Girl Scout."

Phyliss gasped and started to weep silently.

"Dad, now look what you've done. Phyliss, I'm eating better than ever, and I have all the clothes I could possibly need."

"Money?"

"I'm doing just great. Wonderful, in fact. I don't need anything."

"Are you happy, baby?"

"Very happy," Sherry assured them both.

"Where are you—at least tell me where you are," her stepmother cried.

Before she could answer, the operator came back on the line. "It will be another $1.25 for the next three minutes."

"I've got to go."

"Sherry," Phyliss pleaded. "Remember to eat your garlic."

"I'll remember," she promised. "Goodbye, Dad. Goodbye, Phyliss." At age twenty-five she didn't require a babysitter, although Phyliss seemed convinced otherwise. As the good daughter, Sherry had done her duty.

Gently she replaced the telephone receiver, feeling much relieved. Looking up she discovered Roarke advancing toward her across the lawn in long, angry strides. Just the way he moved alerted her to his mood. She stiffened with apprehension and waited.

"Miss White." His gaze traveled from the telephone to her and then back again. "Who's staying with the girls?"

"I...they're all asleep. I didn't think it would matter if I slipped out for a couple of minutes. I'd be able to hear them if there was a problem," she went on hurriedly, trying to cover her guilty conscience. She really hadn't been gone more than a few minutes.

The anger left Roarke as quickly as it came. He knew he was being unreasonable. The source of his irritation wasn't that Sherry had stepped outside her cabin. It was the fact that she'd made a phone call, and he strongly suspected she'd contacted a male friend.

Self-consciously, Sherry lowered her head. "You're right, I shouldn't have left the girls. I'll make sure it doesn't happen again."

"It's a pleasure to have you agree to something I say," Roarke said, his face relaxing into a lazy smile.

Sherry's heart lifted in a strange, weightless way. She'd been tense, conscious once more that she'd done something to irritate him.

"I'll walk you back to your cabin," he suggested softly.

"Thank you." It wasn't necessary, for the cabin was within sight, but she was pleased Roarke chose to keep her company.

"I saw you on the phone," he commented, without emotion, a few minutes later. "I suppose you were talking to one of your boyfriends."

"No," she corrected, "that was my family."

Roarke cleared his throat and straightened. "Is there a boyfriend waiting for you back…where was it again?"

"Seattle, and no, not anyone I'm serious about." Sherry went still, her heart thundering against her breast. "And you? Do y-you have someone waiting in Berkeley?"

Roarke shook his head. There was Fiona, another professor whom he saw socially. They'd seen each other in a friendly sort of way for a couple of years, but he hadn't experienced any of the physical response with Fiona that he did with Sherry. Come to think of it, Fiona's views on romance were much like his own. "There's no one special," he said after a moment.

"I see." From the length of time that it took him to tell her that, Sherry suspected that there was someone. Her spirits dipped a little. Good grief, did she think he lived like a hermit? He couldn't! He was too good-looking.

Roarke's gaze studied her then, and in the veiled shadows of the moon, Sherry noted that it was impossible to make out the exact color of his eyes. Green or tawny, it didn't seem to matter now that they were focused directly on her. Her breathing became shallow and she couldn't draw her gaze away from him. Finally, she dragged her eyes from his and looked up at the stars.

Neither spoke for several minutes, and Sherry found the quiet disarming.

"You seem to have adjusted well to the camp," Roarke commented. "Other than a few problems with mornings, that is."

"Thank you."

"How did the lessons go this evening? Wasn't it statistics you told me you were planning to discuss?"

Sherry swallowed down her apprehension and answered in a small, quiet voice. "Everything went well."

Roarke's eyes narrowed as he watched her struggle to keep the color from invading her cheeks. She might think herself clever, but he wasn't completely ignorant of her creative efforts.

"I may have deviated a little," she admitted finally.

"A little?" Roarke taunted. "Then let me ask you something."

"Sure." She tried to make her voice light and airy, belying her nervousness.

"Who got stuck with the queen of spades?"

"Gretchen," she returned automatically, then slapped her hand over her mouth. "You know?"

"I had a fair idea. A little friendly game of hearts, I take it?"

She nodded, studying him. "And canasta and gin rummy, while I was at it."

He did nothing more than shake his head in a gesture of defeat.

"Are you going to lecture me?"

"Will it do any good?"

Sherry laughed softly. "Probably not."

"That's what I thought."

She relaxed, liking him more by the minute. "Then you don't mind?"

Roarke sighed. "As long as you don't fill their minds with romantic tales, I can live with it. But I'd like to ask about the lesson plans you handed in to me."

"Oh, I was planning to do everything I wrote down… I'm just using kind of…unorthodox methods."

"I figured as much." His face relaxed into a languorous smile. "I'd guess that the night you intend a study on finances is really a game of Monopoly."

"Yes…how'd you know?" He didn't sound irritated, and that lent Sherry confidence.

"I have my ways."

"Do you know everything that goes on in this camp?" She'd never met anyone like him. Roarke seemed to be aware of every facet of his organization. How he managed to keep tabs on each area, each cabin, was beyond her.

"I don't know everything," he countered, "but I try…"

As his voice trailed off the beauty of the night demanded their attention. Neither spoke for a long moment, but neither was inclined to leave, either.

"I find it surprising that you don't have someone special waiting for you." Roarke's voice was low, slightly bewildered.

"It's not so amazing." A few men had been attracted to her—before Phyliss had drilled them on their intentions, invited them to dinner and driven them crazy with her wackiness. A smile touched the corner of Sherry's mouth. If there was anyone she wished to discourage, all she need do was introduce him to her loony stepmother. "I'm attending Seattle Pacific full-time, and I'm involved in volunteer work. There isn't much opportunity to date."

While she was speaking, Roarke couldn't stop looking at her. Her profile was cast against the moon shadows of the dark violet sky. The light breeze flirted with her hair, picking up the wispy strands at her temple and puffing them out and away from her face. Her dark hair was thick and inviting. He thought about lifting it in his hands, running the silky length through his fingers, burying his face in it and breathing in its fresh, clean scent. From the moment she'd first entered his office he'd thought she was pretty. Now, Roarke studied her and saw much more than the outward loveliness that had first appealed to him. Her spirit was what attracted him, her love of life, her enthusiasm.

He'd never seen a cabin enjoy their counselor more. Sherry was a natural with the children. Inventive.

Clever. Fun. A hundred times since she'd arrived at camp, he'd been angered enough to question the wisdom of having hired her. But not tonight, not when he was standing in the moonlight with her at his side. Not now, when he would have given a month's wages to taste her lips and feel her softness pressed against him. She was a counselor and he was the camp director, but tonight that would be so easy to forget. He was a man so strongly attracted to a woman that his heart beat with the energy of a callow youth's.

Sherry turned and her gaze was trapped in Roarke's. At his tender look, her breath wedged in her lungs, tightening her chest. Her heart thudded nervously.

"I guess I should go inside," she said, hardly recognizing her own voice.

Roarke nodded, willing her to leave him while he had the strength to resist her.

Sherry didn't move; her legs felt like mush and she sincerely doubted that they'd support her. If she budged at all, it was to lean closer to Roarke. Never in all her life had she wanted a man to hold her more. His gaze fell to her mouth and she moistened her lips in invitation, yearning for his kiss.

Roarke groaned inwardly and closed his eyes, but that only served to increase his awareness of her. She smelled of flowers, fresh and unbelievably sweet. Warmth radiated from her and he yearned to wrap his arms around her and feel for himself her incredible softness.

"Good night, Sherry," he said forcefully, bounding to his feet. "I'll see you in the morning."

Sherry sagged with relief and watched as Roarke marched away with the purposeful strides of a marine drill sergeant, his hands bunched into tight fists at his side.

Chapter 6

"I demand that we form a search party," Wendy cried, crossing her arms over her chest and glaring at Sherry. "You did when Ralph was missing."

"Wendy, sweetheart," Sherry said, doing her best to keep calm. "Ralph is a living, breathing animal."

"A *rodent hamustro* actually," Sally informed them knowingly.

"Whatever. The thing is—a misplaced Ken doll doesn't take on the urgency of a missing rodent."

"But someone stole him."

Sherry refused to believe that any of the girls would want Ken badly enough to pilfer him from their cabin mate. "We'll keep looking, Wendy, but for now that's the best we can do."

Hands placed on her hips, the youngster surveyed

the room, her eyes zeroing in on her peers. "All right, which one of you crooks kidnapped Ken-Richie?"

"Wendy!"

"I refuse to live in a den of thieves!"

"No one stole your doll," Sherry said for the tenth time. "I'm sure you misplaced him."

Wendy gave her a look of utter disgust. "No one in their right mind would misplace the one and only love of Barbie-Brenda's life."

"Oh, brother," Sherry muttered under her breath.

"I think Longfellow might have done it," Pamela inserted cautiously. "It's just the kind of thing a ghost would do."

"Longfellow?"

"Right," Jan and Jill chimed in eagerly. "Longfellow."

Wendy considered that for a moment, then agreed with an abrupt nod of her head and appeared to relax somewhat. "You know, I bet that's exactly what did happen."

Over the next two days the standard response to any problem was that Longfellow was responsible. Soon the entire camp was buzzing with tales of the make-believe ghost Sherry had invented.

"My mattress has more bumps than a camel," Gretchen claimed one morning.

Six preteens glanced at the chronic complainer and shouted in unison, "Longfellow did it!"

Ralph's cage door was left open to Pamela's dismay. "Longfellow," the girls informed her.

At breakfast, the Cream of Wheat had lumps. The girls looked at one another across the table, nodded once and cried, "Longfellow."

Every time Sherry heard Longfellow's name, she cringed inwardly. That Roarke hadn't heard about the friendly ghost was a miracle in itself. Sherry had already decided that when he did, she would give an Academy Award performance of innocence. By now, news of the spirit had infiltrated most of the cabins, although Sherry couldn't be certain which counselors had heard about him and who hadn't. She did notice, however, that the boys from Fred Spencer's cabin were unusually quiet about the ghost.

Since the night she'd met Roarke at the pay phone, their relationship had gone from a rocky, rut-filled road to a smooth-surfaced freeway. He'd shocked her by ordering coffee served at their early-morning meetings. Although he hadn't specifically said it was for her benefit, Sherry realized it was.

"I don't think I ever thanked you," she told him one morning early in the week, when the staff had been dismissed from their dawn session.

"Thanked me?" He looked up from reading over his notes.

"For the coffee." She gestured with the foam cup, her gaze holding his.

Roarke grinned and his smile alone had the power to set sail to her heart.

"If you'll notice, I haven't been late for a single meeting since the coffee arrived. Fact is, I don't even need to open my eyes. The alarm goes off, I dress in the dark and follow my nose to the staff room."

"I thought that would induce you to get here on time," he said, his gaze holding hers.

Actually, the coffee hadn't a single thing to do with it. She came because it was the only time of day she could count on seeing Roarke. Generally, they didn't have much cause to spend time with each other, because Roarke was busy with the running of the camp and Sherry had her hands full with her seven charges. That he'd become so important to her was something of a quandary for Sherry. The minute he discovered she'd falsified her references, she'd be discharged from Camp Gitche Gumee. More than once Lynn had specifically told her that Mr. Roarke could forgive anything but dishonesty. Sherry had trouble being truthful with herself about her feelings for Roarke for fear of what she'd discover.

"I'm pleased the coffee helped." Dragging his eyes away from her, Roarke closed his notebook and walked out of the building with her. "Have you spent much time stargazing lately?"

She shook her head and yawned. "Too tired."

"Pity," he mumbled softly.

It would have been so easy for Sherry to forget where they were and who they were. She hadn't ever felt so strongly attracted to a man. It was crazy! Sometimes she wasn't completely sure she even liked him. Yet at all hours of the day and night, she found herself fantasizing about him. She imagined him taking her in his arms and kissing her, and how firm and warm his mouth would feel over her own. She dreamed about how good it would be to press her head against his shoulder and lean on him, letting his strength support her. She entertained fleeting fantasies even while she was doing everything in her power to battle the unreasonable desires.

"By the way," Roarke said, clearing his throat, "one

of the references you gave me came back marked 'no such address.'"

"It did?" Sherry's heart pounded, stone-cold. She'd prayed he wouldn't check, but knowing how thorough Roarke was made that wish nothing short of stupid. She was going to have to think of something, and quick.

"You must have listed the wrong address."

"Yes... I must have."

"When you've got a minute, stop off at the office and you can check it over. I'll mail it out later."

"Okay."

They parted at the pay phone, Sherry heading toward her cabin and Roarke toward the mess hall.

The cabin was buzzing with activity when Sherry stepped inside, but when the girls spied their counselor the noise level dropped to a fading hum and the seven returned to their tasks much too smoothly.

Suspicious, Sherry paused and looked around not knowing exactly what she expected to find. The girls maintained a look of innocence until Sherry demanded, "What's going on here?"

"Nothing," Sally said, but she was smiling gleefully.

Sherry didn't believe it for a moment. "I don't trust you girls. What are you up to?" Her gaze swept the room. Never in her life had she seen more innocent-looking faces. "Ginny?" Sherry turned her questions to the teenager who replaced her in the early mornings when she attended the staff meetings.

"Don't look at me." The teenager slapped her sides, looking as blameless as the girls.

"Something's going on." Sherry didn't need to be a psychic to feel the vibrations in the air. The seven wizards were up to something, and whatever it was seemed to have drawn them together. All through breakfast they were congenial and friendly, leaning over to whisper secrets to one another. Not a single girl found fault with another. Not even Gretchen! Their eyes fairly sparkled with mischief.

Sherry studied them as they left the mess hall for their classes. Her group stayed together, looking at one another and giggling with impish delight without provocation.

"Hi." Lynn pulled out a bench and sat across the table from Sherry.

Sherry pulled her gaze away from her wizards. "How's it going?"

Lynn shrugged. "I'm not sure."

"Have you been seeing Peter?"

"Are you kidding?" Lynn asked and snorted softly. "We know better. Oh, we see each other all the time, but never alone."

"That's wise."

"Maybe, but it sure is boring." Lynn lifted her mug to her lips and downed her hot chocolate. "It's getting so bad that the eighth-grade boys are beginning to look good to me."

Despite the seriousness of her friend's expression, Sherry chuckled. "Now that's desperate."

"Peter and I know the minute we sneak off, we'll get caught—besides we aren't that stupid." She sagged against the back of her chair. "I don't know what it is, but Mr. Roarke has this sixth sense about these things. He always seems to know what's happening. Peter's convinced that Mr. Roarke is aware of everything that goes on between us."

"How could he be?"

Lynn shrugged. "Who knows? I swear that man is clairvoyant."

"I'm sure you're exaggerating." Sherry's stomach reacted with dread. She was living with a time bomb ticking away—she'd been a fool to have tried to slip something as important as references past Roarke.

"Since Peter and I haven't seen a lot of each other," Lynn continued, "we've been writing notes. It's not the same as being alone with each other, but it's been… I don't know…kind of neat to have his thoughts there to read over and over again."

Sherry's nod was absent.

"Well, I suppose I'd best get to work." Lynn swung her leg over the bench and stood.

"Right," Sherry returned, "work."

"By the way, I think the signs are cute."

Sherry's head shot up. "Signs? What signs?"

"The ones posted outside the cabins. How'd you ever get Mr. Roarke to agree to it? Knowing the way he feels about fairy tales, it's a wonder—"

Rarely had Sherry moved more quickly. She'd known her girls were up to something. Signs. Oh, good heavens! By the time she was outside the mess hall, she was able to view exactly what Lynn had been talking about. In front of each cabin a large picket had been driven into the ground that gave the cabin a name. The older boys' quarters was dubbed Pinocchio's Parlor, the younger Captain Hook's Hangout. Cinderella's Castle was saved for the older girls. But by far the largest and most ornate sign was in front of her own quarters. It read: The Home of Sherry White and the Seven Wizards.

The quality of the workmanship amazed Sherry. Each letter was perfectly shaped and printed in bright, bold colors. There wasn't any question that her girls were responsible, but she hadn't a clue as to when they'd had the time. It came to her then—they hadn't painted the markers themselves, but ordered them. Gretchen had claimed more than once that her father had given her her own American Express card. She'd flashed it a couple of times, wanting to impress the others. Of all the girls, Gretchen had taken hold of the tales of fantasy with rare enthusiasm. She loved them, and had devoured all the books Sherry had given her.

"Miss White," Roarke's voice boomed from across the lawn.

Her blood ran cold, but she did her best not to show her apprehension. "Yes?"

He pointed in the direction of his headquarters. "In my office. Now!"

The sharp tone of his voice stiffened Sherry's spine. If she'd been in a less vulnerable position, she would have clicked her heels, saluted crisply and marched toward him with her arms stiffly swinging at her sides. Now, however, was not the time to display any signs of resistance. She could recognize hot water when she saw it!

It seemed the entire camp came to a halt. Several children lingered outside the classrooms, gazing her way anxiously. Teachers found excuses to wander around the grounds, a few were in a cluster, pointing in Sherry's direction. Fred Spencer, the counselor who had made his opinion of Sherry's ideas well-known, looked on with a sardonic grin. Each group paused to view the unfolding scene with keen interest.

Before Sherry had a chance to move, Roarke was at her side. Over the past few weeks, she'd provoked the stubborn camp director more times than she could count, but never anything like what he suspected she'd done this time. A muscle worked its way along the side of Roarke's jaw, tightening his features.

"M-maybe it would be best to talk about this after you've had the opportunity to cool down and think matters through. I realize it looks bad, but—"

"We'll discuss it *now*."

"Roarke, I know you're going to have trouble believing this, but I honestly didn't have anything to do with those signs."

His lip curled sardonically. "Then who did?"

Sally and Gretchen hurried up behind the couple. "Don't be angry with Miss White," Gretchen called out righteously. "She told you the truth. In fact, the signs are a surprise to her, too."

"Then just who is responsible?" Roarke demanded.

The two youngsters looked at each other, grinned and shouted their announcement. "Longfellow!"

"Who?"

Sherry wished the ground would open so she could dive out of sight and escape before anyone noticed. If Roarke had frowned upon her filling the girls' heads with fairy tales as "romantic nonsense," then he was sure to disapprove of her creating a friendly spook.

"Longfellow's our ghost," Sally explained, looking surprised that the camp director wouldn't know about him. "Longfellow, you know—he lives here."

"Your what? Who lives where?" Roarke managed to keep his voice even, but the look he gave Sherry could have forced the world into another ice age.

"The ghost who lives at Camp Gitche Gumee," Sally continued patiently. "You mean, no one's ever told you about Longfellow?"

"Apparently not," Roarke returned calmly. "Who told *you* about him?"

"Miss White," the girls answered in unison, sealing Sherry's fate.

"I see."

Sherry winced at the sharpness in his voice, but the girls appeared undaunted—or else they hadn't noticed.

"You aren't upset with Miss White, are you?" Sally asked, her young voice laced with concern. "She's the best counselor we ever had."

"The signs really were Longfellow's idea," Gretchen added dryly.

Roarke made a show of looking at his watch. "Isn't it about time for your first class? Miss White and I will discuss this matter in private."

The children scurried off to their class, leaving Sherry to face Roarke alone. Having two of her charges defend her gave her ego a boost. Roarke was so tall and overpowering that she realized, not for the first time, how easily he could intimidate her. Sherry squared her shoulders, thrust out her chin and faced him head-on.

She turned to squarely face him, hands on her hips, feet braced. "I have other plans this morning. If you'll excuse me, I would—"

"The only place you're going is my office."

"So you can shout at me?"

"So we can discuss this senselessness," he said through gritted teeth.

It wouldn't do any good to argue. He turned and left her to follow him, and because she had no choice, she did as he requested, dreading the coming confrontation. For the past few days at camp, Sherry had come to hope that things would be better between her and Roarke. The night he'd walked her back from the pay phone had blinded her to the truth. They simply didn't view these children in the same way. Roarke saw them as miniature adults and preferred to treat them as such. Sherry wanted them to be children. The clash was instinctive and intense.

Roarke held the office door open for her and motioned with his hand for her to precede him. Sherry remembered what Lynn had said about Roarke firing people in the mornings. Well here she was, but she wasn't going down without an argument. Of all the things she had expected to be dismissed over— falsified references, misleading lesson plans, ghost stories—now it looked as if she was going to get the shaft for something she hadn't even done.

"I already told you I had nothing to do with the signs," she spoke first.

"Directly, that may be true, but indirectly there's no one more to blame."

Sherry couldn't argue with him there. She was the one who had introduced the subject to her seven wizards.

"If you recall, I specifically requested that you stop filling the children's heads with flights of fancy."

"I did," she cried.

"It's all too obvious that you didn't." His shoulders stiff, he marched around the desk and faced her. Leaning forward, he placed his hands on the desktop and glared in her direction. "You're one of those people who request an inch and take a mile."

"I…"

"In an effort to compromise, I've given you a free hand with the nine-and ten-year-old girls. Against my better judgment, I turned my head and ignored gin rummy taught in place of statistics classes. I looked the other way while you claimed to be studying frozen molecules when in reality you were sampling home-made ice cream."

"Don't you think I know that? Don't you think I appreciate it?"

"Obviously, you don't," he insisted, his voice gaining volume with each word. "Not if you stir up more problems by conjuring up a…a ghost. Of all the insane ideas you've come up with, this one takes the cake."

"Longfellow's not that kind of spook."

His eyes narrowed with a dark, furious frown. "I suppose you're going to tell me—"

"He's a friendly spirit."

Roarke muttered something she couldn't hear and raked a hand through his hair. "I can't believe I'm listening to this."

"The girls have a hundred complaints a day. Wendy's Ken-Richie doll is missing—one of the ten she brought to camp."

"Ken who?"

"Her Ken doll that she named Ken-Richie."

"What the devil is a Ken doll?"

"Never mind, that's not important."

"Anything you do is important because it leads to disaster."

"All right," Sherry cried, losing patience. "You want to know. Fine. Ken-Richie is the mate for Barbie-Brenda. Understand that?"

* * *

Roarke was growing more frustrated by the minute. There had been a time when he felt he had a grip on what was happening at camp, but from the minute Sherry had arrived with her loony ideas, everything had slid downhill.

"Anyway," Sherry continued, "it's so much easier to blame Longfellow for stealing Ken-Richie than to have a showdown among the girls."

"Who actually took the…doll?"

"Oh, I don't know—no one does. That's the point. But I'm sure he'll turn up sooner or later."

"Do you actually believe this… Longfellow will bring him back?" Roarke taunted.

"Exactly."

"That's pure nonsense."

"To you, maybe, but you're not a kid and you're not a counselor."

"No, I'm the director of this camp, and I want this stupidity stopped. Now."

Sherry clamped her mouth closed.

"Is that understood, Miss White?"

"I can't."

"What do you mean you can't? You have my direct order."

She lifted her palms and shrugged her shoulders. "It's gone too far. Almost everyone in the entire camp knows about Longfellow now. I can't put a stop to the children talking about him."

Roarke momentarily closed his eyes. "Do you realize what you've done?"

"It was all in fun."

He ignored that. "This camp has a reputation for academic excellence."

"How can a make-believe ghost ruin that?"

"If you have to ask, then we're in worse trouble than I thought."

Sherry threw up her hands in disgust. "Oh, honestly!"

"This is serious."

Now it was Sherry's turn to close her eyes and gain control of her temper. She released a drawn-out sigh. "What is it you want me to do?" she asked, keeping her voice as unemotional as possible. "I realize that within a few weeks, I've managed to ruin the reputation for excellence of this camp—"

"I didn't say that," he countered sharply.

"By all rights I should be tossed out of here on my ear..."

Roarke raised both hands to stop her. They glared at each other, each daring the other to speak first. "Before this conversation heats up any more, I think we should both take time to cool down," Roarke said stiffly.

Sherry met his gaze defiantly, her heart slamming against her breast with dread. "Do you want me to leave?"

He hesitated, then nodded. "Maybe that would be best."

Tears burned the backs of her eyes and her throat grew tight with emotion. "I'll...pick up my check this afternoon."

Roarke frowned. "I want us to cool our tempers— I'm not firing you."

Sherry's head snapped up and her heart soared with hopeful expectation. Roarke wasn't letting her go! She felt like a prisoner who'd been granted a death row pardon by the governor at the last minute. "But it's morning—you mean, you don't want me to leave Camp Gitche Gumee?"

Roarke looked confused. "Of course not. What are you talking about?"

The flood of relief that washed over her submerged her in happiness. It took everything within Sherry not to toss her arms around his neck and thank him.

With as much aplomb as she could muster, she nodded, turned around and walked across the floor, but paused when she reached the door. "Thank you," she whispered, sincerely grateful.

It seemed the entire camp was waiting for her. A hush fell across the campus when she appeared. Faces turned in her direction and Lynn gestured with her hands, wanting to know the outcome.

Sherry smiled in response, and it seemed that everyone around released an elongated sigh. All except Fred Spencer, who Sherry suspected would be glad to see her leave. Until that moment, Sherry hadn't realized how many friends she'd made in her short stay at Camp Gitche Gumee. Her legs felt weak, her arms heavy. Although she'd been fortunate enough to hold on to her job, Roarke remained furious with her. More than anything she wanted to stay for the entire camp session. And not because she was running away from Phyliss, either.

She'd left Seattle because of her crazy, wonderful stepmother, seeking a respite from the woman she loved and didn't wish to offend. But Sherry wanted to stay in California for entirely different reasons. Some of which she sensed she didn't fully understand herself.

At break time, Sally, Gretchen and two other girls came storming into the cabin.

"Hi," Sherry said cheerfully. "What are you guys doing here?"

The girls exchanged meaningful glances. "Nothing," Wendy said, swinging her arms and taking small steps backward.

"We just wanted to be sure everything was okay."

Sherry's answering grin was wide. She winked and whispered, "Things couldn't be better."

"Good!" A breathless Jan and Jill arrived to chime in unison.

Producing a stern look was difficult, but Sherry managed. She pinched her lips together and frowned at her young charges. The last thing she needed was to do something else to irritate Roarke. "Aren't you girls supposed to be in class?"

"Yes, but…"

"But we wanted to see what happened to you."

"It's too hot to sit inside a classroom, anyway," Gretchen grumbled.

"Gretchen's right," Sally added, looking surprised to agree with the complainer.

"Scat," Sherry cried, "before I reach for my machine gun."

The girls let loose with a shriek of mock terror and ran from the cabin, down the steps and across the lawn. Sherry grinned as she watched them scatter like field mice before a prowling cat.

It was then that she noticed the signs in front of each cabin had been removed. She crossed her arms, leaned against the doorjamb and experienced a twinge of regret. Cinderella's Castle was far more original than Cabin Three, even Roarke had to admit that.

After such shaky beginnings, the morning progressed smoothly. Sherry dressed to work out in the exercise room, then ate lunch with the girls, who chatted easily. Sherry took a couple of minutes to joke about the signs, hoping to reassure them that everything was fine. But she didn't mention Longfellow, although the name of the make-believe ghost could be heard now and again from various tables around the mess hall.

Throughout the meal, Sherry had only a fleeting look at Roarke. He came in, made his announcements and joined the teachers at their table for the noontime meal. He spoke to several counselors, but went out of his way to avoid Sherry, she noted. She hadn't expected him to seek her out for conversation, but she didn't appreciate being ignored, either.

Following lunch, Sherry slipped into the exercise room. Ginny was already there working out with the weights.

"Hi," the young assistant greeted, revealing her pleasure at seeing Sherry.

"Hi," Sherry returned, climbing onto the stationary bicycle and inserting her feet into the stirrups. Pedaling helped minimize the effects of all the fattening food she was consuming at camp.

Ginny, strapping a five-pound belt around her own waist, studied Sherry. "You should wear weights if you expect the biking to do any good."

"No thanks," Sherry said with a grin. "I double-knot my shoelaces; that's good enough."

The teenager laughed. "I heard you had a run-in with Mr. Roarke this morning. How'd you make out?"

"All right, I suppose." Sherry would rather let the subject drop with that. The events of the morning were best forgotten.

"From what I heard, he's been on the warpath all day."

"Oh?" She didn't want to encourage the teenager to gossip, but on the other hand, she was curious to discover what had been happening.

"Apparently one of the kids got caught doing something and was sent into Mr. Roarke's office. When Mr. Roarke questioned him, the boy said Longfellow made him do it. Isn't that the ghost you told the girls about not so long ago?"

Sherry's feet went lax while the wheel continued spinning. Oh dear, this just wasn't going to be her day.

"Something else must have happened, too, because he looked as mad as a hornet right before lunch."

Sherry had barely had time to assimilate that when Lynn appeared in the doorway, her young face streaked with tears.

"Lynn, what happened?"

Sherry's friend glanced at Ginny and wiped the tears from her pale cheeks. "Can we talk alone?"

"Sure." Sherry immediately stopped pedaling and climbed off the bike. She placed her arm around the younger girl's shoulders. "Tell me what's upset you so much."

"I-it's Mr. Roarke."

"Yes," she coaxed.

"He found some of the notes I'd written to Peter.

He wants to talk to us first thing in the morning…the morning—we both know what that means. I…I think we're both going to be fired."

Chapter 7

Sherry woke at the sound of the alarm and lay with her eyes open, savoring the dream. She'd been in a rowboat with Roarke in the middle of the lake. The oars had skimmed the water as he lazily paddled over the silver water. Everything was different between them. Everything was right. All their disagreements had long since been settled. The pros and cons of a friendly ghost named Longfellow were immaterial. All that mattered was the two of them together.

The looks they'd shared as the water lapped gently against the side of the small boat reminded Sherry of the evening they'd sat on the porch and gazed into the brilliant night sky. Stars were in Sherry's eyes in her dream, too, but Jeff Roarke had put them there.

With a melancholy sigh, she tossed aside the covers and sat on the edge of the mattress. It was silly to be so affected by a mere dream, but it had been so real and so wonderful. However, morning brought with it the chill of reality, and Sherry was concerned for Lynn and Peter. She had to think of some way to help them.

After dressing, she held in a yawn and walked across the thick lawn to the staff room. Her arms were crisscrossed over her ribs, but Sherry couldn't decide if it was to ward off a morning chill or the truth that awaited her outside her dream world. Birds chirped playfully in the background and the sun glimmered through the tall timbers, casting a pathway of shimmering light across the dewy grass, giving Sherry hope.

At the staff room, Sherry discovered that only a couple of the other counselors had arrived. Roarke was there, standing at the podium in the front, flipping through his notes.

With the warm sensations of the dream lingering in her mind, Sherry approached him, noted his frown and waited for him to acknowledge her before she spoke. Uncomfortable seconds passed and still Roarke didn't raise his head. When he did happen to look up, his gaze met hers, revealing little. Sherry realized that he hadn't forgotten their heated discussion. He'd been the one to suggest that they delay talking because things were getting out of hand. But from the narrowed, sharp appraisal he gave her it was all too apparent that his feelings ran as hot today as they had the day before.

"Miss White." He said her name stiffly.

Sherry grimaced at the chill in his voice. "Good morning."

He returned her greeting with an abrupt nod and waited. There had never been a woman who angered

Roarke more than Sherry White. This thing with the ghost she'd invented infuriated him to the boiling point, and he'd been forced to ask her to leave his office yesterday for fear of what more he'd say or do. His anger had been so intense that he'd wanted to shake her. *Wrong*, his mind tossed back—it had taken every ounce of determination he possessed, which was considerable, not to pull her into his arms and kiss some common sense into her.

The power she had to jostle his secure, impenetrable existence baffled him. He'd never wanted a woman with the intensity that he wanted Sherry, and the realization was frightening. A full day had passed since their last encounter, and he still wasn't in complete control of his emotions. Even with all this time to cool his temper, she caused his blood to boil in his veins.

No other counselor had been granted the latitude he'd given her. He'd turned a blind eye to her other schemes, accepting lesson plans that stated she would be teaching a study on centrifugal force when he knew she was planning on cooking popcorn. The evening sessions weren't the only rule he'd stretched on her behalf. The other counselors would question the integrity of his leadership if they knew about Ralph. But the ghost—now that was going too far. The truth about Longfellow had driven him over the edge. She'd abused his willingness to adapt to her creativity and in the process infuriated him.

Although his emotions were muddled, no woman had intrigued him the way Sherry did, either. He couldn't seem to get her out of his mind. He had enough problems organizing this camp without entertaining romantic thoughts about one impertinent counselor.

"You wanted something?" he asked, forcing his voice to remain cool and unemotional.

"Yes…you said yesterday that you thought it'd be best if we continued our discussion later."

Roarke glanced at his watch. "There's hardly time now."

"I didn't mean this minute exactly," Sherry answered. He was making this more difficult than necessary.

"Is there something you'd like to say?"

"Yes."

"Then this afternoon would be convenient," Roarke said coldly. He might be agreeing to another meeting, he told himself, but he couldn't see what they had left to say. He'd been angry, true, but not completely unreasonable. Nothing she could say would further her cause.

Sherry tried to smile, but the effort was too much for her. "I'll be there about one o'clock."

"That would be fine."

By now the small room was filled to capacity, and she walked to the back, looking for a chair. Lynn had saved her a seat, and Sherry sank down beside her friend, disappointed and uncomfortable. Twenty minutes into the day and already her dream was shattered. So much for lingering looks and meaningful gazes. She might as well be made of mud for all the interest Jeff Roarke showed her.

The announcements were dealt with quickly, but

before Roarke could continue, Fred Spencer, the counselor for the older boys, raised his hand.

"Fred, you had a question?"

"Yes." Fred stood and loudly cleared his throat.
"There's been talk all over camp about Longfellow.
Who or what is he?"

Sherry scooted so far down in her chair that she was
in danger of slipping right onto the floor. Fred Spencer was a royal pain in the rear end as far as Sherry
was concerned.

"Longfellow is a friendly ghost," Roarke explained
wryly. "As I understand it, he derived his name from
Henry Wadsworth Longfellow, the poet."

Still Fred remained standing. "A ghost?" he shouted.
"And just whose idea was this nonsense?" A hum of
raised voices followed, some offended, others amused.
"Why, I've heard of nothing else for the past twenty-
four hours. It's Longfellow this, Longfellow that. The
least bit of confusion with kids can become a major
catastrophe. These children come to this camp to learn
responsibility. They're not gaining a darn thing by
placing the blame on an imaginary spirit."

Unable to endure any more, Sherry sprang to her
feet. "I believe you're putting too much emphasis on a
trivial matter. The camp is visited by a friendly ghost.
It doesn't need to be made into a big deal. Longfellow is for fun. The children aren't frightened by him,
and he adds a sense of adventure to the few weeks
they're here."

"Trivial," Fred countered, turning to face Sherry
with his hands placed defiantly on his hips. "I've had
nothing but problems from the moment this...this
Longfellow was mentioned."

"Sit down, Fred," Roarke said, taking control.

Fred ignored the request. "I suppose you're responsible for this phantom ghost, Miss White? Just like you were with those ridiculous signs?"

Sherry opened and closed her mouth. "Yes, I invented Longfellow."

"I thought as much," Fred announced with profound righteousness.

Again the conversational hum rose from the other staff members, the group quickly taking sides. From bits and pieces of conversations that Sherry heard, the room appeared equally divided. Some saw no problem with Longfellow while others were uncertain. Several made comments about liking Sherry's style, but others agreed with Fred.

Roarke slammed his fist against the podium. "Mr. Spencer, Miss White, I would greatly appreciate it if you would take your seats."

Fred sat, but he didn't remain silent. "I demand that we put an end to this ghost nonsense."

A muscle in Roarke's jaw twitched convulsively and his gaze lifted to meet and hold Sherry's. "I'm afraid it's too late for that. Word of Longfellow is out now, and any effort to do away with him would only encourage the children."

Grumbling followed, mostly from Fred Spencer and his cronies.

"My advice is to ignore him and hope that everyone will forget the whole thing," Roarke spoke above the chatter.

"What about Miss White?" Fred demanded. "She's been nothing but a worry from the moment she arrived. First those ridiculous signs and now this. Where will it end?"

"That's not true," Lynn shouted, and soared to her feet in an effort to defend her friend. She gripped the back of the chair in front of her and glared at the older man. "Sherry's been great with the kids!"

"Miss Duffy, kindly sit down," Roarke barked, raising his hands to quiet the room. The noise level went down appreciably, although the controversy appeared far from settled. He spoke to Fred Spencer with enough authority to quickly silence the other man. "This is neither the time nor the place to air our differences of opinion regarding another counselor's teaching methods."

Sherry wasn't fooled. Roarke wasn't defending her so much as protecting the others from criticism should Fred take exception to another's techniques. Fred Spencer's reputation as a complainer was as well-known as Gretchen's.

"If the staff can't speak out, then exactly whose job is it?" Fred shouted.

"Mine!" Roarke declared, and the challenge in his voice was loud and infinitely clear.

"Good, then I'll leave the situation in your hands."

From her position, Sherry could see that Fred wasn't appeased. Nor did she believe he would quietly drop the subject. From the beginning, she'd known he disagreed with her efforts with the children. Whenever he had the chance, he put down her ideas and found reason to criticize her.

The remainder of the meeting passed quickly, but not fast enough as far as Sherry was concerned. She and Lynn walked out of the staff room together.

"I can't believe that man," Lynn grumbled. "His idea of having fun is watching paint dry."

"Miss Duffy."

Roarke's cold voice stopped both women. The teenager cast a pleading glance at Sherry before turning around to face her employer.

"I believe we have an appointment."

"Oh, yes," Lynn said with a wan smile. "I forgot."

"I'm afraid that's part of the problem," Roarke returned with little humor. "You seem to be forgetting several things lately."

Sherry opened her mouth to dilute his sarcasm, but one piercing glare from Roarke silenced her. This wasn't her business. She didn't want to say or do anything to irritate him any more. Her greatest fear was that after the events of the morning, Roarke wasn't in any mood to deal kindly with Lynn and Peter. With a heavy heart, Sherry returned to her cabin.

Ginny had roused the girls and there was the typical mad confusion of morning. As usual there was fighting over the bathroom and how long Jan and Jill hogged the mirror to braid each other's hair.

"My mattress has got more lumps than the Cream of Wheat we had the other day," Gretchen muttered, sitting on the side of the bed and rubbing the small of her back.

Pamela was stroking Ralph's head with one finger inserted between the bars of the cage; both girl and rodent appeared content.

Sally and Wendy were already dressed, eager to start another day, while Diane slumbered, resisting all wake-up notices.

Sherry walked over to the sleeping youngster's bunk

and pulled out the Hardy Boys novel and flashlight from beneath her pillow. Once she'd turned the ten-year-old on to Judy Blume, Beverly Cleary and other preteen series books, there had been no stopping her. Diane's favorite had turned out to be John D. Fitzgerald's Great Brain books. The dry textbook material had been replaced by fiction, and a whole new world had opened up to the little girl. Now Sherry had to teach Diane about moderation. "Sleeping Beauty," she coaxed softly, "rise and shine."

"Go away," Diane moaned. "I'm too tired."

"Ken-Richie hasn't shown up yet," Wendy muttered disparagingly. "I wonder if Longfellow's ever going to bring him back." She might have mentioned the ghost, but her narrowed gaze surveyed the room, accusing each one who was unlucky enough to fall prey to her eagle eye.

"Hey, don't look at me," Sally shouted. "I wouldn't take your stupid Ken-Richie if someone paid me. *Batrachoseps attenuatus* are my thing."

"What?" Gretchen demanded.

"The California Slender Salamander," Wendy informed her primly. "If you were really so smart you'd know that."

"I'm not into creepy crawly things the way you are."

"I noticed."

"If my American Express card can't buy it, I don't want it," Gretchen informed her primly.

"It's nearly breakfast time," Sally encouraged Diane, roughly shaking the other girl's shoulder. "And Wednesday's French toast day."

"I don't want to eat," Diane murmured on the tail end of a yawn. "I'd rather sleep."

"Listen, kiddo," Sherry said, bending low and whispering in the reluctant girl's ear, "either you're up and dressed in ten minutes flat, or I won't loan you the other books in the Hardy Boys series."

Diane's dark brown eyes flew open. "Okay, okay, I'm awake."

"Here." Sally handed her a pair of shorts and matching top and Sherry looked on approvingly. The girls were developing rich friendships this summer. Even Gretchen, with her constant complaining and her outrageous bragging, had mellowed enough to find a friend or two. She still found lots of things that needed to be brought to Sherry's attention, like lumpy mattresses and the dangers of sleeping too close to the window. Her credit card was flashed for show when her self-worth needed a boost, but all in all, Gretchen had turned into a decent kid.

Feeling sentimental, Sherry looked around at the group of girls she'd been assigned and felt her heart compress with affection. These seven little wizards had securely tucked themselves into the pocket of her heart. She would long remember them. The girls weren't all she'd recall about this summer, though. Memories of Roarke would always be with her. Her stay at the camp was nearly half over and already she dreaded leaving, knowing it was doubtful that she'd see Roarke again. The thought brought with it a brooding sense of melancholy. For all their differences, she'd come to appreciate him and his efforts at the camp.

Much to Sherry's surprise, and probably Fred Spencer's too, the occupants of Cabin Four arrived in the dining hall precisely on time without stragglers. French toast was a popular breakfast, and when the girls had finished, Pam slipped Sherry an extra piece of the battered bread and asked if she would feed it to Ralph.

"Sure," Sherry assured the child. "But I'll tell him it's from you."

The blue eyes brightened. "He likes you, too, Miss White."

"And I think he's a great mascot for our cabin," she admitted in a whisper.

Once the mess hall had emptied, Sherry poured herself a steaming cup of coffee and paused to savor the first sip. She had just raised the cup to her lips when Lynn entered the room, paused to look around and, seeing Sherry, hurried across the floor.

"How'd it go?"

Lynn bit her lower lip and dejectedly shook her head. "Not good, but then I didn't expect it would with Mr. Roarke in such a lousy mood."

"He didn't fire you, did he?"

"I'm afraid so."

"But..." Sherry was so outraged she could barely speak. She hadn't believed he'd do something so unfair. True, the two had broken camp rules, but so had she, so had everyone. It wasn't as though Lynn and Peter were overtly carrying on a torrid romance. No one was aware that they cared for each other. If Roarke hadn't found their notes, he wouldn't even have known they were interested in each other.

"I have to pack my bags," Lynn said calmly, but her voice cracked, relaying her unhappiness. "But before I go I just wanted to tell you how much I enjoyed working with you." Tears briefly glistened in the other girl's eyes.

Flustered and angry, Sherry ran her fingers through her hair and sadly shook her head. "I don't believe this."

"He was upset, partly because of what happened this morning, I think, and other problems. There's a lot more to being camp director than meets the eye."

Sherry wasn't convinced she would have been so gracious with Roarke had their circumstances been reversed.

"Listen," Sherry said and braced her hands against her friend's shoulders. "Let me talk to him. I might be able to help."

"It won't do any good," Lynn argued. "I've never known Mr. Roarke to change his mind."

While chewing on her lower lip, a plan of action began to form in Sherry's befuddled mind. Sure, she could storm into Roarke's office and demand an explanation, but they'd just end up in another shouting match. As the camp director, he would no doubt remind her that whom he chose to fire or hire was none of her concern. The risk was too great, since he could just as easily dismiss her. Following the events of the past few days, she would be cooking her own goose to openly challenge him.

Her plan was better. Much better.

"Don't pack yet," Sherry said slowly, thoughtfully.

"What do you mean?"

"Just that. Go to your quarters and wait for me there."

"Sherry—" Lynn's brow creased with a troubled frown "—what do you have in mind? You don't look right. Listen, Mr. Roarke isn't having a good day—I don't think this would be the time to talk to him."

Lynn paused, set her teeth to chewing at the corner of her mouth and sighed. "At least tell me what you have in mind."

Sherry shook her head, not wanting to answer in case her scheme flopped. "Don't worry. I'll get back to you as soon as possible."

"Okay," Lynn agreed reluctantly.

Sherry headed directly to Roarke's office, knocking politely.

"Yes."

Sherry let herself inside. "Hello."

He hesitated, then raised his pen from the paper. This morning was quickly going from bad to worse. He'd been angry when he'd talked to Lynn and Peter. Angry and unreasonable. He'd dismissed them both unfairly and had since changed his mind. Already, he'd sent a message to the two to return to his office. He never used to doubt his decisions. Everything had been cut-and-dried. Black or white. Simple, uncomplicated. And then Sherry had tumbled into his peaceful existence with all the agility of a circus clown, and nothing had been the same since. He wanted to blame her for his dark mood. She occupied his mind night and day. Fiona was insipid tea compared to Sherry's sparkling champagne.

Sherry tempted him to the limit of his control. A simple smile left him weak with the longing to hold her. The energy it required for him to keep his hands off her was driving him crazy and weakening him. The situation between them was impossible, and his anger with Lynn and Peter had been magnified by his own level of frustration. And here she was again.

"Is there something I can do for you, Miss White?"

Her steady gaze held his. "I came to apologize."

"What have you done this time?"

His attitude stung her ego, but Sherry swallowed down her indignation and continued calmly. "Nothing new, let me assure you."

"That's a relief."

Her hand touched the chair. "Would you mind if I sat down?"

Pointedly, he glanced at his watch. "If you insist."

Sherry did, claiming the chair. "Things haven't gone very smoothly between us lately, have they?" she began in an even, controlled voice. "I decided that perhaps it would be best if we cleared the air."

"If it's about Longfellow—"

"No," she interrupted, then sadly shook her head. "It's more than that."

For several moments, he was silent, giving Sherry time to compose her thoughts. She'd come on Lynn and Peter's behalf, yearning to turn circumstances so he would rehire the two teenagers. That had been her original intention, but now that she was in his office, she couldn't go through with it. What she felt for this man was real, and their minor differences were quickly forming a chasm between them that might never be spanned unless she took the first leap. She turned her palms up and noted that his hard-sculpted features had relaxed. "I'm not even sure where to start."

"Miss White—"

"Sherry," she cried in frustration. "My name is Sherry and you know it." Abruptly, she made a move to stand, her hands braced on the chair arms. "And this is exactly what I'm talking about. I don't call you Mr.

Roarke, yet you insist upon addressing me formally, as if I were... I don't know, some stiff, starched counselor so unbending that I refuse anyone the privilege of using my name."

Roarke's gaze widened with her outburst. "You came to apologize?" He made the statement a question, confused by her irrational behavior. Sherry was too gutsy to be ambivalent. Whatever it was she had to say was real enough to sincerely trouble her.

"That was my original thought," she said, standing now and facing him. "But I'm not sure anymore. All I know is that I want things to be different between us."

"Different?"

"Yes," she cried, "every day, it seems, there's something that I've done to displease you. You can't even look at me anymore without frowning. I don't want to be a thorn in your side or a constant source of irritation."

"Sherry—"

"Thank you," she murmured, interrupting him with a soft smile. "I feel a thousand times better just having you say my name."

The frown worrying Roarke's brow relaxed, and a slow, sensuous smile transformed his face. "Although I may not have said it, I've always thought of you as Sherry."

"But you called me Miss White."

"The others..."

Briefly, she dropped her eyes, remembering Fred Spencer's dislike of her. "I know."

"I haven't been angry with you; it's just that circumstances have been working against us."

"I realize I haven't exactly made things easier."

* * *

Sherry didn't know the half of it, Roarke thought. At least once a day he'd been placed in the uncomfortable position of having to defend her from the jealousy and resentment of some others. But she was by far the most popular counselor in camp, and neither he nor anyone else was in any position to argue her success.

"I know, too," she continued, "that you've turned your head on more than one occasion while I've bent the rules and disrupted this camp."

"Bent the rules," he repeated with a soft laugh. "You've out-and-out pulverized them."

Sherry sighed with relief; she felt a hundred times better to be here with him, talking as they once had in the moonlight. How fragile that truce had been. Now, if possible, she wanted to strengthen that.

"It's important to me, Roarke—no matter what happens at camp—that we always remain friends."

Looking at her now, with the sunlight streaming through her chestnut hair, her dark eyes imploring his, searing their way through the thickest of resolves, it wasn't in Roarke to refuse her anything.

"You can be angry with me," she said. "Heaven knows I've given you plenty of reasons, but I have to feel deep down that as long as we share a foundation of mutual respect it won't matter. You could call me Miss White until the year 2020 and it wouldn't bother me, because inside I'd know."

Roarke was convinced she had no idea how lovely she was. Beautiful. Intelligent. Witty. Fun. He felt like a boy trapped inside on a rainy day. She was laughter and sunshine, and he'd never wanted a woman as badly as he did her at this moment.

He stood and moved to her side. Her gaze narrowed with doubt when he placed his hands on her shoulders and turned her to face him. "Just friends?" he asked softly, wanting so much more. After the first week he'd thought to send her straight back to Seattle, because in a matter of only a few days, she'd managed to disturb his orderly life and that of the entire camp. He hadn't. Her candor and wit had thrown him off balance. But staring at her now, he realized her eyes disturbed him far more. She had beautiful, soulful eyes that could search his face as though she were doing a study of his very heart.

Sherry's palms were flattened against Roarke's hard chest; her head tilted back to question the look in his eyes. Surely she was reading more than was there—yet what she saw caused her heartbeat to soar. "Roarke?" she questioned softly, uncertain.

"I want to be more than friends," he answered her, lowering his mouth to hers. "Much more than friends."

Her lips parted under his, warm and moist, eager and curious. For weeks, she'd hungered to feel Roarke's arms around her and experience the taste of his kiss. Now that she was cradled securely in his embrace, the sensation of supreme rightness burned through her. It was as though she'd waited all her life for exactly this moment, for exactly this man.

His arms tightened around her slender frame as he deepened the kiss, his mouth moving hungrily over hers, insistently shaping her lips with his own. Roarke's spirit soared and his heart sang. She'd challenged him, argued with him, angered him. And he loved her, truly loved her. For the first time in his life, he was head over heels in love. He'd thought himself exempt from the emotion, but meeting Sherry had convinced him otherwise.

"Sherry," he groaned. His hands pushing the hair back from her face, he spread eager kisses over her face.

Sherry's world was spinning and she slid her hands up his chest to circle his neck, clinging to the very thing that caused her world to career out of control. She was lost in a haze of longing.

Roarke groaned as she fit her body snugly to his. His mouth crushed hers, sliding insistently back and forth, seducing her with his moist lips until hers parted.

Sherry thought she'd die with wanting Roarke. He tore his lips from hers and held her as though he planned never to let her go. His arms crushed her, but she experienced no pain. Physical limitation prevented her from being any closer, and still she wasn't content, seeking more. His arms were wrapped around her waist, locked at the small of her back. She rotated her hips once, seeking a way to satisfy this incredible longing.

"Sherry, love," he groaned, "don't."

"Roarke, oh, Roarke, is this real?"

"More real than anything I've ever known," he answered, after a long moment.

She moved once more and he moaned, drew in a deep, audible breath and held it so long that she wondered if he planned ever to breathe again.

Raising her hands, she lovingly stroked his handsome face. "I feel like I could cry." She pressed her forehead to his chest. "I'm probably not making the least bit of sense."

Gently, he kissed the crown of her head. "I've wanted to hold you forever."

"Roarke," she said solemnly, raising her eyes to meet his. Her heart was shining through her gaze. "You can't fire Lynn and Peter. Please reconsider."

The words were like a knife ripping into his serenity. Roarke released Sherry and stepped back with such abruptness that she staggered a step. "Is that what this is all about?"

Her eyes mirrored her bewilderment. "No, of course not," she murmured, but she couldn't meet the accusing doubt in his eyes. "Originally I came because Lynn told me you'd dismissed both her and Peter, but…"

"So you thought that if you could get me to kiss you, I'd change my mind."

That was so close to the truth that Sherry yearned to find a hole, curl up in it and magically disappear. The words to explain how everything had changed once she'd arrived at his office died on her lips. It would do no good to deny the truth; Roarke read her far too easily for her to try to convince him otherwise.

She didn't need to say a word for him to read the truth revealed in her eyes. "I see," he said, his voice heavy with resentment.

Sherry flinched. She had to try to explain or completely lose him. "Roarke, please listen. I may have thought that at first, but…"

The loud knock against the door stopped her.

His face had become as hard as stone and just as implacable. "If you'll excuse me, I have business to attend to."

"No," she cried, "at least give me a chance to explain."

"There's nothing more to say." He walked across the room and opened the door.

Lynn and Peter stood on the other side. Instantly Lynn's gaze flew to Sherry, wide and questioning.

"Come in," Roarke instructed, holding open the door. "Miss White was just leaving."

Arching her back, Sherry moved past Peter. As Sherry neared Lynn, the other girl whispered, "Your plan must have worked."

"It worked all right—even better than she dared hope," Roarke answered for her with a look of such contempt that Sherry longed to weep.

Chapter 8

"Sherry, I'm sorry," Lynn said for the tenth time that day. "I didn't think Mr. Roarke could hear me."

Sherry's feet pedaled the stationary bike all the more vigorously. She'd hoped that taking her frustration out on the exercise bike would lessen the ache in her heart. She should have known better. "Don't worry about it. What's done is done."

"But Mr. Roarke hasn't spoken to you in a week."

"I'll survive." But just barely, she mused. When he was through being angry, they'd talk, but from the look of things it could be some time before he cooled down enough to reason matters through. There was less than a month left of camp as it was. For seven, long, tedious days, Roarke had gone out of his way to avoid her. If she were in the same room, he found something important to distract him. At the staff meetings, he didn't call upon her unless absolutely necessary and said "Miss White" with such cool disdain that he might as well have stabbed a hot needle straight through her.

By the sheer force of her pride, Sherry had managed to hold her head high, but there wasn't a staff member at Camp Gitche Gumee who wasn't aware that Sherry White had fallen from grace. Fred Spencer was ecstatic and thrived on letting smug remarks drop when he suspected there was no one else around to hear. Without Roarke to support her ideas, Fred was given free rein to ridicule her suggestions. Not a single thing she'd campaigned for all week had made it past the fiery tongue of her most ardent opponent.

When Sherry proposed a sing-along at dusk, Fred argued that such nonsense would cut into the cabin's evening lessons. Roarke neither agreed nor disagreed, and the suggestion was quickly dropped. When she'd proposed organized hikes for the study of wildflowers, there had been some enthusiasm, until Fred and a few others countered that crowding too many activities into the already heavy academic schedule could possibly overextend the counselors and the children. A couple debated the issue on Sherry's behalf, but in the long run the idea was abandoned for lack of interest. Again Roarke remained stoically silent.

"Maybe you'll survive," Lynn said, breathing heavily as she continued her sit-ups, "but I don't know about the rest of us."

"Roarke hasn't been angry or unreasonable." Sherry was quick to defend him, although he probably wouldn't have appreciated it.

"No, it's much worse than that," Lynn said with a tired sigh.

"How do you mean?"

"If you'd been here last year, you'd notice the difference. It's like he's built a wall around himself and is closing everybody off. He used to talk to the kids a lot, spend time with them. I think he's hiding."

"Hiding?" Sherry prompted.

"Right." Lynn sat upright and folded her arms around her bent knees, resting her chin there. "If you want the truth, I think Mr. Roarke has fallen for you, only he's too proud to admit it."

Sherry's feet pumped harder, causing the wheel to whirl and hiss. A lump thickened in her throat. "I wish that were true."

"Look at the way he's making himself miserable and, consequently, everyone else. He's responsible for the morale of this camp, and for the past week or so there's been a thundercloud hanging over us all."

To disagree would be to lie. Lynn was right; the happy atmosphere of the camp had cooled decidedly. As for Roarke caring, it was more than Sherry dared hope. She wanted to believe it, but she sincerely doubted that he'd allow a misunderstanding to grow to such outrageous proportions if he did.

"Have you tried talking to him?" Lynn said next. "It couldn't hurt, you know."

Maybe not, but Jeff Roarke wasn't the only one with a surplus of pride. Sherry possessed a generous portion of the emotion herself.

"Well?" Lynn demanded when Sherry didn't respond. "Have you even tried to tell him your side of it?"

The door to the exercise room opened, and both

women turned their attention to the tall, muscular man who stepped inside the room.

"Roarke," Sherry murmured. Her feet stopped pumping, but the rear wheel continued to spin.

He was dressed in faded gray sweatpants and a T-shirt, a towel draped around his neck. Just inside the door, he paused, looked around and frowned.

"Here's your chance," Lynn whispered, struggling to her feet. "Go for it, girl." She gave Sherry the thumbs-up sign and casually sauntered from the room, whistling a cheery tune as she went.

Sherry groaned inwardly; Lynn couldn't have been any more obvious had she openly announced that she was leaving to give the two time to sort out their myriad differences. Sherry nearly shouted for her to come back. Talking to Roarke in his present frame of mind would do no good.

While continuing to pedal, Sherry cast an anxious look in Roarke's direction. He ignored her almost as completely as she strove to ignore him. Lifting the towel from his neck he tossed it over the abdominal board of the weight gym and turned his back to her. The T-shirt followed the towel and he proceeded to go about bench-pressing a series of weights.

Without meaning to watch him, Sherry unwillingly found her gaze wandering over to him until it was all she could do to keep from staring outright. The muscles across his wide shoulders rippled with each movement, displaying the lean, hard build.

The inside of Sherry's mouth went dry; just watching him was enough to intoxicate her senses. His biceps bulged with each push.

The bike wheel continued to spin, but Sherry had

long since given up pedaling. She freed her feet from the stirrups and climbed off. Her legs felt shaky, but whether it was from the hard exercise or from being alone with Roarke, Sherry couldn't tell.

"Hello," she said, in a voice that sounded strange even to her own ears. Nonchalantly, she removed the helmet with the tiny side mirror from her head. "I suppose you're wondering why I'd wear a helmet when I'm pedaling a stationary bike," she said, hoping to make light conversation.

Sweat broke out across Roarke's brow, but it wasn't from the exertion of lifting the weights. It demanded all his concentration to keep his eyes off Sherry. Ignoring her was the only thing that seemed to work. "What you wear is none of my concern," he returned blandly.

"I—I don't feel like I'm really exercising unless I wear the helmet," she said next, looking for a smile to crack his tight concentration. She rubbed her hand dry against her shorts. The helmet hadn't been her only idea. She'd strapped a horn and side mirror onto the handlebars of the bike and had later added the sheepskin cover to pad the seat.

Roarke didn't comment.

He looked and sounded so infuriatingly disinterested that Sherry had to clear the tears from her throat before she went on.

"Roarke," she pleaded, "I hate this. I know you have good reason to believe I plotted...what happened in your office." She hesitated long enough for him to consider her words. "I'll be honest with you—that had been exactly my intention in the beginning. But once I got there I realized I couldn't do it."

"For someone who found herself incapable of such a devious action, you succeeded extremely well." He paused and studied her impassively.

"I w-want things to be different. I don't think we'll ever be able to settle anything here at camp, so I'm proposing that we meet in town to talk. I'll be in Ellen's Café tomorrow at six…it's my day off. I hope you'll meet me there."

Roarke wanted things settled, too, but not at the expense of his pride and self-respect.

"Answer me, Roarke. At least have the common courtesy to speak to me." His manner was so distant, so unconcerned that Sherry discovered she had to look away from him or lose her composure entirely.

"There's nothing to say," he returned stiffly.

The prolonged silence in the room was as irritating as fingernails on a blackboard. Sherry couldn't stand it any more than she could tolerate his indifference.

"If that's the way you wish to leave matters, then so be it. I tried; I honestly tried," she said, with such dejection that her voice was hardly audible.

Pointedly, Roarke looked in another direction.

With the dignity of visiting royalty, Sherry tucked her helmet under her arm, lifted her chin an extra notch and left the room. Jeff Roarke was a fool!

"Miss White, Miss White!" Diane ran across the campus to her side and stopped abruptly, cocking her head as she studied her counselor. "You're crying."

Sherry nodded and wiped the moisture from her face with the back of her hand.

"Are you hurt?"

"In a manner of speaking." Diane was much too perceptive to fool. "Someone hurt my feelings, but I'll be all right in a minute."

"Who?" Diane demanded, straightening her shoulders. From the little girl's stance, it looked as though she was prepared to single-handedly take on anyone who had hurt her friend and counselor.

"It doesn't matter who. It's over now, and I'll be fine in a minute." Several afternoons a week, Sherry sat on the lawn and the children from the camp gathered at her feet. As a natural born storyteller, she filled the time with make-believe tales from the classics and history. The children loved it, and Sherry enjoyed spending time with them. "Now what was it you needed?"

Shyly Diane looked away.

Sherry laughed. "No, let me guess. I bet you're after another book. Am I right?"

The youngster nodded. "Can I borrow the last book in the Great Brain series?"

"One great brain to another," Sherry said, forcing the joke.

"Right. Can I?"

Sherry looped her arm around the child's small shoulders. "Sure. This story is really a good one. Tom contacts the Pope…well, never mind, you'll read about it yourself."

They'd gone about halfway across the thick carpet of grass when a piercing scream rent the air. Startled, Sherry turned around and discovered Sally running toward her, blood streaming down her forehead and into her eyes, nearly blinding her.

"Miss White, Miss White," she cried in terror. "I fell! I fell!"

Sherry's stomach curdled at the sight of oozing blood. "Diane," she instructed quickly, "run to the cabin and get me a towel. Hurry, sweetheart."

With her arms flying, Diane took off like a jet from a crowded runway.

"I saw it happen," Gretchen cried, following close on Sally's heels and looking sickly pale. "Sally slipped and hit her head on the side of a desk."

"It's fine, sweetheart," Sherry reassured the injured youngster. She placed her hand on the side of Sally's head and found the gash. Pressing on it gently in an effort to stop the ready flow of blood, she guided the girl toward the infirmary.

"Gretchen, run ahead and let Nurse Butler know we're coming."

"It hurts so bad," Sally wailed.

"I'm sure it does, but you're being exceptionally brave."

Breathless, Diane returned with the towel. Sherry took it and replaced her hand with the absorbent material.

The buzzer rang in the background, indicating that the next class was about to start.

Gretchen and Diane exchanged glances. "I don't want to leave my friend," Gretchen murmured, her voice cracking.

Both Gretchen and Diane were frightened, and sending them away would only increase their dismay and play upon their imaginations, Sherry reasoned.

"You can stay until we're all sure Sally's going to be fine. Now, go do what I said."

Gretchen took off at a full run toward the nurse's office, with Diane in hot pursuit. By the time Sherry reached the infirmary, Kelly Butler, the wife of the younger boys' counselor, had been alerted and was waiting.

"Miss White, I'm scared," Sally said, and sniffled loudly.

"Everything's going to be fine," Sherry assured her mini-scientist, standing close to her side.

"Will you stay with me?"

"Of course." Sally was her responsibility, and Sherry wouldn't leave the child when she needed her most—no matter how much blood there was.

"This way." Kelly Butler motioned toward the small examination room.

While maintaining the pressure to the gash, Sherry helped Sally climb onto the table. Gretchen and Diane stood in the doorway, looking on.

"You two will have to stay outside until I'm finished," the nurse informed the girls.

Both girls sent pleading glances in Sherry's direction. "Do as she says," Sherry told them. "I'll be out to tell you how Sally is in a few minutes."

Halfway through the examination Sherry started to feel light-headed. Her knees went rubbery, and she reached for a chair and sat down.

"Are you all right?" Kelly asked her.

"I'm fine," she lied.

"Well, it isn't as bad as it looks," the nurse said. She paused to smile at the youngster. "We aren't going to need to take you into Arrow Flats for stitches, but I'll have to cut away your bangs to put on a bandage."

"Can I look at it in a mirror?" The shock and pain had lessened enough for Sally's natural curiosity to take over. "If I don't become a biochemist, then I might decide to be a doctor," Sally explained haughtily.

Sherry's nauseated feeling continued, and forcing a smile, she stood. "I'll go tell Diane and Gretchen that Sally's going to recover before they start planning her funeral."

"Thanks for staying with me, Miss White," Sally said, gripping the hand mirror.

"No problem, kiddo."

"You're going to make a great mom someday."

The way she was feeling caused Sherry to sincerely doubt that. The sight of blood had always bothered her, but never more than now. Taking deep breaths to dispel the sickly sensation, she stood and let herself out of the examination room.

Her two charges were missing. Sherry blinked, but Jeff Roarke, who sat in their place, didn't vanish. The light-headed feeling persisted, and she wasn't sure if he was real or a figment of her stressed-out senses.

"How is she?" he asked, coming to his feet.

"Fine." At the moment, Sally was doing better than Sherry. "Head wounds apparently bleed a lot, but it doesn't look like she's going to need stitches."

Roarke nodded somberly. "That's good."

"Where are Diane and Gretchen?"

"I sent them back to class," he told her. "I heard how you took control of the situation."

Sherry bristled. "I suppose you'd prefer to believe that I'd panic when confronted with a bleeding child."

"Of course not," he flared.

Trying desperately to control the attack of dizziness, Sherry reached out and gripped the edge of a table.

"You've got blood on your sweatshirt," Roarke said.

Sherry glanced down and gasped softly as the walls started spinning. She wanted to comment, but before she could the room unexpectedly went black.

Roarke watched in astonishment as Sherry crumpled to the floor. At first he thought she was playing another of her silly games. It would be just like her to pull a crazy stunt like that. Then he noted that her coloring was sickly, almost ashen, and immediately he grew alarmed. This wasn't any trick, she'd actually fainted! He fell to his knees at her side and tossed a desperate look over his shoulder, thinking he should call the nurse. But Kelly was already busy with one patient.

He reached for Sherry's hand and lightly slapped her wrist. He'd seen someone do this in a movie once, but how it was supposed to help, he didn't know. His own heart was hammering out of control. Seeing her helpless this way had the most unusual effect upon him. All week he'd been furious with her, so outraged at her underhandedness that he'd barely been able to look at her and not feel the fire of his anger rekindled. He wasn't particularly proud of his behavior, and he'd chosen to blame Sherry for his ill-temper and ugly moods all week. He'd wanted to forget she was around, and completely cast her from his mind once the summer was over.

Seeing her now, he felt as helpless as a wind-tossed leaf, caught in a swirling updraft of emotion. He was falling in love with this woman, and pretending otherwise simply wasn't going to work. She was a schemer, a manipulator...and a joy. She was fresh and alive and unspoiled. The whole camp had been brought to life with her smile. Even though this was her first year as a counselor, she took to it as naturally as someone who had been coming back for several summers. Her mind was active, her wit sharp and she possessed a genuine love for the children. They sensed it and gravitated toward her like bees to a blossoming flower.

She moaned, or he thought she did; the sound was barely audible. Roarke's brows drew together in a heavy frown, and he gently smoothed the hair from her face. He'd never seen anyone faint before and he wasn't sure what to do. He elevated her head slightly and noted evidence of fresh tears. Dealing with Sally's injury hadn't been the source of these. From everything Gretchen and Diane had told him, Sherry had handled the situation without revealing her own alarm. No, he had been the one who'd made her cry by treating her callously in the exercise room.

Roarke's eyes closed as hot daggers of remorse stabbed through him. The urge to kiss her and make up for all the pain he had caused her was more than he could resist. Without giving thought to his actions, he secured his arms beneath her shoulders and raised her. Then tenderly, with only the slightest pressure, he bent to fit his lips over hers.

Chapter 9

Sherry didn't know what was happening, but the most incredible sensation of warmth and love surrounded her. Unless she was dreaming, Roarke was kissing her. If this was some fantasy, then she never wanted to wake up. It was as though the entire week had never happened and she was once again in Roarke's arms, reveling in the gentleness of his kiss. The potent feelings were far too wonderful to ignore, and she parted her lips, wanting this moment to last forever. She sighed with regret when the warmth left her.

"Sherry?"

Her eyes blinked open and she moaned as piercing sunlight momentarily blinded her. She raised her hand to shield her vision and found Roarke bending over her.

"Roarke?" she asked in a hoarse whisper. "What happened?"

"You fainted."

She surged upright, bracing herself on one elbow. "I did what?"

Roarke's smile was smug. "You fainted."

It took a moment for her to clear her head. "I did?"

"That's what I just said."

"Sally…"

"Is fine," he reassured her. "Do you do this type of thing often?"

Sherry rubbed a hand over her face, although she remained slightly disoriented. "No, it feels weird. I've never been fond of the sight of blood, but I certainly didn't pass out because of it."

"When was the last time you had something to eat?"

Sherry had to think. Her appetite had been nil for days. She wasn't in the habit of eating breakfast unless it was something like a quick glass of orange juice and a dry piece of toast. This morning, however, she hadn't bothered with either breakfast or lunch.

"Sherry?" he prompted.

"I don't know when I last ate. Yesterday at dinnertime, I guess." She'd been so miserable that food was the last thing she'd wanted.

Roarke's frown deepened, and his arm tightened around her almost painfully. "Of all the stupid—"

"Oh, stop!" She jerked herself free from his grip and awkwardly rose to her feet. "Go ahead and call me stupid…but why stop with that? You've probably got ten other names you're dying to use on me."

Roarke's mouth thinned, but he didn't rise to the bait. The last thing he'd expected was for her to fight him. This woman astonished him. She was full of surprises and…full of promise. Even when she was semiconscious, she had shyly responded to his kiss. He was embarrassed by the impulse now. Who did he think he was—some kind of legendary lover?

"You're coming with me," he commanded.

"Why? So you can shout at me some more?" she hissed at him like a cat backed into a corner, seeking a means of escape.

"No," he returned softly. "So I can get you something to eat."

"I can take care of myself, thank you very much."

Roarke snickered. "I can tell. Now stop arguing."

Sherry closed her mouth and realized what a fool she was being. For an entire week, she'd wanted to talk to him, spend time alone with him, and now when he'd suggested exactly that, she was making it sound like a capital offense.

Roarke led the way out of the infirmary, and Sherry followed silently behind him. The cooking staff were busy making preparations for the evening meal, and the big kitchen was filled with the hustle and bustle of the day. Roarke approached the cook, who glanced in Sherry's direction and nodded as Roarke said something to him.

Roarke returned to her. "He's going to scramble you some eggs. I suggest you eat them."

"I will," she promised, then watched helplessly as Roarke turned and walked out of the mess hall, leaving her standing alone.

Ellen's Café in Arrow Flats was filled with the weeknight dinner crowd. Sherry sat at a table by the window and studied the menu, although she'd read it so many times over the past twenty minutes that she could have recounted it from memory.

"Do you want to order, miss?" the young waitress in the pink uniform asked. "It looks like your friend isn't going to make it."

"No, I think I'll hold off for a few more minutes, if you don't mind."

"No problem. Just give the signal when you're ready."

"I will." Sherry felt terrible. More depressed than she could remember being in months. She'd really hoped tonight with Roarke would make a difference. She'd put such high hopes in the belief that if they could get away from the camp to meet on neutral ground and talk freely, then maybe they could solve the problems between them.

Just then the café door whirled open. Sherry's gaze flew in that direction, her heart rocketing to her throat as Roarke stepped inside. His gaze did a sweeping inspection of the café, and paused when he found Sherry. He sighed and smiled.

To Sherry it seemed that everyone and everything else in the restaurant faded from view.

"Hi," he said, a bit breathlessly, when he joined her. He pulled out the chair across the table from her and sat. "I apologize for being late. Something came up at the last minute, and I couldn't get away."

"Problems at the camp?"

Forcefully, he expelled his breath and nodded. "I don't want to talk about camp tonight. I'm just a lonely college professor looking for a quiet evening."

"I'm just a sweet young thing looking for a college professor seeking a quiet evening."

"I think we've found each other." Roarke's grin relaxed the tight muscles in his face. He'd convinced himself that Sherry had probably left when he didn't show. They both needed this time away from camp. He'd been miserable and so had she.

He was here at last, Sherry mused silently. Roarke was with her, and the dread of the past pain-filled minutes was wiped out with one Jeff Roarke smile.

"Have you ordered?"

Sherry shook her head and lowered her gaze to the memorized menu. "Not yet."

Roarke's eyes dropped, too, as he studied his own. Choosing quickly, he set the menu beside his plate. "I highly recommend the special."

"Liver and onions? Oh, Roarke, honestly." She laughed because she was so pleased he was there, and because liver and onions sounded exactly like a meal he'd enjoy.

"Doubt me if you will, but when liver hasn't been fried to a crisp, it's good."

Sherry closed her menu and set it aside. "Don't be disappointed, but I think I'll go with the French dip."

Roarke grinned and shook his head. "I never would have believed Miss Sherry White could be so boring."

"Boring!" She nearly choked on a sip of iced tea.

"All right, all right, I'll revise that." Laugh lines formed deep grooves at the corners of his eyes. "I doubt that you'll ever be that. I can see you at a hundred and ten in the middle of a floor learning the latest dance step."

Sherry's hand circled her water glass. "I'll accept that as a compliment." But she didn't want to be on any dance floor if her partner wasn't Jeff Roarke, she added silently.

The amusement drained from his eyes. "What you said yesterday hit home."

Sherry looked up and blinked, uncertain. "About what?"

"That you wanted things to be different between us. I do too, Sherry. If we'd met any place but at camp things would be a lot easier. I have responsibilities—for that matter, so do you. Camp isn't the place for a relationship—now isn't the time."

Nervously, her fingers toyed with the fork stem. She didn't know what to say. Roarke seemed to be telling her that the best thing for them to do was ignore the attraction between them, pretend it wasn't there and go on about their lives as though what they felt toward each other made no difference.

"I see," she said slowly, her high spirits sinking to the depths of despair.

"But obviously, that bit of logic isn't going to work," Roarke added thoughtfully. "I've tried all week, and look what happened. I can't ignore you, Sherry, it's too hard on both of us."

The smile lit up her face. "I can't ignore you, either. As it turns out, I'm here and you're here."

His eyes held hers. "And there's no place else I'd rather be. For tonight, at least, we're two people with different tastes and lifestyles who happened to meet in an obscure café in Arrow Flats, California."

Sherry smiled and nodded eagerly.

The waitress came and took their order, and Sherry and Roarke talked throughout the meal and long after they'd finished. They lingered over coffee, neither wanting the evening to end.

They left the café when *the* Ellen herself appeared from the kitchen and flipped the sign in the window to Closed. She paused to stare pointedly at them.

"I have the feeling she wants us to leave," Roarke muttered, looking around and noting for the first time that they were the only two customers left in the café.

Sherry took one last sip of her coffee and placed her paper napkin on the tabletop.

Roarke grinned and scooted back his chair to stand, and Sherry rose and followed him out of the restaurant.

"Where are you parked?" he asked.

"Around the corner."

He reached for her hand, lacing her fingers with his own. The action produced a soft smile in Sherry. Something as simple as holding her hand would be out of the question at camp. But tonight it was the most natural thing in the world.

"It's nearly ten," Roarke stated, surprise lifting his husky voice.

It astonished Sherry to realize that they'd sat and talked for more than three and a half hours. Although they hadn't touched until just now, she'd never felt closer to Roarke. When they were at camp it seemed that their differences were magnified a thousandfold by circumstances and duty. Tonight they could be themselves. He'd astonished her. Amused her. Being with Roarke felt amazingly right.

He hesitated in front of the SUV. The camp logo was printed on the side panel.

Roarke opened the driver's side for her, and Sherry

tossed her purse inside. They stood with the car door between them.

"Roarke?" she whispered, curious. "This may sound like a crazy question, but yesterday when I fainted... did you kiss me?"

His grin was slightly off center as he answered her with a quick nod. He'd felt like a fool afterward, chagrined by his own actions. He wasn't exactly the model for Prince Charming, waking Sleeping Beauty with a secret kiss.

"I thought you must have," Sherry said softly. She'd felt so warm and secure that she hadn't wanted to wake up. "I was wondering is all," she added, a little flustered when he didn't speak.

Roarke caressed her cheek with his right hand. "Are you worried you'll have to pass out a second time before I do it again?"

She smiled at that. "The thought had crossed my mind."

"No," he said softly, sliding his hand down her face to the gentle slope of her shoulder. "Just move out from behind the car door."

Smiling, she did, deliberately closing it before walking into his arms. Roarke brought her close, breathed in the heady female scent of her and sighed his appreciation. His lips brushed against her temple, savoring the marvelous silken feel of her in his arms and the supreme rightness of holding her close. He kissed her forehead and her cheek, her chin, then closed her eyes with his lips.

His gentleness made Sherry go weak. She slipped her arms up his chest and around his neck, letting his strength absorb her weakness.

Roarke paused to glance with irritation at the street-light, and suddenly decided he didn't care who saw him with Sherry or any consequences he might suffer as a result. He had to taste her. He kissed her then, deeply, yearning to reveal all the things he couldn't say with words. Urgently, his lips moved over hers with a fierce tenderness, until she moaned and responded, opening her mouth to him with passion and need.

Sherry's husky groan of pleasure throbbed in Roarke's ears and raced through his blood like quick-silver. He kissed her so many times he lost count, and she was weak and clinging to his arms. His own self-restraint was tested to the limit. With every vestige of control he possessed, he broke off the kiss and bur-ied his face in her shoulder. He drew in a long breath and slowly expelled it in an effort to regain his wits and composure. He couldn't believe he was kissing her like this, in the middle of the street, with half the town looking on. Holding her, touching her, had been the only matters of importance.

"I'll follow you back to camp," he said, after a long moment.

Still too befuddled to speak, Sherry nodded.

Roarke dropped his arms and watched reluctantly as she stepped away. It was all he could do not to haul her back into his arms and kiss her senseless. From the first moment that he'd watched her interact with the children, Roarke had known that she was a natu-ral. What he hadn't guessed was that this marvelous woman would hold his heart in the palm of her hand. He couldn't tell Sherry what he felt for her now; to do so would create the very problem he strove to avoid between staff members. Romance and camp were like oil and water, not meant to mix. To leave her doubting was regrettable, but necessary until the time was right. Never, in all the years that he'd been camp director, had Roarke more looked forward to August.

Roarke was busy all the following day. Even if he'd wanted, he wouldn't have been able to talk to Sherry. They passed each other a couple of times but weren't able to exchange anything more than a casual greeting. Now, at the end of another exhausting day, he felt the need to sit with her for a time and talk. For as long as he could, he resisted the temptation. At nine-thirty, Roarke decided no one would question it if they saw him sitting on her porch talking.

As he neared her cabin, he heard the girls clamoring inside.

"I saw Buttercup," one of the girls cried, the alarm in her voice obvious.

Roarke glanced around, and sure enough, there was his calico, snooping around the cabin, peeking through the window. Naturally, Sherry's girls would be concerned over the feline, since they continued to house the rodent mascot. Every other cabin had welcomed Buttercup, but the cat had made his choice obvious and lingered around Sherry's, spending far more time there than at all the others combined. Roarke wasn't completely convinced it was solely the allure of Ralph, the hamster, either. Like almost everyone else in camp, the feline wanted to be around Sherry. Roarke watched with interest whenever Fred Spencer voiced his objections. It was obvious to Roarke that the man was jealous of Sherry's popularity, and his resentment shone through at each staff meeting.

"I saw him, too!" The commotion inside the cabin continued.

Roarke climbed the three steps that led to the front door and crouched down to pick up his cat.

"Now," Sherry's excited voice came at him from inside the cabin.

Just as he'd squatted down the front door flew open, and he looked up to find Sherry standing directly in front of him, pointing a Thompson submachine gun directly at his chest.

Before he could shout a warning, a piercing blast of water hit him square in the chest.

Chapter 10

The blast of water was powerful enough to knock Roarke off balance. Crouched as he was, the force, coupled with the shock of Sherry aiming a submachine gun at him, hurled him backward.

"Roarke," Sherry screamed and slapped her hand over her mouth, smothering her horror, which soon developed into an out-and-out laugh.

Buttercup meowed loudly and scrambled from Roarke's grip, darting off into the night.

"Who the hell do you think you are?" Roarke yelled. "Rambo?" With as much dignity as he could muster, he stood and brushed the grit from his buttocks and hands.

"Mr. Roarke said the H-word." Righteously, Gretchen turned and whispered to the others.

Six small heads bobbed up and down in unison. Unlike Sherry, they recognized that this wasn't the time to show their amusement. Mr. Roarke didn't seem to find the incident the least bit humorous.

"I'm going to say a whole lot more than the H-word if you don't put that gun away," he shouted, his features tight and impatient.

Doing her utmost to keep from smiling, Sherry lowered her weapon, pointing the extended barrel toward the hardwood floor. "I apologize, Roarke, I wasn't aiming for you. I thought Buttercup was alone."

"That cat happens to be the camp pet," he yelled. He paused and inhaled a steadying breath before continuing. "Perhaps it would be best if we spoke privately, Miss White. Girls, if you'd kindly excuse us a moment."

"Oh, sure, go ahead," Gretchen answered for the group, and the others nodded in agreement.

"Sure," Jill and Jan added.

"Feel free," Sally inserted.

"Why not?" Diane wanted to know.

The amusement drained from Sherry's eyes. So much for the new wonderful understanding between them and the evening they'd spent together in town. Roarke knew how much she hated it when he sarcastically called her Miss White. No one did it quite the way he did, saying her name with all the coldness of arctic snow. Snow White. That's what the girls liked to call her when she wasn't around, although they didn't think she knew it.

Sherry stepped onto the porch and Roarke closed the door. "I do apologize, Roarke." Maybe if she said it enough times he'd believe her.

"I sincerely doubt that," he grumbled, swatting the

moisture from his shirt. "Good grief, woman, don't you ever do anything like anyone else?"

"I was protecting Ralph," she cried, growing agitated. "What was I supposed to do? Invite Buttercup in for lunch and break seven little girls' hearts?"

"I certainly don't expect you to drown him."

"Fiddlesticks!" she returned, staring him down. "You're just mad because I got you wet. Believe me, it was unintentional. If I'd known you were going to be on the other side of the door, do you honestly think I would have pulled the trigger?"

"You'll do anything for a laugh," he countered.

Sherry was so angry, she could barely speak. "I might as well have, you're a wet blanket anyway." Following that announcement, she marched into the cabin and slammed the door.

Regret came instantly. What was she doing? Sherry wailed inwardly. She'd behaved like a child when she so much wanted to be a woman. But Roarke always assumed the worst of her, and his lack of trust was what hurt most.

Roarke had half a mind to follow her. He opened his mouth to demand that she come back out or he'd have her job, but the anger drained from him, leaving him flustered and impatient. For a full minute he didn't move. Finally he wiped his hand across his face, shrugged and headed back to his quarters, defeated and discouraged.

That night, Roarke lay in bed thinking. Sherry possessed more spirit than any woman he'd ever known. He would have loved to get a picture of the expression on her face once she realized she'd blasted him with that crazy weapon. But instead of laughing as they should have, the episode had ended in a shouting match. It seemed he did everything wrong with this woman. Maybe if he hadn't kept his nose buried in a book most of his life he'd know more about dealing with the opposite sex. Fiona was so much like him that they'd drifted together for no other reason than that they shared several interests. As he lay in bed, Roarke wasn't sure he could even remember what Fiona looked like.

He'd never been a ladies' man, although he wasn't so naive as to not realize that the opposite sex found him attractive. The scars of his youth went deep. The bookworm, four-eyes and all the other names he'd been taunted with echoed in the farthest corners of his mind. As an adult he'd avoided women, certain that they would find his intelligence and his dedication to the child genius a dead bore. He was thirty-six, but when it came to this unknown, unsettling realm of romance, he seemed to have all the social grace of a sixteen-year-old.

"Miss White," Pamela called into the dark silence.

"Yes?" Sherry sat upright and glanced at the bedside clock. Although it was well past midnight, she hadn't been able to sleep. "Is something wrong, honey?"

"No."

The direction of the small voice told Sherry that Pamela's head hung low. "Come here, and we can talk without waking the others." Sherry patted the flat space beside her and pulled back the covers so Pam could join her in bed.

The little girl found her way in the dark and climbed

onto the bed. Sherry sat upright and leaned against the thick pillows, wrapping her arm around the nine-year-old's shoulders.

"It's Ralph's fault, isn't it?" Pamela said in a tiny, indistinct voice.

"What is?"

"That Mr. Roarke yelled at you."

"Honey," Sherry said with a sigh, "how can you possibly think that? I squirted Mr. Roarke with a submachine gun. He had every right to be upset."

"But you wouldn't have shot him if it hadn't been for Ralph. And then he got mad, and it's all my fault because I smuggled Ralph on the airplane without anyone knowing."

"Mr. Roarke had his feathers ruffled is all. There isn't anything to worry about."

Pamela raised her head and blinked. "Will he send you away?"

Knowing that Roarke could still find out that she'd deceived him on the application form didn't lend her confidence. "I don't think so, and if he does it'd be for something a lot more serious than getting him wet."

Pamela shook her head. "My mom and dad shout at each other the way you and Mr. Roarke do."

"We don't mean to raise our voices," Sherry said, feeling depressed. "It just comes out that way. Things will be better tomorrow." Although she tried to give them confidence, Sherry's words fell decidedly flat.

Throughout the staff meeting the following morning Sherry remained withdrawn and quiet. When Roarke didn't seek her out when the session was dismissed, she returned to her cabin. The girls, too, were quiet, regarding her with anxious stares.

"Well?" Gretchen finally demanded.

"Well, what?" Sherry asked, pulling a sweatshirt over her head, then freeing her hair from the constricting collar. When she finished, she turned to find all seven of the girls studying her.

"How did things go with Mr. Roarke?"

"Is he still angry?"

"Did he yell at you again?"

Sherry raised her hands to stop them. "Everything went fine."

"Fine?" Seven thin voices echoed hers.

"All right, it went great," Sherry sputtered. "Okay, let's move it—it's breakfast time."

A chorus of anxious cries followed her announcement as the girls scrambled for their sweaters, books and assorted necessities.

For most of the day Sherry stayed to herself, wanting to avoid another confrontation with Roarke. However, by late afternoon, she felt as if she was suffering from claustrophobia, avoiding contact with the outside world, ignoring the friends she'd made this summer. There had to be a better way!

Most of the classes had been dismissed, and Sherry sat on the porch steps of her cabin, watching the children chasing one another about, laughing and joking. The sound of their amusement was sweet music to her ears. It hadn't been so long ago that she'd wondered about these mini-geniuses, and she was pleased to discover they were learning to be children and have fun. Several of the youngsters were playing games she'd taught them.

A breathless Gretchen soon joined Sherry, sitting on the step below hers. As was often the case when

Sherry was within view of the children, she was soon joined by a handful of others.

"Will you tell me the story about how the star got inside the apple again?" Gretchen asked. "I tried to tell Gloria, but I forgot part of it."

"Sure," Sherry said with a grin and proceeded to do just that. Someone supplied her with an apple and a knife, and she took the fruit and cut it crosswise at the end of the story, holding it up to prove to the growing crowd of children that there was indeed a star in every apple.

Fred Spencer approached as she was speaking, pursing his lips in open disapproval. Sherry did her best to ignore him. She didn't understand what Fred had against her, but she was weary of the undercurrents of animosity she felt whenever he was near.

"Shouldn't these children be elsewhere?" he asked, his voice tight and sightly demanding.

Sherry stood and met the glaring dislike in the other man's eyes. "Okay, children, it's time to return to your cabins."

The small group let out a chorus of groans, loudly voicing their protest. Reluctantly, they left Sherry's side, dragging their feet.

"Oh, Miss White," Gretchen murmured. "I forgot to give you this." She withdrew an envelope from her pocket. The camp logo was stamped on the outside. "Mr. Roarke asked me to give this to you. I'm sorry I forgot."

"No problem, sweetheart." Sherry reached for the letter, her heart clamoring. Although she was dying to read what Roarke had written, Sherry held off, staring at her name, neatly centered on the outside of the business-size envelope. Fleetingly, she wondered if Roarke had decided to fire her. Then she realized that he wouldn't have asked Gretchen to deliver the notice; he had more honor than that.

With trembling fingers and a pounding heart, she tore off the end of the envelope, blew inside to open it and withdrew a single sheet. Carefully unfolding it, she read the neatly typed sentence in the middle of the page: Midnight at Clear Lake. Jeff Roarke.

Sherry read the four-word message over and over again. Midnight at the lake? It didn't make sense. Was he proposing that she meet him there? The two of them, alone? Surely there was some other hidden meaning that she was missing. After the incident with Buttercup, he had her so flustered she couldn't think straight.

During the evening, Sherry flirted with the idea of ignoring the note entirely, but as the sun set and dusk crept across the campgrounds, bathing the lush property in golden hues, she knew in her heart that no matter what happened she'd be at the lake as Jeff Roarke had requested.

At five minutes to midnight, she checked her seven charges to be sure they were sleeping and woke Ginny long enough to tell her she was leaving. As silently as possible, Sherry slipped from the cabin. The moon was three-quarters full and cast a silken glow of light on the pathway that led to the lake's edge.

Hugging her arms, Sherry made her way along the well-defined walkway. Roarke's message hadn't been specific about where she was to meet him, although she'd read the note a hundred times. She pulled the letter from the hip pocket of her jeans and read the four words again.

"Sherry."

Roarke's voice startled her. Alarmed, Sherry slapped a hand over her heart.

"Sorry, I didn't mean to frighten you."

"That's all right," she said, quick to reassure him. "I should have been listening for you." He looked so tall and handsome in the moonlight, and her heart quickened at the sight of him. Loving him felt so right. A thousand times over the past few days she'd had doubts about caring so much for Roarke, but not now. Not tonight.

"Shall we sit down?"

"It's a beautiful night, isn't it?" Sherry asked as she lowered herself onto the sandy beach. They used an old log to lean against and paused to gaze into the heavens. The lake lapped lazily a few yards from their feet, and a fresh cool breeze carried with it the sweet, distinctive scent of summer. The moment was serene, unchallenged by the churning problems that existed between them.

"It's a lovely evening," he answered after a moment. He drew his knees up, crossed his legs and sighed expressively. "I'm pleased you did this, Sherry. I felt badly about the episode with the squirt gun."

"You're pleased I did this?" she returned. "What do you mean?"

"The note."

"What note? I didn't send you any note, but I did receive yours."

"Mine!" He turned then to study her, his gaze wide and challenging.

"I have it right here." Agilely, she raised her hips and slipped the paper from her pocket. It had been folded several times over, and her fingers fumbled with impatience as she opened it to hand to him.

Roarke's gaze quickly scanned the few words. "I didn't write this."

"Of course you did." He couldn't deny it now. The stationery and envelope were both stamped with the Camp Gitche Gumee logo.

"Sherry, I'm telling you I didn't write that note, but I did receive yours."

"And I'm telling you I didn't send you one."

"Then who did?"

She shrugged and gestured with her hand. She had a fair idea who was responsible. Her wizards! All seven of them! They'd plotted this romantic rendezvous down to the last detail, and both Roarke and Sherry had been gullible enough to fall for it. It would have angered Sherry, but for the realization that Roarke had wanted these few stolen moments badly enough to believe even the most improbable circumstances.

Roarke cleared his throat. He could feel Sherry's mounting agitation and sought a way to reassure her. He wasn't so naive as not to recognize that her girls must be responsible for this arrangement. The fact was, he didn't care. She was sitting at his side in the moonlight, and it felt so good to have her with him that he didn't want anything to ruin it.

"It seems to me," he said slowly, measuring his words, "that this is Longfellow's doing."

"Longfellow?" Sherry repeated. Then she relaxed, a

smile growing until she felt the relief and amusement surge up within her. "Yes, it must be him."

"Camp Gitche Gumee's own personal ghost—Longfellow," Roarke repeated softly. He paused, lifted his arm and cupped her shoulder, bringing her closer into his embrace.

Sherry let her head rest against the solid strength of his shoulder. Briefly she closed her eyes to the swelling tide of emotion that enveloped her. Roarke beside her, so close she could smell his aftershave and the manly scent that was his alone. He was even closer in spirit, so that it was almost as if the words to communicate were completely unnecessary.

Silence reigned for the moment, a refreshing reprieve to the anger that had so often unexpectedly erupted between them. This was a rare time, and Sherry doubted that either would have allowed anyone or anything to destroy it.

"We do seem to find ways to clash, don't we?" Sherry said, after a long moment. They'd made a point of not talking about life at camp when they'd had dinner, but tonight it was necessary. "Roarke, I want you to know I've never intentionally gone out of my way to irritate you."

"I had to believe that," he said softly, gently riffling his fingers through her soft dark hair. "Otherwise I would have gone a little crazy. But maybe I did anyway," he added as an afterthought.

"It just seems that everything I do—is wrong."

"Not wrong," he corrected, his voice raised slightly. "Just different. Some of your ideas have been excellent, but a few of the other counselors…"

"Fred Spencer." Roarke didn't need to mention names for her to recognize her most outspoken opponent. Almost from the day of her arrival, Fred had criticized her efforts with the children and challenged her ideas.

"Yes, Fred," Roarke admitted.

"Why?"

"He's been with the camp for as long as we've been operating, dedicating his summers to the children. It's been difficult for him to accept your popularity. The kids love you."

"But I don't want to compete with him."

"He'll learn that soon enough. You've shown admirable restraint, Sherry. The others admire you for the way you've dealt with Fred." He turned his head just enough so that his lips grazed her temple as he spoke. "The others nothing; *I've* admired you."

"Oh, Roarke."

His arm around her tightened, and Sherry held her breath. The magic was potent, so very potent. His breath fanned her cheek, searing her flushed skin. Without being aware that she was rotating her head toward him, Sherry turned, silently seeking his kiss.

Roarke's hand touched her chin and tipped her face toward him. Sherry stared up at him, hardly able to believe what she saw in his eyes and felt in her heart. His gaze was full of warmth and tenderness and he was smiling with such sweet understanding. It seemed that Roarke was telling her with his eyes how important she was to him, how much he enjoyed her wit, her creativity. Her.

Slowly he bent his head to her. Sherry slid her hands up his shoulders and tilted her head to meet him halfway. He groaned her name, and his lips came down to caress hers in a long, undemanding, tender kiss that robbed her lungs of breath.

The kiss deepened as Roarke sensually shaped and molded her lips to his. Sherry gave herself over to him, holding back nothing. He kissed her again and again, unable to get enough of the delicious taste of her. She was honey and wine. Unbelievably sweet. Sunshine and love. He kissed her again, then lifted his head to tenderly cup her face between his large hands and gaze into her melting brown eyes.

"Roarke?" she said his name, not knowing herself what she would ask. It was in her to beg him not to stop for fear that something would pull them apart as it had so often in the past.

"You're so sweet," he whispered, unable to look away. His mouth unerringly found hers, the kiss lingering, slow and compelling so that by the time he raised his head Sherry was swimming in a sea of sensual awareness.

"Roarke, why do we argue?" Her hands roamed through his hair, luxuriating in the thick feel of it between her fingers. "I hate it when we do."

"Me, too, love. Me, too." His tongue flickered over the seam of her lips, teasing them at first, then urging them apart. "Sherry, love," he whispered, and inhaled deeply. "We have to stop."

"I know," she answered and nodded.

But neither loosened the embrace. Neither was willing to forsake the moment or relinquish this special closeness growing between them.

Roarke rubbed his moist mouth sensuously against hers. Back and forth, until Sherry thought she would faint with wanting him. When she could tolerate it no longer, she parted her lips and once again they were tossed into the roiling sea of sensual awareness.

Without warning, Roarke stopped.

Kissed into senselessness, Sherry could do nothing to protest. Breathing had taken on an extraordinary effort, and she pressed her forehead to his chest while she gathered her composure.

"Roarke," she whispered.

"In a minute."

She raised her gaze enough to view the naked turmoil that played so vividly across his contorted features.

"I'm sorry," she told him. "So sorry for what happened with Lynn and Peter that day. Sorry for so many things. I can't have you believing that I'd use you like that. I couldn't... I just couldn't."

His smile was so gentle that Sherry felt stinging tears gather in her eyes.

"I know," he said softly. "That's in the past and best forgotten."

"But, Roarke, I..."

He placed his index finger across her lips, stopping her. "Whatever it is doesn't matter."

Sherry's wide-eyed gaze studied him. She dreaded the moment he learned the whole truth about her. "But I want to be honest."

"You can't lie," he said as his hands lovingly caressed the sides of her face. "I've noticed that about you."

"But I have—"

"It doesn't matter now, Sherry. Not now." Unable

to resist her a moment longer, he bent low and thoroughly kissed her again.

Any argument, any desire for Sherry to tell him about the falsified references was tossed aside as unimportant and inconsequential. Within a few weeks the camp session would be over, and if he hadn't discovered the truth by then, she would simply trust that he never would. Later, much later, she'd tell him, and they could laugh about it, her deception would be a source of amusement.

Roarke stood, offering Sherry his hand to help her to her feet. She took it and pulled herself up, then paused momentarily to brush the sand from her backside and look out over the calm lake. This summer with Roarke would always be remembered as special, but she didn't want it to end. The weeks had flown past, and she couldn't imagine ever being without him now.

With a sigh of regret to be leaving the tranquil scene, Roarke draped his arm over her shoulder and guided her back to the main campgrounds.

"My appreciation to Longfellow," he whispered outside her cabin door.

They shared a secret smile, and with unspoken agreement resisted the urge to kiss good-night.

"I'll tell the girls—Longfellow—you said so," she murmured.

Roarke continued to hold her hand. "Good night, Sherry."

"Good night, Roarke." Reluctantly he released her fingers, moved back and turned away.

"Roarke?" she called, anxiously rising onto her tiptoes.

He turned around. "Yes?"

She stared at him, uncertain; her feet returned to the porch. It was in her mind to ask his forgiveness for everything she'd done that had been so zany and caused him such grief. She yearned to confess everything, clean the slate, but anxiety stopped her. She was afraid that a confession now would ruin everything. She could think of only one thing to say. "Friends?"

"Yes," he answered and nodded for emphasis. Much more than friends, he added silently. Much more.

Things changed after that night. Roarke changed. Sherry changed. Camp Gitche Gumee changed.

It seemed to Sherry that Roarke had relaxed and lowered his guard. Gone was the stiff, unbending camp director. Gone was the tension that stretched between them so taut that Sherry had sometimes felt ill with it. Gone were the days when she'd felt on edge every time they met. Now she eagerly anticipated each meeting.

Roarke spent less time in his office and was often seen talking to the children. The sound of his amusement could frequently be heard drifting across the campgrounds. He joked and smiled, and every once in a while, he shared secret glances with Sherry. These rare moments had the most curious effect upon her. Where she'd always been strong, now she felt weak, yet her weakness was her strength. She'd argued with Roarke, battled for changes, and now she was utterly content. The ideas she'd fought so long and hard to instill at the camp came naturally with her hardly saying a word.

The late afternoons became a special time for Roarke and Sherry with the camp kids. All ages would gather around the couple, and Sherry would lead an impromptu songfest, teaching them songs she'd learned as a youngster at camp. Some were silly songs, while others were more serious, but all were fun, and more than anything, Sherry wanted the children of Camp Gitche Gumee to have fun.

Soon the other counselors and staff members joined Sherry and Roarke on the front lawn, and music became a scheduled event of the day, with two other musically inclined counselors taking turns leading the songs. Within a week, as if by magic, two guitars appeared, and Sherry played one and Lynn the other, accompanying the singers.

Someone suggested a bonfire by the lake, and the entire camp roasted marshmallows as the sky filled with twinkling stars.

When they'd finished the first such event in the history of the camp, Gretchen requested that Sherry tell everyone about Longfellow, and after a tense moment, Sherry stepped forward and kept the group spellbound with her make-believe tales.

To her surprise, Roarke added his own comical version of a trick the friendly spook had once played on him when he'd first arrived at the camp. Even Fred Spencer had been amused, and Sherry had caught him chuckling.

The night was such a success that Sherry was too excited to sleep. Her charges were worn-out from the long week and slept peacefully, curled up in their cots. Sherry sat on top of her bed and tried to read, but her thoughts kept wandering to Roarke and how much had changed between them and how much better it was to be with him than any man she'd ever known.

The pebble against her window caught her attention.

"Sherry?" Her name came on a husky whisper.

Stumbling to her feet, she pushed up the window and leaned out. "Who's there?"

"How many other men do you have pounding on your window?"

"Roarke?" Her eyes searched the night for him, but saw nothing. "I know you're out there."

"Right again," he said, and stepped forward, his hands hidden behind his back.

Sherry sighed her pleasure, propped her elbows against the windowsill and cupped her face with her hands. "What are you doing here?"

He ignored the question. "Did you enjoy tonight?"

Sherry nodded eagerly. "It was wonderful." *He* was wonderful!

"Couldn't you sleep?" he asked, then added, "I saw your light on."

"No, I guess I'm too keyed up. What about you?"

"Too happy."

Sherry studied the curious way he stood, with his hands behind him. "What have you got?"

"What makes you think I have anything?"

"Roarke, honestly."

"All right, all right." He swept his arm around and presented her with a small bouquet of wildflowers.

The gift was so unexpected and so special that Sherry was speechless. For the first time in years she struggled to find the words. She yearned to let him know how pleased she was with his gift.

"Oh, Roarke, thank you," she said after a lengthy moment. "I'm stunned." She cupped the flowers in her hand and brought them to her face to savor the sweet scent.

"I couldn't find any better way to let you know I think you're marvelous."

Their eyes held each other's. "I think you're marvelous, too," she told him.

He wanted to kiss her so much it frightened him—more than the night they'd sat by the lake. More than the first time in his office. But he couldn't. She knew it. He knew it. Yet that didn't make refusing her easy.

"Well, I guess I'd better get back."

Sherry's gaze dropped to the bouquet. "Thank you, Roarke," she said again, with tears in her throat. "For everything."

"No." His eyes grew dark and serious. "It's me who should be thanking you."

He'd been gone a full five minutes before Sherry closed the window. She slumped onto the end of her bed and released a sigh. In her most farfetched dreams, she hadn't believed Jeff Roarke could be so wonderfully romantic. Now she prayed nothing would happen to ruin this bliss.

Chapter 11

"Sleepy and Grumpy are at it again," Wendy told Sherry early the next morning. "Diane doesn't want to wake up and Gretchen's complaining that she didn't sleep a wink on that lumpy mattress."

With only a week left of camp, the girls seemed all the more prone to complaints and minor disagreements. Sherry and the other counselors had endured more confusion these past seven days than at any other time in the two-month-long session of Camp Gitche Gumee.

"Say, where'd you get the flowers?" Jan and Jill blocked the doorway into Sherry's room. Jill had long since lost her tooth, making it almost impossible to tell one twin from the other.

Sherry's gaze moved from Jan and Jill to the bouquet of wildflowers Roarke had given her. They had withered long before, but she couldn't bear to part with them. Every time she looked at his gift she went all weak inside with the memory of the night he'd stood outside her window. The warm, caressing look in his eyes had remained with her all week. She'd never dreamed Jeff Roarke could be so romantic. Pulling herself up straight, Sherry diverted her attention from the wilted wildflowers and thoughts of Roarke. If she lingered any longer, they'd all be late to the mess hall.

Taking charge, Sherry stepped out of her room and soundly clapped her hands twice. "All right, Sleeping Beauty, out of bed."

"She must mean me," Gretchen announced with a wide yawn and tossed aside her covers.

"I believe Miss White was referring to Diane," Wendy said, wrinkling up her nose in a mocking gesture of superiority.

"I was speaking to whoever was still in bed," Sherry said hurriedly, hoping to forestall an argument before it escalated into a shouting match.

"See," Gretchen muttered and stuck out her tongue at Wendy, who immediately responded in kind.

"Girls, please, you're acting like a bunch of ten-year-olds!" It wasn't until after the words had slipped from her mouth that Sherry realized her wizards *were* ten-year-olds! Like Roarke, she'd fallen into the trap of thinking of them as pint-size adults. When she first arrived at camp, she'd been critical of Roarke and the others for their attitudes toward the children. She realized now that she'd been wrong to be so judgmental. The participants of Camp Gitche Gumee weren't normal children. Nor were they little adults, of course, but something special in between.

Moving at a snail's pace that drove Sherry near the

brink of losing her control, the girls dressed, collected their books and headed in an orderly fashion for the dining hall. Sherry sat at the head of the table, and the girls followed obediently into their assigned seats.

"I hate mush," Gretchen said, glaring down at the serving bowl that steamed with a large portion of the cooked cereal.

"It's good for you," Sally, the young scientist, inserted.

Diane nodded knowingly. "I read this book about how healthy fiber is in the diet."

Gretchen looked around at the faces staring at her and sighed. "All right, all right. Don't make a big deal over it—I'll eat the mush. But it'll taste like glue, and I'll probably end up at Ms. Butler's office having my stomach pumped."

When Roarke approached the front of the mess hall and the podium, the excited chatter quickly fizzled to a low murmur and then to a hush.

Sherry's gaze rested on the tall director, and even now, after all these weeks, her heart fluttered at the virile sight he made. She honestly loved this man. If anyone had told her the first week after her arrival at camp how she'd feel about Jeff Roarke by the end of the summer, she would have laughed in their face. She recalled the way Roarke had irritated her with his dictatorial ways—but she hadn't known him then, hadn't come to appreciate his quiet strength and subtle wit. She hadn't sat under the stars with him or experienced the thrill of his kisses.

Now, in less than a week, camp would be dismissed and she'd be forced to return to Seattle. Already her mind had devised ways to stay close to Roarke in the next months. A deep inner voice urged her to let him speak first. Most of the times they'd clashed had been when Sherry had proceeded with some brilliant scheme without discussing it with Roarke first. No—as difficult as it would be, she'd wait for him to make the first move. But by heaven that was going to be hard.

When Roarke's announcements for the day were completed, the children were dismissed. With an eager cry, they crowded out of the mess hall door to their first classes.

Sherry remained behind to linger over coffee. Soon Roarke and Lynn joined her.

"Morning," Sherry greeted them both, but her gaze lingered on Roarke. Their eyes met in age-old communication, and all her doubts flew out the window and evaporated into the warm morning air. No man could look at her the way he did and not care. Her tongue felt as if it was stuck to the roof of her mouth and her insides twisted with the potency of his charm.

"The natives are restless," Lynn groaned, cupping her coffee mug with both hands.

"Yes, I noticed that," Roarke commented, but his gaze continued to hold Sherry's. With some effort he pulled his eyes away. Disguising his love for her had become nearly impossible. Another week and he would have the freedom to tell her how much he loved her and to speak of the future, but for now he must bide his time. However, now that camp was drawing to a close, he found that his pulse raced like a locomotive speeding out of control whenever he was around her. His hands felt sweaty, his mouth dry. He'd discovered the woman with whom he could spend the rest of his life and he felt as callow as a boy on his first date.

"The kids need something to keep their minds off the last days of camp," Sherry offered.

"I agree," Lynn added. "I thought your suggestion about a hike to study wildflowers was a good one, Sherry. Whatever became of that?"

Fred Spencer had nixed that plan at a time when Roarke might have approved the idea, had he not been so upset with Sherry. She couldn't remember what had been the problem: Longfellow or their first kiss. Probably both. It seemed she'd continually been in hot water with Roarke in the beginning. How things had changed!

"Now that I think about an organized hike, it sounds like something we might want to investigate," Roarke commented, after mulling over the idea for a couple of minutes.

Sherry paused, uncertain, remembering Fred. "What about...you know who?"

"After a couple more days like this one, Fred Spencer will be more than happy to have you take his group for an afternoon."

"We could scout out the area this morning," Lynn suggested, looking to Sherry for confirmation.

"Sure," Sherry returned enthusiastically. She'd had a passion for wildflowers from the time she was ten and camped at Paradise on Washington state's Mount Rainier with her father; hiking together, they'd stumbled upon a field of blazing yellow and white flowers.

"Then you have my blessing," Roarke told the two women, grinning. "Let me know what you find and we'll go from there."

* * *

When Sherry and Lynn returned to camp after their successful exploratory hike of the area surrounding the camp and the lake, there was barely time to wash before lunch. Although Sherry was eager to discuss what she'd found with Roarke, she was forced into joining her girls in the mess hall first.

The wizards chattered incessantly, arguing over a paper napkin and a broken shoelace. Wendy reminded everyone that Ken-Richie was still in the hands of a no-good, lily-livered thief and she wasn't leaving camp until he was returned.

The meal couldn't be over soon enough to suit Sherry. The minute the campers were excused, she eagerly crossed the yard to Roarke's office. He hadn't made an appearance at the meal, which was unusual, but it happened often enough not to alarm Sherry.

When she reached his office, she noted that he was alone and knocked politely.

"Come in." His voice was crisp and businesslike.

He looked up from his desk when Sherry walked into the room, but revealed no emotion.

"Is this a bad time?" she asked, hesitant. She could hardly remember the last time he'd spoken to her in that wry tone. Nor had he smiled, and that puzzled her. Her instincts told her something was wrong. His eyes narrowed when he looked at her, and Sherry swallowed her concern. "Do you want me to come back later?"

"No." He shook his head for emphasis. "What did you find?"

"We discovered the most beautiful flowers," she said, warming to the subject closest to her heart. "Oh, Roarke, the trail is perfect. It shouldn't take any more than an hour for the round trip, and I can show the kids several different types of wildflowers. There are probably hundreds more, but those few were the ones I could identify readily. The kids are going to love this."

Her eyes were fairly sparkling with enthusiasm, Roarke noted. Seeing her as she was at this moment made it almost impossible to be angry. His stomach churned, and he looked away, hardly able to bear the sight of her. The phone call had caught him off guard. He'd had most of the morning to come to grips with himself and had failed. Something had to be done, but he wasn't sure what.

"When do you think we could start the first hikes? I mean if you think we should, that is." He was so distant—so strange. Sherry didn't know how she should react. When she first entered the office she'd thought he was irritated with her for something, but now she realized it was more than anger. He seemed distressed, and Sherry hadn't a clue if the matter concerned her or some camp issue. Several times over the past couple of months, she'd been an eyewitness to the heavy pressures placed upon Roarke. He did a marvelous job of managing Camp Gitche Gumee and had gained her unfailing loyalty and admiration.

"Roarke?"

"Hmm?" His gaze left the scene outside his window and reluctantly returned to her.

"Is something wrong?"

"Nothing," he lied smoothly, straightening his shoulders. "Nothing at all. Now regarding the hike, let's give it a trial run. Take your girls out this afternoon and we'll see how things go. Then tomorrow morning you can give a report to the other counselors."

Sherry clasped her hands together, too excited to question him further. "Thank you, Roarke, you won't regret this."

His stoic look was all the response he gave her.

As Sherry knew they would, the girls, carrying backpacks, grumbled all the way from the camp to the other side of the small lake. The pathway was well-defined, and they walked single file along the narrow dirt passage.

"Just how long is this going to take?"

"My feet hurt."

"No one said the Presidential Commission on Physical Fitness applied at Camp Gitche Gumee."

Listening to their complaints brought a smile to Sherry's features. "Honestly," she said with a short laugh, "you guys make it sound like we're going to climb Mount Everest."

"This is more like K-2."

"K-what?" Jan and Jill wanted to know.

"That's the highest peak in the Himalayas," Sally announced with a prim look. In response to a blank stare from a couple of the others, she added, "You know? The mountain system of south-central Asia that extends fifteen hundred miles through Kashmir, northern India, southern Tibet, Nepal, Sikkim and Bhutan."

"I remember reading about those," Diane added.

Gretchen paused and wiped her hot, perspiring face with the back of her hand. "You read about everything," she told her friend.

"Well, that's better than complaining about everything."

"Girls, please," Sherry said, hoping to keep the peace. "This is supposed to be fun."

"Do we get to eat anything?" Jan muttered.

"We're starved," Jill added.

The others agreed in a loud plea until Sherry reminded them that they'd left the mess hall only half an hour before.

"But don't worry," she said, "it's against camp policy to leave the grounds without chocolate chips." Sherry did her best to hide a smile.

Pamela laughed, and the others quickly joined in.

For all their bickering, Sherry's wizards were doing well—and even enjoying themselves. With so much time spent in the classroom in academic ventures, there had been little planned exercise for the girls.

"We'll take a break in a little bit," Sherry promised.

"It's a good thing," Gretchen muttered despairingly.

"Really," Sally added.

"Don't listen to them, Miss White," Pamela piped in, then lowered her voice to a thin whisper. "They're wimps."

"Hey! Look who's calling a wimp a wimp!"

In mute consternation, Sherry raised her arms and silenced her young charges. Before matters got out of hand, she found a fallen log and instructed them to sit.

Grumbling, the girls complied.

"Snack time," Sherry told them, gathering her composure. She slipped the bulky backpack from her tired shoulders. "This is a special treat, developed after twenty years of serious research."

"What is it?" Sally wanted to know, immediately interested in anything that had to do with research.

Already Gretchen was frowning with practiced disapproval.

Sherry ignored their questions and pulled a full jar of peanut butter from inside her pack. She screwed off the lid and reached for a plastic knife. "Does everyone have clean hands?"

Seven pairs of eyes scanned seven pairs of hands. This was followed by eager nods.

"Okay," Sherry told them next, "stick out an index finger."

Silently, they complied and shared curious glances as Sherry proceeded down the neat row of girls, spreading peanut butter on seven extended index fingers. A loud chorus of questions followed.

"Yuk. What's it for?"

"Hey, what are we suppose to do with this?"

"Can I lick it off yet?"

Replacing the peanut butter in her knapsack, Sherry took out a large bag of semisweet chocolate chips.

"What are you going to do with that?"

"Is it true what you said about not leaving camp without chocolate chips?"

"Scout's honor!" Dramatically, Sherry crossed her heart with her right hand, then tore open the bag of chocolate pieces, holding it open for the girls. "Okay, dip your finger inside, coat it with chips and enjoy."

Gretchen was the first to stick her finger in her mouth. "Hey, this isn't bad."

"It's delicious, I promise," Sherry told her wizards as she proceeded from one girl to the next.

"It didn't really take twenty years of research for

this, did it?" Sally asked, cocking her head at an angle to study her counselor.

Sherry grinned. "Well, I was about twenty when I perfected the technique." She swirled her finger in the air, then claimed it was all in the wrist movement.

The girls giggled, and the sound of their amusement drifted through the tall redwoods that dominated the forest. Sherry found a rock and sat down in front of her wizards, bringing her knees up and crossing her ankles.

"When I was about your age," she began, "my dad and I went for a hike much like we're doing today. And like you, I complained and wanted to know how much farther I was going to have to walk and how long it would be before I could have something to eat and where the closest restroom was."

The girls continued licking the chocolate and peanut butter off their fingers, but their gazes centered on Sherry.

"When we'd been gone about an hour, I was convinced my dad was never going back to the car. He kept telling me there was something he wanted me to see."

"Can you tell us what it was?"

"Did you ever find it?"

"Yes, to both questions," Sherry said, coming to her feet. "In fact, I want to show you girls what my father showed me." She led them away from the water's edge. The girls trooped after her in single file, marching farther into the woods to the lush meadow Sherry had discovered with Lynn earlier in the day.

A sprinkling of flowers tucked their heads between the thick grass, hidden from an untrained eye.

"This is a blue monkshood," Sherry said, crouching down close to a foot-tall flower with lobed, toothed leaves and a thin stalk. Eagerly the girls gathered around the stringy plant that bloomed in blue and violet hues.

"The blue monkshood can grow as tall as seven feet," Sherry added.

"That's even bigger than Mr. Roarke," Diane said in awe.

At the sound of Jeff Roarke's name, Sherry's heart went still. She wished now that she'd taken time to talk to him and learn what he'd found so troubling. His eyes had seemed to avoid hers, and he'd been so distant. The minute they returned to camp, Sherry decided, she was going directly to his office. If she wasn't part of the problem, then she wanted to be part of the solution.

"Miss White?"

"Yes?" Shaking her head to clear her thoughts, Sherry smiled lamely.

"What's this?" Wendy pointed to a dwarf shrub with white blossoms and scalelike leaves that was close by.

"These are known as cassiopes." Sherry pronounced the name slowly and had the girls repeat it after her. "This is a hearty little flower. Some grow as far north as the arctic."

"How'd you learn so much about wildflowers?" Gretchen asked, her eyes wide and curious.

"Books, I bet," Diane shouted.

"Thank you, Miss White," Gretchen came back sarcastically.

"I did study books, but I learned far more by combining reading with taking hikes just like the one we're on today."

"Are there any other flowers here?"

"Look around you," Sherry answered, sweeping her arm in a wide arc. "They're everywhere."

"I wish Ralph were here," Pamela said with a loud sigh. "He likes the woods."

"What's this?" Sally asked, crouched down beside a yellow blossom.

"The western wallflower."

Gretchen giggled and called out, "Sally found a wallflower."

"It's better than being one," came the other girl's fiery retort.

"Girls, please!" Again Sherry found herself serving as referee to her young charges.

"I don't want camp to end," Wendy said suddenly, slumping to the ground. She shrugged out of her backpack and took out her Barbie and Ken dolls, holding them close. "But I want to go home, too."

"I feel the same way," Sherry admitted.

"You do?" Seven faces turned to study her.

"You bet. I love each one of you, and it's going to be hard to tell you all goodbye, but Camp Gitche Gumee isn't my home, and I miss my friends and my family." As much as she'd yearned to escape Phyliss, Sherry knew what she was saying was in fact true. She did miss her father and her individualistic stepmother. And although California was beautiful, it wasn't Seattle.

"Are you planning to come back next year, Miss White?" Pam asked timidly.

Sherry nodded. "But only if you and Ralph will be here."

"I come back every summer," Gretchen said. "Next year I'm going to have my mother request you as my counselor."

Sherry tucked her arm around the little girl's shoulders and gently squeezed. "What about the lumpy mattress?"

"I said I was going to request you as my counselor, but I definitely don't want the same bed."

Sherry laughed at that, and so did the others.

The afternoon sped past, and by the time they returned to camp, Pam had gotten stung by a bee, Jan and Jill had suffered twin blisters on their right feet and Sally had happened upon two varieties of skipper moths. With a little help from her friends, she'd captured both and brought them back to camp to examine under her microscope.

The tired group of girls marched back into camp as heroes, as the other kids came running toward them, full of questions.

"Where did you guys go?"

"Will our counselor take us on a search for wildflowers, too?"

"How come you guys get to do all the fun stuff?"

"Miss White."

Jeff Roarke's voice reached Sherry, and with a wide, triumphant grin she turned to face him. The smile quickly faded at the cool reception in his gaze, and his dark, brooding look cut through her like a hot needle.

"You wanted to see me?" Sherry asked.

"That's correct." He motioned with his hand toward his office. "Lynn has agreed to take care of your girls until you return."

Lynn's smile was decidedly weak when Sherry's

gaze sought out her friend's. Sherry paused, heaved in a deep breath and wiped the grime off the back of her neck with her hand. Her face felt hot and flushed. So much for her triumphant entry into Camp Gitche Gumee.

"Would you mind if I washed up first?" she asked.

Roarke hesitated.

"All right. A drink of water should do me."

They paused beside the water fountain, and Sherry took a long, slow drink, killing time. She straightened and wiped the clear water from her mouth. Again, Roarke's gaze didn't meet hers.

"I-it's about the references, isn't it?" she asked, trying her best to keep her voice from trembling. "I know I shouldn't have falsified them—I knew it was wrong—but I wanted this job so badly and—"

It didn't seem possible that Roarke's harsh features could tighten any more without hardening into granite. Yet, they did, right before her eyes.

"Roarke," she whispered.

"So you lied on the application, too."

Sherry's mind refused to cooperate. "Too? What do you mean, too? That's the only time I ever have, and I didn't consider it a real lie—I misled you is all."

His look seared her. "I suppose you 'misled' me in more than one area."

"Roarke, no...never." Sherry could see two months of a promising relationship evaporating into thin, stale air, and she was helpless to change it. She opened her mouth to defend herself and saw how useless it would be.

"Are you finished?" Roarke asked.

Feeling sick to her stomach, Sherry nodded.

"This way. There are people waiting to see you."

"People?"

At precisely that moment the door to Roarke's office opened and Phyliss came down the first step. With a wild, excited cry, she threw her arms in the air and cried, "Sherry, baby, I've found you at last."

Before Sherry had time to blink, she found herself clenched in her stepmother's arms in a grip that would have crushed anyone else. "Oh, darling, let me look at you." Gripping Sherry's shoulders, the older woman stepped back and sighed. "I've had every detective agency from here to San Francisco looking for you." She paused and laughed, the sound high and shrill. "I've got so much to tell you. Do you like my new hairstyle?" She paused and patted the side of her head. "Purple highlights—it drives your father wild."

Despite everything, Sherry laughed and hugged her. Loony, magnificent Phyliss. She'd never change.

"Your father is waiting to talk to you, darling. Do you have any idea what a wild-goose chase you've led us on? Never mind that now…we've had a marvelous time searching for you. This is something you may want to consider doing every summer. Your father and I have had a second honeymoon traveling all over the country trying to find you." She paused and laughed. "Sherry, sweetheart," she whispered, "before we leave, you and I must have a girl-to-girl talk about the camp director, Mr. Roarke. Why, he's handsome enough to stir up the blood of any woman. Now don't try to tell me you haven't noticed. I know better."

Flustered, Sherry looked up to find Roarke watching them both, obviously displeased.

Chapter 12

"Roarke, please try to understand," Sherry pleaded.

A triumphant Phyliss and Virgil White had left Camp Gitche Gumee only minutes before. Her stepmother had evidently decided to look upon Sherry's disappearance as a fun game and had spent weeks tracking her down. It was as if Phyliss had won this comical version of hide-and-seek and could now return home giddy with jubilation for having outsmarted her stepdaughter.

As if that wasn't enough, Phyliss stayed long enough to inspect the camp kitchen and insist that Sherry tint her dark hair purple the minute she returned to Seattle—it was absolutely the in thing. She also enumerated in embarrassing detail Sherry's "many fine qualities" in front of Roarke, then paused demurely to flutter her lashes and announce that she'd die for a stepson-in-law as handsome as he was.

Sherry was convinced the entire camp sighed with relief the minute Phyliss and her father headed toward the exit in their powder-pink Cadillac. As they drove through the campgrounds, Phyliss leaned over her husband and blasted the horn in sharp toots, waving and generously blowing kisses as they went.

During the uncomfortable two hours that her parents were visiting, Sherry noted that Roarke didn't so much as utter a word to her. He carried on a polite conversation with her father, but Sherry had been too busy keeping Phyliss out of mischief to worry about what her father was telling Roarke.

Now that her parents were on their way back to Seattle, Sherry was free to speak to the somber camp director. She followed him back to his office, holding her tongue until he was seated behind the large desk that dominated his room.

"Now that you've met Phyliss you can understand why I needed to get away. I love her…in fact, I think she's wonderful, but all that mothering was giving me claustrophobia."

Roarke's smile was involuntary. "I must admit she's quite an individual."

Without invitation, Sherry pulled a chair close to Roarke's desk and sat down. She crossed her legs and leaned forward. "I—I'm sorry about the references on the application."

"You lied." His voice was a monotone, offering her little hope.

"I—I prefer to think of it as misleading you, and then only because it was necessary."

"Did you or did you not falsify your references?"

"Well, I did have the good references, I just equivocated a little on the addresses..."

"Then you were dishonest. A lie is a lie, so don't try to pretty it up with excuses."

Sherry swallowed uncomfortably. "Then I lied. But you wouldn't have known," she added quickly, before losing her nerve. "I mean, just now, today, when I mentioned it, you looked shocked. You didn't know until I told you."

"I knew." That wasn't completely true, Roarke thought. He'd suspected when the post office returned the first reference and then two of the others; but rather than investigate, Roarke had chosen to ignore the obvious for fear he'd be forced to fire her. Almost from the first week, he'd been so strongly attracted to her that he'd gone against all his instincts. Now he felt like a fool.

Sherry's hands trembled as she draped a thick strand of hair around her ear. She boldly met his gaze. "There are only a few days of camp left. Are...are you going to fire me?"

Roarke mulled over the question. He should. If any of the other counselors were to discover her deception, he would be made to look like a love-crazed fool.

"No," he answered finally.

In grateful relief Sherry momentarily closed her eyes.

"You understand, of course, that you won't be invited back as a counselor next summer."

His words burned through her like a hot poker. In one flat statement he was saying so much more. In effect, he was cutting her out of his life, severing her from his emotions and his heart. The tight knot that formed in her throat made it difficult to speak. "I understand," she said in a voice that was hardly more than a whisper. "I understand perfectly."

Sherry made her way to her cabin trapped in a haze of emotional pain. Lynn's words at the beginning of the camp session about Roarke's placing high regard on honesty returned to taunt her. The night they'd sat by the lake under the stars and kissed brought with it such a flood of memories that Sherry brushed the moisture from her cheek and sucked in huge breaths to keep from weeping.

"Miss White," Gretchen shouted when Sherry entered the cabin. "I liked your stepmother."

"Me, too," Jan added.

"Me, three," Jill said, and the twins giggled.

Sherry's smile was decidedly flat, although she did make the effort.

"She's so much fun!" Wendy held up her index finger to display a five-carat smoky topaz ring.

Costume jewelry, of course, Sherry mused. Phyliss didn't believe in real jewels, except her wedding ring.

"Phyliss told me I could have the ring," Wendy continued, "because anyone who appreciated Barbie and Ken the way I did deserved something special."

"She gave me a silk scarf," Diane said with a sigh. "She suggested I read Stephen King."

"Is her hair really purple?"

"She's funny."

Sherry sat at the foot of the closest bunk. "She's wonderful and fun and I love her."

"Do you think she'll visit next year?"

"I…I can't say." Another fib, Sherry realized. Phyliss wouldn't be coming to Camp Gitche Gumee because Sherry wouldn't be back.

"She sure is neat."

"Yes," Sherry said, and for the first time since she'd spoken to Roarke, the smile reached her eyes. "Phyliss is some kind of special."

"Miss White, Miss White, give me a hug," Sally cried, her suitcase in her hand. Sally was the first girl from Sherry's cabin to leave the camp. Camp Gitche Gumee had been dismissed at breakfast that morning. The bus to transport the youngsters to the airport was parked outside the dining room, waiting for the first group.

"Oh, Sally," Sherry said, wrapping her arms around the little girl and squeezing her tight. "I'm going to miss you so much."

"I had a whole lot of fun," she whispered, tears in her eyes. "More than at any other camp ever."

Tenderly, Sherry brushed the hair from Sally's forehead. "I did, too, sweetheart."

Goodbyes were difficult enough, but knowing that it was unlikely she would ever see her young charges again produced an even tighter pain within Sherry. She'd grown to love her girls, and the end of camp was all part of this bittersweet summer.

"Miss White," Gretchen cried, racing out of the cabin. "Miss White, guess what?"

Wendy followed quickly on Gretchen's heels. "I want to tell her," the other girl cried. "Gretchen, let me tell her."

A triumphant Wendy stormed to Sherry's side like

an unexpected summer squall. "Look!" she declared breathlessly and held up the missing Ken-Richie.

"Where was he?" Sherry cried. The entire cabin had been searching for Ken-Richie for weeks.

"Guess," Gretchen said, hands placed on her hips. She couldn't hold her stern look long, and quickly dissolved into happy giggles. "I was sleeping on him."

Sherry's eyes rounded with shock. "You were sleeping on him?"

"I kept telling everyone how lumpy my mattress was, but no one would listen."

"Little wonder," Wendy said. "You complain about everything."

"Ever hear the story of the boy who cried wolf?" Sally asked.

"Of course, I know that story. I read it when I was three years old," Gretchen answered heatedly.

"But how'd Ken-Richie get under Gretchen's mattress?" Sherry wanted to know.

Wendy shuffled her feet back and forth and found the thick grass of utmost interest. "Well, actually," she mumbled, "I may have put him there for safekeeping."

"You?" Sherry cried.

"I forgot."

A pregnant pause followed Wendy's words before all four burst into helpless peals of laughter. It felt so good to laugh, Sherry decided. The past few days had been a living nightmare. In all that time, she hadn't spoken to Roarke once. He hadn't come to her. Hadn't so much as glanced in her direction. It was as though she were no longer a part of this camp, and he had effectively divorced her from his life.

Past experience in dealing with Roarke had taught

Sherry to be patient and let his anger defuse itself
before she approached him. However, time was running out; she was scheduled to leave camp the following day.

"The bus is ready," Sally said, and her voice sagged
with regret. She hugged Sherry's middle one last time,
then climbed into the van, taking a window seat.
"Goodbye, Miss White," she cried, pressing her face
against the glass. "Can I write you?"

"I'll answer every letter, I promise."

Sherry stood in the driveway until the van was out
of sight, feeling more distressed by the moment. When
she turned to go back to her cabin, she found Fred
Spencer standing behind her. She stopped just short
of colliding with his chest.

He frowned at her in the way she found so irritating.

"One down and six to go," she said, making polite
conversation.

"Two down," he murmured, and turned to leave.

"Fred?" She stopped him.

"Yes?"

She held out her hand in the age-old gesture of
friendship. "I enjoyed working with you this summer."

He looked astonished, but quickly took her hand
and shook it enthusiastically. "You certainly added
zip to this year's session."

She smiled, unsure how to take his comment.

"I hope you don't think my objections were anything personal," the older man added self-consciously.
"I didn't think a lot of what you suggested would work,
but you proved me wrong." His gaze shifted, then returned to her. "I hope you come back next summer,
Miss White. I mean that."

Fred Spencer was the last person she'd ever expected to hear that from. "Thank you."

He tipped his hand to his hat and saluted her. "Have a good year."

"You, too."

But without Roarke, nothing would be good.

By three that afternoon, Sherry's cabin was empty. All her wizards were safely on their way back to their families. The log cabin that had only hours before been the focal point of laughter, tears and constant chatter seemed hollow without the sound of the seven little girls.

Aimlessly, Sherry wandered from one bunk to another, experiencing all the symptoms of the empty-nest syndrome. With nothing left to do, she went into her room and pulled out her suitcase. Feeling dejected and depressed, she laid it open on top of her mattress and sighed. She opened her drawer, but left it dangling as she slumped onto the end of the bed and reread the book the girls had written for her as a going-away present. Tenderly, her heart throbbing with love, she flipped through each page of the fairy tale created in her honor.

The girls had titled it *Sherry White and the Seven Wizards*. Each girl had developed a part of the story, drawn the pictures and created such a humorous scenario of life at Camp Gitche Gumee that even after she'd read it no less than ten times, the plot continued to make her laugh. And cry. She was going to miss her darling wizards. But no more than she would miss Roarke.

A polite knock at the front of the cabin caught Sherry by surprise. She set the book aside and stood.

"Yes." Her heart shot to her throat and rebounded against her ribs at the sight of Jeff Roarke framed in the open doorway of the cabin.

"Miss White."

He knew how she detested his saying her name in such a cool, distant voice, she thought. He was saying it as a reminder of how far apart they were now, telling her in two words that she'd committed the unforgivable sin and nothing could be the same between them again.

"Mr. Roarke," she returned, echoing his frigid tone.

Roarke's mouth tightened into a thin, impatient line.

"Listen," she said, trying again. "I understand and fully agree with you."

"You do?" His brows came together in a puzzled frown. "Agree with me about what?"

"Not having me back next year. What I did was stupid and foolish and I'll never regret anything more in my life." Her actions had cost her Roarke's love. Because there was nothing else for her to do, Sherry would leave Camp Gitche Gumee and would wonder all her life if she'd love another man with the same intensity that she loved Jeff Roarke.

"Fred told me the two of you had come to terms."

Sherry rubbed her palms together. Fred had smiled at her for the first time all summer. Sherry could afford to be generous with him.

"He isn't so bad," she murmured softly.

"Funny, that's what he said about you."

Sherry attempted a smile, but the effort was feeble and wobbly at best.

With his hands buried deep within his pockets, Roarke walked into the cabin and strolled around the room. The silence hung heavy between them.

Abruptly, he turned to face her. "So you feel I made the right decision not to ask you back."

She didn't know why he insisted on putting her through this. "I understand that I didn't give you much of a choice."

"What if I made another request of you?"

Sherry's gaze held his, daring to hope, daring to believe that he would love her enough to overcome her deception. "Another request?"

"Yes." In an uncustomary display of nervousness, Roarke riffled his fingers through his hair, mussing the well-groomed effect. "It might be better if I elaborate a little."

"Please." Sherry continued to hold herself stiff.

"Camp Gitche Gumee is my brainchild."

Sherry already knew that, but she didn't want to interrupt him.

"As a youngster I was like many of these children. I was too intelligent to fit in comfortably with my peers and too immature to be accepted into the adult community."

Sherry just nodded.

"The camp was born with the desire to offer a summer program for such children. I regretted having hired you the first week of camp, but I quickly changed my mind. Maybe because I've never experienced the kind of fun you introduced to your girls, I tended to be skeptical of your methods." He paused and exhaled sharply. So many things were rummaging around in his head. He didn't know if he was saying too much or not enough.

"I'm not sure I understand," Sherry said.

"I'd like you to come back."

"As a counselor?"

"No." He watched the joy drain from her eyes and tasted her disappointment. "Actually I was hoping that you'd consider becoming my partner."

"Your partner?" Sherry didn't understand.

Silently, Roarke was cursing himself with every swearword he knew. He was fumbling this badly. For all his intelligence he should be able to tell a woman he loved her and wanted her to share his life. He rubbed his hand along the back of his neck and exhaled again. None of the things he longed to tell her were coming out right. "I'm doing this all wrong."

"Doing what? Roarke," she said. "You want me to be your partner—then fine. I'd do anything to come back to Camp Gitche Gumee. Work in the kitchen. Be a housekeeper. Even garden. All I want in the world is here."

"I'm asking you to be my partner for more reasons than you know. The children love you. In a few weeks' time, you've managed to show everyone in the camp, including me and Fred Spencer, that learning can be fun. There wasn't a camper here who doesn't want you back next year."

"As your partner what would be my responsibilities?"

"You'd share the management of the camp with me and plan curriculum and the other activities that you've instigated this summer."

Some of the hope that had been building inside her died a silent death. "I see. I'd consider it an honor to return in any capacity."

"There is one problem, however."

"Yes?"

"The director's quarters is only a small cabin."

"I understand." Naturally, he'd want his quarters.

Roarke closed his eyes to the mounting frustration. He couldn't have done a worse job of this had he tried. Finally he just blurted it out. "Sherry, I'm asking you to marry me."

Joy crowded her features. "Yes," she cried, zooming to her feet. Her acceptance was followed by an instantaneous flood of tears.

"Now I've made you cry."

"Can't you tell when a woman is so overcome with happiness that she can't contain herself?" She wiped the moisture from her cheeks in a furious action. "Why are you standing over there? Why aren't you right here, kissing me and holding me?" She paused and challenged him, almost afraid of his answer. "Jeff Roarke, do you love me?"

"Dear heaven, yes."

They met halfway across the floor. Roarke reached for her and hauled her into his arms, burying his face in the gentle slope of her neck and shoulder while he drew in several calming breaths, feeling physically and mentally exhausted. He'd never messed anything up more in his life. This woman had to love him. She must, to have allowed him to put her through that.

Being crushed against him as she was made speaking impossible. Not that Sherry minded. Her brain was so fuddled and her throat so thick with emotion that she probably wouldn't have made sense anyway.

Roarke tucked his index finger beneath her chin and raised her mouth to meet his. His hungry kiss rocked her to the core of her being. Countless times, his mouth feasted on hers, as though it were impossible to get enough of her. Not touching her all these weeks had been next to impossible, and now, knowing that she felt for him the same things he did for her made the ache of longing all the more intense.

Freely, Sherry's hands roved his back, reveling in the muscular feel of his skin beneath her fingers. All the while, Roarke's mouth made moist forays over her lips, dipping again and again to sample her sweet kiss.

"Oh, love," he whispered, lackadaisically sliding his mouth back and forth over her lips. "I can't believe this is happening." He ground his hips against her softness and sharply sucked in his breath. "Nothing can get more real than this."

"Nothing," she agreed and trapped his head between her two hands in an effort to study him. "Why?"

"Why do I love you?"

Her smile went soft. "No, how can you love me after what I did?"

"I met Phyliss, remember?"

"But…"

"But it took me a few days to remember that you'd tried to tell me about the references."

"I did?"

Resisting her was impossible, and he kissed the tip of her pert nose. "Yes. The night at the lake. Remember? I knew then, or strongly suspected, but I didn't want to hear it, didn't want to face the truth because that would have demanded some response. Yet even when I was forced to look at the truth, I couldn't send you away. Doing that would have been like sentencing my own heart to solitary confinement for life."

"Oh, Roarke." She leaned against him, linking her hands at the base of his spine. "I do love you."

"I know."

Abruptly, her head came up. "What about school?"

"What about it?"

"I've only got one year left."

"I wouldn't dream of having you drop out," he rushed to assure her. "You can transfer your credits and finish here in California."

Sherry pressed her head against his heart and sighed expressively. "I can and I will." Being separated from him would be intolerable. Roarke met the intensity of her gaze with all the deep desire of his own. He wanted Sherry to share his life. She was marvelous with the youngsters, and having her work with him at Camp Gitche Gumee would be an advantage to the camp and the children. But with all of his plans, he hadn't paused to think that one day he would have a child of his own. The love he felt for Sherry swelled within him until he felt weak with it. And strong, so strong that he seemed invincible.

"Someday we'll be sending our own wizards to this camp," Sherry told him.

Roarke's hold on her tightened.

"The girls told me you were my prince," she said, her gaze falling on the book her wizards had created.

"We're going to be so happy, Sherry, my love."

"Forever and ever," she agreed, just as the book said.

* * * * *

Also by Lee Tobin McClain

Love Inspired

Redemption Ranch

The Soldier's Redemption
The Twins' Family Christmas
The Nanny's Secret Baby

Rescue River

Engaged to the Single Mom
His Secret Child
Small-Town Nanny
The Soldier and the Single Mom
The Soldier's Secret Child
A Family for Easter

HQN

The Off Season

Cottage at the Beach
Reunion at the Shore
Christmas on the Coast
Home to the Harbor

Safe Haven

Low Country Hero
Low Country Dreams
Low Country Christmas

Visit the Author Profile page at Harlequin.com,
or leetobinmcclain.com, for more titles!

THE SOLDIER'S REDEMPTION

Lee Tobin McClain

To the staff and volunteers at Animal Friends of Westmoreland. Thank you for letting me work alongside you to learn how a dog rescue operates... and thank you for being a voice for those who cannot speak for themselves.

And the people, when they knew it, followed him: and he received them, and spake unto them of the kingdom of God, and healed them that had need of healing.

—*Luke* 9:11

Chapter 1

Finn Gallagher leaned his cane against the desk and swiveled his chair around to face the open window. He loved solitude, but with overseeing Redemption Ranch's kennels, dealing with suppliers and workers and the public, he didn't get enough of it. These early-morning moments when he could sip coffee and look out across the flat plain toward the Sangre de Cristo Mountains were precious and few.

He was reaching over to turn on the window fan—June in Colorado could be hot—when he heard a knock behind him. "Pardon me," said a quiet female voice. "I've come about the job."

So much for solitude.

He swiveled around and got the impression of a small brown sparrow. Plain, with no identifying markers. Brown tied-back hair, gray flannel shirt, jeans, no-brand sneakers.

Well, she was plain until you noticed those high cheekbones and striking blue eyes.

"How'd you find us?" he asked.

"Ad in the paper." She said it Southern style: "Aaa-yud." Not from around here. "Kennel assistant, general cleaning."

"Come on in. Sit down," he said and gestured to a chair, not because he wanted her there but because he felt rude sitting while she was standing. And his days of getting to his feet the moment a lady walked into the room were over. "I'm Finn Gallagher. I run the day-to-day operations here at the ranch."

"Kayla White." She sat down like a sparrow, too, perching. Ready for flight.

"Actually," he said, "for this position, we were looking for a man."

She lifted an eyebrow. "That's discriminatory. I can do the work. I'm stronger than I look."

He studied her a little closer and noticed that she wore long sleeves, buttoned down. In this heat? Weird. She looked healthy, not like a druggie hiding track marks, but lately more and more people seemed to be turning in that desperate direction.

"It's pretty remote here." He'd rather she removed herself from consideration for the job so he wouldn't have to openly turn her down. She was right about the discrimination thing. With all their financial troubles, the last thing Redemption Ranch needed was a lawsuit. "A good ten miles to the nearest town, over bad roads."

She nodded patiently. And didn't ask to be withdrawn from consideration.

"The position requires you to live in. Not much chance to meet people and socialize." He glanced at her bare left hand.

"I'm not big on socializing. More of a bookworm, actually."

That almost made him like her. He spent most of his evenings at home with a dog and a good book, himself. "Small cabin," he warned.

"I'll fit." She gestured at her petite self as the hint of a smile crossed her face and was just as quickly gone. "I'm relocating," she clarified, "so living in would be easier than finding a job and a place to stay, both."

So she wasn't going to give up. Which was fine, really; there was no reason the new hire had to be male. He just had a vision of a woman needing a lot of attention and guidance, gossiping up a blue streak, causing trouble with the veterans.

Both his mother and his boss would have scolded him for that type of prejudice.

Anyway, Kayla seemed independent and not much of a talker. The more Finn looked at her, though, the more he thought she might cause a little interest, at least, among the guys.

And if she were using… "There's a drug test," he said abruptly and watched her reaction.

"Not a problem." Her response was instant and unambiguous.

Okay, then. Maybe she was a possibility.

They talked through the duties of the job—feeding and walking the dogs, some housekeeping in the offices, but mostly cleaning kennels. She had experience cleaning, references. She liked dogs. She'd done cooking, too, which wasn't a need they had now, but they might in the future.

Now he wasn't sure if he wanted to talk her into the job or talk her out of it. Something about her, some hint of self-sufficiency, made him like her, at least as much as he liked any woman. And they did need to hire someone soon. But he got the feeling there was a lot she wasn't saying.

Would it be okay to have a woman around? He tested the notion on himself. He didn't date, didn't deserve to after what he'd done. That meant he spent almost no time around women his age. A nice, quiet woman might be a welcome change.

Or she might be a big complication he didn't need.

"What's the living situation?" she asked. "You said a cabin. Where's it located?"

He gestured west. "There's a row of seven cabins. Small, like I said. And a little run-down. Seeing as you're female, we'd put you on the end of the row— that's what we did with the one female vet who stayed here—but eventually they'll fill up, mostly with men. Veterans with issues."

She blanched, visibly.

He waited. From the bird feeder outside his window, a chickadee scolded. The smell of mountain sage drifted in.

"What kind of issues?" Her voice came out a little husky.

"PTSD related, mostly. Some physical disabilities, too. Anything that would cause a vet to give up hope, is how the owner of the ranch puts it. We give residents a place to get their heads together, do some physical labor and help some four-legged critters who need it. The idea is to help them get back on their feet."

She looked away, out the window, chewing on her lower lip.

He took pity. "We don't allow any firearms. No drugs or alcohol. And we have a couple of mental health specialists and a doctor on call. Planning on a chaplain, too." *Once we start bringing in enough money to hire one*, he almost added, but didn't. "If somebody's problems seem too much for us to handle, we refer them elsewhere."

"I see." She looked thoughtful.

They should've put what kind of nonprofit it was in the ad, to screen out people who were scared of veterans. But the truth was, they'd limited the ad to the fewest words possible, economizing.

"I can show you around," he said. "If you like what you see, we can talk more."

He was pretty sure that conversation wouldn't happen, judging by the way her attitude had changed once their focus on veterans had come up.

He hoisted himself to his feet, grabbed his cane and started toward the door.

She'd stood up to follow, but when she saw him full-length, she took a step back.

It shouldn't surprise him. Even with the inch or so he'd lost from the spinal surgery, he was still six-four. And he'd been lifting to work off some steam. Pretty much The Incredible Hulk.

It had used to work in his favor with women, at least some of them, way back when that had mattered.

"You're military?" she asked as he gestured for her to walk out ahead of him.

"Yep." He waited for the fake *thank you for your service*.

She didn't say it. "What branch?" she asked.

He was closing the door behind them. When he turned to answer, he saw that she'd moved ahead and was kneeling down in front of a little boy who sat on the floor of the outer office, his back against the wall, holding a small gaming device.

Finn sucked in a breath, restrained a surprised exclamation, tried to compose himself.

Kid looked to be about five. Freckle faced and towheaded.

Just like Derek.

His emotions churning, he watched her tap the boy's chin to get his attention. Odd that such a small boy had been so quiet during the, what, half hour that they'd been talking. Derek could never have done it.

"My son, Leo," she said, glancing up at Finn. And then, to the boy: "We're going to walk around with Mr. Gallagher. We might have a place to stay for a bit, a tiny little house."

The boy's eyes lit up and he opened his mouth to speak. Then he looked over at Finn and snapped it shut. He scooted farther behind his mother.

Could the kid be afraid of his limp or his cane? Could Kayla? But if she couldn't deal with that, or her kid couldn't, then they needed to take themselves far away from Redemption Ranch. His problems were minor compared to some of the veterans who would soon be staying here.

And beyond that, what kind of risks would a young kid face in a place like this? The vets he wasn't really worried about, but a little kid could be trouble around dogs—if he was too afraid of them, or not afraid enough.

No kids were going to be hurt on Finn's watch. Never again.

"This way," he said, his voice brusque. He'd show them around, because he had said he would. Unlike a lot of people, he didn't retract his promises.

He touched her back to guide her out. As he felt the ridge of her spine through the shirt, she looked up at him, eyes wide and startled.

He withdrew his hand immediately, his face heating. He hadn't meant his touch to be flirtatious, but apparently it had come off some weird way.

He could already tell this wasn't going to work.

Kayla pulled Leo close beside her as she walked ahead of the square-shouldered soldier into the open air. Her mind raced at strategic pace.

She'd gotten a good feeling about the job when she'd seen it, reading the *Esperanza Springs Mountaineer* in the café where they'd had an early breakfast. Live in—check. They needed a place to live. A good thousand miles away from Arkansas, remote and off the beaten path—check. That was the big priority. Work she could handle—check. She liked dogs, and she liked working hands-on.

A wholesome, healthy, happy environment that would help Leo heal… Of that, she wasn't yet sure.

As for her own healing from her terrible marriage, she wasn't expecting that, and it didn't matter. She wasn't the type to elicit love from anyone, her son the exception. She knew that for sure, now.

The man striding beside her—and how did a guy

stride with a cane, anyway?—looked a little too much like her bodybuilding, short-haired, military-postured ex. Finn had spooked her son to the point where, now, Leo pressed close into her side, making it hard to walk.

But it wasn't like she was going to become best friends with this Finn Gallagher, if she did get this job and decide to take it. It wasn't like she'd reveal anything to him, to anyone, that could somehow lead to Mitch finding them.

The mountains rose in a semicircle around the flat basin where the ranch was situated, white streaks of snow decorating the peaks even at the end of June. There was a weathered-looking barn up ahead of them, and off to the right, a pond with a dock and a rowboat.

This place drew her in. It was beautiful, and about as far from Little Rock as they could reasonably go, given the car she was driving. If she were just basing things on geography, she'd snap this job up in a minute.

But the military angle worried her.

"Would we live there?" Leo pointed. His voice was quiet, almost a whisper, but in it she detected a trace of excitement.

They were approaching a small log cabin with a couple of rustic chairs on a narrow porch. As Finn had mentioned, it was the end of a row of similar structures. Sunlight glinted off its green tin roof. One of the shutters hung crooked, but other than that, the place looked sturdy enough.

"This is the cabin you'd live in if this works out," Finn said, glancing down at Leo and then at her. "The vet who lived here before just moved out, so it should be pretty clean. Come on in."

Inside, the cabin's main room had a kitchen area—

sink and refrigerator and stove—along the far wall. A door to one side looked like it led to a bathroom or closet. A simple, rough-hewn dining table, a couch and a couple of chairs filled up the rest of the small room. With some throw rugs and homemade curtains, it would be downright cozy.

"Sleeping loft is upstairs," Finn said, indicating a sturdy, oversize ladder.

Leo's head whipped around to look at Kayla. He loved to climb as much as any little boy.

"Safe up there?" she asked Finn. "Anything that could hurt a kid?" She could already see that the sleeping area had a three-foot railing at the edge, which would prevent a fall.

"It's childproof." His voice was gruff.

"No guns, knives, nothing?" If Finn were like Mitch, he'd be fascinated by weapons. And he wouldn't consider them a danger to a kid.

"Of course not!" Finn looked so shocked and indignant that she believed him.

"Go ahead—climb up and take a look," she said to her son. Leo had been cooped up in the car during the past four days. She wanted to seize any possible opportunity for him to have fun.

She stood at the bottom of the ladder and watched him climb, quick and agile. She heard his happy exclamation, and then his footsteps tapped overhead as he ran from one side of the loft to the other.

Love for him gripped her hard. She'd find a way to make him a better life, whether here or somewhere else.

"I'm not sure this is the right environment for a child," Finn said in a low voice. He was standing close enough that she could smell his aftershave, some old-fashioned scent her favorite stepfather had used. "We need someone who'll work hard, and if you're distracted by a kid, you can't."

"There's a camp program at the church in Esperanza Springs. Thought we'd check that out." Actually, she already had, online; they had daily activities, were open to five-year-olds and offered price breaks to low-income families.

Which they definitely were.

Finn didn't say anything, and silent men made her nervous. "Leo," she called, "come on down."

Her son scrambled down the ladder and pressed into her leg, looking warily at Finn.

Curiosity flared in the big man's eyes, but he didn't ask questions. Instead, he walked over to the door and held it open. "I'll show you the kennels." His face softened as he looked down at Leo. "We have eighteen dogs right now."

Leo didn't speak, but he glanced up at Kayla and gave a little jump. She knew what it meant. Eighteen dogs would be a cornucopia of joy to him.

They headed along the road in front of the cabins. "Is he comfortable with dogs?" Finn asked.

"He hasn't been around them much, but he's liked the ones he's met." Loved, more like. A pet was one of the things she'd begged Mitch for, regularly. She'd wanted the companionship for Leo, because she'd determined soon after his birth that they'd never have another child. Fatherhood didn't sit well with Mitch.

But Mitch hadn't wanted a dog, and she'd known better than to go against him on that. She wouldn't be the only one who'd suffer; the dog would, too, and Leo.

"We're low on residents right now," Finn said. He waved a hand toward a rustic, hotel-like structure half-hidden by the curve of a hill. "Couple of guys live in the old lodge. Help us do repairs, when they have time. But they both work days and aren't around a whole lot."

"You going to fill the place up?"

"Slowly, as we get the physical structures back up to code. These two cabins are unoccupied." He gestured to the two that were next to the one he'd just shown them. The corner of one was caving in, and its porch looked unstable. She'd definitely have to set some limits on where Leo could play, in the event that this worked out. "This next one, guy named Parker lives there, but he's away. His mom's real sick. I'm not sure when he'll be back."

Across the morning air, the sound of banjo and guitar music wafted, surprising her. She looked down at Leo, whose head was cocked to one side.

They found the source of the music on the porch of the last cabin, and as they came close, the men playing the instruments stopped. "Who you got there?" came a raspy voice.

Finn half turned to her. "Come meet Willie and Long John. Willie lives in the cabin next door, but he spends most of his time with Long John. If you work here, you'll see a lot of them."

As they approached the steps, the two men got to their feet. They both looked to be in their later sixties. The tall, skinny, balding one who'd struggled getting up had to be Long John, which meant the short, heavy-set one, with a full white beard, his salt-and-pepper hair pulled back in a ponytail, must be Willie. Both wore black Vietnam veteran baseball caps.

Finn introduced them and explained why Kayla was here.

"Hope you'll take the job," Long John said. "We could use some help with the dogs."

"And it'd improve the view around here," Willie said, a smile quirking the corner of his mouth beneath the beard.

Finn cleared his throat and glared at the older man.

Willie just grinned and eased down onto the cabin's steps. At eye level with Leo, he held out a hand. "I'm pleased to meet you, young man," he said.

"Shake hands," Kayla urged, and Leo held out his right hand.

"Pleased to meet you, sir," he said, his voice almost a whisper, and Kayla felt a surge of pride at his manners.

After a grave handshake, Willie looked up at her. "Wouldn't mind having a little guy around here. Always did like to take my grandkids fishing." He waved an arm in the direction of the pond she'd seen. "We keep it stocked."

Kayla's heart melted, just at the edges. Grandfather figures for Leo? A chance for him to learn to fish?

There was a low *woof* from inside the screen door and a responding one from the porch. A large black dog she hadn't seen before lumbered to its feet.

"About time you noticed there's some new folks here," Long John said, reaching from his chair to run a hand over the black dog's bony spine. "Rockette, here, don't pay a whole lot of attention to the world these days. Not unless her friend Duke wakes her up."

Willie opened the screen door. A gray-muzzled pit bull sauntered out.

"Duke. Sit." Willie made a hand gesture, and Duke obediently dropped to his haunches, his tongue lolling out. Willie slipped a treat from the pocket of his baggy jeans and fed it to the dog.

Leo took two steps closer to the old black dog, reached out and touched its side with the tips of his fingers.

"One of our agreements, for anyone who lives in the cabins, is that they take in a dog," Finn explained. "Gives them a little extra attention. Especially the ones not likely to be adopted."

Leo tugged Kayla's hand. "Would *we* have a dog?"

"Maybe." She put seriousness into her voice so he wouldn't get his hopes up. "It all depends if Mr. Gallagher decides to offer me the job, and if I take it. Those are grown-up decisions."

"Sure could use the help," Long John said, lowering himself back into his chair with a stifled groan. "Me and Willie been doing our best, but..." He waved a hand at a walker folded against the porch railing. "With my Parkinson's, it's not that easy."

"Hardly anyone else has applied," Willie added. "Don't get many out-of-towners around these parts. And the people who live in Esperanza Springs heard we're gonna have more guys up here. They get skittish." He winked at Kayla. "We vets are gentle as lambs, though, once you get to know us."

"Right." She had direct experience to the contrary.

At first, before her marriage had gone so far downhill, she hadn't translated Mitch's problems into a mistrust of all military personnel. Later, it had been impossible to avoid doing just that.

When Mitch had pushed his way into her place well

after their divorce was final—talking crazy and rough-ing her up—she'd gone to the police.

She hadn't wanted to file a complaint, which had been stupid. She'd just wanted to know her options, whether a protection order would do any good.

What she hadn't known was that the police officer she'd spoken with was army, too. Hadn't known he drank with Mitch at the Legion.

The cop had let Mitch know that she'd reported him, and she still bore the bruises from when he'd come back over to her place, enraged, looking for blood.

Shaking off her thoughts, she watched Long John talk with Finn while Willie plucked at his guitar and then held it out to show Leo. The two veterans did exude a gentle vibe. But then, their wartime experi-ences were distant, their aggressions most likely tamed through age and experience.

"Let's take a look at the kennels," Finn said and nodded toward the barn. "Later, guys."

Just outside the barn, Finn turned and gestured for Leo to stand in front of him. After a nod from Kayla, Leo did, his eyes lowered, shoulders frozen in a slump.

"I want you to ask before you touch a dog, Leo," he said. "Most of them are real nice, but a couple are nervous enough to lash out. So ask an adult first, and never, ever open a kennel without an adult there to help you. Understand?"

Leo nodded, taking a step closer to Kayla.

"Good." Finn turned toward the barn door and beckoned for them to follow him.

Much barking greeted their entry into the dim barn. Finn flicked on a light, revealing kennels along both sides of the old structure and more halfway up the middle. One end of the barn was walled off into what looked like an office.

Finn walked down the row of dogs, telling her their names, reaching through some of the wire fencing to stroke noses. His fondness for the animals was obvious in his tone and his gentle touch. "All of them are seniors," he explained over his shoulder. "Which is about seven and up for a big dog, eight or nine for a little one."

"Where do they come from?" she asked. The barking had died down, and most of the dogs stood at the gates of their kennels, tails wagging, eyes begging for attention.

"Owner surrenders, mostly. Couple of strays."

She knelt to look at a red-gold dog, probably an Irish setter mix. "Why would anyone give you up, sweetie?" She reached between the cage wires to touch the dog's white muzzle, seeming to read sadness in its eyes.

"Lots of reasons," Finn said. "People move. Or they don't have money for food and vet bills. Sometimes, they just don't want to deal with a dog that requires some extra care." He knelt beside her. "Lola, here, she can't make it up and down stairs. Her owner lived in a two-story house, so…"

"They couldn't carry her up and down?"

"Apparently not."

"Can I pet her, too, Mom?" Leo asked, forgetting to be quiet.

Kayla looked over at Finn. "Can he?"

"She's harmless. Go ahead."

As Leo stuck fingers into the cage of the tail-wagging Lola, Finn turned toward Kayla. "Most of our dogs *are* really gentle, just like I was telling Leo. The ones that are reactive have a red star on their cages." He pointed to one on the cage of a medium-sized brown dog, some kind of Doberman mix. "Those, you both stay away from. If the job works out, we'll talk about getting you some training for handling difficult dogs."

If the job worked out. Would it work out? Did she want it to?

Finn had moved farther down the row of cages, and he made a small sound of concern and opened one, guiding a black cocker spaniel out and attaching a leash to her collar. He bent over the little dog, rubbing his hands up and down her sides. "It's okay," he murmured as the dog wagged her tail and leaned against him. "You're okay."

"What's wrong?"

"Her cage is a mess. She knocked over her water and spilled her food." He scratched behind her ears. "Never has an accident, though, do you, girl?"

Kayla felt her shoulders loosen just a fraction. If Finn was that kind and gentle with a little dog, maybe he was a safe person to be around.

"Could you hold her leash while I clean up her cage?" he asked, looking over at Kayla. "In fact, if you wouldn't mind, she needs to go outside."

"No problem." She moved to take the leash and knelt down, Leo hurrying to her side.

"Careful," Finn warned. "She's blind and mostly deaf. You have to guide her or she'll run into things."

"How can she walk?" Leo asked, squatting down beside Kayla and petting the dog's back as Finn had done. "Mom, feel her! She's soft!"

Kayla put her hand in the dog's fur, shiny and luxuriant. "She *is* soft."

"She still has a good sense of smell," Finn explained to Leo. "And the sun and grass feel good to her. You'll see." He gestured toward the door at the opposite end of the barn. "There's a nice meadow out there where the dogs can run."

She and Leo walked toward the barn's door, guiding the dog around an ancient tractor and bins of dog food. In the bright meadow outside, Kayla inhaled the sweet, pungent scents of pine and wildflowers.

"Look, Mom, she's on her back!" Leo said. "She likes it out here!"

Kayla nodded, kneeling beside Leo to watch the little black dog's ecstatic rolling and arching. "She sure does. No matter that she has some problems—nobody likes to be in a cage."

A few minutes later, Finn came out, leading another dog. "I see you've figured out her favorite activity," he said. "Thanks for helping."

The dog he was leading, some kind of a beagle-basset mix, nudged the blind dog, and they sniffed each other. Then the hound jumped up and bumped her to the ground.

"He's hurting her!" Leo cried and stepped toward the pair.

"Let them be." Finn's hands came down on Leo's shoulders, gently stopping him.

Leo edged away and stood close to Kayla.

Finn lifted an eyebrow and then smiled reassuringly at Leo. "She's a real friendly dog and likes to play. Wish I could find someone to adopt her, but with her disabilities, it's hard. Willie and Long John can only handle one dog each. I have one of our problem dogs at my place—" He waved off toward a small house next to a bigger one, in the direction of the lodge. "And Penny—she owns the ranch—has another at hers. So for now, this girl stays in the kennel."

If she and Leo stayed here, maybe they could take the black dog in. That would certainly make Leo happy. He'd sunk down to roll on the ground with the dogs, laughing as they licked his face, acting like a puppy himself. He hadn't smiled so much in weeks.

And Kayla, who always weighed her choices carefully, who'd spent a year planning how to divorce Mitch, made a snap decision.

This place was safe. It was remote. Mitch would never find them. And maybe Leo could have a decent childhood for a while. Not forever, she didn't expect that, but a little bit of a safe haven.

She looked over at Finn. He was smiling, too, watching Leo. It softened his hard-planed, square face, made him almost handsome. But as he watched, his mouth twisted a little, and his sea-blue eyes got distant.

She didn't want him to sink into a bad mood. That was never good. "If I can arrange for the summer camp for Leo," she said, "I'd be very interested in the job."

He looked at her, then at Leo, and then at the distant mountains. "There's paperwork, a reference check, drug tests. All that would have to be taken care of before we could offer you anything permanent."

"Not a problem." Not only did she have good references, but they were sworn to secrecy as to her whereabouts.

"I'll have to talk to our owner, too." His voice held reluctance.

Time to be blunt. "Is there some kind of problem you see in hiring me?"

"I'm withholding judgment," he said. "But we *do* need someone soon, since our last assistant quit. Until everything's finalized, how about a one-week trial?"

"That works." Even if the job didn't come together, she and Leo would get a week off the road.

With dogs.

Meanwhile, Finn's extreme caution made her curious. "You never did mention what branch of the military you served in," she said as he bent over to put leashes back on the two tired-out dogs.

"Eighty-Second Airborne."

Kayla sat down abruptly beside Leo, pulling her knees to herself on the grassy ground. She knew God was good and had a plan, but sometimes it seemed like He was toying with her.

Because this perfect new job meant involvement with a man from the same small, intensely loyal division of the US Army as her abusive ex.

Chapter 2

"You sure you're not making a big mistake?" Penny Jordan asked Finn two days later.

It was Saturday afternoon, and they were sitting in Penny's office, watching out the window as Kayla's subcompact sputtered up the dirt road to cabin six, leaving a trail of black exhaust in its wake.

"No." Finn watched as Kayla exited the car and opened the back door. Leo climbed out, and they opened the hatch and stood, surveying its contents. Leo looked up at her, listening seriously, like an adult. "I think it probably *is* a mistake, but I couldn't talk her out of wanting the job. So I went with the one-week trial."

"But she's moving in." Penny, ten years older than Finn but at least twenty times wiser, took a gulp of black coffee from her oversize cup. "That doesn't seem like a trial thing to do."

"They were staying at the campground up toward Harmony." He eased his leg off the chair where he'd been resting it, grimacing. "Afternoon thunderstorms are getting bad. At least they'll have a roof over their heads."

"You're skirting the issue." Penny leaned forward, elbows on the table. "She has a young son."

"I know, and even though she says she's got a plan for childcare, I don't know that it's safe for him—"

"Finn." Penny put a hand on his arm. "You know what I'm talking about."

He wasn't going there. "Guess I'd better get up there and help 'em move in."

"You're going to have to face what happened one of these days," she said, standing up with her trademark speed and grace. "I'll come, too. Gotta meet the woman who broke through your three-foot-thick walls."

"She didn't break through—it's a *trial*," he emphasized. "She knows the deal. And yes, you should meet her, because when she's not working kennels she can do housekeeping for you. Free you up for the real work."

Penny put her hands on her hips and arched forward and sideways, stretching her back. She was slim, with one long braid down her back and fine wrinkles fanning out from the corners of her eyes, the result of years spent outdoors in the Western sun. Not a trace of makeup, but she didn't need it; she was naturally pretty. Big heart, too.

She didn't deserve what had happened to her.

"Speaking of the real work," she said, "we might

have two more vets coming in within the next six weeks."

"Oh?"

"Guy's classic PTSD, right out of Iraq. The woman…" Penny shook her head. "She's been through it. Scarred up almost as bad as Daniela was." Penny walked over to the window and looked out, her forehead wrinkling. "I'm going to put her in the cabin next to your new hire. She'll be more comfortable farther away from the guys."

Finn nodded. Daniela Jiminez had only recently left the ranch to marry another short-term resident, Gabriel Shafer. They'd stopped in to visit after their honeymoon, and their obvious joy mostly made Finn happy. He'd never experience that for himself, didn't deserve to, but he was glad to have had a small part in getting Gabe and Daniela together.

They walked down the sunny lane to the cabins. Finn kept up with Penny's quick stride even though he wasn't using his cane; it was a good day.

When they were halfway down, Willie's truck came toward them and glided to a halt. "Hitting the road-house for dinner and then a little boot scootin'," Willie said out the window. "You should come along, Finn. Meet somebody."

Penny rolled her eyes. "Men."

"Like Finn's gonna get a lady friend," Long John said from the passenger seat.

"You think you've got better odds?" Finn asked, meaning it as a joke. Everyone knew he didn't go out, didn't date. Those who pushed had gotten their heads bitten off and learned a lesson. Willie and Long John, though, were more persistent than most.

"We've both got better odds because we know how

to smile and socialize," Willie said. "Ladies around here love us."

That was probably true. Unlike Finn, they both had the capacity for connection, the ability to form good relationships. He, on the other hand, didn't have the personality that meshed easily with a woman's. Too quiet, too serious. Deirdre had thrown that fact at him every time he caught her cheating.

"Y'all be careful, now," Penny said, giving the two men a stern look. "You know we don't hold with drinking at the ranch, and that roadhouse is the eye of the storm."

"Rum and coke, hold the rum," Willie promised.

"Scout's honor," Long John said, holding up a hand in mock salute.

The truck pulled away, and a couple of minutes later Finn and Penny reached the cabin driveway where Kayla was unloading her car. She put down her box, picked up a red rubber ball and squatted in front of her son. "You say hello," she told the boy, "and then you can go throw the ball against the house."

The little boy swallowed, and his eyes darted in their direction and away. "Hi," he said and then grabbed the ball and ran to the side of the cabin.

"He's a little shy," Kayla said. She extended a hand to Penny. "I'm Kayla White. Are you Penny?"

"That's right." Penny gave Kayla a frank appraisal. "I'm glad to meet you. Looking forward to having a little help around here. See how you like the work. And how the work likes you. Cleaning up after dogs isn't for everyone."

"I've done worse." Kayla's color rose, like she'd read a challenge under Penny's words. "I appreciate the chance to stay in the cabin, but we're not going to really settle in until the trial week's over. I know the job wasn't intended for a mother and child."

"Sometimes the Good Lord surprises us," Penny said. "Now, what can we do to help you move in?"

"Not a thing." Kayla brushed her hands on the sides of her jeans. "I'm about done. And I can do some work tomorrow, although it'll be limited by Leo. I'm going to have him try that church camp on Monday." She shaded her eyes to watch her son as he threw the ball against the house, caught it and threw it again.

Looking at young Leo, Finn felt the lid on his memories start to come loose. Derek had loved to play ball, too. Finn had spent a lot of time teaching him to throw and catch and use a bat. Things a father was supposed to teach his son.

His throat tightened, and he coughed to clear it. "We'll take care of the work your first day here. You can start on Monday." He was feeling the urge to be away from her and her child.

She looked from Finn to Penny. "Well, but you're giving me a place to stay early. I don't want to be beholden." She pushed back a strand of chocolate hair that had escaped her ponytail and fallen into her eyes.

She was compact, but strong, with looks that grew on you slowly. Good thing she wasn't his type. Back when he was in the market for a woman, he'd gone for bigger, bouncier, louder ladies. The fun kind.

Yeah, and look where that got you.

"I'm with Finn on having you start Monday, but I'll tell you what," Penny said. "We all go down to church on Sundays. Why don't you join us? It'll give your son a chance to get to know some of the other kids while you're still nearby. That should make his first day at camp a little easier."

Finn turned his face so Kayla couldn't see it and glared at Penny. Yeah, he'd hired Kayla—temporarily—but that didn't mean they had to get all chummy in their time off.

Still, it was church. He supposed he ought to be more welcoming. And he knew Penny missed her grown daughter, who for inexplicable reasons had sided with her father when Penny's marriage had broken up. If Penny wanted to mother Kayla a little, he shouldn't get in the way.

Kayla bit her lip. "I'd like to get Leo to church," she said. "We went some back home, but...well. It wasn't as often as I'd have liked. I want to change that, now."

So she'd be coming to church with them every Sunday if she took the job? It wasn't as if there was much of a choice; Esperanza Springs had only two churches, so it was fifty-fifty odds she'd choose theirs.

Unless she wanted to get some breathing room, too.

Or maybe she'd leave after a week. He intended to make sure the work was hard and long, so that she didn't get too comfortable here.

Because something about Kayla White was making *him* feel anything but comfortable.

As the church service ended in a burst of uplifting piano music, Kayla leaned back in the pew. Her whole body felt relaxed for the first time in weeks. Months, really.

The little church had plain padded benches and a rough-hewn altar. Outside the clear glass windows, the splendor of the mountains put to shame any human effort at stained glass artistry.

Leo had sat with her for half the service, reluctantly gone up to the children's sermon and then followed the other kids out of the sanctuary with a desperate look back at Kayla. She'd forced herself not to rescue him and had made it ten minutes before giving in to her worries and going to check on him. She'd found him busily making crafts with the other young children, looking, if not happy, at least focused.

Now beside her Penny stretched, stood and then sat back down. "Hey, I forgot to mention that Finn and I help serve lunch after church to the congregation and some hard-up folks in the community. Would you like to join us? If you don't feel like working, you can just mingle until lunch is served."

The pastor—young, tanned and exuberant—had been visiting with the few people remaining in the pews, and he reached them just as Penny finished speaking. "We find we get more people to come to church when we offer a free meal," he said and held out a hand to Kayla. "Welcome. We're glad to have you here. I'm Carson Blair."

"Kayla White. I enjoyed your sermon."

He was opening his mouth to reply when two little girls, who looked to be a bit older than Leo, ran down the aisle at breakneck speed. They flung themselves at the pastor, one clinging to each leg, identical pouts on their faces.

"Daddy, she hit me!"

"She started it!"

The pastor knelt down. "Skye, you need to go sit right there." He indicated a pew on the left-hand side.

"And, Sunny, you sit over here." He pointed to the right.

"But…"

"We wanted to play!" The one he'd called Sunny looked mournfully at her twin.

"Sit quietly for five minutes, and you can play together again."

Kayla smiled as the pastor turned back toward the small circle of adults. "Good tactics," she said. "I have a five-year-old. I can't imagine handling two."

Finn pushed himself out of the pew and ended up standing next to Kayla, leaning on his cane, facing the pastor. "Had a phone message from you," he said to the pastor. "I'm sorry I didn't return it. Weekend got away from me."

"We all know your aversion to the phone," the pastor said, reaching out to shake Finn's extended hand.

"To conversation in general," Penny said. "Finn's the strong, silent type," she added to Kayla.

"Don't listen to them," Finn advised and then turned back toward the pastor. "What's up?"

"I was hoping to talk to you about your chaplain position. I know you can't pay yet, but I'd be glad to conduct vespers once a week, or do a little counseling, as long as it doesn't take away from my work here."

"I'll keep that in mind."

Finn's answer didn't seem very gracious for someone who'd just been offered volunteer services.

The pastor looked at him steadily. "Do that."

"We certainly will," Penny said. "But speaking of work, that lunch won't get served without us. You coming?" she asked Kayla.

"Absolutely. Lunch smells wonderful. I'm happy to help, if it will get me a plate of whatever's cooking."

"We all partake," the pastor said, shaking her hand again vigorously. "We're glad to have you here. It's rare that we get a fresh face."

"Won't be so rare soon," Penny warned. "We have a couple of new veterans coming in. And I'm working on getting Long John and Willie to church, too."

"You know the church does a van run," the pastor said. "Sounds like you'll need it. And we'll gladly welcome the men and women who served our country."

Finn jerked his head to the side. "Let's go."

In the church kitchen, organized chaos reigned. Finn handed aprons to Kayla and Penny and then donned one himself, choosing it from a special hook labeled with his name.

"Why do you get your own apron?" she asked, because there didn't seem to be anything special about it.

"It's king-size," he said ruefully. "Those little things barely cover a quarter of me. Last Christmas, the volunteers went together to buy me this tent."

"And in return," a white-haired woman said, "we make him carry all the heavy trays and boxes. Isn't that right, Finn?"

"Glad to, as long as you save me a piece of your strawberry-rhubarb pie, Mrs. Barnes."

Kayla was put to work dishing up little bowls of fruit salad while Penny helped Mrs. Barnes get everyone seated and Finn pulled steaming trays of chicken and rice from the ovens. A couple of other ladies carried baskets of rolls to each table and mingled with the guests, probably fifty or sixty people in all.

It wasn't a fancy church. As many of the congregation members wore jeans as dresses and suits, and seating for the meal was open. That meant there was no distinction between those who'd come just for the food and those who'd come for the service first. Nice.

The children burst into the room and took over one corner, stocked with toys and a big rug. Kayla waited a minute and then went to check on Leo. She found him banging action figures with another kid in a zealous pretend fight.

"Hey, buddy," she said quietly, touching his shoulder.

He flinched and turned. She hated that he did that. No matter what, she was going to make sure he gained confidence and stopped feeling like he was at risk all the time. Mitch had never hit him, to her knowledge, but yelling and belittling were almost as bad. And that last time, when he'd broken into their place and beaten Kayla, she'd looked up from the floor to see Leo crouched in the doorway, pale and silent, tears running down his cheeks.

"Leo is quiet, but he seems to fit in," said the woman who'd run the children's program. "He's a very polite little boy. I understand he's going to do the day camp, too?"

Kayla nodded. "Thank you for taking care of him."

"He's welcome to sit at the kids' table and eat. Most of the children do, though a few go sit with their parents."

Kayla turned back to Leo. "What do you think, buddy? Want to sit here with your new friends, or come sit with me and Miss Penny and Mr. Finn?"

Leo considered.

The other boy whacked his action figure. "AT-TACK!" he yelled.

Leo made his figure strike back, and the other boy fell on the floor, pretending he'd been struck.

"I'll stay with the kids," Leo said and dived down to the floor to make his action figure engage in some hand-to-hand combat with the one the other boy was holding.

Kayla watched them play for a moment as realization struck her. If she did, indeed, build a better life for Leo, it would mean he'd become more and more independent. He wouldn't be tied to her by fear. He'd have regular friendships, sleepovers at other boys' homes, camping trips.

And where did that leave her, who'd centered her life around protecting her son for the past five years?

It'll leave me right where I should be, she told herself firmly. It would be good, normal, for Leo to gain independence. And if that made her nostalgic for his baby years of total reliance on her, that was normal, too. She could focus on the healthy ways parents and children related, instead of walking on eggshells to avoid offending Mitch.

The lunch went quickly, partly because the serving staff ate in shifts and then hurried back to the kitchen to help with refills and cleanup. Kayla didn't mind. She liked the camaraderie of working with others. And she liked having her stomach—and her son's—full of delicious, healthy food.

She was washing dishes when Mrs. Barnes came up beside her, towel in hand. "I'll dry and put away," she said. "Where are you from, dear?"

"Arkansas," Kayla said vaguely. "Small town." Mrs.

Barnes seemed harmless, but Kayla didn't want to get into the habit of revealing too much.

"And what brought you to Esperanza Springs? We don't get a whole lot of newcomers."

Kayla was conscious of Finn nearby, carrying big empty serving dishes back to the sinks to be washed. "I was looking for a change," she said. "I've always loved the mountains, so we thought we'd take our chances in Colorado."

"And what did you do back in Arkansas?"

Kayla didn't see malice in the other woman's eyes, only a little too much curiosity. "I worked for a cleaning company," she said. "Cleaning houses and offices and such." No need to mention that she'd started it, and that it had been doing well. She hoped Janice, who'd taken it over, was managing okay. She'd been avoiding calling her, afraid word would get back to Mitch, but she needed to stop being afraid. She'd call Janice tonight.

The kitchen was getting hotter, and Kayla dried off her hands and unbuttoned her sleeves. As she rolled them up, Mrs. Barnes went still. Behind her, Finn stared, too.

Too late, she looked down and saw her arms, still a traffic wreck of bruises.

"Oh, my, dear, what happened?" Mrs. Barnes put a gentle hand on Kayla's shoulder.

She didn't look at either of them. "I fell."

It wasn't a lie. Each time Mitch had hit her, she'd fallen.

Someone called Mrs. Barnes to the serving counter. She squeezed Kayla's shoulder and then turned away, leaving Finn and Kayla standing at the sink.

He frowned at her, putting his hands on his hips. "If someone hurt you—"

An Eighty-Second Airborne tattoo peeked out from under the sleeve of his shirt. The same tattoo Mitch had.

She took a step backward. "I need to go check on Leo," she said abruptly and practically ran out of the kitchen, rolling down her sleeves as she went.

Leo was drawing pictures with the same boy he'd been playing with before, but he jumped up and hugged her when she approached. "Mom! Hector goes to the day camp here, too! He's gonna get me the cubby next to his and bring his Skytrooper tomorrow!" He flopped back down on the floor, propped on his arms, drawing on the same large piece of paper as his new friend.

"That's great, honey." Kayla backed away and looked from Leo to the kitchen and back again. She was well and truly caught.

Her whole goal was to provide a safe, happy home for Leo. And it looked like maybe she'd found that place. The ranch, the dogs, the church people, all were bringing out her son's relaxed, happy side—a side she'd almost forgotten he had.

But on the other hand, there was Finn—a dangerous man by virtue of his association with Mitch's favorite, dedicated social circle. She knew how the Eighty-Second worked.

She grabbed a sponge and started wiping down tables, thinking.

Finn had seen her bruises and gotten suspicious. If she let slip too much information, he might just get in touch with Mitch.

On the other hand, maybe his tattoo was old and

so was his allegiance. Maybe he'd gotten involved in broader veterans affairs. Not everyone stayed focused on their own little division of the service.

She had to find out more about Finn and how committed he was to his paratrooper brothers. And she had to do it quickly. Because Leo was already starting to get attached to this place, and truthfully, so was she.

But she couldn't let down her guard. She had to learn more.

As she wiped a table, hypnotically, over and over, she concocted a plan. Once she'd finalized it, she felt better.

By this evening, one way or another, she'd have the answer about whether or not they could stay. For Leo's sake, she hoped the answer was yes.

Chapter 3

Late Sunday afternoon, Finn settled into his recliner and put his legs up. He clicked on a baseball game and tried to stop thinking.

It didn't work.

He kept going back to those bruises on Kayla's arms, the defensive secrecy in her eyes. All of it pretty much advertised a victim of abuse.

If that were the case, he was in trouble. His primary responsibility was to the veterans here, and some angry guy coming in to drag Kayla away would up the potential for violence among a group of men who'd seen too much of it.

That was bad.

But worse, he was starting to feel responsible for Kayla and the boy. They were plucky but basically defenseless. They needed protection.

If he sent them away, he'd be putting them at risk.

His phone buzzed, a welcome break from his worries. He clicked to answer. "Gallagher."

"Somethin' curious just happened." It was Long John's voice.

Finn settled back into his chair. "What's that, buddy?" Unlike Willie, Long John had no family, and with his Agent Orange–induced Parkinson's, he couldn't get out a lot. He tended to call Finn with reports of a herd of elk, or an upcoming storm, or a recommendation about caring for one of the dogs.

It was fine, good, even. Finn didn't have much family himself, none here in Colorado, and providing a listening ear to lonely vets gave him a sense of purpose.

Long John cleared his throat. "That Kayla is mighty interested in you."

"What do you mean?" For just a second, he thought Long John meant romantic interest, but then he realized that wasn't likely to be the case. Kayla was young, pretty and preoccupied with her own problems. She wouldn't want to hook up with someone like him. Long John was probably just creating drama out of boredom.

"She came over for a little chat," Long John said. "Talked about the weather a bit and then got right into questions about you."

"What kind of questions?"

"Where'd you serve. How active are you in the local chapter. How many of your military buddies come around. Did you ever do anything with the Eighty-Second on the national level. That kind of stuff."

"Weird." Especially since she'd seemed to have an aversion to all things military.

"Not sure what to make of it," Long John said. "She's a real nice gal, but still. All kinds of people trying to take advantage. Thought you should know."

"Thanks." He chatted to the older man for a few more minutes and then ended the call.

Restless now, he strode out onto his porch. The plot thickened around Kayla. If she'd been treated badly by someone, why would she now be seeking information about Finn? Was she still attached to her abuser? Was he making her gather information for some reason?

As he sat down on the porch steps to rub his leg— today was a bad day—he saw Kayla sitting with Penny at the picnic table beside Penny's house. Talking intently.

More information gathering?

Leo played nearby, some engrossing five-year-old game involving rocks and a lot of shouting. Kid needed a playmate. They should invite the pastor's little girls up here.

Except thinking of the widowed pastor hanging around Kayla rubbed him the wrong way.

And why should any of that matter to him? Impatient with himself, he got down on the ground and started pulling up the weeds that were getting out of control around the foundation of his place, like everywhere else on the ranch. Kayla wasn't his concern. She was here on a temporary pass. And even if they did give her the full-time job—which he still questioned—he didn't need to get involved in how she ran her life and raised her kid.

Penny stood and waved to him. "I'll be inside, doing some paperwork, if anybody needs me," she called.

He stood, gave her a thumbs-up and watched her walk inside. That was how they ran the place, spelling each other, letting each other know what they were doing. It'd be quiet on a Sunday, but they liked for at least one of them to be on call, phone on, ready to help as needed.

From the garden area just behind him, he heard a thump, a wail—"Mommy!"—and then the sound of crying. Leo. Finn spun and went to the boy, who was kneeling on the ground where Finn had been digging. His hand was bleeding and his face wet with tears.

Finn beckoned to Kayla, who'd jumped up from the picnic table, and then knelt awkwardly beside the little boy. "Hey, son, what happened?"

Leo cringed away, his eyebrows drawing together, and cried harder.

"Leo!" Kayla arrived, sank down and drew Leo into her arms. "Oh, no, honey, what happened?"

"It hurts!" Leo clutched his bloody hand to his chest.

"Let me see."

The little boy held up his hand to show her, but the sight of it made him wail louder. "I'm bleeding!"

Kayla leaned in and examined the wound, and Finn did, too. Fortunately, it didn't look too serious. The bleeding was already stopping. "Looks like he might have cut it on the weed digger. Is that what happened, buddy?"

The boy nodded, still gulping and gasping.

"I have bandages and antibiotic cream inside, if you want to bring him in." He knew better than to offer to carry the boy. Only a mother would do at a time like this.

Kayla got to her feet and swung Leo up into her arms. "Come on. Let's fix you up."

There was a buzzing sound, and Finn felt for his phone.

"It's mine," Kayla said. "I'll get it later."

"You can sit in there." Finn indicated the kitchen. "I'll grab the stuff."

Moments later, he was back downstairs with every size of Band-Aid in his cupboard and three different types of medical ointment.

Kayla had Leo sitting on the edge of the sink and was rinsing his hand.

Leo howled like he was being tortured.

"I know, honey, it hurts, but we have to clean it. There. Now it'll start feeling better." She wrapped a paper towel around the boy's hand and lifted him easily from the sink to a kitchen chair.

She'd been right. She *was* stronger than she looked, because Leo wasn't small.

"Let's see," Finn said, giving the little boy a reassuring smile.

Leo shrank away and held his hand against his chest.

"I won't touch it. I just want to look." To Kayla he added, "I have first-aid training from the service. But it's probably fine. Your call."

"Let Mr. Finn look, honey. Let's count one-two-three and then do the hard thing. Ready?"

Leo looked up, leaned into her and nodded. "Okay."

Together, they counted. "One, two, three." And then Leo squeezed his eyes shut and held out his hand.

Finn studied the small hand, the superficial cut across two fingers. He opened his mouth to reassure Kayla and Leo.

And then memory crashed in.

He'd put a Band-Aid on Derek's hand, not long before the accident. He'd cuddled the boy to his chest as he held the little hand—just like Leo's—in his own larger one. Carefully squeezed the antibiotic on the small scrape, added a superhero Band-Aid and wiped his son's tears.

"It looks fine," he said to Kayla through a suddenly tight throat. "You go ahead and dress it." He shoved the materials at her, limped over to the window and looked out, trying to compose himself.

Normally, he kept a lid on his emotions about his son. Especially his son. Deirdre, yes, he grieved losing her, but she was an adult and she'd made a lot of bad choices that had contributed to her death.

His son had been an innocent victim.

"There. All fixed!" Kayla's voice was perky and upbeat. "You keep that Band-Aid on, now. Don't go showing that cut to your friends. It's a big one."

"It *is* big," Leo said, his voice steadying. "I was brave, wasn't I, Mommy?"

Finn turned back in time to see her hug him. "You were super brave. Good job."

Leo came over to Finn and, from a safe distance, held up his hand. "See? It was a really big cut!"

"It sure was," Finn said and then cleared the roughness out of his throat. "Sorry I don't have any fun Band-Aids. Not many kids come around here."

And there was a good reason for that. Having little boys around would tear him apart.

Change the subject. "You want to watch TV for a few minutes, buddy? I need to talk to your mom."

Leo's head jerked around to look at Kayla. "Can I, Mom?"

She hesitated. "I guess, for a few minutes. If we can find a decent show." She looked at Finn pointedly. "I actually don't allow him to watch much TV."

"Sorry." He headed into the living room and clicked the TV on, found a cartoonish-looking show that he remembered his son liking and looked at Kayla. "This okay?"

She squinted at the TV. "Yeah. Sure."

Her phone buzzed again, but she ignored it.

In the kitchen, she looked at him with two vertical lines between her eyebrows. "What's up?"

"Why'd you grill Long John about me?" he asked her abruptly.

At the sharp question from Finn, Kayla's mind reeled. "What do you mean?" she asked, buying time.

She knew exactly what he meant.

Long John must have gotten on the phone the moment she'd left his cabin. And wasn't that just like a soldier, to report anything and everything to his military buddies.

They're friends, an inner voice reminded her. She'd just met Long John, while Finn had probably known him for months if not years.

Finn let out a sigh. "Long John let me know you were asking all kinds of questions about me. I wondered why."

She studied him for signs of out-of-control anger and saw none. In which case, the best defense was a good offense. "You have a problem with me checking my employer's references the same way you and Penny are checking mine?" she bluffed.

He looked at her for a moment. "No. That's not a problem. It's just that some of your questions seemed pointed. All about my military service."

"That's part of your background," she said.

Finn shook his head. "I'm just not comfortable with having you here if you have any sort of attitude toward the military," he said. "The veterans are the most important thing to us, and believe it or not, they're sensitive. Especially the ones we get here. I don't need a worker who's cringing away from them or, on the other hand, overly curious."

She nodded. "That makes sense." She should have known this wouldn't work. It was too perfect.

The thought of going back on the road filled her with anxiety, though. Her supply of money was dwindling, and so was Leo's patience.

This place was *perfect* for Leo.

She tried to hang on to the pastor's words from this morning. What was the verse? *I know the plans I have for you...*

God has a plan for us.

She straightened her spine. "We'll get our things together tonight and move on tomorrow."

Her phone buzzed for about the twentieth time. Impatient, she pulled it out. She read through the texts from her friend Janice, back in Arkansas, her anxiety growing.

Don't come back under any circumstances.
He tore up your place.
He's raving that he's going to find you.
Get a PFA, fast.

She sank into a kitchen chair, her hand pressed to her mouth, her heart pounding. What was she going to do now?

"Listen, Kayla, I didn't mean you had to leave this minute," Finn said. "You can stay out the week, like we discussed. We can even help you figure out your next step. I just don't think…" He paused.

There was a brisk knock at the screen door, and then Penny walked in. "I called the last reference, and they raved about you," she said to Kayla. "So as far as I'm concerned, you're hired."

Kayla glanced up at Finn in time to see his forehead wrinkle. "Temporarily," he said.

"Long-term, as far as I'm concerned." Penny gave him an even stare.

"We need to talk," he said to Penny.

"All right." She put a bunch of paper in front of Kayla. "Start signing," she said. "Look for the *X*s."

Finn and Penny went out onto the porch, and she heard the low, intense sound of an argument.

From the living room, she heard Leo laughing at the television.

Finn didn't want to hire her. That was clear, and it

wasn't only because she'd been nosy. Something else about her bothered him.

Which was fine, because he kind of bothered her, too. She didn't think he was dangerous himself, but he was clearly linked up to the veteran old boys' network. If Mitch started yelling at one of his meetings about how they were missing, the word could get out. Paratroopers were intensely loyal and they helped each other out, and a missing child would definitely be the type of thing that would stir up their interest and sympathy.

She needed to be farther away, but for now, the protection offered by the ranch was probably the safest alternative for Leo. A week, two, even a month here would give her breathing room.

Or maybe Mitch's rage would burn out. Although it hadn't in the year since the divorce he'd fought every inch of the way.

Finn didn't want her here, but she was used to that. She'd grown up in a home where she wasn't wanted.

And Penny had seemed to intuit some of her issues when Kayla had probed about Finn and the ranch during a lull before the church service. She'd said something about men, how women needed to stick together. Penny was on her side.

She could deal with Finn. She didn't need his approval or his smiles.

And she didn't want to depend on anyone. But here, she could work hard, pull her weight.

Finn and Penny came back in. Finn's jaw jutted out. Penny looked calm.

"You can have the job," Finn said.

"However long you want it," Penny added, glancing over at Finn.

Kayla drew in a deep breath, looking at them. "Thank you."

Then, her insides quivering, she picked up the pen and started signing.

Chapter 4

Finn headed for the kennels around eight o'clock the next morning, enjoying the sight of the Sangre de Cristos. He could hear the dogs barking and the whinnying of a horse. They only kept two, and Penny cared for them up at the small barn, but she sometimes took one out for a little ride in the morning.

Up ahead, Kayla's cabin door opened, and she and Leo came out.

He frowned. He wasn't thrilled about her working here, but he was resigned to it. He just had to stay uninvolved, that was all.

He watched her urge Leo into the car. Leo resisted, turning away as if to run toward the cabin, but she caught him in a bear hug.

Uh-oh. Wherever they were going—probably down to the church day camp—Leo wasn't on board.

She set Leo down and pointed at the back seat, and with obvious reluctance, the boy climbed in. Through the car's open windows, he heard Leo complain, "I can't get it buckled."

She bent over and leaned in, and he noticed she didn't raise her voice even though Leo continued to whine. She spoke soothingly but didn't give in.

Finn looked away and tried to think about something other than what it would be like to parent a kid Leo's age.

Derek's age.

When she tried to start the car, all that happened was some loud clicking and grinding. A wisp of smoke wafted from the front of the vehicle.

She got out and raised the hood. From inside the car, Leo's voice rose. "If I have to go, I don't want to be late!"

By now, Finn had reached the point where her cabin's little driveway intersected with the road. He looked out over the valley and sniffed the aromatic pines and tried to stay uninvolved. She hadn't seen him. He could walk on by.

He tried to. Stopped. "Need a jump?"

She bit her lip, its fullness at odds with her otherwise plain looks and too-thin figure. She looked from him to Leo. As clear as the brightening blue sky, he could see the battle between her desire for independence and her child's needs.

"I think my starter's bad."

"You need to call for a tow?" He stood beside her and pretended to know what he was looking at. Truth was, despite the fact that he'd sold farm machinery in one of his jobs, car repair wasn't in his skill set.

She shook her head. "I can fix it, if I can get down to town and get the part."

He looked sideways at her. "You sure?"

She blew out a *pfft* of air and nodded. "Sure. Just takes a screwdriver and a couple of bolts. Trouble is, Leo needs to get to camp."

His glance strayed to her mouth again but he looked away quickly, glancing down to the cross around her neck. She wasn't a girl up for grabs, obviously, and even if she were, he couldn't partake. One, because she was sort of his employee—Penny was technically her boss, but he was her direct supervisor. And two, because of what he'd done. He didn't deserve to connect with a woman. He needed to remember his decision in that regard.

No one had ever tested it before, not really.

But there was nothing wrong with giving her and the boy a ride, was there? Any Good Samaritan would do that.

"I planned to head down into town anyway," he said. "I can move up my schedule. Come on. Grab his booster seat and we'll hop in my truck."

She hesitated and looked toward Leo, who appeared very small even in the compact car. "Okay. Thank you. That would be a big help." She leaned in. "Hustle out, buddy. Mr. Finn's going to give us a ride."

"Is our car broken?"

"Yes, but I can fix it," she said, her voice confident. Leo nodded. "Okay."

Finn carried the booster seat and Kayla held Leo's hand as they walked down the dirt road toward Finn's place and the truck. The piney breeze felt fresh against his face. A mountain bluebird flashed by, chirping its *TOO-too, TOO-too.*

Other than that, it was quiet, because Kayla wasn't a person who had to talk all the time. As a quiet man himself, he appreciated that.

The ride to town got too quiet, though, so he turned on a little country music. When his current favorite song came on, he saw her tapping a hand against her jean-clad thigh. He was tapping the steering wheel, same rhythm, and when their eyes met, she flashed a smile.

They got close to town, and there was a sniffling sound in the back seat. Kayla turned half-around. "What's wrong, buddy?"

"I don't want to go." Leo's voice trembled.

"It's hard to do new things," she said, her voice matter-of-fact.

"My tummy hurts."

"Sometimes that happens when you're scared." She paused, then added, "Anyone would be a little bit afraid, meeting a lot of new people. But we know how to do things anyway, even when we're scared."

"I don't want to." His voice dripped misery.

The tone and the sound brought back Finn's son, hard. He remembered taking Derek to his first T-ball practice, a new team of kids he didn't know. Finn had comforted him in the same way Kayla was comforting Leo.

His breath hitched. He needed to stop making that dumb kind of equation. "You'd better stop crying," he said to Leo. "Buck up. The other boys will laugh at you."

Finn looked in the rearview mirror, saw the boy's

narrow shoulders cringe and wanted to knock himself in the head.

Leo drew in a sharp, hiccupy breath.

Kayla was giving Finn the death stare. "Anyone worth being your friend will understand if you're a little scared the first day," she said over her shoulder.

But Leo kept gasping in air, trying to get his tears under control. And that *was* good; the other kids wouldn't like a crybaby, but still. Finn had no right to tell Leo what to do.

No rights in this situation, at all.

And now the tension in the truck was thicker than an autumn fog.

He'd created the problem and he needed to fix it. "Hey," he said, "when do you want the dog to come live with you?"

The snuffly sounds stopped. Kayla glanced back at Leo, then at Finn, her eyes narrowed.

He could tell she was debating whether or not to trust him and go along with this or to stay angry. He'd seen that expression plenty of times before, with his wife. She'd have chosen to hold on to her anger, no question.

"I don't know." Kayla put on a thoughtful voice. "I'd rather wait until this evening when Leo's home from camp. That way, he can help me handle her. That is…" She turned half-around again. "Do you think we're ready to take care of a dog? You'd have to help me."

"Yeah!" Leo's voice was loud and excited. "I know we can do it, Mom."

"Hey, Leo," Finn said, "I don't know the dog's name. She needs a new one. Maybe the other kids at camp could help you pick one out." Actually, the former owners *had* told Finn the dog's name. It was a common curse word. Even now, thinking of their nasty laughs as they'd dumped the eager, skinny, blind-and-deaf dog at the ranch, his mouth twisted.

"Okay!" Leo said as they pulled into the church parking lot. "I'll ask them what we should name her!" He unfastened his seat belt as soon as the truck stopped, clearly eager to get on with his day.

"Wait a minute," Kayla warned Leo as he reached for the door handle. "I need to take you in, and we have to walk on the lines in the parking lot. It's for safety. The teacher told me when I talked to her."

"I'll be here," Finn said as Kayla got nimbly out of the truck and then opened the back for Leo to jump down. They walked toward the building holding hands, Leo walking beside her, moving more slowly as they got closer.

Watching them reminded him of dropping off his son.

He couldn't make a practice of getting involved with Kayla and Leo, he told himself sternly. It hurt too much. And it gave his heart crazy ideas about the possibility of having a family sometime in the future.

That wasn't happening, his head reminded him.

But his heart didn't seem to be listening.

Kayla walked out of the church after dropping Leo off at the camp program, her stomach twisting and tears pressing at her eyes.

If only she didn't have to start him in a new program so soon after arriving in town. But she had to work; there wasn't a choice about that.

He'll be fine. He has to grow up sometime.

But he'd looked so miserable.

The lump in her throat grew and the tears overflowed.

To her mortification, two of the other mothers—or maybe it was a mother and a grandmother—noticed and came over. "What's wrong, honey?" the older, redheaded one asked.

The younger woman came to her other side and startled Kayla by wrapping her in a hug. "Are you okay?"

What kind of a town was this, where complete strangers hugged you when you were sad? Kayla pulled back as soon as she graciously could and nodded. "I just hate…leaving him…in a new place."

"Gotcha," the older woman said without judgment and handed her a little packet of tissues. "I'm Marge. Just dropped off my Brenna in the same classroom your boy was in. It's a real good program."

Kayla drew in big gasps of air. "I'm sorry." She blew her nose. "I feel like an idiot."

"Oh, I know what you're going through," the mother who'd hugged her said. "I cried every single day of the first two weeks at kindergarten drop-off." She patted Kayla's shoulder. "I'm Missy, by the way. What's your name? I haven't seen you around."

"I'm Kayla. Pleased to meet you." She got the words out without crying any more, but barely.

"Now, me," Marge said, "I jumped for joy when Brenna started kindergarten. She's my sixth," she added, "and I love her to pieces, but it was the first time I had the house to myself in fifteen years. I don't want to give up the freedom come summer, so all my kids are in some kind of program or sport."

Kayla tried to smile but couldn't. Leo had gone willingly enough with the counselor in charge, no doubt buoyed up by the prospect of telling the other children he was getting a dog. But as they'd walked away, he'd shot such a sad, plaintive look over his shoulder. That was what had done her in.

For a long time, it had been her and Leo against the world. She had to learn to let him go, let him grow up, but she didn't have to like it.

In the past year of starting and running her little business, cleaning houses for wealthy people, she'd paid attention to how they cared for their kids. Lots of talking, lots of book reading. That had been easy for her to replicate with Leo.

A couple of the families she'd really admired had given their kids independence and decision-making power, even at a fairly young age. That was harder for Kayla to do, given how she and Leo had been living, though she could see the merits of it. "Maybe I should go back in and check on him," she said, thinking aloud.

"Don't do it," Missy advised. "You'll just make yourself miserable. And if he sees you, he'll get more upset."

"He'll be fine." Marge waved a hand. "They have your number to call you if there's anything wrong. Enjoy the time to yourself."

One of the other mothers, a tall, beautifully made-up blonde, drifted over. "Some of us are going to Flexible Coffee for a bit," she said to Kayla. "I noticed you're new. Want to come?"

More small-town friendliness? Kayla appreciated it, but she didn't quite feel comfortable. She didn't want to go socialize for an hour or two; she had a car starter to buy and install.

Before she could beg off, Marge lifted an eyebrow and pinned the woman with a steady stare. "Glad you're willing to bury the hatchet, Sylvie—that is, if you're inviting all of us. You haven't spoken to me since Brenna gave Jocelyn that surprise haircut last year."

Sylvie shuddered. "Right before she had a pageant. She could have won."

Marge snorted. "Don't pin that on me. Jocelyn wears a wig to those things, just like every other little beauty queen."

"I wouldn't expect *you* to understand." Sylvie's once-over, taking in Marge's faded T-shirt and cutoff shorts, wasn't subtle.

Missy rolled her eyes. "Would you two stop fighting? You're going to give Kayla here a bad impression of our town."

The gorgeous Sylvie glanced out into the parking lot and then looked at Kayla speculatively. "That looked like Finn Gallagher's truck. Are you two seeing each other?"

"No!" Heat climbed Kayla's cheeks. All three women looked at her and she realized she'd spoken too loudly. "I work for him, that's all," she said quickly, trying to sound casual. "I'm having car trouble, so he gave me and my son a ride to town."

"Think I'll go say hello." Sylvie sashayed over to Finn's truck.

"One of these days, she's going to land him," Marge said.

"Not sure she's his type," Missy said.

"Long-legged blondes are every guy's type." Marge stretched. "You two going to take her up on her coffee invite?"

"I have to work," Missy said, turning toward the row of cars. "But if you go, call me later with all the gossip, okay?"

"Will do," Marge called after her. Then she turned to Kayla. "How about you. Want to come?"

"I have to work, too." And Kayla wasn't sure she wanted to get in the middle of a lot of gossip. Back in high school, she'd envied the girls who knew everything about everyone and felt comfortable in the spotlight, but no more.

Now she just wanted peace. And peace, for her, definitely meant staying *out* of the spotlight.

"Well, it was nice meeting you. Think I'll go just to see what news Sylvie's gathered," Marge added. "Unless she decides to hook up with Finn right here and now." She nodded toward Finn's truck.

Sylvie had propped her crossed arms on the open window and was leaning in. She ran a hand through her long blond hair, flipping it back.

Kayla felt a surge of the old jealousy. There were women who stood out and got noticed. And then there were women like her. As good-looking as Finn Gallagher was, he'd definitely go for the showier type.

Which didn't matter, of course. Finn could date whomever he chose, and it wasn't her business. She just hoped he could still give her a ride back to the ranch before taking off with Sylvie.

But Sylvie backed away quickly, spun and headed toward the main parking lot where Kayla and Marge still stood.

"Did you get a date?" Marge asked her bluntly.

"Marge! And no. He blew me off again." Sylvie sighed dramatically. "If only I didn't have this attraction to unavailable men. Are we going for coffee or not?"

"I'll meet you over there," Marge said.

"How about you, Kayla?" Sylvie studied her a little too hard. "Come on—join us. I'd like to get to know you."

No way. "Thank you," she said in the fake-nice voice women like Sylvie always inspired in her. "I appreciate the coffee offer, but I really do need to get going. Thank you for helping me with my meltdown," she added to Marge. "I'll see you at pickup, or maybe another day this week. 'Bye, Sylvie."

She hurried off toward Finn's truck, hoping she hadn't been too abrupt.

"What went on just now?" Finn asked as soon as she'd settled inside and fastened her seat belt.

She shrugged. "They asked me for coffee, but I told them I needed to work."

"You know, your shift doesn't start until ten. You could've gone."

"No, thanks."

He looked at her speculatively but didn't ask any questions. "I'd like to take you to breakfast," he said instead.

That jolted her inner alarm system but good. "Why?"

"Because I'm guessing you haven't eaten, and you have a long day of work ahead." He hesitated, then added, "And because I upset Leo, and I want to make it up to you."

"That's not necessary. You fixed it." What did he want with her, inviting her to a meal?

He must have read her wariness, because he spread his hands. "No big deal. I often stop at the Peak View Diner for breakfast. It's cheap, and Long John and Willie will probably be there. They'd love to have a new audience."

Oh. Well, if Long John and Willie would be there…

"Best bacon biscuits in the state." He offered a winning smile that made her breath catch.

Her stomach growled. "Well…"

"Look," he said, "I'm not asking you out, if that's what's worrying you. It's just that Esperanza Springs is a sociable little town. People are curious about you, and it's better for them to meet you than to gossip among themselves."

"Bacon biscuits, huh?" She grinned and lifted her hands, palms up. "I can't turn that down. Just as long as you and Long John and Willie protect me from the gossip hounds."

"Believe me," he said, "nobody can get a word in around those guys' stories, but they really are popular. If people see you're with them—"

"And with you?" she interrupted.

"To a lesser extent, yes. So we'll make an appearance, eat a couple of biscuits and then get back to the peace and solitude I think we both prefer."

She looked at him sideways and gave a slow nod. "Okay," she said and then looked away, afraid of revealing the surge of emotion that had welled up in her at his words.

It wasn't that often that people paid enough attention to Kayla to figure out what she was like inside.

And it was even less often that someone shared the same preferences and tastes.

Unfortunately, Kayla was finding Finn's attention and understanding just a little bit too appealing.

That night, Kayla spooned up another sloppy joe for Leo. She sat back in her chair at the little table, pushed her own empty plate away and stretched.

Despite her sore muscles and tiredness, she had a sense of accomplishment.

Working in the kennel had been physical and sometimes hard, but she loved the sweet old dogs already. And she was relieved to know that she could do the work, that it wasn't too hard for her. Finn's directions were clear and easy to understand, and he'd left her to do her job rather than hovering over her.

After work, she'd put the new starter in her car. *Thank you, online videos.* Paying someone to fix something simple like that just wasn't in the budget.

She looked around the bare cabin. That might be her next project, making it look a little homier.

It would be a while before she found a spare hour to dig out her old camera and explore the ranch, take some shots. She was an amateur, but she enjoyed photography. Living in such a beautiful place was making her itch to capture some images.

But for today, she'd gotten the car fixed and dinner on the table and started a job, and that was enough. She'd sleep well tonight.

Leo wiped a napkin across his face and chattered on about his day at camp, his new friends and potential names for the dog. She didn't have the heart to correct him for talking with his mouth full. Fortunately, he seemed to have forgotten that Finn had said he'd bring the dog around tonight, because that didn't seem to be happening.

Or maybe he was just used to men disappointing him, as Mitch had so many times when he'd failed to pick Leo up for visits as planned.

We're free from all that now. She pushed thoughts of her ex away. Instead, she listened to her son chatter and let her shoulders relax, stretching her neck from side to side. She'd better get these dinner dishes washed before she got so sleepy she was tempted to just let it go. This cabin was way too small for that, especially since the kitchen, dining room and living room were just one connected space.

There was a knock on the door, a little scuffling.

Her shoulders tensed again.

"It's Finn, with a special visitor," came the deep voice that was already becoming familiar to her.

"The *dog*!" Leo shouted and jumped up from the table. "May I be 'scused?"

"You may." She smiled and stood up.

Leo ran to the door and flung it open. "Hi, dog!"

"She's here for you if you're ready," Finn said to Kayla, restraining the black cocker spaniel just inside the doorway. "If not, tonight can just be a visit."

Kayla laughed and rubbed Leo's back. "You think you'll be able to get her out of here again? We're as ready as we'll ever be." She knelt down, and Finn dropped the leash, and the dog walked right into her arms.

"She's so sweet!" Kayla rubbed her sides and turned a little, encouraging the dog to go to Leo, who reached out to hug her tight.

"Gentle!" Kayla laughed as the dog gave Leo a brief lick. "Let her go and we'll see what she does."

The dog started to explore, keeping her nose to the floor as she trotted around. She bumped into a kitchen chair, backed up and continued on her quest as if nothing had happened.

When she reached Leo again, she was ready to examine him. She licked his hands and face while he squealed and laughed.

Kayla laughed, too. "Leo must smell like dinner," she said and then looked up at Finn. "Would you like a plate? We have plenty of sloppy joes and corn on the cob." She flushed a little as she named the humble fare. Finn was probably used to better.

Finn looked over at the table, and for a moment something like longing flashed across his face. But it was gone so quickly that she might have imagined it. "It does smell good," he said, "but I already ate with Penny and a couple of the guys. We do meals together occasionally."

Leo rolled away from the friendly dog, and she knelt in a play bow and uttered a couple of short barks.

"She's deaf, but she still barks?" Kayla asked.

"She's not entirely deaf. And she barks when she's excited." He ruffled Leo's hair. "She's excited now. I think she likes you."

Leo looked up at Finn, eyes positively glowing.

Finn slid a backpack off and set it on the floor. "If you're sure you're ready, I'll get out her stuff."

Kayla nodded. "That's fine. I'm just going to get the dinner dishes cleaned up." She hoped Finn would pick up on the fact that she wanted Leo to be as involved as possible.

He seemed to read her mind. "Leo, I need help," Finn said. "If you can just let the dog explore for a few minutes, we'll get out her supplies."

"Supplies?" Leo's eyes widened.

Finn pulled out a food dish and large water bowl. "Now, the thing about dogs and food," he said to Leo, "is that you never want to come between them. This one's gentle, but she's been hungry before and she probably remembers it. Dogs can get a little bit mad if they think you're taking their food."

Kayla couldn't resist: she walked over and knelt to hear the lesson. The dishes could wait.

"Did you choose a new name for her?" Finn asked.

"Shoney," Leo said, looking up at Kayla. "It's the place where my dad and me liked to go for dinner."

Kayla stared blankly at her son. She hadn't realized that was why he liked the name. And wasn't it amazing that a kid could love a dad as mean and inattentive as Mitch had been? He'd taken Leo out for a meal exactly once since the divorce.

If Finn felt those undercurrents, he ignored them. Instead he continued with the lesson, explaining the leash and the toys and the brush for the dog's hair.

Kayla's shoulders relaxed. Finn was a steady man. He'd arrived when he'd said, bringing the dog, bringing the supplies they needed. He showed Leo how to gently lead Shoney around so that she didn't get hurt running into things. He pulled out a blanket, ragged but clean, and explained that it was the blanket Shoney had been using in the kennel, and would help her feel more comfortable in a new place.

"I used to have a blanket," Leo said, "but we put it

away." He hesitated, then added, "I only use it sometimes. In 'mergencies."

Finn nodded. "Makes sense."

Finn wasn't like other men she'd known, her mother's boyfriends or the teasing boys at school, or Mitch. In fact, she'd never met a man like him before.

He glanced over, and she flushed and looked away. She focused on the paneled walls, the curtainless windows, through which she could see the sun turning the tops of the mountains red, making the pasturelands golden. Crisp evening air came through the screen door, a welcome coolness for her warm face.

Leo filled the dog bowl with water and set it in the corner on a towel just as Finn had instructed, pausing often to pat Shoney. Then he returned to the backpack to check out the rest of Shoney's supplies.

"Your son's careful," Finn said approvingly.

"He's had to be." Unbidden, a memory from Leo's younger days pushed into her awareness.

Leo had just turned four, and he'd spilled a glass of juice at the table. Just a few drops had hit Mitch's phone before Kayla had swooped in with a towel, but he'd jumped up, shouted at Leo and raised his fist.

She'd intercepted the blow, but her heart still broke thinking of how Leo had tried to stifle his tears.

"Look, Mom!" His voice now was worlds away from that fearful one, and happiness bloomed inside her.

"What do you have there?" She stood and walked over to him.

"There's a scarf for her!" He held up a pink-checked neckerchief.

"Cool! See how it looks on her."

As Leo crossed the room to where Shoney had flopped down, Kayla looked over at Finn. "You dress your dogs?" she asked teasingly, lifting an eyebrow.

He shrugged and a dimple appeared in his cheek. His gaze stayed fixed on hers. "I like a girl in nice clothes."

"Oh, you do?"

They looked at each other for a moment more, until several realizations dawned on Kayla at once.

She was flirting. She *never* flirted.

She didn't have nice clothes, another fact that put Finn out of her league.

And this situation, living in close proximity to Finn here at the ranch, could get out of control all too easily.

She looked away from him, her cheeks heating.

No surprise that he turned and walked over to Leo, ensuring that their slightly romantic moment was over. "Here's a scoop for dog food," he explained while Kayla finished clearing up the dinner dishes. "She gets one scoop in the morning and one in the evening."

"How can Shoney find her food, if she's blind?" Leo asked.

"Because of her super sense of smell," Finn explained, then put a piece of food on the floor near Shoney. Sure enough, the shaggy black dog found it almost immediately.

Kayla's heart melted, not in a flirty way now, but in a grateful way. As Leo experimented with having Shoney find bits of food, she walked over to Finn and knelt beside him to watch.

"He's being gentle," Finn said. "You've taught him well."

That meant the world to Kayla, for someone to say

she'd done a good job. Especially on gentleness, since his male role model had been anything but. "You're really good with him yourself," she said. "Have you spent a lot of time around kids?"

All the joy drained out of Finn's face. He looked away, then rose smoothly to his feet and picked up his now-empty backpack. "You good for now?" he asked, his voice gruff.

"Um, sure. I think so." What had she said wrong?

"Then I'll leave you alone with your new family member. See you, Leo." Finn was out the door almost before Leo could offer a wave.

As she petted the dog and helped Leo get to know her, she mused over the encounter in her mind. It was when she'd mentioned kids that he'd closed off.

There was some kind of story there. And God help her, but she wanted to know it.

Chapter 5

The next morning, Kayla tried not to notice Finn's very muscular arms as he pulled the truck into a parking lot in town, just beneath the Esperanza Springs Fourth of July Community Celebration banner.

"Like I said, I'm sorry to make you work on a holiday," Finn said, in the same friendly but utterly impersonal tone he'd taken all morning. "But once we get the dogs settled, you can hang out with Leo and do whatever, until the parade starts." He was acting differently toward her, after the awkward ending to their evening last night. She'd replayed it in her mind, and she didn't think she'd said anything to offend him. Maybe he was just moody. Or maybe she was imagining his distance.

Trying to match his businesslike cordiality, she gave him a quick, impersonal smile as she climbed down from the truck and got Leo out of the back. "No problem. I think it'll be a fun day."

"Will Shoney be okay?" Leo asked. He'd been loath to leave her alone, and truthfully, Kayla had felt the same. Shoney had followed them to the door, and when Kayla had nudged her back inside so she could close it, the dog had cried mournfully.

Finn nodded down at Leo. "Shoney's been staying in a little cage in the kennel for a few weeks. She'll be thrilled to have your whole cabin to herself for a little while."

Kayla focused on the intensely blue sky and the bright sun that illuminated the broad, flat valley, framed by the Sangre de Cristos. Even on the prettiest summer day in Arkansas, the air didn't have this refreshing crispness to it. "Come on," she said to Leo. "Let's go find Miss Penny. She said you could hang around with her while Mom works."

"Okay," he said agreeably, and Kayla sent up a prayer of thanks for Leo's accepting, nonconfrontational demeanor.

They didn't have far to look, because as soon as they'd turned toward the celebration's central area, Penny approached them. "Hey, Leo, I think they've got some good fry bread for breakfast. Have you ever had Native American food?"

Leo looked up at Kayla, puzzled.

"No, he hasn't," Kayla said to Penny, "and neither have I. But we're both in favor of bread and fried food, so I'm sure he'll love it."

"Come on, kiddo. Let's go!" And the two were off into the small line of food vendors, most still setting up, along the edge of the town park.

Kayla helped Finn lift down the crates. They'd brought five dogs, well-socialized ones who could handle the crowds and noise, healthy ones more likely to be adopted.

"We'll put them in the shade, out of the way, and let them out one at a time to move around and get some exercise. If you can stay and do that while I park the truck, there won't be that much more to do."

So she let each dog out and strolled around, keeping them leashed but letting them greet people politely. It would be great if all five found homes today.

Suddenly, Axel, the ancient rottweiler Kayla was walking, started barking and pulling at the leash. Kayla got him under control as the other dogs chimed in, barking from their crates. She looked around to see what was causing the ruckus.

Two women walked in their direction, each with two large Alaskan malamutes on leashes. It took a minute, but Kayla recognized the taller woman as Marge from the previous day's camp drop-off.

She stood still as the pair slowly approached, keeping Axel close and smiling a greeting. And then she saw the lettering on Marge's shirt, identical to that of the other woman: Mountain Malamutes.

"We breed 'em," the other woman explained, gathering both of her leashes in one hand and leaning forward to greet Kayla. "I'm Rosa. We're teaming up with you and Finn today to try and get your guys adopted."

"Great, but how?" Kayla was struggling to keep Axel from pulling her off her feet and to speak above the noise of the crated dogs. Meanwhile, the malamutes stood panting, tongues out, alert but quiet. "And how on earth do you get your dogs to behave so well?"

Marge laughed. "Thousands of years of breeding, for starters," she said. "They're work dogs. Plus, we train 'em hard. But Rosa and I, we feel bad about breeding dogs when there are so many rescues who need homes, so we help where we can."

A group of men in Western shirts walked by, most carrying musical instruments, and Kayla recognized Long John's shuffling gait. Willie was beside him, and the two stopped and greeted Kayla as if they'd known her for years instead of days.

"You and young Leo should come hear us play," Willie said, patting her arm.

"That you should," Long John agreed. "We're at eleven and then again at three, right over on the stage they're setting up." He waved a hand toward a flurry of activity at the center of the park.

"I will," Kayla promised, warmed by their friendliness.

As the men walked on, a little girl about Leo's size rushed over and wrapped her arms around Marge's legs. "Mommy!" she cried, sounding upset. She buried her face in Marge's leg.

Marge extracted herself, knelt and studied the little girl's upset face. "What's wrong, baby?"

"Sissy and Jim won't play with me. So I got mad and ran away from them."

Marge's eyes narrowed as she scanned the area. "I'm gonna speak my piece to those two when I find 'em." She looked up at Kayla. "Two of my older kids. They're supposed to be taking care of Brenna."

"Hi, Brenna," Kayla said, smiling at the adorable little redhead. "I think you were in camp with my son, Leo, yesterday."

"Uh-huh." Brenna sucked a finger. "We played on the swings."

"Matter of fact," Marge said, "I think I see him right over there on the playground. Want to run over and see if he wants to play?" Marge turned to Kayla. "Is that okay?"

"I'm sure it is. Let me just text Penny." She did, and the answer came back immediately: Send her over. The more, the merrier.

Brenna took off for the play area, and when she got there, she hugged Leo. And then they started climbing a multilevel wooden structure.

A volley of rapid Spanish rang out nearby, and Hector, the boy who'd played with Leo at church, ran to join Leo and Brenna.

Kayla's breath caught as gratitude swept over her. Some small towns could be clannish, but Esperanza Springs had welcomed her and Leo with open arms.

She was well on her way to falling in love with this place. The natural beauty and the distance from Arkansas were great, but more than that, she already felt like part of a community.

Moments later, Finn returned, in time to direct another truck their way. Then they all helped unload five empty dog crates on wheels, made to look like circus animal carts, but cunningly arranged with harnesses. As Finn and Rosa tested out one of the carts, hooking up a malamute and putting in Charcoal, the largest dog they'd brought from the ranch, Kayla couldn't help clapping her hands. "That's so adorable!"

Marge nodded. "Exactly the reaction we're looking for. And the next step we're hoping for is that people who get swept away with the cuteness will want to adopt the dog."

"And buy a malamute," Rosa called.

"It's a win-win." Finn adjusted the cart, and they all watched while the malamute trotted in a circle, tail and ears high, pulling the silver-muzzled Lab mix.

"It's working. If it works for Charcoal, it'll work for all the dogs." Finn let Charcoal out of the cart and urged him back into his crate. "Kayla, if you want to take some time off, you're welcome. I'd just need a little assistance at twelve thirty, when the parade's lining up."

"Thanks, boss." She added a sassy smile, forgetting for a moment to be businesslike and keep her distance.

He lifted an eyebrow, the corners of his own mouth turning up.

Kayla forced herself to turn away. She strolled through the grounds, savoring the sights, smells and sounds of a small-town Fourth of July. She'd grown up in Little Rock, and if the city had offered such events back then, her mother hadn't known about them. She and Mitch had taken Leo to a few Fourth of July gatherings, but the kind Mitch favored involved a lot of drinking. They didn't have this wholesome feel.

"Hey." Sylvie, the pretty blonde who'd issued the coffee invite the day before, fell into step beside her. "How's it going? Having fun with our Podunk event?"

"I love it, actually," Kayla said.

"Is your son here?" Sylvie looked sideways at her.

"Yes. He's on the playground." Kayla reached up and ran her fingers along the soft, low branches of a cottonwood tree, enjoying the ambling freedom of walking through the park.

"Hey, listen," Sylvie said. "I know Finn seems like a nice guy, but you should be careful. Especially being a single mom and all."

Kayla straightened. "Why?"

Sylvie looked at her like she was dense. "Well, because no one knows anything about his history, of course!" She opened her mouth as if to say more, but a handsome cowboy waved to her. "Gotta go," she said.

Kayla's walk slowed as she approached the playground. She replayed what Sylvie had said. Was there something she didn't know about Finn? Was he a risk?

That was hard to believe. He seemed safe and trustworthy.

So did Mitch. When they'd first started dating, he'd been so attentive that Kayla had felt like she was living in a fairy tale. Roses, candlelight dinners, unexpected visits just to tell her he was thinking of her. For a girl who'd felt like a mistake all her life, all that romance had been heady stuff. Accepting his proposal had been a no-brainer. He was the only man who'd ever seemed to care.

But even during their engagement, she'd started to feel a little constricted. She'd realized his love was possessive, probably too possessive. She'd told herself it was because he loved her, that at least he wasn't running around on her or burying himself in his work.

Everything had changed when they'd had Leo. Having to share her affections had brought out the crazy in Mitch. And rather than getting used to parenting, growing into it, he'd gotten worse and worse.

She hesitated and then walked over to where Penny was sitting, checking her phone and glancing up at the kids often.

"Thanks so much for watching him," she said. "Can I ask you something?"

"Sure."

"Is there something I should know about Finn? Something that would make me or Leo at risk around him?"

Penny frowned. "Not a thing. Why do you ask?"

"This other mom, Sylvie. She said I should be careful around Finn."

"Nope. He's fine. He…" Penny hesitated. "He's had some heartache in his past. Tragedy, really. But I wouldn't say he's dangerous."

Tragedy. She'd sensed that about him.

She trusted Penny. And the truth was, she trusted Finn.

Mostly.

"Mom!" Leo ran over and hugged her. "This is fun!" He grabbed her hand and pulled her toward the wooden climbing structure. "Watch how high I can go!"

He climbed rapidly to the lookout tower, and Kayla had to force herself to smile and wave rather than climb up herself and make him come down. He was growing up, and this was a safe place. She had to let him spread his wings and fly.

Then he shouted, "Dad!"

Kayla's heart stopped. What on earth? Could Mitch be here?

Leo scrambled down to the ground and she met him there, but before she could grab him, he ran, hard, across the park's grassy area.

She ran after him, arms and legs pumping almost as fast as her heart. She caught up with him at the same moment that he reached a man in military fatigues and a maroon Airborne beret.

Not Mitch. Just the same uniform.

"You're not…" Leo looked up and then backed off of the man. "You're not Daddy." His eyes filled with tears.

"Oh, honey." Kayla's fear turned to sadness for her son. Despite all Mitch's failings as a dad, he was all Leo knew.

"So this little one is an Airborne kid, is he?" The soldier knelt. "Come on—want to try on my hat?" He put it on Leo's head.

"So cute!" Someone snapped a picture. Then another woman, who turned out to be the soldier's wife, took a photo of the soldier and Leo together.

Anxiety bloomed in Kayla's chest. She turned to the soldier's wife, trying to keep the first one in her sights. "What are the photos for?"

"Oh, do you want me to send them to you?" The woman smiled. "You must be his mom. I'm Freida."

Kayla hated to quell the friendliness, but safe was safe. "I don't like photos of my son to be out and about, actually. Would you mind deleting them?"

The woman stared. "I was only trying to be nice. I wasn't going to put them up online or anything."

"Of course. I'm sure you wouldn't. It's just… I'm sorry."

The woman clicked a couple of buttons on her phone. "There. Gone." Her voice was cool, and her meaningful glance toward her husband showed that there was going to be plenty of talk about this at the dinner table tonight.

Kayla shook off her concern, because Leo was crying. She knelt and put her arms around him. "What's wrong, honey?"

"I thought it was Daddy!"

"You miss him, don't you?"

"Yeah. When are we gonna see him?"

That was the question. "Remember how we talked about it. Daddy's not safe for us right now."

"But I miss him."

Her heart broke for a little boy whose father wasn't worthy of the name. But he'd always loom large in Leo's thoughts, just as her own parents did. "I'm sure he misses you, too," she said. It might be true. As damaged as Mitch was, he still had to have some human feeling for his flesh and blood. Didn't he? "I have an idea. Let's make a scrapbook of pictures of you and the things we're doing. Maybe later, we can send it to him."

Leo nodded, but he was slumped as they walked back across the park.

Fortunately, the presence of the malamutes and the parade cheered him up, and he seemed to forget his sadness as he watched the parade and helped with the dogs. Then they ate their fill of hot dogs and baked beans and potato chips.

Finn approached just as they were scooping up the last of their brownies and ice cream. "Looks good," he said.

"Sit down and join us?" she invited before thinking better of it.

"I'd like to, but I'd better not. Listen, Willie's driving the truck back with the dogs. Long John, too. Dogs don't do so well with fireworks. In fact, a lot of our guys, Willie included, don't like them, either."

"Fireworks?" Leo's eyes widened. "Daddy loved those!"

"Why wouldn't the guys...? Oh," she said as realization dawned.

"Right. The loud noises and flashing lights remind them of..." He hesitated and looked at Leo. "Of some bad things in their pasts."

She smiled to show her appreciation of his tact. He wanted to protect Leo from harsh realities, just like she did. It was breathtakingly different from being with Mitch. And whatever Sylvie said, Kayla felt that Finn was basically a good guy.

"I want to stay for the fireworks, Mom. I miss Daddy."

She bit her lip. What would be the harm in staying?

"I'm meeting with some of my fellow Airborne Rangers," Finn said. "I'll drive back probably around eleven."

Right. She had to remember, and keep remembering, that Finn was loyal to his own kind. Not to her.

Also, she didn't need for Leo to be getting more memories of Mitch, becoming more unhappy and discontent. "I think we'll go ahead and leave with Willie," she decided.

"No!" Leo jumped up and kicked the picnic table, hard. "Ow!" he cried, obviously feeling the blow through his thin sneakers, the word ending in a wail as he plopped down on the ground to hold his foot. "I wanna stay for fireworks! Daddy would let me!"

She blew out a sigh. This day, that had started out so nicely, was going rapidly downhill. And she didn't know if she was making the right decisions. Didn't know if she was keeping him safer or sending him to the psychiatrist's couch. That was the problem of being a single parent: there was no one to consult with.

She dearly longed to consult with Finn, who was watching sympathetically as she patted Leo's shoulder and studied his foot to make sure he hadn't really hurt himself.

But she had to remember that Finn wasn't someone she should get close to, because his loyalty would inevitably be toward his military brothers, not a civilian woman and child.

Sighing, she turned her back on Leo and walked a few steps away, denying him the attention he was seeking. Finn nodded once and left the scene, too. He understood that much, at least, and she was grateful.

Leo's crying turned to hiccups and then stopped, and she turned back to him and held out a hand. "Come on. Let's go get in the car with the dogs and Mr. Willie. We'll see how Shoney's doing and take her for a walk." As she'd hoped, the idea of their new dog distracted Leo.

As for Kayla, she wished for all the world that she could stay and simply enjoy the warmth and fun of a small-town holiday.

The next Saturday, Finn came outside and was surprised to see Kayla laughing, standing close to a tall man whose back was turned. Even with her hair in its usual messy braid, she looked beautiful.

In the yard in front of the main house, Leo played with two little girls.

His chest tightened, and he had to force himself not to clench his fists. He started toward the pair, then stopped to take a calming look at the countryside, the flat basin surrounded by white-capped mountains.

Kayla wasn't his, no way. And he had no right to feel jealous that she was spending time with someone else.

He drew in a breath and continued on down. Halfway there, he recognized the pastor.

Which didn't necessarily make him feel any better. Carson Blair was good-looking and well respected, the father of twins just a bit older than Leo. He wasn't such a hulk as Finn, so he and Kayla were better matched physically.

More than that, the pastor wasn't carrying the load of guilt Finn did. On the contrary, he was a good man, a servant of God who had every right to happiness.

All of those logical thoughts didn't stop Finn's feet from moving toward them to see what was going on.

"Hey, Finn," the pastor said, smiling. "We've had an offer of some fishing. Would you like to join us?"

"An offer from whom?" He knew he sounded grouchy. "You need to sign a waiver if your kids are visiting the ranch. Liability issues."

"Didn't even think of that." The pastor gave an easy smile. "Where do I sign?"

Kayla was looking at him, confusion on her face. "Willie invited him, and Leo, too," she said. "He said he's had his grandkids fishing at the pond here. I didn't think you'd mind."

She was wearing her typical kennel uniform, jeans and a T-shirt. As usual, it made her look like a teenager.

It also meant she wasn't dressing up for the pastor.

"No problem, just covering our backs," Finn said. "The ranch can't afford a lawsuit."

Kayla gave him a look as if to say that Carson Blair was hardly going to sue them. "I'll go get the waiver. Isn't Penny in the office?"

"Good idea."

That left him standing alone with Carson. "How are the girls?" he asked, just to avoid an awkward silence and the pastor's know-too-much eyes.

"They're doing pretty well. Life's a scramble, though. It sounded nice to come up here and relax for a little while. Get out some of their energy."

Leo chose that moment to glance over. He'd been shouting, but when he saw Finn, he lowered his voice.

Just the effect he wished he didn't have on kids. Although it *was* a useful reminder. Kids might not know exactly *why* he was scary, but they were right to be scared. He wasn't safe to be around.

Kayla came back, forking fingers through her hair with one hand while holding out the waiver with the other. In the past week, her bruises had faded to the point where she let her arms show. Finn could still see them, though. It reminded him that she'd been through a lot and didn't need him adding to her problems.

After the pastor had signed the waiver and run it back inside, they all headed down toward the pond where Willie was waiting, several fishing rods in hand.

"Okay, kids," Willie said, clearly in his element. "I'm going to give you each a fishing pole and show you how to bait it."

"With *worms*?" Carson's daughter—Skye, maybe?—stared into a Styrofoam container, horrified fascination on her face. The other twin and Leo peeked in, too, and a lively discussion broke out, amiably moderated by Willie.

Finn strolled away from the group. Just the smell of the lake, the fresh air, the smile on the old man's face, helped him get some perspective.

He was still raw from losing his wife and child, and probably always would be. What he wasn't used to was developing any kind of feelings for another woman and child. This was the first time his heart had come out of hibernation.

There were bound to be some missteps, some difficulties. He'd made the decision not to get involved again, but it had never been tested before. So this was a new learning experience.

Behind him there was a shout. A splash.

Finn spun and saw Leo struggling and gasping in the reeds at the lake's edge. Kayla was a few steps farther away, but she ran toward Leo, the pastor right behind her.

Finn got there first, tromped into the mud and reeds, yanking his feet out of the sucking mud with each step. "I'm coming, buddy," he called, keeping his voice calm. "I've got you."

Everyone on the shore was shouting, the two little girls were screaming, but he blocked it all out and focused on Leo. He got his hands around the boy's torso and lifted, and was rewarded with a punch in the face.

He shook it off like you'd shake off a buzzing bee, ignored the boy's flailing and carried him toward shore. Once Leo realized he was safe, he started to cry in earnest and clung to Finn.

The feeling of a little boy in his arms, the relief of saving him, of not losing another kid on his watch, overwhelmed Finn and he hugged Leo right back. Then he put the boy into Kayla's arms.

She sank to the ground, holding and cuddling Leo. "You're okay, you're okay," she said, stroking his hair, using the edge of her sleeve to wipe mud and tears from his face.

He was okay. Praise God.

Kayla looked up at Finn. "Thank you."

He shook his head. "I should have been clear about the safety rules." He'd thought Willie was in charge of the trip and would have told them to stay away from that soggy edge, but apparently not, and he shouldn't rely on someone else. When would he learn that it was his responsibility to keep kids safe?

"That's not a way to end a fishing trip," Willie said. "Let's take a lunch break. The two of you can grab some clean clothes and come back."

"I'll dry right off in the sun," Finn said. "Leo can change if he wants, and then I'd like to see if I could help him catch a fish."

For whatever reason, the boy was afraid of him, and for whatever reason, Finn seemed to want to stop that. So be it. It didn't have to mean anything.

"I'll dry off here, too," Leo said, straightening up and stepping away from Kayla. Trying to be a little man. Finn's throat tightened.

He was hunting around for a bobber in Willie's fishing box when he noticed a small laminated photo. "Who's this?" he asked.

Willie looked at the photo and shook his head. "My granddaughter who died."

Finn stared at the little blonde, obscured by cracked and yellowing laminate. "I didn't know. I'm sorry."

Willie shrugged. "I don't talk about it much, but there's not a day I don't think of her." He sighed. "You get used to it. Not over it, but used to it."

"I haven't."

Willie nodded. "It takes time."

Finn looked at the older man, always upbeat, always quick with a helping hand or a joke to cheer up other people. It was a good reminder: Finn wasn't the only person in the world who'd suffered a loss.

After they'd fished and each of the children had caught at least one, Kayla offered to take the kids to her cabin to get them cleaned up and give them a snack. "And you can meet our new dog," she said to the twins, earning squeals of delight.

Leo and the pastor's twins were getting to be friends. That meant that Kayla and Carson would become friends, too; that was how it went when you were the parents of young children.

It made sense. But he didn't have to like it.

He didn't like the way the departing kids' laughter woke up his memories, either. Derek would have loved to fish and play with dogs. But thanks to Finn's own carelessness, he'd never get to do it.

Finn didn't deserve the kind of happiness that came to good people like the pastor and Kayla.

He roused himself from his reverie and started gathering the remaining gear to take back to his cabin. His leg ached, and he stopped to rub it.

"You're hurting today." Carson Blair knelt and picked up a few loose pieces of fishing gear.

"Yeah." Finn straightened. "Thought you'd be going up to Kayla's with your girls."

"She and Willie said they can handle them for a

bit," Carson said. "I'll help you carry stuff up to the main house. It'll give me the chance to talk to you."

He was going to speak to Finn about Kayla. "No need," he said. "I'm fine."

"Are you sure about that?"

The man was annoying. "Yes, I'm sure."

"Well, I'm not," Carson said. "You've got some kind of issue with me, and I'd like to know what it is. I think we could work together, make good things happen, at church and in town and at this ranch, but not if you're mad about something I don't even understand."

The words burst out before Finn could stop them. "You need to leave my employees alone."

Carson raised an eyebrow. "Is that what Kayla is to you? An employee?"

"Yes, and she's got a job to do here. She doesn't need any distractions."

"Funny, she told me she was off today."

"You calling me out?" Finn's fists clenched.

Carson raised a hand like a stop sign. "I'm not calling you out. I'm a pastor. It's sort of against the rules." A slight smile quirked his face. "Besides which, I know my limits. I couldn't take you." He turned and started walking. "Come on. I'll help you carry this stuff up."

Finn hesitated and then fell into step beside the man. The momentary break gave him time to think. He didn't have any right to Kayla, and there was no good reason for him to be throwing his weight around, setting limits.

"Sorry," he said as he fell into step beside the pastor. "Didn't mean to act like a thug."

Carson chuckled. "You're hardly that." He paused.

"But…if I might make a suggestion, have you considered talking to someone about your grief issues?"

Finn's ire rose again. "I've got my issues under control."

"Do you?" The pastor's question was mild, but his face showed skepticism. "You seem a little quick to anger. A lot of times, that's about something other than the issue at hand. Although," he added, "I can see why you'd be defensive of Kayla. She's a lovely woman."

Finn glowered.

"And I'm interested in a purely pastoral sense. I don't have time for anything more. But you—" he turned and faced Finn down "—you need to get yourself straight with God before you have anything to offer a good woman like Kayla."

Finn schooled his face for a sermon. And closed his mind against the tiny ray of hope that wanted in. Because getting himself straight with God wasn't going to happen, no matter what a flowers-and-sunshine pastor had to say.

On Monday morning, Kayla took her time strolling toward the kennel for her morning shift.

Magpies chattered and barn swallows skimmed the fields, low and graceful in the still-cool morning air. She lifted her face and sent up a prayer of thanks.

Leo had gone eagerly to camp this morning, none the worse for his tumble into the pond two days before. Just the memory of it sent a shudder through Kayla, but it was rapidly followed by more gratitude, this time for Finn.

He'd been instantly alert and had rescued Leo almost before Kayla had realized the gravity of the situation. Willie and Pastor Carson had rushed in to provide sympathy and comfort.

Having all that support had melted Kayla. She'd been raising Leo virtually alone since his birth. Mitch hadn't been a partner, but a threat to be wary about. And he'd cut her off from most of her old friends.

Kayla was independent; she'd had to be, growing up with her parents.

The sudden, warm feeling she'd gotten, that she and Leo were part of a caring community—that was something she treasured, something she felt a timid wish to build. She'd made a start yesterday at church, introducing herself to more people and signing up for a women's book discussion later in July.

She felt the urge to build something with Finn, too, but she wasn't willing to explore that. Neither, from the looks of things, was he.

He did give her a friendly wave when she walked into the kennel. "I'm putting the dogs from the first row out into the run. I'll supervise 'em if you clean?"

"Sure." She smiled at him. It was nice he'd phrased it as a question, when in reality he was the boss and could call the shots.

She started removing toys and beds and dishes from the kennels in preparation for hosing them down. The cleaning protocol they'd set up helped prevent disease, and it also made for a nice environment for the animals. For many, it was the best place they'd ever lived.

She opened the door to the last kennel on the end and saw something dark on the floor. Blood.

"Finn!" She left everything where it was and headed to the doorway. "I think that new dog, Winter, is sick."

She scanned the field and located the big female, sitting watchful, away from the other dogs.

"What's going on?" Finn had been kneeling beside Axel, but now he stood and came over. "Is she acting different?"

"Take a look at her kennel. I'll watch the dogs."

He went inside and she knelt and called to Winter. She'd been dropped off the previous day by a couple of guys, neighbors of her owner. They'd rescued her from what they said was an abusive situation, but Finn, who'd talked with them, hadn't offered up any more details.

The dog looked over, ears hanging long, cloudy eyes mournful.

"Come here, girl," Kayla encouraged and felt in her pocket for a treat. She checked to make sure no aggressive dogs were nearby and then held it out to Winter.

The dog came closer, walking with a hunched, halting gait, but stopped short and cringed back as Finn emerged from the kennel. He held up his phone. "That was blood. I called the vet," he said. "Her new-dog appointment was supposed to be today, but he had to cancel. He says he can come out but he has to bring his baby boy."

She nodded, still watching the wary dog. "What do you think is wrong with Winter?"

Finn shook his head slowly, his mouth twisting. "The story is that she had a litter of stillborn pups. The owner got mad and started beating her."

Kayla gasped. "Who *does* that?" Sudden tears blurred her vision. The dog was beautiful, one of God's innocent creatures. That someone would feel he had the right to abuse her...

"The guys who dropped her off say they're going to call him up on animal abuse charges. But they wanted to make sure she was safe first." He studied the dog. "I'll step away. She's probably afraid of men, and for good reason. Maybe you can get her to come over."

It took continued encouragement and the tossing of several treats before the dog got close enough for Kayla to touch her.

"Be careful," Finn said quietly from his position on the other side of the dog run. "She's been treated badly. She may bite."

Kayla clicked her tongue and held out another treat, then carefully reached out to rub the dog's chest. Winter let out a low whine.

"Here, baby. Have a snack." She waved the remaining treat, gently.

The dog grabbed it from her hand and retreated to a safe distance to eat.

"You stay out here with her," Finn said. "I'll get the rest of the kennels clean and then bring the other dogs in. I worry about contagion. No telling what she's picked up."

So Kayla sat in the sun, sweet-talking the old dog. After Finn took the other dogs in, as the day warmed up, Winter approached close enough that Kayla could scratch her ears.

She patted the ground. "Go ahead—relax. Just rest."

But the dog remained alert, jumping up when a chipmunk raced past, then sinking back down on her haunches, head on front paws, eyes wary.

Kayla knew how *that* felt. "It's hard to relax when you're worried for your safety, isn't it?" she crooned. "It's all right. We'll protect you here."

What was true for the dog might be true for Kayla, too. Sometimes, during the past week, she'd felt her habitual high-alert state ebb away. Even now, the hot sun melted tension from her shoulders.

After half an hour, she heard a vehicle approach and a door slam. Soon Finn appeared with a jeans-clad man he introduced as Dr. DeMoise.

"Call me Jack," the tall vet said easily, shifting a wide-eyed baby from one shoulder to the other so he could shake her hand.

"Your son's beautiful," Kayla said. Without her willing it, her arms reached for the baby boy. "Do you think he'll let me hold him?"

"Most likely." The vet smiled his thanks. "He's not real clingy yet."

She lifted the baby from his arms. The child—probably about six months old—stared at her with wide eyes and started to fuss a little. Kayla walked and hummed and clucked to him. Comforting a baby must be like riding a bike: it came back easily. Leo had been colicky, and she'd spent a lot of time soothing him.

Now, holding the vet's baby close and settling him, longing bloomed inside her. She hadn't let herself think about having another baby, not when she was with Mitch, and not in the difficult year after getting divorced, when she'd been struggling to start a business and fend him off. Now desire for another little one took her breath away.

Forget about it, she ordered herself.

But with Leo growing up so fast...

The baby stiffened and let out a fussy cry, probably sensing her inner conflict. She breathed in and out slowly and walked him around the field.

Once she'd gotten the baby calmed down, she watched as Jack squatted near the dog, who seemed to be in increasing distress. Finn leaned against the fence several feet away, watching.

"I'm wondering if she's got another pup," the vet said finally. "You said her litter was stillborn?"

"And her owner beat her right after she gave birth."

The vet grimaced. "I'm going to need to take her in, but let's see what she's trying to do now, first. Couple of clean towels?"

Finn went inside and the doctor examined the dog and pressed her abdomen gently.

Kayla walked over, swaying gently with the baby. "Is she going to be okay?"

The vet frowned. "I hope so. It's good you called."

"Could she have another live pup?"

"No. Not after almost a day, not likely." He rubbed the dog's ears, gently. "But we'll do our best to take care of Mama, here. She doesn't deserve what happened to her."

"Nobody does." Kayla leaned closer and saw a couple of wounds on the dog's back and leg.

Finn handed the towels to the doctor and then came over to stand by Kayla. He smiled at Jack's baby, reached out and tickled his leg, and the baby allowed it.

"This one's not afraid of you. Lots of babies are scared of men. At least…" At least, they'd been afraid of Mitch.

"Sammy's been raised by his dad for the last six months," Finn explained as they both watched the vet work with Winter. "He and his wife adopted him, but she passed away, so now he's a single dad."

"Awww." She swayed with the baby to keep him calm.

"Jack is the only vet within thirty miles, so he has a busy practice. When his wife died and he had to care for Sammy full-time... It's been rough."

"Day care?"

"He's got a part-time nanny, but apparently, she's not working out."

The vet rose and walked over to them. "I'll drive my van to the gate so we can get her into the clinic. If one of you wants to come along..."

"I can," Kayla said instantly. "I can take care of Sammy and help with the dog."

"No." Finn frowned. "I'll go."

"But—" She didn't want to let the baby out of her arms.

"I need you to finish up here," he said abruptly.

Jack gave them both a quizzical look. "Whatever you two decide. I'll be right back with the van. Just make sure the dog stays still."

After he'd left, Kayla spoke up. "I just thought, since I've got the baby calmed down—"

"I don't want you going into town with Jack. People will make something of it." His face was set.

Kayla pressed her lips together. It was almost as if Finn felt possessive of her. Which didn't make any sense.

But it *did* feel familiar, and scarily so. Mitch had started out just a little possessive, but that had expanded until he got outraged if she had a conversation with a male cashier or said "thank you" to a guy holding open a door for her.

Finn's attitude was probably about something else. There was no reason a man like Finn should have any feelings at all about her, possessive or otherwise.

But she needed to be careful, and stay alert, and not get too involved. Just in case Finn bore any similarity to Mitch.

Chapter 6

That Friday evening, Finn turned his truck into the road that led to Redemption Ranch with mixed feelings—mixed enough that he pulled over, telling himself he needed to check on Winter and her new foster puppy, crated in the back.

Truth was, he wanted to get his head together before he got back to the ranch.

The trip to pick up Winter from the vet clinic had been a welcome opportunity to escape from a work environment that had him in close proximity to Kayla for much of the day.

He opened the back of the pickup and checked on the two dogs. Winter lay still, but with her head upright and alert. The young pup beside her had been a surprise, but so right that Finn had quickly agreed to take both back to the ranch.

He took his time adjusting the crates and rubbing Winter's head through the side bars, aware that he was just procrastinating on returning to the ranch and Kayla. He wanted to stay uninvolved, but he couldn't seem to pull it off. When he'd seen Kayla holding that baby earlier in the week, he'd gotten gushy, romantic, old-movie feelings, until memories crashed in and washed them away in a sea of cold guilt. And then, just to top off his own ridiculousness, he'd gone caveman on her, refusing to allow her to go help Jack. Which was just plain stupid. Jack was single, and eligible, and deserving of happiness, and why *wouldn't* he like Kayla, especially when she'd shown such tenderness toward his son?

But before he'd had the sense to think that through, he'd gotten in Jack's face, insisting that Kayla couldn't go into town with Winter, that he, Finn, had to be the one to go himself.

What was wrong with Finn, that he was acting like a Neanderthal around this woman whose personal life was absolutely none of his business?

Possessive stuff. No matter what his brain said, his emotions wanted to mark her as his.

It was almost like he wanted to be a husband and father again.

Finn pushed the thoughts away by turning up the country music louder. And then was rewarded with songs about hurting love. He released a huff and started the truck again.

He pulled up toward the kennel and tried not to look to the right, at Kayla's place. But there were Penny and Willie, carrying a table from the next cabin down the road and into the yard in front of Kayla's porch. He rolled down a window to see what was going on, and the smell of grilling meat sent his stomach rumbling.

"Come on—join in," Willie called, beckoning with his free arm.

What could he do but pull over and stop the truck? The cessation of movement started Winter barking, so he had to get her out of the crate. And then the pup cried, so he had to be brought out, too.

And that brought everyone running over to see.

Finn knelt beside Winter and the fragile pup, trying to help them get their bearings. Trying to get his own, as well.

Leo shouted and reached out, and the puppy cringed.

"Careful!" Finn said.

Only when Leo shrank back did Finn realize he'd boomed out the word too loudly.

"You left with one and came back with two?" Penny asked, kneeling to see the dogs and, not coincidentally, putting herself at Leo's height. She put a hand on the kid's shoulder. "That's not her pup, is it?"

"It is now." Finn couldn't help but smile as the puppy yapped up at Winter and she gave him a chastening slurp of her tongue, knocking him into his place. Quickly, he explained how the unlikely pairing had come to pass.

Willie was setting up horseshoes, and Long John sat in a chair, shucking corn. "Looks like a party," Finn said, loud enough for the two older veterans to hear.

"Cooking out. It's Friday." Willie grinned. "Not that I've worked that hard all week, but habit is habit."

"Do you need a blanket for the dogs to rest on?" It was Kayla's husky voice, and when he turned toward her, he saw that she already had one in hand. Of course, she'd seen the need and filled it, quietly and efficiently. That was who she was.

They settled the dogs off to the side of the picnic table. "Why is there a pup, Mom?" Leo asked, pressing against Kayla's side. "You said she had babies that died."

"I don't know. Ask Mr. Gallagher."

But Leo pressed his lips together and stayed tight by Kayla's side.

Great. Finn had managed to spook the poor kid. "Winter wasn't feeling well after her puppies didn't make it," he said, simplifying and cleaning it up for young ears. "And Dr. Jack had a pup at the clinic who didn't have a mom."

"The Good Lord has a way of working things out," Willie said. "Joy out of sorrow." He gave Finn a meaningful look.

Finn's jaw tightened, because he knew what Willie was thinking. That Finn was supposed to find some kind of redemption out of the loss he'd faced.

It wasn't happening. Not now, not ever.

"This corn's ready to throw on the grill," Long John called.

"Chicken's almost done," Penny said.

"Ooh, I've got to check on my apple cobbler." Kayla hurried inside.

Willie came over to where Finn stood. "You as hungry as I am?"

Finn noticed Leo watching them. On an impulse, he clutched his hands across his abdomen and fake-fell to the ground. "Starving!" he groaned.

Willie laughed and nudged Finn with his boot. "Get up, boy. Them that don't work, don't eat."

Finn jumped to his feet. By now, Leo was smiling, just a little. "I'll do anything," Finn said, "for apple cobbler."

"Then get inside and help her carry out the dishes, and make it snappy." Willie rolled his eyes at Leo. "Think I'll ever be able to make this big lug behave?"

Leo laughed outright. "He's a grown-up! He doesn't have to behave."

"That's where you're wrong," Willie said. "Grown-ups have to behave even better than kids. Right, Finn?"

"I'm going, I'm going." He glanced over at Leo, who was still smiling. "Keep an eye on those dogs for me, will you?"

"Yeah!" Leo hurried in their direction. Finn waited just long enough to see that the boy knelt carefully, not getting too close.

"I'll keep an eye, too," Willie murmured to Finn. "Now, I'm serious. If you want dinner, you'd better help the lady get it on the table."

Finn reached Kayla's small kitchen just in time to see her lift the cobbler out of the oven. Her cheeks were pink and her eyes bright, and he wondered how he'd ever thought her plain.

She met his eyes, and it seemed to him her color heightened. "I... Dinner's almost ready. I hope you'll join us."

"I'd like to." His playful mood from trying to jolly Leo up lingered, and he assumed a hangdog look. "But Willie told me I can't unless I do my share of the work. Give me a job?"

She chuckled, and the sound ran along his nerve

endings. "There's never a shortage. You can carry out the plates and silverware. Then come back, and I'll have more for you to do."

"Yes, ma'am." He inhaled. "That smells fantastic."

"I have some talents."

"I can see that."

Their eyes locked for a moment, and Finn was sure he detected some sort of interest, not just casual, in hers. His own chest almost hurt with wanting to get closer to this woman. And he could barely remember why he'd thought that was a bad idea.

She turned away from him, laughing a little. "Go on. Get to work."

So he carried out the flatware and plates, and then went back for several more loads. Penny called him into action to help at the grill, and then Willie remembered there was a fresh pitcher of lemonade down at his cabin. Long John offered to get it, going so far as to stand up, but Finn waved off the offer and walked down to get it. Limp or no, he was still more able-bodied than Long John.

It felt like a party, but more than that, it felt like family. And Finn, whose relatives all lived back East, hadn't had that sense in years.

Two years, to be specific. Since Deirdre and Derek had died.

But for the first time in a long time, that thought didn't send him into darkness. He set it aside, because he wanted to focus on the here and now, just for a little bit longer.

So they ate their fill of grilled chicken and corn on the cob, Long John's famous coleslaw, and potato salad Penny had picked up from the deli in town. She'd gotten ice cream, too, so when the main meal was over, there was that for the cobbler.

The dogs, Winter and the new pup as well as Shoney, went up and down the long table, begging. Finn couldn't be sure, but he suspected that all the dogs had gotten a few scraps. Himself, he'd concentrated on sneaking food to Shoney, who couldn't see the many crumbs and pieces that dropped to the ground.

Finally, they'd all eaten their fill, and more. Leo asked to be excused and was soon rolling on the ground with the dogs. Penny started clearing dishes. When Finn stood to help, she waved him away. "Take it easy for a bit," she said. "The kitchen's only big enough for one. You, too, Kayla. Sit back and relax."

"No, I'll wash and you can dry," Kayla compromised.

"Seems to me," Willie said, his eyes twinkling, "that a boy of Leo's age might like to play a little Frisbee or catch. But my old bones ache too much to do a game justice." He looked at Finn. "How about you?"

Finn hadn't missed how Leo's eyes lit up. "It'd be good to work off some of this fine food," he said and glanced up at Kayla. "Okay with you?"

"Of course, if he wants to." She turned toward Leo and then shrugged. "Just ask him."

It was tacit permission for Finn to form his own relationship with Leo. And while he knew it wasn't a good idea long-term, some lazy, relaxed, happy part of himself couldn't worry about that just now.

"Think I've got a couple of mitts and a softball down in my storage cupboard," Willie said and started to get up.

"I'll get it if you tell me where." This time, Finn

took his cane, wanting to save his leg for the actual game of catch.

And that was how Finn ended up teaching Leo how to throw like a pitcher and how to hold his mitt, while Willie and Long John relaxed in lawn chairs and offered advice.

It felt like an unexpected blessing. Leo, who seemed at times timid as a mouse, was smiling and laughing and, to all appearances, enjoying himself enough that he didn't seem to want to stop.

Out here, tossing a softball back and forth as the sun sank behind the Sangre de Cristos, it was easy for Finn to focus on what was good in his life. This work that benefited other creatures, both human and canine, in a concrete way. This place, with its open spaces and views of the jagged mountain range that seemed to point the way directly to heaven. These people, who'd struggled enough in their lives to understand others rather than judge them.

Back in Virginia, after everything had gone so terribly wrong, he'd sunk too deep into himself, to where he could only see what was bad and wrong inside him. It was the kind of shame and guilt that threatened to make you want to do away with yourself, and although it would have been deserved, and he'd come close, some faint inner light had told him it was wrong. He'd dragged himself to church and talked to the pastor, older than Finn and wiser, about getting a fresh start. He was suffocating in Virginia, and all he'd felt the smallest shred of desire for was the open spaces of the West, where he'd sometimes traveled for work. Next thing, the pastor had been calling his old high school friend, Penny. The job had fallen into place so neatly that Finn, who didn't normally put much stock in God reaching down from the sky and fixing things, felt there'd been some of that going on.

Maybe Kayla and Leo's arrival had been a God thing, too.

Finally, he felt the chill in the darkening air and realized that Leo was yawning, and wondered aloud whether it was time to go inside.

"Not when there's a fire to be built." Willie got up and dragged an old fire-pit bowl from the back of the house. "Hey, Leo, can you give me a hand picking up sticks?"

"And I'll get the logs," Finn said with a mock sigh.

As they taught Leo how to build a fire—with appropriate safety warnings—Finn had a reluctant realization.

He hadn't wanted to get involved with people, especially women and kids. He'd come to Redemption Ranch to focus on making retribution, giving something back to a world from which he'd taken so much away. To lose himself amid the mountains that made even a hulk like him feel small. Not to grow close to a pair of souls who tugged at him, made his heart want to come alive again.

But want to or not, it had happened.

Kayla washed the last dish and handed it to Penny, then let the water out of the sink. "Thanks for helping," she said. "We got done in half the time."

"Yes, we did." Penny hung the pan on the overhead hook.

"No thanks to you," she scolded Shoney, who'd been roaming the kitchen and generally getting underfoot, looking for dropped food and occasionally finding it. Kayla dried her hands, knelt to rub the dog's shaggy head, and then stood and headed for the door. "I'd better go see how Leo's doing."

"He's doing fine." Penny put a hand on Kayla's arm, stopping her. "I can see him out the window. He's with Willie and Finn."

"And he's not acting scared of Finn?"

"Come see." Penny gestured out the window.

Kayla looked and sucked in a breath.

In the background, the setting sun made rosy fire on the mountains. Swallows skimmed and swooped, catching insects for an evening snack, chirring and squeaking their pleasure. The dogs sprawled on the blanket she'd brought out, the new puppy spooned in close to Winter.

And there was Leo, laughing up at something Willie had said, while Finn looked on fondly.

They weren't related by blood, but they were interacting like three generations. It was what she'd always wanted for Leo.

"Does he have a grandpa?" Penny asked.

Kayla shook her head. "His father's parents have both passed, and my dad..."

Penny was wiping off the counter, but at Kayla's pause she stopped and looked at her.

"My dad's in prison for life." She said it all in a rush, as she did every time she had to discuss her dad with anyone. Then she knelt and pulled Shoney against her, rubbing the shaggy head.

"That's rough." Penny leaned back against the counter, her face sympathetic rather than judgmental. "Did that happen when you were a kid, or later?"

"When I was twelve." She'd remember the day forever, even though she'd tried to push it out of her mind. Coming home from school to police cars every which way in the front yard. The neighbors whispering and gawking. And then her father, coming out of the house, swearing and fighting the two officers who were trying to control him.

It had been another couple of years before she'd gotten her mother to tell her the charge. "He shot a convenience-store clerk," she said now to Penny. "A robbery gone bad. Drugs." She looked at the floor. "The man he killed was the father of three kids. And he disabled a police officer trying to escape."

"Oh, honey." Penny held out her arms, and when Kayla didn't stand to walk into them, she came right over and wrapped her arms around Kayla and Shoney both. "That must have been so hard."

Kayla felt a little pressure behind her eyes, but she had no intention of crying. She cleared her throat and took a step back. "It *was* hard. Kids can be cruel."

"Did you have brothers and sisters?"

"Nope. Just me. I was a mistake."

Penny stared and slowly began shaking her head back and forth. "Oh, no. No, you weren't. God doesn't make mistakes."

Kayla waved a hand. "I know. I know. It's fine. It's just…that's how my parents looked at it, is all."

"You ever talk to anyone about that?" Penny asked.

Kayla's eyebrows came together. "I'm talking to you."

"I mean a therapist."

"No. No way." Her dad's issues, and her mom's

problems after the arrest, were part of a big box of heartache she didn't want to open.

"So your parents had issues, let you know they hadn't planned to have you." Penny lifted an eyebrow. "How old were you when you married the abuser?"

Kayla's jaw about dropped. "What? What does that have to do with my folks?"

Penny took the dish towel from Kayla's hands, folded it once and hung it on the stove handle. "I just think it's interesting that you chose a man who didn't value you properly, after being with parents who maybe did the same. Patterns." Penny looked out the window. "We repeat patterns."

The older woman's words hit too close to home. After her father had gone to prison, Kayla had tried to stay close to her mother, as close as the multiple boy-friends and stepfathers would permit. But when her mom had been killed in a drinking-related car acci-dent...yeah. Kayla had connected with Mitch almost immediately, drawn to his self-assurance and domi-nant personality.

Kayla didn't want to think about what that all might mean, psychologically. Instead, she turned the tables. "Are you speaking from experience?"

"Touché," Penny said. "I sure am. And one day, you and I can sit down and talk about it, maybe. All I know is, I'm not quick to put my trust in any man. But it's important to trust someone. I want you to know you can trust me."

"Why?" Kayla asked bluntly. She didn't understand why Penny was being intrusive, and she *really* didn't understand why she was being kind.

"I've watched how you interact with your son for

a couple of weeks now. You're a good mom." Penny smiled at her. "And more relevant to me, you're a good worker. I'd like to keep you around."

A sudden thickness settled in Kayla's throat. "Thanks."

"And when I said what I did about men, I wasn't talking about Finn. He's one of the good ones. So are Long John and Willie, for that matter."

Kayla nodded but didn't speak. Penny might think these men were good, and trustworthy, and probably on some level they were. But on the flip side, they were military men and loyal to their band of brothers.

Men like Mitch.

"We're done in here," she said instead of answering. "Want to go outside by the fire?"

"For a bit, sure." Penny's eyes were hooded, and Kayla was suddenly sorry she hadn't pursued Penny's remarks about men. She got the feeling that the older woman had a story that was plenty interesting, not to mention a few issues of her own.

She led the way, but when she got to where she could see the fire, she stopped. Penny almost ran into her.

Willie was playing guitar, softly, and Long John picked harmony on his banjo. The fire burned low, sending the warm, friendly smell of wood smoke in their direction.

And Leo was sleeping in Finn's arms.

Kayla drew in a deep breath and let it out slowly. There was something about a man who was good with kids. Something about a man big enough to hold a five-year-old boy with no problem, and confident enough in his masculinity to be nurturing.

Penny walked past and perched on a log beside Willie. They spoke for a moment, low, and then Willie launched into another song, a love song Kayla remembered from when she was a kid.

Penny stared into the fire, a remote expression on her face.

Kayla walked over to Finn's side. "Are you okay holding him?" she asked. "He can get heavy."

"It's not a problem." But his face was serious, his eyes a little…sad? Troubled?

So they all sat around for a little while longer, huddling in the warmth of the fire. A circle of humans in the light of the moon, seeking warmth, needing each other.

In the distance, there was a howl.

"What's that?" she asked.

"Coyote," Long John said. "Keep the dogs and the boy near home tonight."

Kayla shivered and scooted her log a little closer to the fire's warmth.

She looked around at the faces, old and young. She'd gotten almost close to these people in the past two weeks, and she never got close. She liked being here, liked being with them.

She especially liked being with Finn, if she were honest with herself. They'd fallen into an easy routine, working together in the kennels, sharing information about the dogs and the weather and the ranch. They laughed at the same jokes on the country-music station, liked the same songs. Both of them usually carried a book around for slow moments, and he'd turned her on to Louis L'Amour.

All the connections were something to enjoy, but

also something to be cautious about. She'd liked being around Mitch and his friends at first, too.

Of course, looking back at it, she couldn't miss the warning signs. Why had she chosen Mitch?

There was the obvious fact that no one else had wanted her. And that she'd wanted to have a baby like nobody's business. Still, she should have had more sense.

Unless Penny was right, and it had to do with her parents, her childhood.

Willie played a last riff on his guitar and then looked over at Long John, who'd fallen silent. "That's it for me," he said. "These old bones are ready for bed, early as it is."

"It's not early when you get up for chores." Penny arched her back and stretched.

Both of the older men watched her, identical longing expressions on each weathered face.

Oh. So it was that way. And yet the two were best of friends, and Penny seemed oblivious to the way they'd been looking at her.

As they put their instruments away, Penny stood. "Thanks, everyone. See you tomorrow."

Willie cleared his throat. "Walk you home?"

Penny paused a beat. "No. Thanks, but I'm fine." She turned and headed for the road at a good clip.

"Can't blame a guy for trying," Willie muttered.

Long John gave him a look. "She's the same age as your daughter." He started to heave himself up out of his chair, then sank back with a sigh.

Willie held out a hand, and Long John hesitated, then grasped it and got to his feet. Willie picked up both musical instruments, and the two of them headed back toward their cabins.

That left Kayla alone with Finn, who still held the sleeping Leo in his arms. "I... I'll put out the fire." She felt absurdly uncomfortable.

He nodded. His face was hard to read. Was he enjoying holding Leo or was it a burden for him?

His face suggested something else entirely, but she wasn't sure what.

Finn watched as Kayla hauled a bucket of water to the metal fire pit. She was tiny, but she lifted the heavy bucket easily and poured it on.

That was Kayla—however vulnerable she appeared on the outside, there was solid strength hidden beneath.

She straightened and put her hands to the small of her back. "I should probably bring another bucket of water, right?"

"Just to be sure. I'm sorry I can't help you."

"You're helping, believe me." She gave her sleeping child a tender glance before taking the bucket back over to the outside spigot.

Finn felt the weight of the five-year-old boy against him as if it were lead. Pressing him down into the lawn chair.

Pressing him into his past.

He'd held his own son just like this. It was such a sweet age, still small enough to fit into a lap and to want to be there.

Leo would soon grow beyond such tenderness.

Derek wouldn't, not ever.

The knowledge of that ached in Finn's chest. Outside of the guilt and the regret, he just plain missed his son.

Would Derek have been shy and quiet, like Leo? Or more blustery and outgoing like his cousins, kids Finn never saw anymore because he couldn't stand his brothers' sympathy?

Kayla sloshed another bucket over the fire pit. "There. No sparks left to cause a fire."

He met her eyes and the thought flashed through him: *there are still some sparks here, just not the fire-pit kind.*

But although it was true, it wouldn't do to high-light the fact. "Do you want me to carry him inside?"

She hesitated, and he could understand why. It was an intimate thing to do. Yet a sleeping five-year-old was substantial, and he could bear the burden more easily than she could. Despite the ache in his leg, he wanted to play the man's role rather than watching a small, slight woman do all the heavy lifting.

Before she could refuse him, he stood, carefully holding Leo's head against his shoulder. The boy stirred a little, then cuddled marginally tighter and relaxed against Finn.

His throat too tight to say anything, he inclined his head, inviting Kayla to lead the way inside.

It was tricky, but he used his free hand and good leg to climb the ladder to the sleeping loft, follow-ing behind Kayla. He had to duck his head beneath the slanted roof. When he went to put Leo down, his leg went out from under him and he lurched, making Kayla gasp. But he caught himself and managed to place the boy carefully on his low, narrow cot, made up with faded race-car sheets.

The sight of those sheets hurt his heart a little. Kayla must have packed them up and brought them along, wanting to give her child a taste of home. "Sorry about that," he said, gesturing at his leg. "I wouldn't drop him."

"No, it's fine, thank you! I forgot that climbing might be hard for you."

He shrugged. "My pleasure."

"I guess he's finally used to you," she said as she pulled the sheets and blankets up to cover Leo's narrow shoulders.

"It took some doing, but yeah."

"He…he's seen some scary things. His father… well."

"Same man that gave you the bruises?" he asked mildly.

Her sharp intake of breath wasn't unexpected, but Finn was tired of the distance between them, the concealment, the connections that weren't getting made. Something about this night made him want to throw caution away and nudge her a little, see if the thing he felt was there for her, too.

She ran a hand over Leo's hair, not looking at Finn. "Yes," she said, her voice so low he had to bend closer to hear it. "Same guy."

"If I could get my hands on him, I'd be tempted to do worse to him than he did to you and Leo." Because the words were confrontational, he kept his tone mild.

She glanced up at him, secrets in her eyes. And then she rose, gracefully, to her feet. "It's late."

Yes, it was, and he didn't want to go. He climbed the ladder down ahead of her, so he could catch her if she fell—odd protective urge, since she was probably up and down the ladder a dozen times a day. At the bottom, he waited.

She stepped off the last rung. The slow way she turned, he could tell she knew he was there, close. "Finn…"

He reached out for her, touched her chin. "You're a good mother and a good cook," he said. "Thank you for tonight."

That was all he meant to do; just thank her. But the unexpectedly soft feel of her skin made his hand linger, and then splay to encompass her strong jawline, her soft hair.

She looked up at him through long, thick lashes. There was a light spray of freckles across her nose.

Finn's heart swelled with tenderness, and he lowered his face toward hers.

Chapter 7

Kayla drew in a panicky breath and reached out, feeling the rough stubble of Finn's face. He was going to kiss her and she wanted him to.

But he stopped short and brushed her cheek with his finger. "Your skin is so soft. I didn't shave. I'm afraid I'll hurt you."

She inhaled the piney, outdoorsy scent of him and her heart thudded, heavy and hard. "You won't hurt me," she whispered.

He narrowed his eyes just a tiny bit, studying her, as if to test her sincerity.

And then he pulled her closer and lowered his lips the rest of the way down to hers.

Tenderness and respect? She'd never experienced kissing this way. It made her want to pull him closer, but she didn't dare. And after a moment, he lifted up to look at her. "You're like a tiny little sparrow, ready to fly away."

His whimsical description amused her, cutting through the moment's intensity. "Sometimes I've wished I could fly," she admitted, her voice still soft, heart still pounding.

"You did fly. You flew here to Redemption Ranch."

Yes, she had. She'd been flying away from something, someone.

From Mitch.

Reluctantly, she stepped back from the warm circle of Finn's arms. She looked at the floor across the room, embarrassed to meet his eyes, because she'd not only enjoyed his kiss, she'd returned it.

"Someday," he said, "I want to hear more about what you flew away from."

She bit her lip. She was starting to trust him, kind of wanted to tell him. Finn's solid protection and support would be such a blessing to her and Leo.

But there, as he crossed his arms and looked at her, was his Eighty-Second Airborne tattoo. She still didn't know how attached he was to his unit, how close the bonds of brotherhood went for him.

Just because of who he was, she'd suspect the ties held tight. He was the loyal type, for sure. "The past isn't important," she said, not looking at him.

Something flashed in his eyes, some emotion. "I'm not sure I agree with you. If you don't deal with the past, you can't move forward."

"Moving forward is maybe overrated."

"Like us kissing?"

She huffed out a fake kind of laugh. "Yeah."

He cocked his head to one side, looking at her, his

expression a little puzzled. "I don't understand women very well," he said. "And it's late. I should be going."

Something inside her wanted to cling on, to cry out, *No, don't go!* But that was the needy part of her that her mom had despised. The part that had experienced Mitch's attention and glommed right on. "See you tomorrow," she said, forcing her voice to sound casual.

"Actually, not much," he said. "After the meeting tomorrow morning, I'll be away for the weekend."

"Oh." Her heart did a little plummet, and that was bad. She was already too attached, expecting to see him every day.

He must have heard something in her voice. "It's a reunion," he said, indicating his tattoo. "Eighty-Second Airborne."

Her heart hit the floor. "Oh."

He laughed a little. "Bunch of old guys telling stories, mostly. But I love 'em. They're my brothers."

Of course they were. He'd do anything for his brothers.

Including, if it came to that, helping one of them find the woman who'd betrayed him and taken away his son. "Finn, about…this," she said, waving a hand, her cheeks heating. "We shouldn't… I mean, I don't—"

His face hardened. "I understand. We got carried away."

"Exactly. I just didn't want you to think…"

"That it meant something?"

It meant everything. "Exactly," she lied.

"Agreed," he said, his bearing going a little more upright and military. "See you."

And he was gone. The little lost girl inside Kayla curled up in a ball and cried at the loss of him.

* * *

She was hiding something.

Finn headed toward Penny's place for the dreaded semiannual meeting with the ranch's finance guy. Bingo, his current dog, loped along beside him.

"You have to act nice if you're coming to the meeting," Finn grumbled to the dog, but Bingo only laughed up at him. "I know. Penny will give you treats to make you behave."

The dog's tail started to wag at the *T* word.

Finn tried to focus on the dog, on the fresh morning air, on anything but the fact that he'd kissed Kayla last night. And she'd responded. She'd liked it.

And then she'd backed right off.

Had she heard the truth about Finn, or remembered it? Was that why she'd pushed him away?

But it wasn't just that. She was secretive, and he wanted to know why. Wanted to know what it was in her past that had her running. If they were going to be involved, he needed to know.

Were they going to be involved?

Probably not. For sure not. He'd made the decision, after losing his wife and son, that he wasn't going to go there again. Up until now, his grief had been so thick and dark that the promise hadn't been hard to keep.

But Kayla and Leo had made their way through his darkness and were battering at the hard shell surrounding his heart. He'd held Leo last night, held him for at least an hour, and the experience had softened something inside him.

Leo needed a father figure. And some part of Finn, apparently, needed a son.

But he didn't deserve a son. He didn't deserve to

look forward, with hope, to the kind of happy new life that Derek and Deirdre would never have.

It was just that holding Kayla, kissing her, had been so very, very sweet. It had brought something inside him back to life.

He reached the main house. A glance at his phone told him he was early, so he settled on the edge of the porch.

If he *did* get involved with Kayla—and he wasn't saying he would, but if it happened—he wanted to know the truth about her. And, he rationalized, she was his employee. He needed to know.

Raakib Khan had served with Finn in the Eighty-Second, and they'd had each other's backs. When Raakib came home, he'd started a little detective agency.

Finn called Raakib, shot the breeze for a minute and then gave him everything he knew about Kayla.

"What is your interest, my friend?" Raakib asked.

"She works for me."

"And is that all?"

Finn let out a disgusted snort. After all they'd been through together, Raakib could read him like a book. "That's all you need to know about," he growled and ended the call.

When he looked up, he saw Kayla walking toward him. His face heated. What had she heard?

She gave him a little wave and walked up the stairs toward the conference room. He got to his feet and followed, the dog ambling behind him.

Penny was in the kitchen, putting doughnuts on a tray, so he veered over her way. "You still sure about having Bingo here?"

"I think it's fine. It keeps us all in a good mood and reminds us of our mission."

He leaned closer. "Why is Kayla here?"

Penny shrugged. "I feel like we need all the ideas we can get. We're in trouble, Finn."

"Worse than I know?"

"You'll hear." She handed him the tray of doughnuts. "Carry this in there, will you? I'll be right in."

Their banker was there. A vet out of the Baltic, but you wouldn't have known it from his suit and dress shoes. Well, he was navy, after all.

He seemed to be grilling Kayla.

Finn wanted to protect her, felt that urge, except that she was holding her own. "No, I've never worked for this exact type of organization before," she admitted to Branson Howe. "But I volunteered with a nonprofit for kids, and I've run a business, so Penny thought I might be able to help. With the website or something."

She'd run a business? That was news to him.

Branson was frowning, arms crossed.

"We can use an outsider perspective," Finn said. "It's been just me and Penny since...well, since everything went haywire." He glanced over at Penny, who'd just walked in. Sometimes he worried about how she was dealing, or not dealing, with what had happened.

"It's okay, Finn—you can talk about it." Penny's abrupt tone called her words into question. "Coffee, everyone? We should get started."

"That's what I've been trying to do." Branson glared at Penny.

Undercurrents. You had to love them. Penny and Branson always circled around each other like two dogs getting ready to fight.

"You called the meeting," she said, "so why don't you tell us what's on your mind?"

Finn glanced at Kayla, who lifted an eyebrow back at him, obviously reading the back-and-forth as personal, the way he was. "I'll get you a cup of coffee," she offered. "Penny, do you need a refill?"

She waved a hand, leaning forward to look at Branson. "What's going on?"

"I just got a notice from the IRS." Branson opened his laptop and accepted a cup of coffee. "We missed a payment, and there's going to be a fine attached to it when we make it. We need to get on it and pay so the IRS doesn't flag us as suspicious. If that happens, we'll be in line for a lot of paperwork and audits."

"I thought the taxes, at least, were fine." Penny frowned. "We had an outside firm do them. They said they'd found enough deductions that we didn't have to pay anything."

Branson dropped his head and looked at her. "And you didn't question that?"

"No. I did pay them, of course... Oh." Penny smacked her forehead. "I'm an idiot."

"What?" Finn had to ask.

"I was going to get someone new for this year, but with as busy as I've been, I didn't. The outside firm was the one Harry chose, and I wonder..." She trailed off. "Again. I'm an idiot."

Harry. Penny's ex, and a poor excuse for a man.

"I looked into your tax people." Branson hesitated and looked at Penny. For the first time, a hint of sympathy twisted the corner of his mouth.

"I'm not made of glass. Give it to me straight."

"Apparently, one of the silent owners of your outside firm was Oneida Emerson. That could be why no forms were filed."

"None?" Penny's voice was casual, but her fists made red spots on her arms.

Again, Branson's eyes portrayed a little sympathy. "I'm hoping this is the last bad news I have to give you, from this situation, but I can't promise that," he said.

"Give it to me straight," Penny said. "Do you think we're going to make it? Or do we give up and shut down?"

"The vets and the dogs need us," Finn protested.

As if understanding his safe haven was at stake, Bingo let out a low whine and rested his head on Finn's knee.

"What about the grant we...you...just got?" Kayla asked.

"Can't be used for anything other than what we applied for. Improvements to the physical facility." Even if what they needed most was money for something else.

"What's the fine and back taxes likely to add up to?" Penny asked.

Branson named a number that was twice their operating budget.

Finn groaned and looked over at Penny. She was shaking her head. "If I could get my hands on Harry and his—" She bit off whatever she'd been going to say, but Finn could guess at it.

Even Bingo sighed and flopped to the floor, looking mournful.

"If you could just get some publicity and success stories out there, you might be able to raise enough in donations," Branson said. "You've barely started fund-raising. But—"

"That's right," Kayla interrupted. "Everyone wants to support vets, and who can resist the dogs?"

"But we have no money for publicity, is the problem," Penny said. "No time to put together a campaign, either."

"Can't get water from a stone." Branson closed his folder. "And neither of you has any background at fund-raising."

"You can't give up." Kayla leaned forward and looked in turn at everyone at the table. "Even if you don't have money, there are ways to get the word out."

Finn's heart squeezed as he looked at her earnest expression. It was sweet that she cared, given the short length of time she'd been here.

"I'm listening," Penny said in a dismissive tone that suggested she wasn't.

"Social media, for one. An updated website, for another."

"We have that stuff. It hasn't helped so far."

"Pardon me for saying so," Kayla said, "but it's all out of date. You—we, I'll help—need to keep that fresh and add new content."

"I know you're right," Penny said, "but I'm not posting pictures of the veterans. That's stood in our way."

"Well, okay, not without permission. But aren't there some who will ham it up for the camera? I'm sure Willie would."

Penny snorted out a laugh. "You're right about that."

"Capitalize on the setting. How warmhearted the community is." She sat up straighter, her cheeks flushing a little. "Maybe have an event that brings the whole community up here. And then photograph and video bits of it to use all year."

"It's a good idea," Penny said, "but wouldn't donations just trickle in? If Branson's right, we need money now."

"A fund-raising event isn't likely to bring in enough to weather this crisis, even if you could really get the word out," Branson said. "And what about when the next crisis comes?"

Finn debated briefly whether to speak up. But Kayla had changed the tone of the meeting and it had made him think of an idea that had been nudging at him. "Let me throw something out there," he said. "That old bunkhouse. If we renovated it, we might be able to host people to come up here."

"A working-ranch type of thing?" Penny looked skeptical. "That would take a lot of time, and our staff is small."

"But it's a possibility," Kayla said.

Penny frowned. "Wouldn't we have to have more ranch-type activities? Like riding horses and roping cattle or something?"

Finn snorted. "Not many ranches run according to that model anymore," he said.

"But," Penny said, "that's what people expect at a dude ranch. My sister worked at one for a while, and the Easterners want all the stereotypes."

Branson was shaking his head. "I don't like the liability issues, if you're having people do actual ranch work."

Kayla looked thoughtful. "I think people would enjoy coming out here for the peace." She waved a hand at the window. "Lots of people just want to get away. Relax. Reflect. This is a great place to do all that."

"This is getting to be pretty pie-in-the-sky," Branson said. "We need to pay our bills. You're talking about a renovation, lots of initial investment. You can't afford that."

"We have to start somewhere, Branson," Penny said impatiently. "Kayla and Finn are just suggesting some ideas. Which is more than I hear you doing."

Finn looked at Penny. She wasn't usually confrontational. He couldn't blame her, given that her husband and his girlfriend had absconded with the ranch's funds. But she shouldn't take it out on Branson, who was, after all, a volunteer.

A volunteer who had a thing for Penny, if Finn's instincts were firing right.

Kayla snapped her fingers. "Crowdfunding. The kids' organization I volunteered for did it."

"I don't like it." Branson shook his head. "My niece tried to crowdfund to pay off her college loans, and then got mad when everyone in the extended family didn't donate."

"But this is a real cause," Penny said. "We're not just trying to avoid our responsibilities. Anyone who knows us knows how hard we work."

"*Do* they know, though?" Kayla asked. "Maybe we should do an open house *and* crowdfunding. People in the community could come up and see what we do, see the dogs and whatever vets are willing. We could talk about our mission. If we put that together with an online campaign, we might at least get some breathing room."

Penny tipped her head to one side, considering.

Then she nodded. "Worth a try, anyway. It might create some buzz."

Branson threw his hands in the air, looking impatient. "You people are dreamers. Some Podunk carnival isn't going to raise the money you need, not in such a limited time frame."

"How limited?" Finn asked.

"The penalty will go up in two weeks. I don't think—"

"Do you have a better idea?" Penny asked him.

"Good fiscal management, maybe?" He stood up and grabbed his papers. "If you'll excuse me, I have some other responsibilities to attend to." He nodded at Kayla and Finn and walked out.

Kayla stared after him and then looked at Finn, one eyebrow raised.

"Don't ask me," he said. "Penny and Branson have some issues that go way back."

"Hello, I'm in the room," Penny said. "You don't have to talk about me like I'm not."

"Plus," Finn went on, ignoring her, "I think Branson takes care of his mother and a special-needs daughter. He's stretched pretty thin."

"He is, but that's not an excuse for shooting down every idea we have." Penny grabbed a chocolate-frosted doughnut and bit into it.

"What do you think of it all?" Finn asked her. "Because if you're in, then I think we should go full bore into this fund-raiser. But we shouldn't make the effort if it's all for nothing. You know more about the books than I do."

"I think it's worth a try," Penny said slowly. "But it would be an all-hands-on-deck sort of situation. That means you, Kayla. You brought up some great ideas. Are you willing to help?"

"Of course," Kayla said. "This place does important work. I would hate to see it go under. And the Lord knows I'm used to working against some odds." She did a half smile.

Finn's heart turned over. *Stick to business.* "I can cancel my weekend trip. This is more important."

Penny bit her lip. "I got a call this morning from my daughter."

"That's a surprise, right?"

Penny nodded. "She's been having some contractions. If it's labor—"

"Then you should go," Kayla said instantly. "We can handle things here."

"Yes," Finn agreed. "We can handle it." Penny never asked for anything for herself, always carried more than her share of the load. If she had the chance to mend things with her daughter—and be there when her first grandchild was born—Finn was all in favor.

"You guys are the best," Penny said. "It's probably Braxton Hicks. I should be able to stick around for a few days and help get this project going. And I can do the online fund-raising part from anywhere. It's just that there will be a lot of on-the-ground organization if we're really going to do an open house."

Finn blew out a sigh. Then he looked over at Kayla. "When should we get started?"

Penny and Kayla looked at each other. "No time like the present," Penny said. "Let's make a list."

Kayla grabbed a legal pad and a pen. "For starters, we need to think of what a good open house would be like. Something other people won't think of."

"That's true," Penny said. "We don't want to resort to carnival games and kettle corn. There's got to be something new that we could do to make people really want to come. If we're asking them to drive all the way up here, we ought to have something interesting and different for them."

"Something with the dogs?" Kayla said.

"Yes, but what?" Penny reached for the pad, but her phone buzzed and she glanced at it. Glanced again. Then she stood so abruptly that her chair tilted and would have fallen if Finn hadn't grabbed it.

"She went into labor," Penny said. "It's too early. I have to go."

"How can we help?" Kayla asked.

"I... I don't even know."

"Come on," Kayla said, taking the older woman's arm. "We'll get your things together."

So Kayla helped Penny pack while Finn called the airport, and within two hours he'd driven her there and gotten home again.

All the while, he was thinking.

He and Kayla were now pretty much committed to setting up an open house, and doing it alone. That was a problem, because every time he was near her he wanted to kiss her.

He had to get himself pulled together and realize, remember, what a bad idea that would be. For him, no; but for Kayla and Leo, most definitely. They'd already been through plenty of problems in their lives, and they didn't need him adding more.

For their sake, he had to keep control of his emotions.

* * *

The next morning, Kayla knelt in the meadow outside the kennels and watched Finn make his way up the road toward her, his gait unsteady. He was using his cane. It must be a bad day with his leg.

On impulse, she lifted her camera lens and started snapping pictures. With the morning sun glowing on the mountains behind him, the image was riveting. Something she could submit to a magazine or contest, if he gave her permission.

When he got closer she let the camera slip into her lap and surveyed the scene. Across the field, scarlet paintbrush flowers bristled toward the sky, while silvery lupine and blue columbine nodded and tossed in the faint breeze. Sage and pine sent their mingled fragrance down from the mountains. She'd brought Willie and Long John's dogs for the shoot, knowing they could be trusted to remain calm. Now Rockette lay at Kayla's side, big black head lifted to survey the scene. Duke, the grizzled pit bull, sniffed around the rocks, displaying a mild interest in a prairie dog that popped out of its burrow to look around.

Finn disappeared into the barn and came out a moment later, with Winter, the female who'd been abused, at his side. He approached Kayla with a half smile, half grimace. "Showing up as ordered."

"I'm sorry." She moved over to offer him a seat on the end of the bench. "You having a bad day?"

"It happens." He lowered himself onto the bench and propped his cane beside him. "What's our game plan?"

He sounded guarded, and she couldn't blame him. In fact, she was feeling the same way. They'd committed to a couple of weeks of working together on an important project, and that meant they'd have to deal with these undertones between them at some time.

If only they hadn't kissed. That had muddied waters that had only just started to clear as they'd adjusted to working together. Now she couldn't look at him without remembering his tenderness, wishing for it to happen again.

But getting close to Finn meant the risk that he'd discover their connection to the Airborne and that Mitch would find out. She couldn't let that happen, for her own safety but especially for Leo's.

Time to get businesslike. "I'd like to video you first."

His jaw literally dropped. "No way. This isn't about me. I thought we were going to video Long John and Willie."

"Later. You first. You can talk about your work here, and about your history as a veteran."

"Nope. Not happening."

She blew out a breath, trying to keep her frustration under control. "We agreed yesterday that we'd make a series of short clips of veterans. Who better to start with than the person who pretty much runs this place?"

"*Willing* veterans. Which I'm not." He rubbed his leg and his face twisted again.

"If you're going to ask others to participate," she said, "you should be prepared to do the same. Tell your story. It will help other vets, and this place, and the dogs."

"My life isn't interesting!" He practically spit out the words and then lowered his voice. "It's a mess."

What was his story?

"Anyway," he grumbled, "I'm not exactly photogenic. I hate being on camera."

"You're inspiring," she said firmly. "And you can have the dogs with you. And we can edit it." She picked up the old video camera and panned the area, adjusting the settings. "Ready?"

He glared at her.

She glared right back.

He drew in a breath and let it out in a sigh. "Where do I stand?"

"Just sit right there." He was on a bench against the wood barn siding, Willie's dog, Duke, beside him, and if he wasn't photogenic she didn't know who was. He'd advertise the place better than anything. And he didn't even consider himself handsome, which was part of his appeal.

Now that he'd agreed, Kayla felt flustered. She was used to being behind a camera, but not to talking. "Let me find the questions I brainstormed," she said and went to her bag. *Be calm, be calm*, she told herself. *It's a job. You're just doing your job.*

And saving a ranch.

And making things right for Leo.

And helping dogs and veterans who need it.

She pulled out the sheet of notebook paper on which she'd jotted some questions and skimmed them over. They seemed kind of…shallow, and weak. She wanted to sparkle for Finn.

You're not a sparkling kind of person, said the voices from her past.

But it wasn't all about her.

She heard Finn's booming laugh and looked over. He was watching the two dogs. Rockette was rolling on her back in the grass, and Duke was poking and prodding her with his paw, letting out intermittent barks. Winter sat watching with mild interest.

She swung her camera around and caught footage of the dogs, then of Finn watching them. She walked closer.

"So, Finn, what do the dogs do for you?" she asked.

He looked more relaxed now, as he gestured toward the silly pair. "They're lighthearted, and always accepting, and they never give up. Old Duke here, he can't stop trying to dominate Rockette. And she won't let herself be dominated."

She quirked an eyebrow at him. "She's aware of the women's movement."

"She's her own dog, that's for sure."

"Could you tell us a little bit about the ranch and its mission?"

As he answered that softball question, he relaxed to his theme and was actually good on camera. His passion for the work showed, and he explained their clientele: vets who had lost hope, dogs who had lost their last chance.

She risked going a little more personal. "And what made you decide to work for the ranch? What is it in your background that makes you feel a connection?"

He frowned for a moment and then nodded. "I know what it is to lose hope," he said. "I served with good people. Some didn't come home, and some came home a lot worse off than I am."

When he came to a natural breaking point, she hazarded a more personal question. "Do you mind telling us about your own injury?"

"Do I have to?"

"Yes. Yes, you do." She put a hand on her hip, trying to look stern, and he laughed, and all of a sudden there was that romantic vibe between them again.

She cleared her throat and pulled herself back to a businesslike mind-set. "Seriously, if you don't mind, it will bring something personal to people."

"Okay." He looked off to the side as if collecting his thoughts, and then faced Kayla and the camera again. "I was caught in a building that had been bombed. A beam fell on me and…" He grimaced. "The fracture was too bad to fix just right."

She studied him. "What were you doing in the building?"

He shrugged. "Civilians were caught inside. One of my buddies, too."

"You went in to help get people out, didn't you?" She knew in her heart that it had gone down that way. Finn was a protector to the core. If he could help someone, he would.

"It needed done," he said. "We were able to get all the kids out. This—" he gestured at his leg "—this didn't happen until the last trip."

"Did you get a medal? Or probably more than one." She thought of Mitch's stories of the actions that had led to his medals.

Finn waved a hand. "Not important."

Maybe not, but she would look up his service record when she got the chance, see what medals he'd earned, or ask Penny. Because she was getting the feeling there was a lot more to his service than he'd mentioned before. And to have that in the video would add to its appeal.

Hearing about his heroism only made her more impressed with him. But she needed to remember her concerns. "Could you tell us a little about your division? Aren't the Airborne a tight unit?"

"Best in the army, at least according to us." He flashed a grin. "We're definitely confident, but you have to be if you're going to step out of a plane over enemy territory."

Kayla's stomach tightened. Of course he was proud of his service and his brothers.

Of course, he was loyal to them. Just as Mitch was.

If they knew each other, they'd be loyal to each other. So she simply had to make sure that never happened.

She heard voices in the kennel and quickly ended the interview. She needed to be careful. She was getting so drawn to Finn. Just looking at him now, she felt like it was hard to catch her breath. "Thank you," she said, feeling shy. "That was...well. I really admire what you did, who you are." She felt like a dork, but she couldn't keep it in.

His face hardened. "Don't get too impressed. There's a lot about me that's far less admirable."

Willie and Long John came out through the kennel door, interrupting the awkward moment. "How'd they do as show dogs?" Willie asked, laughing as Duke jumped up on him.

"They were great. They could be pros." She pointed a stern finger at Long John, then at Willie. "Just so you know, I'll be interviewing you next, after the midday shift. And then we'll cut film into a good video we can use to promote our event."

"I'm ready, willing and able," Willie said, puffing out his chest.

"You're a ham." Long John waved a hand. "Now, me, I'd rather stay offscreen. I'm not the handsome dude I used to be."

Kayla smiled at the lanky man. "You're plenty handsome, and I'd guess the women, especially, will love to see you." She touched his arm. "And more important, your example of working through your issues will be inspiring. Both to donors and to vets who wouldn't otherwise think of coming."

"You're a good little lady," Long John said, his voice gruff. "We struck gold when we got you to come work at the ranch."

The praise warmed the hungry child inside Kayla. She put an arm around Long John's waist. "I feel like *I* struck gold, coming here."

"Yeah, sure, we're in the middle of a gold rush, but we also have to work," Willie said, gesturing back toward the kennel. "Those dogs won't exercise themselves."

"Of course!" Kayla hurried to put her camera away, determined to continue doing well at her regular job in addition to the extra she'd taken on.

"Kayla." Finn spoke quietly. "Why don't you take a break. We can handle the midday shift."

"Oh, no, it's okay. I'm glad to do it."

"Take a break." It wasn't just a suggestion.

He wanted her to leave. He was basically ordering her to leave.

Hot, embarrassing tears prickled the backs of her eyes and she swallowed. "Okay, then," she said. She gathered the rest of her things while the three men went back into the kennel.

She'd thought they had a connection. However reluctantly, Finn had let her in today, at least a little. Revealed something about who he was. She'd had a moment of thinking they were getting closer.

She dawdled on the road back to her cabin, trying to take in the mountains' beauty. Trying not to feel hurt at Finn's rejection.

She was starting to care what he thought, too much. And he was a dangerous man to care about.

But *was* he dangerous?

He didn't seem like the kind of man who would give her up to a fellow soldier. He seemed like he would want to protect her, take care of her.

On the other hand, she hadn't expected betrayal from the police officer she'd gone to when things went south with Mitch. She'd expected an officer of the law to protect her, and look how mistaken she'd been then. She had to remember where these men's loyalties lay.

Faced with an unexpected couple of hours to herself, Kayla walked inside her cabin. Grabbed a glass of iced tea from the fridge—and on impulse, her Bible and devotional book—and went back out onto the porch, Shoney trotting beside her.

She felt confused, like everything was shifting inside her, ready to explode. She didn't have anyone to talk to.

Except God.

She paged through the Bible restlessly, looking out over the fields and mountains. His world. So beautiful and perfect.

She knew He was in charge. You should trust Him. Moreover, there was nothing to do *but* trust Him, since her own power was so limited compared to His.

Her life hadn't been conducive to trusting. Not as a kid, not as an adult.

But God. God wasn't Mitch. God wasn't Finn. God was bigger, incomprehensible and great. He was like the mountains, mysterious, a little scary, and everlasting.

She let her eyes drift over the Psalms until they fell on a line in Psalm 92, one she'd underlined not long ago: *O Lord, how great are thy works! and thy thoughts are very deep.*

She breathed in and out and looked around.

She wasn't going to understand this world. She wasn't going to know what to do, not perfectly.

And no person was going to love away the bad things that had happened to her.

But God could, and would. According to the Book of Revelation, He would wipe away every tear.

She didn't know she was crying until a fat drop splatted on the parchment-thin page. She brushed her knuckles under her eyes and read on.

Read, and prayed, and listened.

Shoney seemed to sense her mood and pressed close against Kayla's legs, and Kayla lifted the dog into her lap. Comfort and affection and unconditional love: God had known she and Leo needed those things, and had provided them through Shoney, whose special needs couldn't take away from her happy, giving spirit.

She nuzzled the dog's soft fur. *Okay, God. I get it. I should be more like Shoney.*

She kept reading and praying all afternoon. It was only when an alarm rang on her phone that she realized she'd have to hustle to go fetch Leo in time.

When she reached her car, she spotted Finn talking to Long John and Willie outside of Willie's cabin. The three men waved, and Willie gestured for her to join them.

She shook her head and mimed pointing at a watch. She got into the car and headed out.

There was a kind of peace in letting it all go, in realizing you weren't in control.

It was something she needed to keep exploring.

When her phone buzzed, she pulled over to take the call, figuring it was Long John asking her to run an errand while she was in town.

She didn't recognize the number. Maybe it was Willie's phone; he didn't use it often, so she'd never put him in her contacts.

"Hello?"

Silence at the other end.

"Hello? Willie?"

More silence. No, not complete silence. Breathing.

Horror snaked through her as she clicked the call off. She fumbled through the settings until she figured out a way to block the number.

She pulled in a breath and let it out slowly.

It was probably nothing. There was no reason to associate a random call with Mitch.

Anyway, once you'd blocked the number there was no way anyone could trace it. Right?

She put the car into Drive and continued on toward town, carefully, both hands on the steering wheel, staying a couple of miles under the speed limit.

She'd better not call attention to herself, lest the law enforcement here be just as corrupt as it had been back in Arkansas.

Chapter 8

Almost two weeks later, Finn listened to the thunderous applause in the community center and smiled over at Kayla, who stood on the other side of the stage. She looked stunning in a white dress that fit her like a glove. Her brown hair fell loose and shiny around her shoulders, and her smile was as joyous as his.

They'd generated so much interest in the ranch, just by talking up the open house with friends and neighbors, that they'd been asked to share their story at the monthly town meeting. The event was tomorrow, and they'd been working like mad, but from the response they were getting, it seemed like it might actually be a success.

As the meeting broke up, people crowded around him, asking questions and offering congratulations.

He looked over and saw a similar group surrounding Kayla.

Funny how conscious he was of her at every moment.

"Well, you done it," Long John said, clapping him on the shoulder. "I think you just got the open house a couple dozen more visitors. Folks are excited."

"That thermometer thing you put online is rising up fast," Willie added, coming up behind Long John and reaching out to shake Finn's hand. In his other hand, he held up his phone, displaying a donation meter already half-full. He squinted over at Long John, then looked back at Finn. "Say, we need to talk to you a minute. In private, like."

"Sure." Finn glanced around, then ushered the two older men toward a quiet corner of the community center. "What's up?"

Long John and Willie glanced at each other. "We've got ourselves an awkward situation," Long John said. "See, we were given a gift card for that new restaurant up Cold Creek Mountain."

"Cold Creek Inn?" Finn whistled. "Nice."

"My daughter wanted to treat us," Willie explained. "Thinks I don't get out enough or some fool thing."

Finn chuckled. "Why don't you ask Dana Dylan to go with you?" He nodded at the white-haired dynamo who'd asked Willie out a number of times.

Willie raised his hands and took a step backward. "No, no way. I don't want to encourage her."

Finn lifted an eyebrow. "Because your heart's somewhere else?"

"His heart ought to go on out with Dana," Long John grumbled.

Finn shouldn't have opened that door. The two men's rivalry over Penny was mostly good-natured, but their friendship was too important to fool with them.

Apparently Willie felt the same way, because he slapped Long John's shoulder. "I'd rather have dinner with my buddy here than any woman. Don't have to clean up my act for him."

"Then you two use the gift card," Finn said. He was still confused about why they'd brought him into it.

"But we don't either of us like that kind of food," Long John said. "Nor a place where you have to get all gussied up to go."

"And it expires tomorrow," Willie said. "If my daughter finds out I didn't use it, she'll be upset."

"So we were thinking…"

"Since you and Kayla are all dressed up," Willie said, "I'd like for you to use it. Tonight." He held out a gilt-edged plastic card with *Cold Creek Inn* embossed in fancy script.

Mixed emotions roiled through Finn's chest. The thought of taking Kayla on a date sounded way too good. Working together as they had been, he was drawn to her more and more. She was a good person—that was the main thing. She tried hard and did the right thing and took care of her son. She said she wasn't a great Christian, that she had a lot to learn, but he'd watched her during church. She had a God-focused heart. The fact that she was gorgeous, at least to him, was just icing on the cake.

But the feelings Finn was having for Kayla were the exact reason he shouldn't be taking her on anything resembling a date. "I think you two should use it," he repeated. "It was meant for you, Willie, not me." And it would be better that way. Better than for him to start something with Kayla that he couldn't finish.

"I'm just not up to it today," Long John said. He gestured down at his body with a disparaging movement of his arm. "My Parkinson's is acting up. I need to get some rest."

"And I'm driving him back," Willie said. "Truth is, I'm worn-out myself. I'd rather sit at home and watch reruns on the TV then go to some fancy place where I have to figure out what fork to use."

"Give it to somebody else, then," Finn said. He was starting to panic at the idea of doing something so romantic with Kayla. No telling where that would lead, but it was a place he couldn't go. "How about the Coopers. Isn't it their anniversary?"

"Nope," Long John said flatly. "Willie and I, we talked it over. We're giving it to you."

"Hey, Kayla," Willie called across the emptying room. "Come here a minute."

"Willie!" Finn scolded in a whisper.

But it was too late. She was already coming over, her high heels clicking, and again Finn was stunned at how gorgeous she was. "What's up?" she asked.

"Finn wants to ask you something," Long John said. "Come on, Willie. I see that old Pete Ramsey. He's always trying to borrow money. I need to get out of here." And the two men turned and walked away.

Although there were other people in the room—and in fact, Long John and Willie didn't go far before finding a couple of chairs—Finn suddenly felt like he was alone with Kayla.

If they went out to the restaurant, they would truly

be alone. The thought created a tsunami of feeling inside him.

He tried desperately to cling to the thought that she might not be trustworthy, that there was some kind of mystery in her past. But he'd just talked to Raakib yesterday, and so far, there was nothing criminal or even dishonest to report.

"Finn?" Kayla was looking at him quizzically. "What's going on?"

She looked so pretty and sophisticated that he felt like a high school boy asking a girl to a dance. The ease he'd felt working with her was nowhere to be found. He held up the gift card. "Willie wants us to use this."

Behind her, Willie made a sweeping motion with his arm while shaking his head vigorously.

And the older man had a point. What a half-baked way to ask a woman out. "What I mean to say is, would you like to go out to dinner with me? At the Cold Creek Inn?"

Color rose in her face as she looked at him and bit her lip.

Oh, man. He *really* wanted to go out with her.

But did her hesitation mean she wanted to go, or that she didn't? He needed to give her an out. "You must be worried about Leo. You probably can't go."

"Actually," she said, holding up her phone, "I just found out he wants to stay a little bit longer at his friend's house. They're roasting marshmallows." She looked so pretty it made his heart hurt. "And his friend lives up Cold Creek Mountain."

"We do have something to celebrate," Finn said, with a smile and a tone he'd kept in cold storage for years. He stepped fractionally closer without even meaning to. "Today went well, and there's no one I'd like to spend the evening with more than you."

Her mouth opened halfway, and he couldn't take his eyes off her. He felt tongue-tied, until he again noticed wild gesturing behind her. Long John, and now Willie, seemed to be conducting a pantomime coaching session; Willie was making a rolling motion with his hands, as if to say, *talk to her more, convince her.*

So he started telling her about the restaurant, how fantastic it was reputed to be. "Apparently it looks out over the valley. They have all kinds of fancy game dishes, venison, and wild boar, and pheasant." But was eating wild game really persuasive to a woman? "I think they're known for their chocolate desserts, too," he said, hoping he'd remembered correctly.

"That sounds good." She gave him a tentative smile.

Finn noticed a couple of nearby people glancing their way. "Come over here," he said and guided her a little bit away from the crowd. "If someone heard us talking about the Cold Creek Inn, there goes your reputation."

"Because of going somewhere with you? Really?"

He thought. Not many people knew about what had happened in his past. And if they did know, would they see it as a reason for her to avoid him? He was starting to wonder. "It's a small town," he said, because he couldn't explain.

Although maybe, someday soon, he would. If anyone would look at his past mistakes with compassion, it was Kayla.

She shrugged. "I don't really care what anyone thinks. Do you?"

He didn't care about anything but her. "Nope," he said. "Let's get out of here." He offered her his arm, and she took it, and he felt like the most fortunate man in the world.

He glanced over his shoulder at Long John and Willie. They were both grinning and fist-bumping and thumbs-upping him. Because of course, they were trying to push him and Kayla together. Matchmaking. He should have realized it before.

He just hoped the two older men knew what they were doing. Because Finn felt like he was diving into a sea of risks, and he couldn't predict the outcome.

When they walked into the Cold Creek Inn, Kayla's breath caught.

The dining room was full of well-dressed people, mostly couples. Waitstaff in white jackets hovered and smiled and carried trays high on one hand—a feat she'd only ever seen in movies. The decor was that of a hunting lodge, with rough-hewn wooden rafters overhead, a pine plank floor and wall hangings depicting hunting scenes.

But most impressive of all was the view. The whole front of the restaurant was glass, a floor-to-ceiling window, and it looked out over the valley. As the sun sank, pink and orange and gold filled the sky, and lights flickered on across the valley.

Breathtaking.

Kayla had read about places like this, had seen them on television, but she had never been. It was way out of her league, and a wave of anxiety washed over her. Would she know how to act, what silverware to use?

Would she spill a glass of water or not know how to ask for the right food?

She was holding Finn's arm, his muscles strong beneath her fingers, and she must have tightened her grip because he looked down at her and patted her sleeve. "Pretty highfalutin for a couple of ranch hands," he said. "But let's just enjoy ourselves, okay?"

As the maître d' led them to a table by the window, she tried to walk with assurance. The man helped her into her seat while Finn took the chair across from hers and thanked him.

Even if she could handle this place, even if she didn't make a fool of herself, she still felt shaky about Finn. Had he really wanted to ask her out? Or was he just using up a gift card?

Regardless, he looked confident and sophisticated in his suit, his shoulders straining a bit at the fabric, his boots making him even taller than usual. Finn dressed up was just plain devastating. And she needed to pull herself together. She focused on the fact that it was a side of him that she hadn't seen before.

"Wait a minute," she said, pleased that she was able to sound light and casual. "I just realized I don't know much about your background before the ranch."

Some of the carefree light went out of his face. *Oh.* She hadn't meant to stir up the bad part of his past. "Did you live in LA or New York or something?" she added hastily. "Did you do client dinners at places like this?"

He laughed. "Far from it," he said. "My family's from Virginia. After the service, I got into agricultural sales. Fertilizer, seeds, stuff like that." He grinned. "At most, I'd take my clients to the town diner."

"But you seem so comfortable here."

He nodded. "My mom saw to it that we all knew not to slurp our soup or reach all the way across the table. Maybe once or twice a year, she'd grill us on our manners and then get Dad to take us to a fancy restaurant as a kind of test."

"That's so nice."

"I was fortunate," he said. "I had a great childhood."

She sensed he was about to ask her about her childhood, and that, she didn't want to talk about. "What does your dad do?" she asked, to forestall him.

"Small-town cop," he said. "Everybody loves him. One of my brothers is a cop in the same department, and the other's a firefighter."

"Back in Virginia."

He nodded.

"Then…why do you live all the way out here?"

He looked out over the valley, now shadowed, with stars starting to appear above. "I'd been out here a few times for work," he said. "Liked the wide-open spaces. And when… Well, I needed a fresh start. Felt like I couldn't breathe, back East."

"I know what you mean," she said.

He looked at her sharply, but seemed to discern that she didn't want to talk about the negatives in her past. So he made her laugh mispronouncing various dishes, and joking about the particularly large trophy moose head that loomed on the wall behind her.

He was trying to make her feel comfortable, and she liked him even better for it.

Through the appetizers he ordered for them, the pheasant dish he recommended, the too-frequent re-fills of their water glasses by their overzealous waiter, he kept the conversation going. And Kayla was both pleased and dismayed to realize that she liked this side of Finn, too. She hadn't known he had a background that would lend itself to a place this classy, but it was nice to relax, knowing that he could handle everything.

"Dessert?" the waiter asked.

"Oh, I couldn't," Kayla said. She was full, and besides, they'd surely used up the gift card now. The prices on the menu had been scandalously high.

Finn looked at her with an assessing gaze. "Maybe we could take a look at the dessert tray."

"Of course, sir." And the waiter hurried away.

"Finn!" She laughed at him. "How are we going to eat dessert?"

A moment later, their waiter returned with a mouthwatering tray of cheesecakes, pastries, cakes and pies.

"That's how," Finn said.

She studied the treats. She'd never before experienced food that literally made her mouth water.

"Change your mind about being too full for dessert?" Finn asked, his voice teasing.

She smiled across the table at him. "Oh, yeah," she said. "I want that one." She pointed at a slice of chocolate cake that was layered with a raspberry filling, with extra chocolate sauce and whipped cream over the top of it.

"Good choice," Finn said. "I'll take the apple pie à la mode."

Of course they had to share their desserts. And of course their hands brushed as they did. Their tones grew lower as the sky outside turned black and candles were lit at each table. They seemed to be embedded in their own little world, a world of smiling and soft laughter and expressive glances miles away from their daily lives at the kennel and the ranch.

When she put down her fork, too full to eat anymore, Finn reached across the table and took her hand. "Kayla, I…" He trailed off.

"What?" One syllable was all she could get out. Even that was an effort, considering that she couldn't breathe.

He kept hold of her hand. "I don't know what's happening between us, but how would you feel about pursuing it?"

She looked at him and tried to remember all the reasons why she didn't want to. Tried to pull them back together into a coherent, reasoned set of ideas. But her doubts had scattered with the same wind that was making the moonlit pine branches below wave gently in the twilight.

It didn't seem like he would do anything to hurt her and Leo. It didn't seem like he would prioritize his military brothers over her. Could she trust him with her story? Was she strong enough to take care of herself and her child if things went south with Finn?

Most of all, could he really want to be with her?

Normally, in the past, she wouldn't have been able to believe it. The years of being unwanted were deeply embedded, so much that they seemed to always be a part of her.

But through her work at the ranch and the spiritual development she was gaining here, she was starting to have a different feeling about herself. A feeling that maybe, possibly, things might go well for her. People might want to be her friend. She might have found a place to belong.

Maybe Finn was a part of all that.

She looked at him and opened her mouth to try to put some of what she was feeling into words. But her phone buzzed with a text, and the waiter brought the check, and the moment was over.

Maybe it was just as well, but she couldn't help regretting it as she reluctantly pulled out her phone and studied the lock screen. "The marshmallow roast is over," she said to Finn. "Leo's ready to go home."

"Of course." He signed the check and stood. Came around the table to pull out her chair for her. "Let's go get him. It's late."

It *was* late. But Kayla's heart was full of promise as they left the restaurant, Finn's hand barely resting on her lower back.

He was a good person, a person she could trust. A person who understood about Leo's needs, and maybe about hers, as well.

Maybe even a person she could build a future with.

After they'd picked up a very sleepy Leo and put him in the booster seat they'd transferred from Kayla's car earlier, Finn drove carefully down the winding mountain road.

A strange warmth surrounded his heart. He'd felt something a little similar with his wife, but way different in degree, like the difference between a candle and a roaring fire.

What he felt for Kayla was explosive, powerful, hot. He didn't want to go back to the friendly coworkers they'd been. He didn't want this night to end.

He heard Kayla murmuring over her shoulder, and

Leo said something almost indistinguishable, and then Kayla spoke back.

"Music okay?" he asked, and when she nodded, he turned on the radio and found some quiet jazz.

It was always good to keep a kid calm right before bed. He remembered having arguments with Deirdre about that, when Derek was just Leo's age. Finn had liked to come home and play with Derek, but the excitement had meant the boy didn't want to go to sleep anytime soon. It had annoyed Deirdre, and now, from a more mature perspective, he could see why.

He'd been young, inconsiderate, all about his own desire to have fun with his son on his own terms.

If he had it to do over again...

He glanced over at Kayla. *Might* he have the chance to do it all over again?

He didn't want to be disloyal to Derek and Deirdre by having a good life when they'd been denied the chance. But his conversations with Pastor Carson over the past weeks had him thinking that maybe, just maybe, he didn't have to pay the price of his sin forever. Maybe the accident hadn't been entirely his fault. Maybe not even very much his fault, and though he'd always blame himself, at least to some degree, light and hope were slowly seeping back into his life. He was starting to live again. And Kayla was the reason why.

Thinking of the dinner they'd just had, he smiled. It wasn't the normal thing they would do together, wasn't something to be repeated often, but they'd made the most of it and they'd had a blast. He wanted that to be the case again, in other contexts. How would she like a rafting trip? A museum? A specialty food tasting? Marge's sled dog show?

He had the feeling that, with Kayla, anything would be fun.

"Leo's out," Kayla said and settled more deeply into her seat, facing forward. "He was exhausted. Thank you again for stopping to pick him up."

"I enjoyed it. I enjoyed the whole evening."

"So did I."

The words seemed to hang in the air between them, floating on soft notes of music. They hadn't gotten to discuss what he'd wanted to—whether she wanted to explore the connection they were feeling—but he'd read interest, at least, in her eyes.

He reached out and squeezed her hand, and the petite size of it in contrast to his own big paw, the mix of soft skin and tough calluses, moved him and made him want to explore her contrasts further.

They had a lot of ground to cover, a lot of background to reveal. He needed to tell her about what had happened with Derek and Deirdre. And he needed to know more about what had happened in her past, what had caused the bruises on her arms when she'd first arrived, what made her jumpy.

Needed her to know that he'd protect her from harm like that in the future.

He eased the truck through a narrow part of the road and came out onto a broad, flat stretch lit by moonlight. Pines loomed on either side of the road, casting shadows in the silvery light.

"It's beautiful," she said softly. "I've never been in a place so beautiful."

"I love Colorado. I wouldn't want to live anywhere else." Then he realized that sounded inflexible. "Though, I guess, for the right reasons—"

"No," she said, putting a hand on his arm. "You fit with this land, and that's a good thing. You're an important part of this community. You belong here."

She got that about him? He drew in a breath and thought he caught a whiff of the flowery scent of her hair. He wanted more than that, though; he wanted to bury his face in its softness, the softness she'd revealed tonight.

Be careful, some part of his mind warned his heart.

They were coming into a section of driveways and houses now, not exactly heavy population, but heavy for this area. Automatically, he slowed.

Suddenly, from a driveway, a car backed out in front of him. *Right* in front of him, going fast.

He slammed on the brake and veered left. He had to avoid the hit at any cost, because if they collided with another car...

Crash.

It was a slight crash, but it made a loud, metal-on-metal impact, and as the car rebounded back and started to rotate, he heard a scream behind him. Leo. Then it was joined by a higher-pitch female scream as the car hit a patch of loose gravel on the road and spun faster.

He kept steering into the spin, his instincts carrying him as his heart and mind freaked out.

It's happening again.

They're going to die.

It's your fault.

He pulled his mind out of that abyss and back into

the present. He saw the cliff's edge coming at them fast, and with superhuman effort, he steered the car away. Time slowed down. They were just a few feet from the edge.

Inches.

Millimeters.

A hair's breadth from the drop-off, the car stopped.

Kayla unsnapped her seat belt and turned to the back seat, basically crawled right over. "Leo. Baby. Baby, it's okay."

She was speaking coherently, so that was one difference.

But Leo's sobs...

He couldn't look back to see what was happening to Leo. Had happened.

There was a knocking sound beside his head, but he couldn't turn to look at it.

He was somewhere else, in another car on another road at another time.

More knocking, then shouting. "Sir! Sir, are you all right?"

"Man, I'm so sorry... Oh, no, Dad, there's a kid in there." Some disassociated part of him heard the hysteria in the adolescent boy's tone.

There were noises. Someone opening the back car door. Voices: Kayla's. A stranger's.

In the distance, the sound of a siren.

His heart was still thudding hard in his chest. Sweat dripped down the middle of his back, soaked his palms that still clenched the steering wheel in a death grip.

With a giant sigh, he let his hands and his shoulders go loose. And then he couldn't hold himself up, or together, anymore.

Finn put his head down on the steering wheel and surrendered to the darkness.

Chapter 9

The next morning, Kayla walked out onto her cabin's porch, coffee in hand, watching the sun break through a bank of clouds and cast its rays over the valley. Gratitude filled her heart.

They were okay. They were all okay.

Leo had a temporary cast on his wrist, and Kayla had a painful, colorful bruise across her shoulder and chest where the seat belt had dug in. She'd been terrified, of course, all through the ambulance ride to the hospital, until the doctors had reassured her that Leo had suffered no ill effects.

As for her resilient son, he'd loved the ambulance ride, the lights and the sirens. Future fireman or EMT, one of the guys had said, laughing as Leo begged to be allowed to sit up front and look at all the buttons and switches.

Finn seemed fine, physically, although he'd made himself scarce at the hospital, after a brusque question about whether she and Leo were all right. But that made sense. Delayed shock reaction, most likely. She couldn't wait to see him today, to talk to him about what had happened. During the car accident, but also beforehand, at the restaurant.

She wrapped her arms around herself, unable to restrain the big smile that spread across her face.

He liked her.

Finn, a real, honorable man, wanted to—how had he put it?—pursue a relationship. With her!

They had a lot to talk about. She was going to have to tell him the history with Mitch, let him know why she'd initially been so guarded. Now that she knew him better, she was pretty sure he would understand.

Behind her, she heard Leo call out, "Mom!" Footsteps pattered and then Shoney's tail thumped. She barked a happy greeting to her boy.

So the day was starting, Kayla would get Leo's breakfast and then help the ranch put on an amazing open house. There was so much to do, and she'd normally have been stressed out about it, but the events of last night had put it all in perspective.

She lifted her face to the sun's warmth and said a silent prayer of thanks: for their safety last night, and their freedom from Mitch, and for the fact that she and her son had found a home.

The day was a whirl of activity. They had almost double the number of visitors as they'd expected, due in part to their social-media sharing and in part to the word that had gotten out after the presentation last night. Everyone had to pitch in. Willie noticed that supplies of hot-dog buns and cola were running low, and took off in the truck to buy more. At the kennel tour, Long John talked up the dogs so positively that people started asking about adopting them. So Kayla set him up at a table with forms to handle that unexpected bit of new business.

Kayla led tours of the ranch, and Finn talked about the veterans' side of it. Penny, who'd just arrived back in town late last night, explained the organizational structure. They all pitched in to keep the free food and drinks coming.

The whole time, people kept coming up to Kayla and hugging her and telling her they'd heard about the accident, and were glad that she and Leo were safe.

When she got a free moment, she asked Missy how everyone knew about the accident.

"Small town," Missy explained. "And Hank Phillips kept telling everyone over and over about it."

She nodded. "He felt awful, and so did his son." The boy, backing out of the driveway on a new learner's permit, had stepped on the gas instead of the brakes, and the car had shot into the road right in front of them. He'd apologized over and over, and had barely managed to restrain tears. "The outcome could have been so much worse. I hope that poor kid doesn't stop driving forever."

"You're such a sweetheart, Kayla," Missy said, hugging her. "A lot of people would be angry. You're really generous, being so understanding."

Kayla waved away the praise, but she felt it. Felt like she and Missy might become friends.

Leo spent much of the day running around with his

buddies from camp and church, making siren sounds and crashing into each other, reenacting the car accident. After a few efforts, she stopped trying to keep him still. Play was his way of processing what had happened, and even though he was fine, it had been a scary thing for all of them.

She hoped for an opportunity to talk with Finn about it, but every time she got a free moment, he was busy. And her own free moments were few, because in between tours, she was creating live videos and posting them.

When people finally started leaving, Penny beckoned her into the offices. "Check it out," she crowed, clicking into the crowdfunding page on the old desktop computer. She spread her hands, pointing them toward the full-to-the-top fund-raising meter. "Ta-da! We have enough to pay the back taxes and more!"

They hugged and did a little jig, taking it out into the driveway, where Leo and other kids saw and laughed and joined in. Then they all escorted the few remaining visitors toward the parking area.

Finally, Finn walked up to her and she started to open her arms. Everyone was hugging, right? But something in his face stopped her.

"Can we talk?" he asked.

"Um, sure." Some of her excitement seeped away as her inner danger alert sprang to attention. "We made a good amount fund-raising. Plenty to pay the taxes."

"Good. Let's walk." His voice was flat, his face without emotion.

She watched as he started away from her, leaning heavily on his cane. Something was different about him. His usual calm now covered over an intense energy.

"Did you get the response you hoped for from the veterans in the group?" she asked his departing back. Hurrying after him, she kept talking. "There were more of them than I expected. All different ages, too."

As soon as they were out of earshot of the others, he turned to her. "Look, it's not going to work between us."

She tilted her head to one side as her heart turned to a stone in her chest. "I don't understand."

He didn't look at her. "It's not complicated. I thought about it and I realized that this—" he waved his hand back and forth between the two of them, still without looking at her "—that this isn't what I want."

The old interior voices started talking. Of course, a man like Finn wouldn't want to be with a woman like her. It had been too much to expect.

But, she reminded herself, she *wasn't* that unwanted girl. She wasn't ugly. She wasn't bland and boring. People in Esperanza Springs liked her. People here at the ranch, too: Penny, and Long John, and Willie.

Finn still wasn't looking at her. Why wouldn't he meet her eyes? "Talk to me," she urged him. "Let's try to work it out, whatever happened."

He shook his head and looked off to the side. Like he didn't even want to see her face. "No."

Confusion bloomed inside. She couldn't understand what had caused him to erect this sudden wall, to refuse to share what he was feeling even though they'd been getting closer and closer these past weeks and especially last night. "Why are you being like this?"

"I'm telling you, it's not going to work."

She put her hands on her hips. "We have something, Finn! What we felt at the restaurant last night, what we've been feeling for a while now, it's worth exploring. You're a good man—"

He held up a hand like a stop sign. "It's *not* real."

"Did someone say something today? One of the visitors?" She couldn't imagine what might have been said, nor that Finn would be so sensitive about hearing it.

"No. The guests were fine." He drew himself up, wincing slightly as he straightened his bad leg. "Look, you did a good job helping with the open house. We worked together, probably more than we should have, and it led us to think we had feelings for each other. That's to be expected."

Tears pressed at her eyelids as she tried to recognize the man she cared about in the squared jaw, the rigidly set shoulders. "Why are you doing this?" she choked out.

"Mr. Finn!" Leo came running up and stopped himself by crashing into Kayla, then bouncing off her to Finn. "Look at my cast!"

Finn closed his eyes for the briefest moment. "I don't want to look at it." He turned and started to walk away, his limp pronounced.

Leo ran a few steps after him. "But, Mr. Finn, I want you to sign it."

"No!" He thundered out the word.

Leo stared after him and then looked back at her, his face sorrowful. "Why is he mad at me, Mommy?"

Kayla sucked in her breath and tamped down the loss that threatened to drown her. "It's okay. Come here." She knelt and opened her arms, and Leo was enough of a little boy that he came running and buried his face in her shoulder. Her bruised, aching shoulder, but never mind. She clung to him fiercely.

Finn had seemed to be different from other men, but apparently, he wasn't. In the end he didn't care enough. The abrupt way he'd pulled back stabbed her like a dull knife to the chest. She might not have believed him, might have thought he was covering something up, except he'd been mean to Leo.

That wasn't the Finn she knew. But maybe she hadn't really known him at all.

She didn't understand it, but she was a person who accepted reality when it stared her in the face. She'd never believed in fairy tales, like some of the girls she'd known in school, imagining knight-like boyfriends who'd sweep them off their feet, visualizing wonderful, romantic wedding days.

But Finn was romantic and wonderful last night, a sad little voice cried from deep inside her heart. *He wanted to pursue a relationship. What happened to that?*

She shook off the weak, pathetic questions so she could focus on the real one: how to go on from here. Should she stay in the best community she'd ever known? The community where Leo had relaxed out of his hypervigilant ways and learned to be a kid again? The place where she'd started to feel at home for the first time in her life?

Could she stay, seeing Finn every day and knowing the brief flame of their relationship was doused for good?

* * *

Two days later, Finn still hadn't gotten over the awful feeling of rejecting Kayla and Leo. Pushing Leo away had been like kicking a puppy. Pushing Kayla away...that had just about ripped out his heart.

But that pain didn't even compare to what he'd felt when the car had spun out of control, when he'd heard Kayla's gasps and Leo's screams.

He'd spent the past two days driving himself hard, getting the kennels cleaned before Kayla got back from dropping Leo off at his camp. When she was around, he made himself scarce by painting a couple of rooms at the main house, mowing grass, even exercising the two horses.

His leg was so bad he couldn't walk without an obvious limp, but he couldn't stop moving. The shame of what he'd started to do—the way he'd almost put another family at risk—just kept eating at him.

Now, near sunset on Monday, he felt a mild panic. Two hours of daylight left and he was out of chores. His leg was throbbing, and he should rest it, but to stop moving would let the thoughts in.

He noticed the old shed behind the main house. They needed to pull it down, build something new on the slab.

He would do that now.

He got his chain saw and carried it around the shed, planning his work. It wasn't hard to see the symbolism: *you're real good at ripping things down, breaking things apart.*

And that's all you're good at.

He destroyed everything he touched.

The last person he wanted to see was Carson Blair,

the pastor, but here he came in his truck, down from the direction of Kayla's cottage. Jealousy burned in Finn. Had she replaced him so quickly, so easily?

"Need some help?" Carson climbed out of his truck and Finn saw he was dressed in work boots and carrying a pair of gloves.

"No. I got this." He revved the chain saw.

"That's not what I heard." Carson crossed his arms and watched Finn as if he could see into his very soul. He probably could. Wasn't that in the job description of a pastor?

Finn started on the posts that held up the shed, taking satisfaction in the harsh vibration as he cut through them. Once he'd gotten through one side, he pushed at the shed with his foot.

"Hey, Finn!" It was Penny, calling from the back door of the main house. "I want some of that wood," she continued as she walked down toward Finn, the pastor and the shed. "It's weathered real nice. Got some things I could make out of it come winter."

"As a matter of fact, I know someone who'd like that door," Carson said. "Mind if I pull it off?"

Finn's intended task, a solitary demolition, was turning into a community event. Fine. He started pulling off some of the boards that were in good shape. "I'll get these cleaned up and bring them over," he said to Penny, hoping she would leave.

She didn't. "What's going on with you and Kayla?" She had her hands on her hips. Vertical lines stood between her brows.

"Nothing that needs to concern you."

"It does concern me," she said, "because they're thinking about leaving."

His head jerked around at that. He wanted to ask, *When? Why? Where will they go?* He wanted a way to patch the hole that her remark had torn in his heart.

But wouldn't it be best if they left?

"Finn," Penny said, "I like you. And I've put up with you and your darkness. The Good Lord knows we all have it. But the way you've treated her beats all." She grabbed a couple of boards and headed toward the house.

Finn glared after her. Maybe he'd been cruel, but it was kindly meant. Kayla and Leo would be better off without him.

He glanced over at the pastor. The man was removing the door from the shed, focused on the task, but Finn had a feeling he'd heard every word.

That impression was reinforced when the pastor spoke. "Anything you want to talk about?" He asked the question without looking at Finn.

"No." Finn walked over to his truck, started it and backed it up to the shed. He found a rope in the back. Tied one end to the truck hitch and the other to a side support of the shed. "Gonna pull it down. Watch out."

He put the truck into gear and gunned it a little, watching his rearview mirror. With a scraping, ripping sound, the shed tilted and then collapsed, boards jumping and bouncing before they settled, the metal roof clanking down.

It wasn't as satisfying as he'd expected it to be.

He stopped the truck, climbed out and limped over to the wreckage. His doctor was going to have his hide for working like this without a rest, messing up his leg worse than it already was. He tugged at the aluminum roof.

Without speaking, the pastor went to the other side and helped him lift the roof off and carry it out of the way.

"Thanks," Finn grunted.

"Why'd you hurt her like that?" Carson went back to the demolished shed and pulled out a couple of jagged pieces of brick.

"To not hurt her." Finn ripped at the corner of the shed that was still standing. The rough wood tore his hands. Good.

"What do you mean?" Carson tossed the bricks into a pile of debris.

"I was driving when my wife and son were killed!"

Carson didn't speak, and when Finn managed to look at his face, there was no judgment there. But, of course, Carson was a pastor. He had to listen to all kinds of horror with a straight face.

Carson came over to help Finn tug at the stubborn corner post. "Does every person who's driving have total control over every circumstance on the road?"

Finn felt like he was choking. The pastor's words were bringing it all back, clear as if he were looking at a movie. He could hear his own voice, yelling at his wife. Her anger, the way she'd shoved at him.

He'd wanted to pull off the road. Why hadn't he pulled off the road?

Because it was a narrow mountain road. There was no place to pull off.

No place to escape the bobtail truck that had come barreling around the curve at a faster speed than it should have.

Just before impact, he'd caught a glimpse of the driver's face. He knew, now, that the driver hadn't died; that after being acquitted of any wrongdoing—although Finn seemed to remember something about a warning from the judge—the man had moved out of state.

The moments after the truck had rammed into them, he couldn't bear to relive. It was bad enough to have experienced the edge of it again when they'd had the near accident with Kayla and Leo.

"Well?" Carson gave the post a final tug and it came loose of its moorings with a scraping sound. He caught his balance and started tugging it toward the pile of debris. When he'd let it fall, he walked back toward Finn. "What do you say? Do you have total control?"

"No, but I should have." He tried to pick up a couple of loose boards, but his leg nearly gave out from under him. With a groan he couldn't restrain, he sat down on a stump. "I should have protected them." The lump in his throat wouldn't let him say more.

"I'm guessing you did the best you could at that moment." The pastor looked at him. "We aren't God."

Finn cleared his throat. "Why did God let that happen?" The words came out way too loud.

Carson looked at him steadily. "Talk to me about it."

"Me, Deirdre, that I can understand. We were fighting, and… But Derek was a kid. An innocent. He didn't deserve to die before he got to live!" Finn heard the anger and harshness in his voice. Anger felt better than raw grief, but not by much.

He hadn't known how angry he was at God until just this moment.

Carson wiped his forehead on the sleeve of his shirt and sat down on a pile of boards, a couple of yards away from Finn, not looking at him. Instead, he stared out toward the mountains. "I wish I had an easy answer, but I don't. Some things, we'll never know, not in this life. But your son is with Him, and I have to believe your wife is, too." He clipped off the words and looked away. "Some things we have to try to believe."

In the midst of his own raw feelings, Finn wondered about the pastor. He was a widower. How much had Carson worked through about his own wife's death?

Because he really couldn't stand on his leg anymore, Finn stayed where he was. He picked up a board, took the hammer from his belt and started pulling out nails.

Carson carried load after load of wood pieces over to the debris pile. When he almost had it cleaned up, he stopped right in front of Finn. "You don't have to suffer forever, you know. Maybe there was some sin in there on your part. There usually is. No one's perfect, but we *are* forgiven."

Forgiven. "Yeah, right."

"It's at the center of the Christian gospel. You know that."

A high-pitched sound came their way. It was laughter, Carson's girls. They ran toward the pastor, Leo right behind them. But when Leo saw Finn, he came to an abrupt stop. He looked at Finn a moment, both fear and reproach in his eyes.

Finn's throat closed up entirely. He busied himself with kneeling down—and man, did that hurt—to pick up some nails. Didn't want the kids to step on them.

"Daddy, come on! We caught a frog and a crawdad, and we wanted to keep them, but Miss Kayla said we better let them stay in the pond. But we took pictures, and Miss Kayla sent them to Miss Penny on her phone. Come see!"

A twin clinging to each leg, Carson looked over his shoulder at Finn. "Catch you later—maybe at the men's Bible study. We deal with some tough questions. Thursday nights." He lifted his hand in a salute-like movement and then followed his girls toward the car.

No way was Finn going to a men's Bible study. Bunch of brainiacs analyzing the deep hidden meaning of some verse of Scripture that no one cared about.

Although come to think of it…now that he was getting to know Carson, Finn realized it wasn't likely to be completely irrelevant.

It was only when he turned to head for his house that he noticed Leo was still standing where Carson's SUV had already pulled away. Looking directly at Finn. His face held sadness and longing and hunger. "Mr. Finn," he called.

That face and that voice made Finn want to run to the boy and scoop him up and hug him, tell him he *was* loved and that men—some of them, at least—could be protective father figures.

Except he wasn't one of those men.

With what felt like superhuman effort, he turned away from Leo and started walking toward his house.

A sound made him look back over his shoulder. Something like a sob. If Leo was crying…

"C'mere, buddy." Kayla knelt near Penny's place. Her voice sounded husky as she spread her arms wide.

Leo ran into them and she held him against her. Over the boy's shaking shoulder, she leveled a glare at Finn. And then her face twisted like she was about to cry herself.

Everything in him wanted to run to them, to hold them, to explain. To ask if they could try again, have another chance.

But that wouldn't be right, because for Finn, there couldn't be another chance. He couldn't *take* another chance.

He turned away and started walking.

It was the hardest thing he'd ever done. It felt like he was ripping his heart out of his chest and leaving it there on the ground, there with Kayla and Leo. But he was doing it for them, even though they didn't know it.

Kayla tried to brace herself for the task at hand. Straightened her spine and made herself move briskly, cleaning the dinner dishes off the table. It was now or never, though; she needed to pack tonight and leave early the next morning.

She drew in a deep breath. "Come sit by Mom, honey," she said to Leo. "We need to talk."

Leo had seemed dejected throughout dinner, and now, as he plodded over to where she was sitting on the couch, he looked resigned. Kids could sense trouble, and it was pretty obvious things had changed here at the ranch. Leo knew: something bad was going to happen.

It was only now she realized he hadn't looked like that in a while. Redemption Ranch had been good for him.

But no more.

"Honey," she said, putting an arm around him, "we have to move away."

She felt him flinch. He was so little to already understand what that meant.

He stared down at his knees. "Why?" His voice sounded whispery.

Because I can't stand being around Finn, loving him, not able to have him. Because I can't stand to see you get your heart broken over and over.

"We need to find a place where we can live full-time," she said. "This job was just for the summer."

"It's still the summer," he said in a very small voice.

"I know."

Was she doing the right thing? There was no question that tearing Leo out of this life would be hard on him. Staying would be hard, too. She was just trying to find the thing that would be the least painful for him. The way he had been getting attached to Finn, the constant rejection was hurting him. He needed to be around men who wouldn't reject him.

And Finn. The conversation she'd had with Penny had cinched her decision. "Don't judge him too harshly," Penny had said. "You and Leo remind him of his losses." She'd hesitated, then added, "His son was just Leo's age."

Penny's words had shaken her, put everything she knew about Finn into a different perspective. Even though she was furious at him for rejecting her and Leo, the deep shadows under his eyes spoke to her, tugged at her heartstrings.

If she and Leo caused Finn pain, it wasn't right for him to have to keep avoiding them. He had been here first. It was his place. He was the veteran. He was the one with the real skills.

"We're going to find another good place," she said to Leo.

"But I like this place," he said. "I like my friends."

"I know you do. You've gotten so good at making friends. You'll be able to make other ones." She tried to force confidence into her voice.

This was killing her.

He shrugged away from her and slid down to the floor. He lay down next to Shoney, who, as usual, was at their feet. The shaggy black dog rolled back into Leo, exposing her belly for a rub. "Shoney doesn't want to move." Leo rubbed the dog's belly and nuzzled her neck.

This was the worst part. "Shoney can't come."

"What do you mean?" Leo stared up at her, his eyes huge. Beside him, Shoney seemed to stare reproachfully, too.

"We're going to be driving a long time, and we'll stay overnight at some places that don't allow dogs." Kayla wasn't sure where they were going, but she'd found a couple of promising job possibilities online. "Once we find a new place to live, we'll have a lot of settling in to do. It wouldn't be fair to Shoney to take her to a brand-new place and leave her alone a lot, even if we were allowed to have a dog wherever we end up."

Kayla made herself watch as Leo started to understand. His eyes filled, brimmed over. She slid down to sit on the floor beside him.

"No, Mom!" Leo wrapped his arms around the dog, who obligingly nuzzled back into her son. "Shoney needed a home and we gave her one. We can't put her back in the kennel."

Kayla cleared her throat and swallowed hard. "We're going to take Shoney to Long John and Willie to look after."

"But Mr. Finn said they can't have another dog. He said it would be too much for them."

"Willie can keep her for a little while. Maybe after we get settled, we can get her back."

Leo buried his face in Shoney's fur. "We'll *never* get her back."

Kayla couldn't even make herself argue, because she knew it was probably true. And how sad that a little boy would have that realistic of an outlook, that he wouldn't be able to be comforted by kind platitudes.

She was kicking herself for letting them settle in this much. Why had she agreed to take Shoney? Of course Leo had gotten attached to her; they both had. But she should have thought ahead enough to know the job wasn't permanent.

To know things probably wouldn't work out, with the job or with Finn.

"I can help more." Leo sat up. "I can take her for more walks. I can feed her and clean up after her. You won't even know she's with us."

Kayla's heart felt like someone was squeezing it, twisting, wringing. She shook her head. "You've been the best helper. But we still can't take her."

Leo buried his head in the dog's side and wailed.

Best to do this fast now. She stood and knelt beside him, rubbing circles on his back. "Do you want to come with me? Help me bring Shoney's stuff up to Willie's place?"

"No! No! I won't go!" He flung his arm to get her away from him, catching her cheekbone with his little fist. Pain spiraled out from the spot. That would be a bruise.

Leo's upset escalated almost instantly into a full-fledged tantrum, and she couldn't blame him. She felt like lying right down on the floor and kicking and screaming alongside him.

But she was the grown-up. Like a robot, she found her phone and called Penny over Leo's screams and sobs. "Can you come up and look after Leo for half an hour?"

"You're really going through with this."

"I have to, Penny."

Kayla loved the older woman for not arguing with her, for just saying, "I'm on my way."

By the time Penny arrived ten minutes later, Kayla had gathered all Shoney's things in a big box. Leo's crying had settled down into brokenhearted sobs, and he wouldn't let Kayla touch or comfort him. He just hung on to Shoney, who, bless her, allowed what amounted to pretty rough treatment without so much as a growl or nip.

"Have you tried to talk to him?" Penny asked, pulling Kayla into the kitchen area, where Leo couldn't hear them.

"He's too upset. He just keeps crying."

"I mean Finn," Penny said. "He's going around looking like someone shot his best friend. If the two of you could hash it all out, you might have a chance."

Kayla hated thinking of Finn being miserable. But he'd get over it, probably just as soon as she and Leo left the area. She shook her head. "The surprise was that he started to act like he liked me," she said. "He's an amazing man. He could have any woman he wanted."

Penny dipped her chin and gave Kayla a pointed

stare. "Doesn't seem like he wants just any woman. What if he wants you?"

"He doesn't. He told me." Kayla shook her head. "And anyway, that just doesn't happen for me."

"Kayla. You've got to work on—"

Kayla held up a hand. "I know. I'm a good person. Working here, getting away from…" She waved a hand in the general direction of the east. "From what was going on back in Arkansas, it's done so much for me. I appreciate your giving me a chance. I know you're the one who talked him into it in the first place."

"Do you know what happened with his wife and child?"

Kayla shook her head. "I don't need to know all that." She was curious, but knowing more details about Finn was likely to just add to her misery.

"You're making a mistake."

"Look, I've just got to take Shoney down to Willie's place before Leo and I both fall apart." She turned away from Penny, clenched her teeth together and walked over to Leo. "Come on, buddy. Let go of Shoney."

"No, Mommy. Please." He looked up at her, his face swollen and red. "Please."

She pressed her lips together to hold back the sobs and wrapped Leo in a hug. This time, his need for comfort overcame his anger and he collapsed into her arms, sobbing. They stayed that way for a couple of minutes. Shoney whined beside them and Kayla cried a little, too.

Be strong for him.

She drew in a gasping breath, then another. "Shoney

will be okay. She'll miss us, but she'll be okay." She stood, staggering under Leo's weight as he clung to her.

Penny came over and reached out. "C'mere, buddy. We've got to let Mom go for a little bit."

Blinking hard against the tears, trying to breathe, Kayla took Shoney's leash off the hook by the door and attached it to the dog's collar. True to form, Shoney jumped and barked and tugged. She loved her walks.

Penny turned away, holding Leo tight. And Kayla walked an eager Shoney out the door.

At the bottom of Willie's porch steps, she knelt down and wrapped her arms around the shaggy black dog. "You've been a good dog," she said, rubbing Shoney's ears and the spots where her collar scratched her neck. Shoney collapsed down on her back, ecstatic with the attention, and Kayla tried to put all the love she felt into this last little bit of doggy affection.

The door of Willie's house opened and he came out onto the porch, backlit by the light from inside. Shoney sensed Willie's presence and jumped up, always ready for the next adventure.

Willie came down, rubbed the dog's head, and then picked up the box of Shoney's belongings and carried them up the steps.

Kayla buried her face in Shoney's coat, so soft and silky.

Shoney couldn't see, and she couldn't hear very well, but she made up for that in an ability to sense emotions. She licked Kayla's face and pressed closer into her arms.

Get it over with.

She picked up the dog, carried her up the porch

steps and set her down, handing the end of her leash to Willie. "Thank you," she whispered.

Willie nodded, his weathered face kind. "I'll take care of her. She'll be all right."

Kayla nodded, turned and walked toward her cabin, her eyes almost too blurred to see. She couldn't go back and help Leo when she was a wreck herself. She stopped in the cool night air and drew in big breaths, trying to pull herself together.

Down at the main house, she saw a few lights. Penny had come in a hurry, leaving the place lit up.

And there was a single light on in Finn's place. The front room. She pictured him there in his recliner, reading. He liked old Westerns and Western history books. Rarely watched TV. They had that in common.

So, yeah, he was probably reading.

But she'd never know what.

The thought of that—that she'd never get to tell him a silly little thing like that she'd finished the Louis L'Amour book he'd lent her—made her shoulders cave in. The loss in her stomach and chest hurt too much. She wrapped her arms around herself.

She'd thought since they had all those weird things in common that they might have something. She'd imagined sharing books and listening to country music together, on into the future.

But it wasn't only about that.

It was about the caring in his eyes. The respect she had for him as a man. The way they both worked hard at life, and tried to overcome past challenges with an upbeat attitude.

In the end, they *hadn't* overcome. She shouldn't be

surprised, but she was. Like a fool, she'd gotten her hopes up.

She looked up at the stars and tried to pray, but God seemed as distant as they were.

She drew in a deep breath and let it out slowly. Then another. Good—she was steadier. She turned and marched toward her cabin.

Through the screen door, she heard Leo sobbing. Her heart gave another great twist.

"I don't know if I can do this, Father," she said to the cold, glittering stars.

But she had to. No choice, when you were a mom. She squared her shoulders and headed into the cabin.

Chapter 10

The men's Bible study, which consisted of a circle of nine or ten men at Willie's house, was breaking up. Men stood, talked, helped Willie to clear away the refreshments he and Long John had made.

It was pretty obvious to Finn that Willie hadn't needed any extra help tonight. Calling Finn and saying he did had been a ruse, probably done in cahoots with the pastor.

Finn didn't really mind. Because one, he had nothing else to do; and two, he'd gotten thought-provoking ideas out of it.

Something bumped against his leg, and he looked down and saw Shoney. A bad feeling came over him. "What's she doing here?" he asked Willie.

"Kayla's leaving tomorrow, and she felt like she couldn't take Shoney along. She doesn't know where they'll land, what kind of place they'll live in or where they might have to stop along the way." He paused. "I put Rockette back in the kennel for now, but I can't leave her there."

That made him sigh, and he knelt and rubbed Shoney's sides, causing her to pant and smile.

She was okay now, with Willie. She was a resilient dog. But going back into the kennel, with her disabilities, wouldn't be a good thing.

And what must it have been like for Kayla and Leo to let Shoney go? They'd gotten so attached. Her blindness and deafness hadn't been any kind of barrier to them; they'd accepted her as she was, and they loved her.

It must have just about killed them to leave Shoney behind. The thought of it put a lump in Finn's throat.

The father of the boy who'd nearly hit their car came over and clapped Finn on the shoulder. "Glad to see you here tonight, because I wanted to thank you again," he said. "Without your driving chops, that accident could have gone a lot worse. If we had to collide with someone, I'm glad it was you."

Finn clenched his teeth to keep himself from snarling at the man. Finn wasn't glad it had been him, because it had broken him apart from Kayla and Leo.

But that was a good thing, right? Because it kept them safe. Safe from the unsafe Finn.

Who this man was saying was actually extra safe. That didn't compute at all.

"My son, man, he's still beating himself up about it," the man continued, oblivious to Finn's inner turmoil. "I wish he'd been here tonight to hear what the pastor had to say. We're none of us in control, not really, are we? Once something's past, you can't keep beating yourself up for it, I told him. You've got to move on."

"Right," he said as the man moved on to talk with someone else.

All the words he'd said swarmed in Finn's head and he didn't know how to process them.

We're none of us in control.

But he wanted to be in control. Wanted to be able to protect anyone on his watch.

He was the man of the family. He was supposed to be able to protect women and children. Back in the Middle East, his was one of the few units that hadn't had a failure in that regard. He hadn't killed any civilians, and neither had any of his men.

He supposed he'd come back cocky, thinking he was superhuman.

The punishment for that arrogance had come real fast.

He folded up the extra chairs and stacked them on the porch to carry down to the main house, then went back inside to see if Willie and Long John needed anything else.

They didn't, of course; they were fine. "Glad you could come," Long John said. "Mighty sad about that gal and her boy leaving us. Sure you can't talk 'em into staying?"

Long John's voice sounded plaintive, and Finn realized that these two old men had grown attached to Kayla and Leo, too. She'd listened to their stories, laughed at their jokes and appreciated their efforts to father her. And Leo had become a grandson to both of them.

"Sure am going to miss them," Willie said.

Everyone liked Kayla and Leo. No one wanted them to leave.

An idea of stopping at her place started to grow in the back of his head. She wasn't likely to forgive him for being so mean to her and Leo, but at least he could explain. Apologize. Pave the way for her to be able to come back for a visit, at least, see the old guys and Penny.

He hoisted the chairs to his shoulder, said good-bye to the last couple of men who were coming out of the cabin.

"Want me to drive those down the hill?" Bowie Briscol asked. "That's what I usually do when we meet here. No need for you to kill yourself hauling them."

Finn started to refuse and then thought, *Why not?* Obviously, Willie and Long John had manufactured the excuse to get him to come, but they'd had a good thought in doing so. They were doing their best to take care of him.

That was what Redemption Ranch was all about. People taking care of each other. And, he realized, he wanted Kayla and Leo to have the chance to be taken care of a little bit, too.

He couldn't repair the fragile thing he and Kayla had started to build, but could he maybe get her to agree to stay on? It had to be safer for her, better for Leo. They needed security and stability. Redemption Ranch could provide that.

He helped load the chairs into the back of Bowie's pickup, waved off the offer of a ride for himself and then strode toward Kayla's cabin, feeling more energized than he had since their falling-out.

There was a car outside Kayla's cabin. Not her old beater, but a late-model, city-style sedan.

Finn stopped and took a few steps back. Under veil of twilight, he watched as a tall, broad-shouldered man in a suit walked up to the door, opened it and went inside.

Heat rushed up Finn's neck. She'd gotten together with another guy this quickly? He'd been having all these *feelings* for her, and she was basically cheating on him?

Like Deirdre?

And with some suit in a fancy car, who probably had enough money to give her the life of luxury she didn't need, but probably wouldn't mind having?

His fists clenched and he hit the road to his place, making it home in record time.

When he got home, he went in the bedroom closet and started digging through boxes, frantic as a loon. He knew what he wanted to find and why.

It was a box of photographs of the years with Deirdre and, later, Derek. He'd hidden them away because it hurt too much to look at them, but he needed to now. Needed to remind himself what it felt like to live with a cheater. To remind himself that women couldn't be trusted.

He pulled out the wedding album, flipped through it and stuffed it back in the box. When those pictures were taken, they'd been happy, of course. Deirdre had been faithful to him, before the wedding and at least through the first year.

It was when he'd gone to the Middle East that she'd changed. He could track it in the pictures she'd sent, that he'd pasted up around his bunk like a fool, showed off to the other guys. She'd lost weight and done up her hair fancy, started wearing high heels.

She'd looked great.

Only when he'd come back had he realized she wasn't doing it for him—not for him alone, anyway.

They'd fought, separated, almost broken up, but then she'd gotten pregnant. It had infuriated her that he'd insisted on a paternity test, but given how much she was running around, it had only made sense to him. When Derek had turned out to be his baby for sure, he'd thought they could mend things between them.

And they had, for a while. The first couple of years of parenthood had been hard, but happy. But when Derek had entered his terrible twos, Deirdre had had her own rebellion.

She'd had issues, obviously. And Finn, young and immature and haughty, hadn't dealt with them well.

He shoved the photos back in the box and leaned against the bed, straightening out his leg, flexing it. The idea that he'd fallen for another cheater…

But even as he had the thought, he was comparing what he'd seen with the reality he knew.

Kayla wasn't the type who'd go into town and pick up some new guy in a bar, just because she'd had a fight with Finn. She just wasn't. And no, he and Kayla hadn't had a relationship, not really, but they'd had the beginnings of one. She'd felt it. She'd said it herself: *we have something here.*

And a woman like Kayla, feeling like that, wouldn't go looking for love somewhere else—not so soon, at least.

There had to be another explanation. A friend,

cousin, brother. It would make sense if she'd called someone to help her out, and he should be glad she had a little male protection.

He didn't *feel* glad, but he knew he should.

As a matter of fact, he should call his detective friend and tell him there wasn't anything more to search for. Whatever secrets hid in her past, he didn't need to know them. Because through all that had happened, he'd actually learned to trust Kayla.

That was some kind of progress, at least.

He walked outside for some air, scrolling through his contacts to make the call, when the familiar, rattly sound of Kayla's car came along the road. It made him smile. He was always glad to hear it, glad she and Leo and that beater of a car had made it back to the ranch in one piece.

No sooner had he thought it than worry tugged at him. When she left the ranch, where would she go? Who would be there to notice she'd made it safely home? To worry if she hadn't?

He'd give her a call later, see if they could talk a little. In preparation for that, he lifted his hand in a wave.

She stared back but didn't wave in response. Her face was set, rigid. She gunned the bad motor and continued up the hill.

Well. Maybe talking to Kayla wouldn't quickly mend the broken bridges between them.

But at least he could call off his watchdog.

He found his friend's name and clicked the number.

Kayla drove the rest of the way up the dirt road that led to her cabin, confused. Why had Finn waved?

She was *not* going to get excited because the man had waved.

Leo, depressed about it being his last day of camp and about Shoney, had finally fallen asleep in the back seat. Fortunately, he hadn't seen Finn's semi-friendly expression. No use getting his hopes up again.

No use getting hers up, either.

Today had been her last day of work, too, and that had been hard; saying goodbye to all the dogs, working alongside Penny because Finn was AWOL.

Her heart was shredded and she had a million things to do and he *waved*?

She glanced back at Leo, his face sweet and relaxed in sleep as it hadn't been since she'd let him know they were leaving. The day-camp group had given him a little goodbye party today, which was sweet. But not surprising. That was the way Esperanza Springs was.

She pulled up to the cabin and stopped the car. When she leaned into the back seat and tried to pull the still-sleeping Leo out, she could barely manage it. Asleep, he seemed to weigh a ton.

It had been so great when Finn had carried him to bed.

She shifted, getting her feet under her, getting him adjusted on her shoulder. She wouldn't have Finn helping her anymore. And guess what: she didn't need him. Her muscles were far stronger now than they'd been six weeks before, when she'd started at Redemption Ranch. And it wasn't only her muscles that were stronger. So was her mind and her confidence.

She shouldered open the front door. It was good to be home. Despite all the turmoil, she'd sleep well tonight.

She took another step and froze, just inches inside.

Why had the door been partly open? She always locked the door when she left.

Even as she reviewed the moments when she'd left the house, she stepped back. One step. Two.

The door swung the rest of the way open. And there, inside, stood Mitch.

She jerked back and Leo stirred, so she forced her body into stillness. How had Mitch found her? How had he gotten into her house? Where was his car? Sweat broke out on her face and back. "What are you doing here?" she asked around a stone of terror that seemed to have lodged in her throat. "Where's your car? How did you find us?"

"I pulled the car around back." He leaned against the door frame and crossed his arms, and his presence in this place felt like a violation. "Oh, and by the way, that was a real cute photo of my son on one of the Eighty-Second sites."

Kayla sucked in a breath. Had *Finn* posted a picture? Surely not, but...

"Nice how the name of the town was right there in the picture," Mitch said, his voice and stance casual, his eyes anything but. "Esperanza Springs Community Days. What kind of a town did you bring him to? It's not even American!"

"The Fourth of July." Kayla closed her eyes, just for a second. That soldier Leo had mistaken for Mitch. Kayla had gotten the man's wife to delete the photos with Leo, but several other people had been around. One of them must have taken a photo and posted it. Probably thinking a closed group website was safe.

No time to wonder why Mitch had been browsing through a random Eighty-Second site. No time to wish she'd been more diligent about keeping cameras away from Leo.

They'd been found. Now she had to find a way to keep her son safe, against all odds.

Seeing Mitch brought back the last time, his big boots kicking her as she'd lain on the floor, trying to breathe, trying not to wake up Leo, gauging the distance to the door, escape, safety even as she'd known she could never leave her son in the house alone with his father, not even for a minute.

She backed to the edge of the porch. The worst thing she could do would be to go inside with him. Out here, with the stars starting to twinkle overhead and the cool, piney breeze from the mountains, she had freedom and a chance.

"Get in here." It wasn't a suggestion, but an order. "Want to talk to you."

Despite his casual posture, his hands were fists and his eyes burned beneath a furrowed forehead. If she ran for it, holding Leo, she'd only make it a few steps before Mitch caught them. Leo would wake up and be afraid.

If Mitch had to fight her and drag her inside, his rage would boil over. If she went inside as he'd asked, it might placate him for a moment.

She nodded and walked through the door and tried not to feel doomed when he closed it behind her. Despair and hopelessness wouldn't save her son. "Let me put Leo down."

Maybe Leo wouldn't have to see this and get traumatized again. Maybe she could talk Mitch down, make promises of seeing him tomorrow, get him to leave tonight. And then she could call Penny and Finn and the pastor and anyone else she could think of to get her out of this bind, because, yeah, she was independent, but she had people to help her now. She wasn't alone.

Mitch stood in front of her, blocking her way, and her stomach twisted. She'd forgotten how big he was. He could knock her out with one blow from his hamlike hand.

She knew. Knew, because he'd done it.

She straightened her spine. "Let me pass. I want to put him down so I can focus on you." *And get you out of here.*

His eyebrows drew together and he looked at her, suspicious, assessing. "Fine." He stepped to the side, not far. She had to walk within a couple of inches, close enough to smell his sweat. Her stomach heaved.

Keep it together. She'd thought to put Leo on his bed in the sleeping loft, but then he'd be a sitting duck, trapped. She didn't want him that far away from her. So she grabbed a blanket off the back of the couch, wrapped it around him and took him into the bathroom. She slid Leo onto the floor and put a towel under his head for a pillow. Thankfully he was a good sleeper.

She turned on the bathroom light, in case he woke up and was scared. *Please, God, whatever happens to me, protect him.*

Mitch stood in the doorway, emanating hostility she could feel like radiant heat. She turned, patting for her cell phone. Good—it was in her back pocket. She'd be able to get to it if he turned his back.

Which, from the hawk-like way he was watching her, didn't seem all that likely.

She walked right up to where he stood in the doorway, knowing that to show weakness would be fatal. "Come sit down," she said, feigning confidence and hospitality.

When he moved out of her way, she closed the bathroom door behind her. Anything to increase the chances that Leo would sleep through this, that he wouldn't get set back from all the progress he'd made.

"Would you like something to drink?" *Would you like to turn your back long enough for me to call for help?*

"Get me a beer," he ordered.

"Don't have any. Soda?"

He snorted in obvious disgust. "Fine." But he followed her to the refrigerator and stood too close, so she dispensed with the idea of a glass and handed him the can. Grabbed one for herself, too. It might come in handy. Lemon-lime carbonated beverage, square in the face, could sting, and a can could work as a missile, too.

She gestured him toward the sitting area and he plopped down on the couch. "Come sit by me."

Um, no. "I'll sit over here," she said, keeping her voice level as she felt for the stand-alone chair and sat down.

"Why are you acting so cold?" He banged his soda down on the end table.

Was he kidding? Hot anger surged inside her, washing away her fear. "You're an uninvited guest. You broke into my cabin. You expect me to roll out the red carpet?" And then she bit her lip. She had to stay calm in order to keep Mitch calm. It was tempting to scream out all the rage she felt at him, but she had to be wise as a serpent here, pretend a gentleness she didn't feel.

"You sure it's not to do with the big guy?"

"What big guy?" she asked, although she knew he must mean Finn.

How did he know about Finn?

"The one that lives right down the road and spends a lot of time with you," he said. "Finn Gallagher."

The surprise must have shown on her face, because he laughed, a high, nasty sound. "Oh, I've been watching you for days now. I know exactly what you've been doing."

She couldn't restrain a shudder. "What do you want with us?"

"You're my wife." His voice rose. "And he's my son. You left me. I have every right to bring you home."

She couldn't let this escalate. Something she'd read in a publication about dealing with aggressive dogs flashed into her mind. She relaxed her muscles and lowered her voice. "Mitch. I'm not your wife. We're divorced."

He glared. Apparently, what worked on dogs wasn't going to work on Mitch. And then his head tilted to one side as he shook it back and forth, and the whites of his eyes showed, and everything inside Kayla froze.

Mitch didn't look stable or sane. He barely looked human.

Every other time he'd been rough with her, he'd seemed angry—enraged, even—but he'd had his senses and he'd known exactly what he was doing.

His expression now made it seem like he'd lost it.

He stood and walked toward her, hands out. "I want you back."

"No, Mitch. Don't touch me."

He kept coming.

She jumped up and away from him and pointed at the door. "Go on. Get out of here or I'll call the police."

He seemed to get bigger, throwing back his head and shoulders and breathing hard. Heavy and threatening, he came at her.

She spun away. "I mean it. I have no problem calling 911."

"What're you going to call with, this?" He reached for the cell phone in her back pocket. She jerked away from his hand and heard her pocket rip.

He had the phone.

Miserable, hopeless thoughts from the past tried to push in: *You deserve whatever he does to you. This is the only kind of man who'll like you. No way can you escape him.*

But she was stronger now. Wasn't she? She *didn't* deserve Mitch's abuse. She wasn't alone; she had friends. She'd even, for a little while, drawn the attention of a good man.

Finn respected her. Finn thought she was a good mother. A good person.

So did Long John and Willie and Penny.

She had to try to get Leo and run. Or maybe she could barricade them in the bathroom. She made a break for it, dodging Mitch, but he grabbed her arm and pulled it, hard. Pain ricocheted from her wrist to her shoulder, and she couldn't restrain a cry.

He took a pair of handcuffs—*handcuffs?*—out of his suit jacket and clicked one side to her wrist, the other to one of the wooden kitchen chairs, forcing her to sit. "Just in case you get any ideas," he said with a sadistic grin.

She tugged, but the cuffs held. And he'd cuffed the arm he'd hurt, so every effort shot pain from her wrist to her shoulder.

"Mommy?" The plaintive voice from the bathroom doorway made them both freeze. "Daddy!" There was an undertone of happiness there, but fear, too.

"Get back in the bathroom," Mitch snarled.

"But…"

"Go!"

Leo edged, instead, toward Kayla. She could see the sweat beaded on his upper lip, the vertical lines between his eyebrows, the shiny tears in his eyes.

"It's okay, honey," she said, trying to put reassurance into her voice and eyes, her free arm reaching for him without her being able to stop it. "It's going to be okay."

Leo took a step toward her and Mitch stepped between. "You pay attention to me, not her!"

He grabbed Leo's shoulder and walked him back into the bathroom, none too gently. Leo started to cry.

There was a swatting sound, and Leo cried harder.

She exploded out of her chair and headed toward the bathroom, dragging the chair behind her.

Mitch emerged, slamming the bathroom door behind him. From the other side, Leo sobbed.

"Stop right there!" Mitch dug in a black case against the wall and turned toward her with an automatic rifle in one hand and a hunting knife in the other.

Kayla froze, then sank back onto the chair. He'd truly gone over the edge. He'd always liked weapons, but he'd restricted their use to shooting ranges or country roads. He'd never pointed one at her, and he wasn't doing that now, but the threat was palpable. Not only to her, but to Leo, because a gun like that could make a wooden door into splinters in a matter of seconds.

A stray thought broke through her terror: not one of the vets she'd met at this ranch—Long John, Willie or Finn—would flaunt weapons so casually. Mitch wasn't a typical vet.

She looked around desperately, wondering how to escape or what to do, aware that if she made a wrong move, it might be her last.

On the counter was the big travel coffee mug Finn had given her when he'd noticed her rinsing and reusing a Styrofoam cup. He was a man of few words, but his actions said it all. He paid attention and tried to make her life a little easier, a little better.

She could trust him because of how he'd treated her. She should have told Finn the truth. Airborne or not, Finn would never have betrayed her to someone like her ex.

Mitch came closer and again she smelled his perspiration, tense and sour. He loomed over her. "You left me and took my son. You can't get away with that. You're going to pay."

He didn't care about Leo, had never been even an okay father, but she didn't dare to say it, not with him this volatile. She pressed her lips together.

Why had she made such a stupid mistake? Maybe if she'd been honest and up front with Finn, he wouldn't have dumped her.

Leo's cries were louder now, breaking her heart.

"Let me go to him," she pleaded. "Just let me talk to him a minute."

Mitch turned toward the bathroom. "Shut up!" he thundered.

But Leo's crying only got louder.

A desperate plan formed in her head, and without a moment's hesitation, she put it into action. "Give him my phone," she said. "He likes to play games on it. He'll quiet right down." And maybe, God willing, he'd use his five-year-old technology skills to call for help. She'd taught him how to use the phone to call 911, and he knew how to call Penny, too.

Mitch hesitated. Leo's wails broke her heart, but they obviously grated on Mitch. He pulled her phone out of his pocket and headed toward the bathroom.

Please, God.

He hesitated at the door and looked back. She tried not to betray anything on her face.

"You're trying to get him to call for help!" He kicked the bathroom door. "You shut up in there, kid, or I'll hurt Mommy."

Leo's cries got quieter. From his gulps and nose-blowing, it was obvious he was trying to stop.

Poor kid. If they could get out of this alive…

Mitch came back over and squatted in front of her. "Suppose you tell me what you thought you were going to gain from leaving Arkansas." He glared at her. "Go on—talk. This ought to be good."

Discouragement pressed down on Kayla.

"Talk!" he yelled, shaking the leg of the chair so that she nearly fell off.

From somewhere inside her, outrage formed and grew. There had been a time when she'd thought she deserved bad treatment, that it was the best she was going to get, but she knew differently now. "I left because I wanted a fresh start for me and Leo," she said, chin up, glaring at him. "I refuse to live a life hiding from you and terrorized by you."

Mitch looked...startled? Was that worry on his face? She'd never stood up to him before.

"You unlock these handcuffs and go back where you came from," she ordered, sweat dripping down her back.

He raised a hand. He was going to punch her.

"Don't. You. Dare." She put every bit of courage and confidence she had into the words.

Mitch stepped back and looked around. "What was that?"

"What?" Was he seriously going to pretend he'd heard something to avoid a confrontation with her? Hope swelled. "You didn't hear anything. Unlock these cuffs!"

"I heard something." He lowered his weapon and moved to the window of the cabin like a cop in a TV movie. A bad movie.

If she could just get to her phone, which he'd left sitting on the chair...

She tried to scoot, quietly, while he leaped around the room, pointing his weapon into every corner. She got within a yard of the phone. If she could move a few inches closer...

"Aha!" he yelled as he leveled the rifle at her.

And Kayla realized two things.

No matter how weak Mitch ultimately turned out to be, he was holding a deadly weapon.

And he *really* didn't act a bit like the veterans she'd

gotten to know over the past two months. "Were you ever even in the Eighty-Second Airborne?" she blurted out before she could think better of it.

He roared something indistinguishable and came at her.

Chapter 11

Finn had been wrestling with God, and God was winning.

Guilt about his past mistakes with his wife, he was realizing, had made him into a worse person. Maybe that was why God forgave mistakes. Because to spend time punishing yourself for all your past sins meant you weren't much good to anybody in the present moment.

Further, he realized that he did want to be involved with people. He wanted to be a husband and father again and do it right this time.

He'd never entirely get over what had happened with Deirdre and Derek. He'd always wonder whether he might have been able to save their lives if only his reflexes had been faster, his speed lower, his focus more intent.

But he wanted to go on living. And that had a lot to do with Kayla and Leo.

His phone buzzed, and he was relieved to escape his own thoughts. He clicked onto the call. "About time you called me back," he said to his friend.

"I have very little to report," Raakib said. "Believe me, my friend, I tried, but I haven't found anything against Kayla. From all accounts, though, her ex-husband, Mitch, is bad news. Quite volatile."

It was nothing more than what he'd expected. He knew Kayla was good. Even without someone vouching for her, he knew it.

Crunching gravel outside the window marked Penny's arrival at her place. Unlike Kayla's car, Penny's had a quiet, well-maintained sound.

Kayla's car. Worry edged into his awareness.

When Finn had been getting jealous of the man in the suit, Kayla hadn't even been in her cabin. So what was the guy doing there? "What does her ex look like?" he asked Raakib.

"Sharp dresser," Raakib said. "Tall, about six-two. Large, because apparently he's obsessed with lifting weights. Though not as large as—"

"Gotta go," Finn said. "I think he's here."

He clicked off the call and grabbed his gun and ran outside. Penny was getting out of her car with a load of groceries.

"Drive me up to Kayla's," he barked. "I think her ex might be here."

Penny's face hardened. She dropped the bags and got back into the car. Finn got into the passenger side, and she gunned the gas the moment he was in.

The car he'd seen before was gone. But Kayla's was there.

So maybe it had just been a friend of hers, who'd visited and left, and Finn would be making an idiot of himself. But he wasn't going to take that risk. Not with Kayla and Leo.

"Whoa—wait," Penny said as she pulled in beside Kayla. "Look at that."

Finn looked in the direction she was pointing. Willie was coming up the road at a pace that was almost a run. Behind him, Long John limped as fast as Finn had ever seen him go, Leo beside him, holding his hand.

It would have looked comical, except for the intent, angry, scared expressions on all three faces.

And the fact that both Long John and Willie had weapons at the ready.

Finn had to salute their courage, but mostly, he had to get to Kayla before they did. "Keep them back," he said to Penny and ran to the cabin door.

Finn walked in on chaos. The man in the suit was on the ground, on top of Kayla. But Kayla was scrambling out from under him. A chair fell and knocked into the man—Kayla almost seemed to be jerking the chair around—and she punctuated that blow with a kick in the man's face.

She might even be winning the fight, but Finn couldn't wait for that to happen, especially with the automatic weapon on the floor near the man.

The man was going for it.

No.

No way. Finn moved faster than he ever had in his

life, leaping onto the man just as his arm reached for the weapon.

The man was strong, burly. He landed a good punch on Finn's face.

"Get the weapon," Finn yelled, and Kayla rolled and stretched her arm and grabbed it.

The door banged open just as Finn started to get the jerk under control. "Sorry," Penny called, "I couldn't hold them back. Leo, wait!"

"Mom!" Leo ran to Kayla.

Finn got the guy into a full nelson. He saw that Penny had secured the gun. Kayla was laughing and crying, one arm wrapped around Leo. "How did you get out?"

Leo puffed out his chest and grinned.

"Kid climbed out the bathroom window," Willie said, shaking his head in obvious admiration. "Came running down and got us."

Finn's prisoner—who had to be Mitch, Kayla's ex—started to struggle.

"I could use a hand here," Finn said, breathing hard. "We need to tie him up."

"I've got some handcuffs," Kayla called, "if you can take them off me and get them onto him."

Only then did Finn realize that Kayla had been fighting this fight while handcuffed to a wooden chair.

Her hair was coming out of its braid, her face red and scratched, the sleeve of her shirt ripped. He had never seen anyone so beautiful.

"Key to the handcuffs," Penny barked at the man, who stopped struggling and actually looked a little cowed. He nodded toward his side pocket.

"I'd get it," Penny said, "but I don't think I can stand to touch him."

Willie extracted the key from the man's pocket, none too gently. Penny freed Kayla and handed the key back to Willie and Long John along with the handcuffs. A moment later Mitch was sitting in the chair, his hands cuffed behind him.

"Those military pins you're wearing," Long John said. "What unit were you in?"

"Eighty-Second Airborne," he mumbled.

Finn's head jerked around at that. "Seriously? Dates of service?" This guy did *not* seem like any paratrooper Finn had ever met. More like one of the wannabes that sometimes hung around veterans' events acting way too aggressive and boastful. "I think we're gonna check on that."

"What's your full name?" Long John, who prided himself on keeping up with the latest technology, had his phone out and was clicking on it.

"It's Mitchell Raymond White," Kayla said.

"Friend in veterans affairs owes me a favor," Willie said. "Think I'll give him a call."

"Where were you stationed?" Finn asked. "And I didn't hear you say your dates of service."

Mitch looked away. "I was on special assignment."

Right. Finn looked over at Kayla and Leo. Kayla met his eyes, her own wide and concerned. But Leo was talking excitedly, explaining how he had climbed out the bathroom window.

Good. The boy wasn't listening. He didn't need to learn about his father's deception this way.

Willie clicked off his phone. "They never heard of him."

"He's not in this record, either," Long John said, scrolling through his phone's screen.

Finn glared at the lowlife cuffed in the chair. "Stolen valor is a pretty serious offense."

"Especially when you've been getting veterans benefits for years," Kayla said from the corner, her voice indignant.

Willie drew himself up to his full height—about five-five—and glowered at Mitch. "Between that crime and what you tried to do to this woman and child, young man, you're going to be behind bars for a good long time."

Penny fussed over Kayla while Willie called the police and Long John tended to some scratches Leo had gotten jumping out the bathroom window.

As for Finn, he sat off to the side, against the wall, his mind reeling.

Something terrible had almost happened, and together, they'd managed to stop it. Kayla and Leo were safe. And he made a decision: he wasn't going to waste another moment.

Whatever Kayla felt, he knew his own heart.

But when he turned and really studied her, he noticed she was holding her arm tight to her side. "Do we need an ambulance?" he asked Penny, who was kneeling beside Kayla, running her hand over her shoulder, arm and wrist.

"Not for me," Kayla answered promptly.

"Maybe a quick visit to the ER or the Urgent Care,"

Penny said. "I don't think your arm is broken, but it's definitely sprained. Here, let it loose."

As Penny held Kayla's arm straight to examine it more carefully, Leo watched with a little too much concern in his eyes. "Hey, Leo," Finn called softly, and the boy looked his way. "You did a real good job today."

A smile tugged at Leo's mouth. And then he ran and jumped into Finn's open arms.

Finn's heart swelled almost to bursting as he held the wiggly little boy, then put him down to hear, again, the story of how Leo had screwed up his courage and climbed out through the window to find help for his mom.

Leo was hungry for praise; well, Finn was glad to give it to him, because what he'd done had been more than praiseworthy.

Finn had a hungry heart, too, and talking to the little boy, commending his quick thinking and agility, seemed to fill it up a little.

He and Leo might be good for each other, he reflected. And as he distracted Leo from the distressing sight of his father being led away in handcuffs, as he talked about ways Leo could help his mom while her arm healed, he felt like he'd been given a second chance.

If only he could convince Kayla to take a chance with him.

A week later, Kayla strolled the midway of the county fair, with Leo holding her hand and Finn beside her.

She wondered what to do.

Rather than packing up the car and moving away, she and Leo had stayed around, at first to give evidence against Mitch, and then to let her arm heal a bit, and now…

Now it was decision time. Tomorrow would be the back-to-school information day. All the kids at Leo's camp were talking about it—the start of first grade was a big deal—and Leo wanted to know: Would he go to school here, or were they moving somewhere else?

She didn't know the answer.

They'd fallen back into their routine here. Leo had been attending camp. Kayla had helped with the dogs as best she could, given her wrenched arm. Shoney had come back, first for a visit, and then an overnight to sleep in Leo's bed, and now somehow she was back to living with them again, her old accepting, ecstatic self.

Finn had been friendly and helpful, but a little guarded. They hadn't really had the chance to talk in depth, because Leo, understandably, was sticking pretty close to Kayla's side.

Mitch had gone to jail, then gone before the judge, and then somehow managed to post bail. With no contacts in Colorado, and forbidden to see Kayla or Leo, he'd gotten permission from the court to go back to his job in Arkansas. Kayla suspected he would also try to destroy evidence of his fraudulent claims of military service, but the likelihood was that he'd be charged with a federal crime. That was because he'd received benefits and discounts he wasn't entitled to.

She still worried about him, and would until he was behind bars. But with Finn, Penny, Long John and Willie on high alert—and friends back in Arkansas reassuring her daily that Mitch was there, going about his routines—she found she was able to relax.

She wouldn't go back there, but she might move on. She liked mountain living, but there were plenty of places, especially here in the West, where she could have it.

The problem was, Finn wouldn't be there.

Penny had talked to her about taking on some additional duties as they worked to expand the ranch. They'd need cleaning and cooking help if they were to open the old bunkhouse.

Everything in Kayla longed to stay in this community where she'd made friends and felt valued, where Leo was happy and social, where the mountains loomed good-heartedly over the flat bowl of the valley, reminding her on a daily basis to look up to God.

But if staying meant watching Finn move on, take up with other women, become a distant friend, she didn't know if she could bear it.

Too much thinking. She squeezed Leo's hand and inhaled the fragrances of cotton candy and fry bread.

"Mom! There's Skye and Sunny!" Leo tugged at her hand. "Can I go see them, please?"

"I'll come with you," she said and then looked questioningly at Finn. "Want to come along?" They'd basically ended up together at the fair by accident, and she didn't want to assume he intended to stay with her and Leo.

But he smiled amiably. "Whatever you two want," he said and followed along.

That was how he'd been acting. Like he wanted to

do things with her and Leo; like he cared. But there was a slight distance. They hadn't talked about why he'd pushed her away before, and it kept a wall between them.

"Leo!" Skye called as they approached. "We're going to go do the pony rides. Can you come?" She clapped a hand over her mouth and looked up at her father. "Oops. I'm s'posed to ask first. Daddy, can Leo come with us?"

Carson fist-bumped her. "Good job remembering, kiddo. And of course Leo can come."

"Can I, Mom?"

Not can *we* go, but can *I* go. He was growing in independence and she was glad and sad all at the same time.

"I'll watch over him," Carson said. "It's run by folks in our church and it's supersafe."

"Sure," she said, and instantly the three children ran toward the other side of the fairgrounds, Carson jogging after them, calling for them to wait.

That left her and Finn, standing together. It felt awkward to Kayla, so she looked out across the valley. The sun was low in the sky, just starting to paint the tips of the mountains red. God's reminder that He lingered with them, even in the dark of night.

"Do you want to ride the Ferris wheel?" Finn asked abruptly. "Over there," he added, gesturing toward the little midway.

How did she respond to that? *Yes, I want to do that because it seems incredibly romantic*? *No, because I don't want to get closer right before we go away?*

"Scared?" he asked, his eyes twinkling down at her. "I'll hold your hand."

That sent a shiver through her. She wanted him to hold her hand, not just now but into the future. He was looking at her funny, and she almost wondered whether he was having the same thought.

But then, as they headed toward it, he kept looking at his watch. Was he bored? Eager to get back to the ranch?

"The line's kind of long," she said, giving him an out in case.

"That'll give us the chance to talk."

Oh. He wanted to talk. Kayla tried to ignore the tremor in her core.

As soon as they got in line, he turned away from the loud family group in front of them. "Why didn't you tell me about Mitch?" he asked quietly.

She looked up at him. "I asked myself the same question, when I thought he'd got us trapped for good. I... I should have. But Airborne Rangers are so loyal, and I'd bought into his story."

Finn's mouth twisted. "Beneath contempt. All of it."

"I know. I still can't believe he maintained that lie for so long. And I feel like a fool for buying into it."

"You had no way of knowing." He shook his head. "Those guys...they're good at concealing what they're doing. He'll pay for it. But, Kayla." He put his hands on her shoulders. "Even if he *had* been a military brother, I would never choose someone else over you."

Kayla's throat tightened and she felt the tears glitter as she looked up into Finn's eyes. He was being sweet; he was being kind.

But she couldn't quite trust his kindness. "Why'd you push me and Leo away, Finn? That really hurt."

He nodded, studying her face. "Do you have some time?"

A half smile tugged at the corner of her mouth. "The line's moving pretty slow." The group ahead of them was playing a guessing game now, Mom and Dad obviously trying to keep their young kids occupied. Behind them, a pair of teenagers stood twined together, clearly focused only on each other.

Finn drew in a deep, slow breath. "You know my family died in a car accident."

She nodded.

"Well, I… I was driving."

"Oh, Finn." She stared at his troubled eyes as the implications of that sank in.

No wonder he was so mired in it—tortured, even. How would you recover from something like that? She took his hands and squeezed them. "I'm so sorry. How awful that must've been."

He nodded. "I was officially exonerated, but…" He shook his head slowly, meeting her eyes briefly, then looking away. "I've lived ashamed for a long time."

His dark sadness, the way he drove himself, all of it made more sense now. Of course Finn would beat himself up, even over an accident that wasn't his fault. He was a protector to the core, and to not be able to protect his family, to have been driving when they were killed… Wow. She put an arm around his waist and squeezed, because she couldn't find anything sufficient to say.

"Next!" The attendant barked out the words.

Finn helped Kayla climb into the narrow-seated cart, and then turned back and spoke to the attendant in a low voice. The attendant looked at him, looked at Kayla and then shook his head.

Finn moved and reached for his wallet. She couldn't see what he was doing. Paying the attendant? They hadn't gotten tickets, but she'd thought rides came with the price of admission.

"Let's get a move on," somebody yelled from the line, the voice good-natured.

Finn climbed into the seat beside her and fastened the bar over them, carefully testing it for security.

"Were you giving that guy a hard time?" Kayla asked.

Color climbed Finn's neck. "You could say that."

As the Ferris wheel slowly filled up, and their car climbed incrementally higher, Kayla looked out over the fair, the town and the broad plain, sparkling with a few lights from far-flung homes and ranches. Her heart gave a painful squeeze.

She loved this place. She loved the land and the people and the discoveries she'd made here, the strength she'd found.

The trouble was, she loved Finn, too. And to stay here loving him… Well, that would be hard and painful. Not just for her, but for Leo, who had also come to care for the big, quiet soldier.

Most likely she *couldn't* stay, but that made her reckless. "Tell me about the accident," she said. "What happened?"

He took a breath and looked around as the Ferris

wheel jolted them to the next level. "You really want to know?"

Something told her that for him to tell it was important, was maybe a key to his healing. If she couldn't be with him, she could at least do that much for him. Be a true friend. She reached for his hand and squeezed it. "I want to know."

He looked down at their interlaced hands. "So I was driving, and we were having a fight. What it was about doesn't matter now."

She nodded, sensing that he needed to tell it his own way, at his own pace. The twilight, the small passenger car, the separation from the noise of the fair, made it seem as if they were alone in the world.

"She took Derek out of his car seat."

"While you were driving?" She stared at him. "What mother would do that?"

"She wanted to get out, wanted me to stop. But it wasn't safe, because there was no shoulder to the road. So I kept driving. I was yelling at her to buckle him in again, to fasten her own seat belt, but instead, she grabbed the steering wheel and jerked it."

"And that's what…" She looked at his square, set jaw, the way he stared unseeingly out across the plain, and knew he was reliving what must've been the worst moment of his life.

He cleared his throat. "We went straight into a semi-truck bobtail."

"And they were both killed." She said the last word steadily, because she sensed that it all needed to come out into the open.

"Instantly." He hesitated, then met her eyes. "I was buckled in. I came out of it with barely a scratch."

"Wow." She'd been holding his hand through the whole recitation, but now she brought her other hand around to grip it, to hold his hand in both of hers. "That must have been so, so awful."

"I wished I had died. So many times. What kind of a man lets his family be killed while he walks around healthy and whole?"

She hesitated, looking up at his face. Around them, the noise and lights seemed to dim. "I don't want to speak ill of someone I don't know, someone who's dead, but it does sound like she caused the accident."

He nodded. "That's what the police report concluded, and I know that in my head. In fact, I'm still angry at her for taking Derek out of his car seat. If he had been buckled in, most likely…" He looked away, his throat working.

"Yeah." She remembered how she'd felt when Mitch had upset Leo, how she'd worried that the hurting would become physical. That was really what had prompted her to leave. But to have a partner actually cause your child's death… Her own throat tightened, and she cleared it. "Nothing I can say can make that better, but I am so sorry."

"It doesn't make you hate me?" He sounded like he really thought she might.

"Of course not!" To see this big, experienced soldier look so insecure, so torn apart… All she could do was put both arms around him. Not as a romantic thing, but for comfort. Friend comfort. It was a short hug, and then she let him go so she could meet his eyes.

"If we were blamed for all the awful things that happened to us, nobody would escape unscathed. Look, I know I'm not to blame for being abused by Mitch. At the same time, I made a bad choice in marrying him. Maybe you made some bad choices, too." She reached up and ran a finger along his square jaw, feeling the roughness of his whiskers. "You're human, Finn. Just like everyone else."

He closed his eyes, nodded slowly and then looked at her. "I've started to make my peace with it."

"The men's Bible study?"

"That, and the pastor, and some thinking and reading I've been doing."

"I'm working on making my peace about Mitch, too." Finn would understand that. He would know that resolving such big issues in your past didn't happen all at once. It was a process, one that would never be fully completed, not in this world.

She'd barely noticed that the Ferris wheel had filled up and that they were moving fast now. But as they went over the top and sank down, her stomach dropped and quivered. She wasn't sure if it was the Ferris wheel or the company, but she squeezed Finn's hand and giggled when it happened again.

He put an arm around her. "You *are* scared," he said. "Chicken!"

"I'm not!" she said with mock indignation. "Look at this." She lifted her arms high in the air.

"Whoa!" He grasped her hands and put them back firmly on the bar in front of them. "Don't do that to me."

So she put her head on his shoulder as the ride continued, then slowed and finished. The cars jerked as people exited the Ferris wheel, but when it was their turn, the operator skipped past them.

"Hey, you missed us," she called back to him, but he didn't seem to be listening.

Oh, well. She didn't mind being here with Finn for a little longer. She looked up at him and noticed beads of sweat on his upper lip. Was *he* the one afraid of the Ferris wheel? Somehow, with his life experiences, she didn't think so.

Now they were back at the top of the Ferris wheel, and it creaked to a stop. She leaned over the edge and looked down. The whole wheel was empty except for them. "Hey," she yelled down. "You forgot us!"

"Kayla."

She jerked around to look at Finn, because there was something strange in his voice.

"Kayla," he said quietly as he took her hand, lifted it to his lips and kissed it. "Kayla, I'm no good at this, but I... I..."

She cocked her head to one side, staring at him. "What? Finn, what is it?"

"It's not a spot to get down on one knee, and anyway, I can't do that too well, not with my bad leg. But..." He reached into his pocket and pulled out a small box. Opened it and then looked into her eyes. "Kayla, I don't want you and Leo to leave. I want you to stay, and not just stay as a coworker. I know it's fast, and I know a lot has been happening in your and Leo's life, but..."

Kayla couldn't breathe.

"So I know it might take you a little time, but for

me, I'm more sure about this than I've ever been about anything in my life. I love you, Kayla. I want to marry you. I want to make a family with you and Leo. And if you say yes—even if you say you'll consider it—I promise to protect you and care for you for the rest of my life."

It was more words than she had heard from Finn, all at once, since she'd met him. Warmth, even a banked fire, shone in his eyes. He was holding her hands so gently.

She felt tongue-tied.

"At least look at the ring?"

"Oh!" She looked down and saw a simple square diamond on a white gold band. She reached out and touched it with one finger, and the sharp hardness of it made her realize that this wasn't a dream, that this was real. The most real thing she'd ever experienced, and the best.

And yes, she should wait and think and make sure. But no way. "Nothing would make me happier than to marry you. And Leo, well, I know he'd be completely thrilled to have you as a dad."

He clasped her to him and held her, and the swelling emotion in her chest made her dizzy. "I want to be a dad to him," he said. "But if he needs to stay in touch with Mitch, I understand that and I will help to make that happen."

Her heart melted at his words. She suspected that Finn could be jealous and possessive, but he was willing to work with Mitch to make things good for Leo. That was selflessness.

He touched her chin, and when she looked up at

him, his face was framed by stars. "Did you really say yes?"

She smiled. "Yes! Yes, I said yes!"

He let out a quiet exclamation and lowered his lips to hers.

As he kissed her with a restrained intensity that warmed her all the way to her toes, she felt like her shoulders were loosening, her chest was opening, and she was free. Free of that feeling of being unwanted. Free of having other people think she was a mistake.

He lifted his head and smiled at her. From the ground, she heard the sound of cheering.

"Do people know what you're doing?" Suddenly it all came together for her. "Did you plan this? Did you tell the attendant?"

A sheepish expression came onto his face. "I'm sorry, but I did have to get a few people involved. Carson knows. That's why he brought the twins by, to help get Leo out of the way."

From below, she heard a shout. "Mom! Did you say yes?"

"Leo knows?"

Finn rolled his eyes and shook his head. "He wasn't supposed to. But I guess Carson let it slip to the girls. That or the ride attendant or the jeweler spilled the news. It's a small town." Then he leaned over the edge of the cart and waved. "Hey, Leo. She said yes. That okay with you?"

Kayla might have been the only one who heard the uncertainty in his voice.

"Yes! Yay!" Leo cheered, and others were talking and laughing and cheering, too. The Ferris wheel slowly rotated their car to the ground and stopped, and there were all the people she cared about: Penny, and Long John and Willie, and Carson and the twins. And of course, Leo. When the attendant opened the bar, Leo ran to them. She opened her arms, and Finn opened his, and Leo leaped into them.

"Want to go for a quick spin as a family?" the ride attendant asked, his eyes crinkling at the corners.

"Yeah!" Leo yelled.

And as they both hugged him, then tucked him carefully in between them, talking and laughing—and in Kayla's case, crying—the warmth and rightness of it overwhelmed her. She looked up at the sky, and the stars seemed a canvas on which God had written His plan. "Thank You," she murmured. "Oh, Father God, thank You."

Epilogue

Four months later

Finn stood at the front of the little church, and even though his fancy tie was half choking him, he couldn't be happier.

"I can't stand weddings," Finn's veterinarian friend Jack DeMoise said from his position behind Finn.

"That's no way to talk, young man," Willie said. It had been a toss-up for Finn which of the two older men should be his best man, but Long John had insisted he didn't want the honor; he had other plans for the wedding. Plans, as it turned out, to walk Kayla down the aisle.

So it was Willie and Jack who stood up with Finn, and Carson who was doing the ceremony. Finn knew what it was to have a band of brothers, but this group wasn't bonded just by fighting; they were bonded by life. They were family.

The changes that being with Kayla and Leo were already working in him felt like a gift from God. He'd been closed in, hurting, before, such that joy couldn't gain a foothold. Now he felt joy every day.

Kayla, too, was changing and growing. She and Leo had been seeing a counselor, trying to deal with Mitch and what he'd done. Both of them seemed to stand taller, as if burdens they'd been carrying had been lifted from their shoulders.

The music changed, and he looked down the church's short aisle. There was Leo, a cute little man in a suit and new cowboy boots, standing straight and serious with his responsibility of carrying the rings. He walked forward slowly, biting his lip, and then he looked up at Finn. Finn gave him an encouraging nod and smile, and Leo started to speed up. Soon, he was running full speed, clutching the satin ring pillow in his fist.

What could Finn do but kneel down and open his arms to the little boy who already seemed like his own son?

He got Leo straightened out and standing in the right place, and looked up in time to see Penny, already halfway down the aisle. Her dress was simple, her hair loose, and behind him, he heard Willie suck in a breath.

Poor Willie. If only everyone in the world could be as happy as Finn was.

Next came Kayla's friend Janice from back in Arkansas. She'd come for the wedding and basically fallen in love with the place, and Finn wouldn't be surprised if she moved out here sometime soon.

And then he lost focus on everything else because there was Kayla. Her classic wedding dress, sleeveless and ivory and fitted, looked incredible. Rather than a veil, she wore a wreath of flowers.

She had a lightness in her steps, a lift to her face that was completely different from when she had arrived at Redemption Ranch. She was radiant, and it wasn't just a figure of speech. She glowed.

She held Long John's arm and Finn wasn't sure who was supporting whom, but they both looked happy.

Kayla caught his eye as she got closer, and love shone out from her eyes, as deep blue as a Colorado sky. This time, he was the one who sucked in a breath.

"You're a blessed man," Carson said, and Finn looked sharply at him.

"It's the simple truth," Jack said from behind him. "You know me and Carson wish you all the happiness in the world." There was a hunger in his voice. Neither Carson nor Jack thought they could have this kind of happiness. They had talked about it a lot in the men's Bible study.

Of course, a year ago, Finn would have never guessed he could have this kind of happiness, either.

As the music swelled, Long John delivered Kayla to Finn. He was taking his fatherly role seriously. "You better be good to this woman," he said to Finn, his voice stern.

"I intend to." Finn watched as Long John sat down and then centered his full attention to Kayla.

Kayla, soon to be his wife.

His heart soared as the pastor began the simple ceremony. Against all his expectations, he'd been given a second chance. With a woman so well suited that they seemed to have been made for each other.

They had both had their share of grief and tribulation. But maybe that just made this happy time all the sweeter.

"I love you," he said to his bride, keeping his voice low.

But not low enough. "You're getting ahead of yourself," Carson said, and the congregation laughed.

"I'm okay with that," Kayla said. "I love him, too."

"Then can we be done and go have cake?" Leo asked.

"Just a few minutes, buddy," Finn said, rubbing Leo's hair.

So Carson made quick work of the ceremony. And then came the cake and congratulations, toasts and dancing. It felt good to be surrounded by their friends, old and new.

But after a couple of hours, Finn pulled Kayla aside. "You had enough of all this?" he asked.

She nodded up at him, her eyes shining. "I can't wait until we're alone together."

He put a hand on either side of her face, leaned down and kissed her lightly. "We're the bride and groom, so we don't have to wait," he said. "What do you say we take off?"

Her eyebrows shot up. "Can we?" she asked. "Without saying goodbye?"

"We have to go through the hall to do it. Should we try?"

Of course, they didn't make it, because Carson and Jack had their eyes open for just such a move. While

Finn and Kayla found Leo and said goodbye to him—
he was staying with Penny, but had plans for daily
visits with Carson and the twins—the news that they
were leaving spread through the crowd.

When they made a run for the borrowed old Cadillac they were taking to their brief mountain honeymoon, they were pelted with birdseed. And sometime
while the reception had been going on, the car had
been decorated with signs, tin cans and shaving cream.

But that was all fitting, because they were starting
their lives together as part of a community. A nosy,
interfering community, but one that wanted the best
for every member, where neighbors were quick to ex-
tend a hand.

Once in the car, Finn leaned over and gave Kayla
the thorough kiss he'd been longing to give all evening, earning catcalls and cheers. He looked into her
eyes. "Are you ready?" he asked.

She nodded, her eyes locked with his. "I'm so
ready," she said. "Let's go."

* * * * *

If you enjoyed The Soldier's Redemption,
keep reading for an extra bonus story from
Lee Tobin McClain!

SECOND CHANCE
ON THE CHESAPEAKE

Lee Tobin McClain

When this project fell completely apart, I turned to my writers' group, especially Kathy, Jackie and Karen, and asked them to help me fix it. As always, they went to work with kindness, creativity and intelligence. Once they let me know (ever so gently) what was wrong, I was able to fix it. This novella is dedicated to them.

Chapter 1

"Time to celebrate our freedom," Gemma McWharter informed her elderly Chihuahua mix, Fang, tucking him more securely against her side. She put down her suitcase so she could ring her cousin's doorbell. Then she stepped back and inhaled deeply.

February on the Chesapeake. Cold, but not the same kind of cold as she'd left behind in north-central Pennsylvania. The air smelled salty and felt a little balmy, and it took her back to childhood summers spent with the poorer—but happier—branch of her family.

She knocked on the door again. "Bisky? Are you there?" Did she have the wrong day? Her ex would've said it was just like her—always screwing up, spacing out, getting things wrong.

Fang gave two short yaps, and she kissed the top of his head and set him down. Only then did she see the note, a torn spot on top suggesting it had fallen down from the nail it had been hanging on.

Come on in, make yourself at home, you know where everything is. I'll be home by six, with wine. We'll have a blast.

Relieved, Gemma smiled and let herself in. Bisky was still Bisky, her favorite cousin. She'd been right to come.

Fang trotted ahead of her into the living room and then looked back, panting. His open mouth revealed his single tooth, the reason for his name. "Go ahead, explore," she encouraged him, and he began sniffing the perimeter of the room.

Gemma kicked off her shoes and looked around Bisky's big, comfortable home, its lived-in style a far cry from the McMansion Gemma had lived in with her husband, or her parents' grand estate. A couple of boat paintings adorned the walls, but the house wasn't overdecorated with nets and shells and fake crab pots, like the tourist places.

A month ago, during a phone conversation, Bisky had mentioned she wanted to redo her attic as a surprise for her teenage daughter, Sunny, while she was away on a school trip. Gemma had jumped at the opportunity to help. Bisky did okay with crabbing and oystering, but there wasn't money for luxuries. Gemma could be useful for her strong, confident cousin, for once.

Besides, she needed practice at redoing spaces for an actual client, and the before-and-after photos would add to the meager collection on her new website.

Visiting the Eastern Shore would give her a break from her family while she decided on her next move. The week away would give Mom time to recover from the fact that Gemma—quiet, backward Gemma—had done what Mom couldn't: leave a marriage to an unfaithful, unloving husband. It would also give her bullying brother, Rob, time to cool down about her divorcing his best friend.

Fang didn't do stairs as well as he used to, so Gemma carried him up the two flights to the attic to get a preliminary look at the week's project.

The scent of newly cut pine came through the open door, and dust particles danced in the slanting beam of late-afternoon light. A dormer looked out over the bay. This was going to be a gorgeous room for a teenager.

She set Fang down and he ran across the space, yapping. She followed him and then recognized all the hazards: sawdust, an open can of paint and even a couple of scattered nails. "Fang, come!" she ordered, but the indulged little dog trotted into the attached bathroom, ignoring her, still yapping.

She hurried after him and felt something sharp pierce the arch of her sock-clad foot. "Ow! Ow! Ow!" She hopped to the wall, watching her step this time, and reached down to disentangle the carpet tack strip that had attached itself to her wool sock and punctured her foot in what felt like several places. "Fang! Get back here!"

Of course, he didn't listen.

She limped toward the bathroom to save him… And ran directly into an enormous, flannel-clad chest.

"Whoa!" She double-stepped back, her heart pounding.

The giant stepped back, too, and picked Fang up.

Fang growled, and the man deposited him in her arms. "Sorry to startle you, ma'am."

That voice was so familiar. She looked more closely at the man in front of her and felt her face heat. "Isaac?"

"Gemma?" he said at the same time. "Are you all right? What happened?"

Fang yapped madly at him from the safety of Gemma's arms while Gemma tried to collect herself. What was Isaac doing here? How had he gotten even better looking than when they'd been friends in their teenage years?

Were he and Bisky an item?

Tucking Fang into the crook of one arm, she gestured toward her foot. "Stepped on some carpet tack," she said. "I wasn't watching where I was going. Are you...do you live here?"

"No!" He laughed like that was funny. "I'm just remodeling the bathroom and putting in a window seat, a few things like that," he explained. "Bisky pulled out the carpet yesterday. I'm sorry I didn't clean up—"

She waved a hand. "Not your fault. I'll be fine."

"That has to sting, though." He frowned down at her foot, then looked at her face. "I didn't know you were visiting Bisky."

"I'm decorating," she said. "Here from Pennsylvania for a week." She stepped backward—she still felt too close to him with his considerable physical presence—and winced as her injured foot hit the ground.

"Come, let me take a look." He gestured her toward the bathroom. "Sit on the edge of the tub and take your sock off. The least I can do is offer first aid."

She did as he'd said and then wished she hadn't. The bathroom was small, and Isaac... Wasn't. She cuddled

Fang, and the little dog alternately cowered close and then craned his neck to try to sniff Isaac.

Isaac knelt in front of her and lifted her foot to look underneath. "Those tacks got you a couple of places," he said. "Nothing deep, and they're bleeding pretty good, so you shouldn't need a tetanus shot. Let me clean them up and put something on them."

"It's okay," she said, but he was already wetting a clean white rag. He added hand soap and then gently lifted her foot.

Her heart thumped. "You don't have to—"

"Gemma. I feel responsible." He looked up at her and she sucked in a breath. Oh, those eyes. Soulful brown eyes that had romanced her into her first kiss— what was it—twenty years ago?

He washed her foot gently and then rinsed the washcloth and wiped the soap away. "Sit still while I grab my first aid kit," he said, and walked out of the bathroom.

Gemma might not have been able to move, anyway. She felt a little limp from the shock of discovering Isaac here.

"Antibiotic and bandages." He came back into the bathroom, knelt down and smeared ointment on her injuries.

"So," he said as he fitted a square of gauze to her foot, then taped it into place, "what have you been doing for the past twenty years?" He looked up at her with a grin, and then she remembered his dimple. Warmth spread through her.

Oh man. She did *not* need to be thinking about how cute he was. This vacation was about her being *free* from men, not getting attracted to an inappropriate one just weeks after her divorce had finally gone through.

"This and that," she said airily. Because, really, what *had* she accomplished? She'd gone to college, married a man preapproved by her parents and older brother, and lived miserably with him. They hadn't been able to have children. He hadn't wanted her to work. "I'm starting a redecorating service, and Bisky is one of my first clients. Well, I'm doing it for her for free, since she's family. Plus, she's putting me up for a week at the shore."

"Fair enough." He patted the bandage and then pulled her sock on again, carefully, as if she were a child. "There you go. All better."

"Thank you." She started to stand, and then he was too close and she sat down again.

Immediately, he backed out of the little bathroom. "I'm going to sweep this place up right now," he said. "Hold on to your dog. I wasn't expecting anyone else here, which is why it's such a mess. Careless of me."

"I'm surprised Bisky didn't tell you I was coming." She looked around, frowning. The room was finished, but bare bones. It needed a lot of work.

Footsteps sounded on the stairs. "Did I hear my name?" Bisky asked, walking in from the hall. "Hey, girl, you're here!" She opened her arms, smiling hugely.

Gemma's shoulders relaxed, and she walked into her cousin's arms for a big hug, Fang growling indignantly as he was squashed between them.

"Girl, you're a sight for sore eyes." Bisky stepped back and studied her. "You let your hair grow! And you've got so much style."

"Thanks." Gemma glanced down at her floral dress, then back at her cousin, clad in a plain, long-sleeved T-shirt and jeans. Bisky was the definition of a natural beauty. "And you're looking great, too. I thought you'd be coming from work."

"Believe me, I wouldn't smell this good just back from a day of oystering. Today I was off. Had to visit a friend and pick up wine." She looked around the attic. "Are we really going to get this done by the time Sunny gets home?"

Gemma studied the room doubtfully. "Depends what you're doing to the floor. If we have to restain it, then I don't see how."

Bisky shook her head. "She likes carpet," she said. "So Isaac's going to put that down, and finish the bathroom and the window seat. Right?" She looked at him. "Can you get away from the hardware store for that long?"

"I can work here every evening. We asked a couple of the part-timers to put in more hours, so I can squeeze in a couple full days as well." Isaac gave her a reassuring smile. "Don't worry, we'll get 'er done."

"Terrific. But what am I thinking? We don't have to stand here." Bisky backed out of the room, beckoning to them. "Come downstairs, and I'll open the wine, and we can figure out how you two are going to get this project done in a week."

Gemma tilted her head and glanced at Isaac, whose brow was furrowed. Obviously, he hadn't known he'd be working with her, just as she hadn't known she'd be working with him.

And how uncomfortable was that, working with the guy who'd given you your first kiss? They'd left things on a weird note all those years ago, and then Gemma had only been back to Pleasant Shores a couple of times—once when a distant relative had married, and once when Sunny was born—to help for a couple of weeks. She hadn't seen Isaac either time. She had no idea of whether he was married or single, what he'd done, how he'd changed.

It was going to be an interesting week.

Chapter 2

Isaac sat at Bisky's kitchen table, turned down the offer of wine and studied Gemma, the woman who'd reappeared in his life after twenty years.

He'd have known her anywhere: porcelain skin, mahogany curls and that shy way she turned her eyes away. He'd thought her gorgeous as a teenager, and she still was, maybe more so. She'd been sweet and kind inside, too, or so he'd thought.

But his family had been right: it was a mistake to get involved with the summer people. Technically, she was more than a summer person; being Bisky's cousin, she wasn't exactly a tourist. But still, she was from a different world. She had expensive clothes. She hadn't had to work. She'd had the accents and speaking style of someone who attended a fancy private school.

And she'd gone on to marry a rich man, just as his

mother had predicted. The same man who'd shown up the last week of the last summer with Gemma's brother, Rob, driving a Porsche and throwing his money around.

So what was she doing back here now, without a wedding ring?

"I'm sorry to spring this on both of you," Bisky said. "I'd thought Isaac would be done with his part by the time you got here, Gem, but it didn't work out that way."

"My fault," Isaac said. "We had a flood at the store, and cleanup had to take priority."

Bisky winced. "Yeah, that was rough. I know you must have taken a financial hit, too. You're good to still make the time to do my project."

Of course he had; he liked Bisky, but additionally, he had to take on all the work he could manage just to keep his mom and his aunt and his store afloat. There was no time for leisure.

No time for dating. No time for a woman like Gemma, who no doubt was used to being wined and dined. She probably lived in a gated community, and he knew from Bisky's updates over the years that she'd traveled the world.

Isaac, by contrast, lived in the house he'd grown up in and had done nothing except stay home and work.

He needed to get his old feelings for Gemma right out of his mind.

"So," Bisky said, reaching for a folder stuffed with papers and magazine clippings, "here are some pictures Sunny showed me a few months ago, when she was begging me to redo her room. I made like I couldn't afford it. So this is going to be a surprise."

Gemma studied the pictures. Isaac leaned over to look, too, and ended up getting a whiff of something flowery from her hair. Resolutely, he moved away.

"Looks like we'll need to do some shopping," Gemma said to Bisky. "Or maybe you'll just send me out for stuff, if you have to work. Then, honestly, it'll be a full-time job to get it all done this week."

"True for me, too," he said.

"Can you work together?" Bisky asked, "or will you just be in each other's way?"

Gemma looked at him the same moment he looked at her, and their gazes tangled for the briefest of moments. Doe eyes, that was what she had. As wild and shy as the sika deer that roamed the Eastern Shore.

"We can work together, I think." Gemma bit her lip. "I mean, I can."

"Me, too." He looked away from her pretty mouth and thought about spending the next few days in close quarters with her. Heat coursed in his veins.

It was going to be quite a week.

After Isaac left, Gemma glared, only half-jokingly, at Bisky. "Did you plan this?"

"Plan what?" Bisky raised her eyebrows, a smile tugging at the corner of her mouth.

"This! Me and Isaac, working together all week!"

"Nope." Bisky held up her hands, palms out. "It truly was an accident. I thought he'd be done by the time you got here. But—" she grinned "—now that it's happening, I think I like it."

"I don't!" Gemma picked up Fang and put him on her lap, where he rolled onto his back for a belly rub. "I'm supposed to be celebrating freedom from men.

Second Chance on the Chesapeake

And now I'm thrown together with Isaac Roberts. The handsomest man alive!"

"He *is* handsome," Bisky agreed. "A really, really good guy, too."

Gemma looked quickly at her cousin. "Do you… Is there anything between you?"

"With Isaac? No. No way. He's like a brother." She paused. "But everyone in town knows how much he's sacrificed for his family. That's all I meant. He's one of the good ones."

Gemma felt unaccountably relieved. "How about you? Are you seeing anyone?"

Bisky shook her head. "You know me. I'm busy raising Sunny and working."

"I thought you sometimes dated when Sunny was away." Gemma took a sip of wine.

Bisky leaned back in her chair, shrugging a little. "It gets old, these short-term things."

She sounded a little sad, and that wasn't like Bisky. "Did something happen?" Gemma asked.

"I just grew up, I guess. Don't worry about me. I'm fine. My life is full." She refilled Gemma's glass and then her own. "But my life's also boring, whereas you… Man, girl, sounds like you've had some excitement. How'd you get the guts to dump *el jerko*?"

"My friend, the high-powered lawyer." Gemma rubbed a finger around the rim of her wineglass. "She told me exactly how to get my money and paperwork together and then file when he was off on a so-called fishing trip. He didn't want to end the marriage because of how it would look, but he also didn't want to be any kind of a husband to me. Not when I'm so boring compared to his special friends at the club."

Bisky snorted. "I assume the special friends were in their twenties and blonde?"

"And busty," Gemma said. "Turns out he likes busty." Which Gemma wasn't.

"Told ya so," Bisky said, but lightly. It was true; on the night before Gemma's wedding, Bisky had taken her out for drinks and had a talk with her.

"Why are you marrying him?" she'd asked bluntly. She'd come up for Gemma's wedding, had only just met Jeff, but she'd disliked him on sight.

"No one else is going to ask me," Gemma had said. She was echoing what her mother and brother had told her, but she knew it was true. She was shy and backward and not that pretty. "I want kids."

"You can have kids other ways." Bisky had sounded completely exasperated. "You have a college degree. Use it! Move somewhere away from your family and get a job. Come to Pleasant Shores and stay with me! Just don't marry a man you don't love."

In some part of herself, Gemma had known she should take Bisky's advice. But the relationship and the wedding had built up a momentum of its own. She hadn't had the courage, back then, to put a stop to it.

"You were right," Gemma said now, rubbing Fang's ears.

"Men." Bisky reached out for Fang, and Gemma passed him over. "You're the best little man, aren't you, buddy?" She held him like a baby, which he tolerated for only a moment before struggling to right himself. Bisky handed him back to Gemma. "You know, I'm generally not that big of a dog person, but I like your little guy. He has attitude."

"He's been great. My best friend through all this."

"I'm glad you have him, then." Bisky gave a great yawn. "Sorry. I can't wait to spend more time hanging out, but for now, I have to go to bed. Four in the morning comes early. Let me show you where you're sleeping."

They cleaned up their glasses and then headed to the second floor, Bisky leading the way, Gemma carrying her suitcase. On the threshold of the guest room, Gemma's throat tightened.

All along one side of the room was baby stuff: a crib, a changing table, a rocker.

"Sorry it's got so much junk," Bisky said. "I cleared out the attic and didn't have anywhere to put this stuff... Oh, hon, what's wrong?"

Gemma shook her head and cleared her throat. "It's nothing. It's just...we were going to adopt, and I had the nursery all ready, and then it fell through." She swallowed hard. "Twice."

"Oh no!" Bisky folded her into a hug. "I'll sleep here, and you take my room."

"No, it's fine. I'll be fine."

"I can't believe you went through that without telling me."

"I actually couldn't talk about it. Still can't. You need to go to bed." She turned her back on the baby furniture, put her suitcase on the bed and opened it.

"Are you okay?" Bisky still had a hand on her shoulder. "To stay in here and to do the attic?"

"Of course! I'm fine. I'll make the attic great for Sunny," Gemma promised.

She'd just have to figure out a way to do that without going crazy working in tight quarters with the man she'd never forgotten.

* * *

A week working closely with Gemma McWharter was going to be even tougher than Isaac had thought.

He'd kept busy finishing the bathroom update as soon as she'd started work on the bedroom, but he couldn't caulk all night. He was supposed to get the bedroom's window seat fitted and planed out today, but she was out there painting walls, cute and sexy in a skimpy tank top and jeans. He wasn't going to be able to pretend she wasn't there.

"Do you need help painting?" he asked finally.

She looked down from the sheet-covered chair she was standing on. "I wouldn't turn it down," she said. "But don't you have things to do yourself?"

"Can't put in the window seat until the walls are done," he said. "May as well help you get there."

"Then sure," she said promptly. "Trim or roller?"

"Roller," he said, and so she continued painting along the edges while he poured paint into a pan and started rolling it onto the wall she'd already edged.

"I'm glad Bisky didn't choose bright purple or pink," Gemma said. "I thought girls usually liked those kinds of colors, but apparently, Sunny prefers neutrals. The gray is going to be gorgeous."

"Sunny's a great kid," Isaac said. "Works hard and helps her mom. And funny."

They painted in silence for a little while, and then she spoke. "If you don't mind my asking... How come you didn't get married and have kids?"

He glanced back over his shoulder at her. He rarely got this question anymore, since everyone in Pleasant Shores knew him and his situation. "I don't even have time to date, what with taking care of Mom and running the store."

"What's going on with your mother?" she asked as she carefully ran her brush along the woodwork that framed the window. "You don't live with her, do you?"

"I do." He stood back to examine the wall he'd just finished painting, looking for bare spots. "Not many women want to date a thirty-seven-year-old man who still lives with his mother. She has Parkinson's," he clarified, "and she can't stay alone anymore. Works for both of us."

He glanced over to see that she'd stopped painting to look at him, her lips turning down. "I'm so sorry. How is she doing?"

"Her spirits are good. She does as much of the housework as she can. Still cooks a mean lasagna."

She clapped her hands lightly. "I remember! Hers was the best."

"Still is," he said, although the truth was, Mom struggled to remember the ingredients these days. It wasn't to the level of cognitive impairment, but she had trouble focusing. "Tell me about you. What's been going on?"

She smiled a little. "Uh-uh, you don't get to change the subject yet," she said. "You don't have kids, and you don't date much, okay. What *do* you do?"

He moved to the next wall and started rolling on paint. "I work," he said.

"At the store?"

He nodded. "Plus I do side jobs like this one."

"So you're putting in, what, twelve hours a day?" Her tone was joking.

He nodded. "At least."

"Is that necessary?" She sounded shocked. "Wow." After a moment's silence, she added, "I'm sorry. I've never been in need, and I don't know what it would be like to work two jobs."

He looked back over his shoulder at her. "We're not in need, exactly. It's important to me to build up enough savings that Mom would be taken care of, if anything happened to me," he said. "Plus, the store has been in the family for decades. It's an important part of the town, but it barely scrapes by."

"Why? Are people hitting the big box stores instead of staying in town?"

He nodded. "Some support us, but it's always a gamble as to whether we'll be in the black any given month. So we don't want to hire outside managers. Me and my aunt, between us, we cover the shifts."

"Isn't she getting kind of old?"

He grinned. "Don't let her hear you say that. She feels and acts young. She's been climbing ladders and lifting boxes her whole life, plus spending most of every day talking to customers. Seems to be a recipe for good health."

"Good for her."

They painted a little while longer, and when he'd done all he could, he put down his roller. Standing beside the sheet-covered dresser in the middle of the room, he took a long draw from his water bottle. "This place is looking good."

She came to the center of the room and turned slowly around, scanning it. Then she smiled up at him. "Thanks for helping me get the painting done. I'll help you with your part however I can."

Their gazes met and held. He could see the gold

circles around her pupils, the pink flush across her cheeks. His heart thumped, then settled into a rapid pounding.

He remembered the first time he'd kissed her, how hard it had been for him to work up the courage, how surprised he'd been that they both seemed to know what to do and that it felt so good.

He should be smoother now, but he wasn't. "You have paint on your chin" was what came out of his mouth. He pulled a bandanna from his back pocket and wiped at it.

He was so close now that he could smell her lemony perfume.

His eyes flickered down to her lips and then back to those gorgeous eyes. He remembered more than the first kiss now; he remembered how quickly things had intensified between them as the summer had gone on, and how hard it had been to pull back.

Her eyes darkened, and he could tell she was remembering it, too.

Mom and Aunt Jean had warned him against getting so close to her, and in the end, they'd been right. Which was why he shouldn't kiss her now.

She made the decision for him. "Well, hey, thanks again!" She stepped away, her cheeks going pinker.

Thanks for what? For almost kissing her? For *not* kissing her? And then he realized she was talking about the painting. "You're welcome. Think I'll go home and check on Mom." His voice sounded a little funny.

As he walked home, he wondered about it. He knew what had made him hesitate, but what had made her back away?

Chapter 3

The next day, Isaac walked into the hardware store two minutes late, knowing he'd hear about it, rubbing his eyes. Trying to rub away the image of Gemma and her full, pretty lips, but that was futile.

"A little help here?" His aunt—great-aunt, really, his mom's aunt—was struggling with a large box.

He hurried over to take it from her. "You should have waited for me."

"I might've," she said, "but Goody is out back waiting for us to load this into her car, and you know how impatient she can get."

He did. He carried the box through the store to the back entrance and loaded it into Goody's ancient, wood-paneled station wagon, trying unsuccessfully to stifle a yawn.

"Glad you saw fit to finally wait on me," Goody

snapped as she drove off. Goody ran the local ice cream shop and was known for being cranky.

Aunt Jean glared after Goody's car, then sighed. "We can't afford to alienate her."

"Sorry I was late." Isaac knew that all too well. If they couldn't offer better service than the big box stores, that was where people would go, and they'd be out of business.

As they walked back inside, she put an arm around him. "You've been working extra, haven't you?"

He nodded. "Things are tight."

He didn't need to say more; Aunt Jean understood. As small business owners, they bought their own insurance, and even the minimal plan was hard to afford. When his mom needed extra treatments, each one was an expense.

"What are you working on?" she asked.

"Bisky's converting her attic into a new bedroom for Sunny. I'm doing some of the woodwork and plumbing."

"I hear her cousin Gemma is there." Aunt Jean frowned.

Isaac nodded. "She's starting a redecorating business. Kind of practicing on Bisky's project."

They'd reached the middle of the store now. A few customers had come in and were strolling the aisles, shopping, but no one was ready to check out yet.

They both walked around then, checking on people, making sure they could find what they needed. Then Aunt Jean came to straighten paint cans beside Isaac. "So you're working with Gemma, spending time with her?"

"A little, looks like. We have to get the remodel and the decorating done this week."

"Bad idea." Aunt Jean shook her head. "I don't like it."

"She's changed. She's nice."

"You stay away from her," Aunt Jean said darkly. "She's not our kind."

"Are we really still doing that?" He pulled out a rag to dust the bottom shelf paint cans. "Separating people out into categories, our kind and the rest?" Gemma had seemed nothing but sweet last night. Sweet, and beautiful.

"Our type and the rich snobs," Aunt Jean snapped. "Like Gemma McWharter and her family. She treated you like dirt before, and she'll do it again. You don't deserve it." She patted his shoulder. It was her version of a hug and he smiled at her.

A movement down the aisle caught his eye as he looked over at his aunt. Gemma stood there, her little dog in her arms, her face stricken. Clearly, she'd overheard.

Gemma stared at Isaac and his aunt. *Our type and the rich snobs. Like Gemma McWharter and her family.*

Was her family viewed that way still? Was she?

It wasn't that far from the mark with her family, she had to admit. Money and status were everything to them. But she was different. Wasn't she?

Reflexively, she hugged Fang closer. She'd thought Isaac liked her, thought he was going to kiss her, but if this was the way he felt...

"Gemma." Isaac stood and approached her, his face compassionate. "Are you okay?"

"I'm fine." She nodded. Best to pretend she hadn't overheard. She didn't want him to pity her.

"Aunt Jean, she's…" He gestured behind him, where his aunt had disappeared. "She's got some outdated views."

He was trying to make her feel better. But that was because he was nice, not because he cared.

He reached out and rubbed the top of Fang's head, the movement of his hand mesmerizing. "Can I help you find something?"

"Uh, yeah." Why was she here again? She fumbled in her pocket. "I need three more screws like this, and a couple of boards sawed to size, if you do that."

"We do that. Screws first." He led her to the area filled with drawers of nails and screws. He held out his hand for her sample, and within seconds, had supplied the size she needed. "Three, you said?"

She nodded, feeling shy as a memory came back to her: shopping for a little project she'd done back home, she'd encountered a hardware store employee who couldn't stop making jokes about screws, loudly, nudging her and making another male employee laugh.

Isaac wouldn't do that, though.

He slid three screws into a tiny plastic bag, then beckoned her to the back of the store, where boards and two-by-fours sat near an old sawhorse. "What length do you need?"

She pulled out her phone, where she'd noted the measurements. "I'm making a hook row and teenagers always have a ton of clothes, so… I think six feet."

He lined up the board she chose and sawed it, and

she had the pleasure of watching his very nice muscles play underneath his olive green T-shirt. Fang struggled, and she put him down. "Now be good," she ordered him. "Stay close to Mama."

"That dog is a hazard." Isaac's aunt bustled over, not meeting Gemma's eyes. "No dogs in the store."

Fang looked directly at her as he lifted his leg.

"No, Fang, no!" Gemma swooped him up just in time. "I took you potty right before we came in. You know better."

Fang looked at Aunt Jean and growled.

"I'll ring you up while Isaac finishes cutting those. I suppose you'll want them delivered, since your little sports car isn't meant for hauling?"

Gemma lifted her chin. "Yes, please." If Mrs. Decker thought she was a snob, she might as well play the part.

As she followed Isaac's aunt to the front of the store, though, her shoulders slumped. Yes, she had to make this redo work. And she would.

But no, Pleasant Shores wasn't going to be an uncomplicated safe haven for her. There was too much backstory, too much history. She didn't fit.

No one but Bisky would love her here.

Her shoulders slumped as her thoughts spiraled. Would anywhere else be any different?

Mrs. Decker rang up her purchase, and Gemma paid with her card. Then, Mrs. Decker looked past her and out the front window of the shop. "Here it comes," she said, her voice disgusted. "Roll out the red carpet. Summer people are starting to show up at all times of the year, more's the pity."

"Nice car," Isaac commented from behind her.

"And we need the summer people's business, Aunt Jean. Paste on that smile." He patted the older woman's shoulder.

Gemma sighed. She herself was one of the summer people that Mrs. Decker was complaining about.

As she walked out the front door, Fang trotting beside her, the door of the expensive dark sedan opened.

When her brother emerged, Gemma's stomach lurched. "Ron! What are you doing here?"

"I saw your note on Bisky's door," he said. "I've come to take you home."

"Come to take me… No. Forget it."

He nodded implacably and gestured toward the car. "Come on, now. Jeff is very upset. So's Mom."

She raised an eyebrow. "Are they, now? And why's that?"

"You've never known where you fit in. We care about you. No one here does." He put an arm around her—something Ron never did—and she had a flash of thinking that maybe he was sincere and wanted what was best for her. That maybe she did fit in better with her family than with the people in this town. People like Mrs. Decker, now glaring through the front window of the hardware store.

No one in this town cared about her the way her family did, difficult as they were.

"Maybe you're right." She sighed and glanced up at Ron's face, seeking comfort.

She didn't find it. Instead, he was smiling, a big, self-congratulatory smile.

It made her pause. Was she really that easy to persuade? "I'll think about what you've said." She stepped away from him. "I'm not sure what I want to do."

"Of course you're not," he said impatiently. "You're never sure."

His tone brought back all the things she didn't like about living with her family. She walked a few feet away.

It was as if the distance removed the spell he'd cast on her. She could leave Pleasant Shores, yes. She probably would. But she'd made a commitment to Bisky, and despite any issues with the people here, with Isaac, despite any reputation her family had, she needed to fulfill her obligation to her cousin.

She opened her mouth to say as much to her brother when he stepped forward and picked up Fang.

"Hey," she said, "he doesn't like it when—"

"I'll just put him in the car," Ron said smoothly, and walked it that direction.

She held on tight to the leash. "Wait a second! You can't—"

"Come on." He pulled on the dog.

Fang's collar tightened and he yelped. The pull on his neck was hurting him. Gemma dropped the leash.

Ron strode faster toward the car.

Gemma's heart turned over. Could Ron really be so awful as to… "Fang!" she cried. "Ron, give him to me this minute!"

But Ron tucked the dog under one arm and opened the car's back door.

Isaac strode toward the exit of the store. He couldn't let her jerk of a brother take her dog.

"Don't involve yourself." His aunt followed him, putting a restraining hand on his arm. "Nothing but heartache that way."

He appreciated his aunt's loyalty: she'd stood by his side, in so many ways, especially running the store and caring for his mom. But she wasn't right about everything. He stopped and gave her shoulders a little squeeze. "Have to help," he said, and marched out, reaching the big dark sedan's back door just as Gemma's brother—Ron, if he recalled correctly—was starting to close it. Inside, Fang whined pitifully.

Isaac shoved the man out of the way and looked across the car at Gemma. "Do you want Fang in here?"

"No!" She rushed around the car, reached in past Isaac and picked up the dog. She cuddled the quivering little creature close to her chest as she walked away from the car, then looked back at Isaac. "Thank you! My poor baby!"

Ron glared at Isaac. "Hands off my car."

Isaac lifted his hands immediately and held them up. "Not interested in your car."

Ron snorted. "Nicest car you'll ever see, working at your mom's hardware store. You locals."

Mom can't work here anymore. But he didn't put words to the thought. That wasn't of interest to Ron, nor to Gemma either, most likely.

And what Ron had said was true: he *was* a local, a small-town man tied to a family business. Gemma and her family were out of his league.

"Loser." Ron's lip curled.

It was what had happened before, years ago: Ron and his friend had made Isaac feel small, and he'd given up. But now, as he looked at Gemma, something reconfigured in his mind, like the pieces clicked together differently.

He looked at Ron's sneering face. "I earn an honest wage and I help people." Maybe it wasn't what would impress this family, including Gemma, but it was who he was.

"That's right." Goody had come out of her shop and now stood beside him. "He keeps the store running, and we need a hardware store here in Pleasant Shores."

"Wow, he keeps a small-town store running?" Ron's snotty implication was clear.

"He gave up everything for his family," Aunt Jean said from the other side of him. "He's worth ten of you."

Isaac stepped back and put an arm around each of the two older women. "Thanks," he said, meaning it, although his feelings were mixed. Someday, it would be nice to impress a woman his own age.

Someone like Gemma. But he wasn't going to wait around for her reaction. He gave Goody and Aunt Jean another quick shoulder squeeze, then turned and went back inside. He had a store to run.

"He saved the day, is what I heard!" Bisky lifted her glass of wine, and Gemma clinked her own against her cousin's. "He's your hero!"

Gemma shook her head. "He would have done the same for anyone. You should have seen how fast he got out of there."

"What did Ron do then?" Bisky asked, frowning. She and Ron had never gotten along.

"He cussed me out and left." Gemma shrugged. "Typical Ron. He doesn't like it when he doesn't get his way." She ran a finger around the edge of her glass. "They look down on me, you know."

"Who?"

"Isaac and his aunt," she said, and told of the remark she'd overheard.

"Oh, Mrs. Decker..." Bisky waved a hand. "She's a fixture in this town, and she's great most of the time, but she does get a little negative about tourists. Outsiders, really. You're not a tourist."

"But I *am* an outsider."

"You don't have to be." Bisky waved at the waiter and held up two fingers. "You know what, you should stay here."

"I *am* staying. I promised you I'd get Sunny's room remodel done, and I will." Although how she was going to work with Isaac, she didn't know.

Oh, he'd saved Fang, but that had been a general act of kindness. He'd left right away, without even responding to her thanks.

"That's great, but I meant you should stay on permanently."

Gemma looked out the window, where the bay shone like a silvery mirror. "Live here, you mean? Mom and Ron would never put up with it."

"Your mom and Ron aren't on your side. They never have been."

"But they're all I've got." Even as she said the words, bleakness settled in on her.

"Gemma. Think back. They shipped you off here every summer because they didn't want to deal with you, but you took what they did and made it a positive," she said. "And we love you. I love you. Sunny and I are family, too."

Gemma's eyes filled. "Thank you. I love you guys, and I love Pleasant Shores."

"It's a wonderful town," Bisky went on. "And I

know, I think that because I live here, but everyone who gets to know the place falls in love with it. You could stay with me and Sunny until you got on your feet." She grinned. "You'd have to redecorate her old bedroom, but that's right up your alley."

"How would I get on my feet, though? It's not like I'm struggling, but I do need to earn a living, eventually. And I don't have the skills for most of the tourist-related jobs…"

Bisky waved a hand. "You don't want a tourist job. They last only six months of the year, so it's an incredible scramble for most. No, you should start your decorating business here."

"In Pleasant Shores? Who would pay me to decorate?"

"There are more and more wealthy people here, on the other side of the peninsula. You could drum up a good business, helping them decorate. They're second homes for most, and they don't have a lot of time to devote to them."

The idea was actually intriguing. But Isaac… Could she live in the same town with him, see him often and know he scorned her? Could her heart take that?

She took a sip of wine and shook her head. "I just don't think I can do it."

Chapter 4

The rest of the week, Isaac and Gemma managed to avoid each other. Which was good, Isaac thought as he approached Bisky's house on the day Bisky's daughter, Sunny, was supposed to come home.

Bisky had insisted that both he and Gemma be present for the big reveal. Which meant he'd see Gemma today, probably for the last time.

He ran his fingers through his hair, always unruly, and knocked on Bisky's door.

Gemma answered, wearing red jeans and a white gauzy shirt, her hair loose around her shoulders. His mouth went dry.

Fang scampered out from the kitchen, barking madly, and she scooped him into her arms.

"Come on in," she said, and she sounded awkward, as awkward as he felt.

He wished things could have been different, wished she could stick around, that she wasn't from a family that had given her such high expectations.

He walked in. "Where's Bisky?"

"She went to Sunny's friend's house to pick Sunny up. She should be right back."

He cast about for something neutral to talk about. "Is everything ready?"

"For the big reveal? Yes, I think so."

Fang strained in her arms, staring at Isaac, struggling toward him.

"Do you want to take him?" she asked. "He's been touchy since the Ron thing."

"Sure." He felt fond of the dog by now, glad he'd been able to protect him from Gemma's brother.

She held out the dog, and Isaac tucked him snugly against his chest. Surprisingly enough, the dog settled immediately.

"We're home!" Bisky's voice came, loud.

"Who are you yelling to?" Sunny sounded cranky. Uh-oh. From what he'd seen of family groups at the hardware store, there was no cranky like teen girl cranky.

"We have company," Bisky said, ushering the girl in the door.

Sunny quickly concealed the irritated expression on her face, but not quickly enough that Isaac didn't see it. Oh well. Sunny was a nice girl, but she'd just gotten back from a school trip. She probably wanted her mom to herself.

"We'll be on our way soon, I promise, hon," Gemma said, giving Sunny the briefest of hugs. "I'm all packed."

She was packed? She was leaving?

She couldn't leave. Something close to panic rose up in Isaac's chest.

"So," Bisky said, "we need to head up to the attic for just a minute. These two are taking a box with them, and I want to make sure it's okay with you."

It seemed like a fairly ridiculous excuse. Sure enough, Sunny balked. "Whatever it is, it's fine," she said, yawning. "I just want to take a nap."

"Soon," Bisky said firmly, and to her credit, Sunny didn't protest anymore. She just sighed and stood up.

They all trooped up the stairs. Sunny glanced into her bedroom and did a double take. "What did you do to my room?"

"I'll explain in a minute. Up here, hon." Bisky ushered Sunny to the stairs that led to the attic. Isaac and Gemma trailed behind.

Bisky stepped aside so Sunny could go first.

Sunny wasn't paying a lot of attention, but when they got to the top, she stopped still, almost causing a pileup of people behind her.

"Mom? What did you do?" Sunny rushed to the window, then spun and looked at the bed, now covered with a pristine white spread and blue pillows. Gauzy curtains hung in the windows, and the carpet he'd put in looked nice, all newly vacuumed. No TV—Bisky had been adamant about that—but there was a low bookshelf holding schoolbooks and paperbacks.

"Just a little surprise," Bisky said, smiling with what looked like satisfaction.

"But how could you...money's so tight..." Sunny burst into tears and flung her arms around her mother. "I love it so much, Mom. Thank you."

Bisky looked shiny-eyed, too, as she held her daughter. Isaac felt more rewarded by this job than he had in ages. It was great to make a family happy.

Deep inside, he longed for a child of his own, because moments like this were what it was all about. Doing things for each other, making each other happy.

He felt an arm snake around his waist and looked down to see Gemma smiling up at him. "Good stuff," he said, and draped an arm over her shoulders.

She felt absolutely, perfectly right at his side.

Sunny was moving around the room now, looking into the bathroom, raving over the wall hangings.

And Bisky was laughing. "Don't give me too much credit," she said, gesturing toward Gemma and Isaac. "It's these two who did all the work."

Sunny came over then and hugged them both. "I can't believe you did this for me," she said. "I can't even tell you how happy I am right now. I'm going to love having this privacy and space."

Isaac saw Bisky's happy expression slip, just for a moment. Maybe she hadn't thought about it, but Sunny was going to spend a lot of time up here, away from her mother. It was right, and the nature of things, but it couldn't be easy for a single mom of one.

Bisky got a phone call and walked over to the far corner of the room to take it. Sunny grabbed Gemma's arm. "I'm worried about Mom."

"Why?" Gemma studied her.

"She had a week to herself. She used to, you know, go out and have fun, but now…"

"Now she just focused on you?" Gemma smiled at Sunny. "You're a sweet child to care so much about her, but she'll be fine."

"But," Sunny said, her eyes filling, "I'm growing up, and I'll go away to college, and who will take care of her then?"

Funny that Sunny thought she took care of her mother rather than the reverse. "Your mom's pretty resourceful," he reminded her.

"And she's strong and smart and beautiful. If she wants companionship, she'll have it. Male or female." Gemma hugged Sunny. "Listen, I'm going to take off," Gemma said. "So glad you're happy with your new space, Sunny. Bisky," she called to her cousin, who'd just ended her phone call, "thanks for all your hospitality and for giving me the opportunity to do this."

"Thank you! It's perfect!" There was more hugging, and then Gemma started down the stairs.

She was leaving. He might never see her again. "I'll walk her out," he told Bisky.

She narrowed her eyes, studied his face for a minute and then nodded. "Sunny and I will be up here," she said. "Go."

Gemma stepped carefully down the stairs, since her eyes were blurry with tears.

She was so happy for Bisky and Sunny. The satisfaction she felt at what she'd created—what they'd created—made her certain that starting her own interior design firm was the right thing to do. Homes helped families, and she wanted to help people have the perfect home.

She had to admit, she wanted a perfect home and perfect family for herself, but it wasn't going to happen. She'd tried and failed. Failed as a wife, and lost her chance as an adoptive mom.

Fang slept in a sunny spot by the window. She picked him up and made her way out to the car, but when she opened the door of it, there was Isaac behind her.

And that was what would make it really hard to leave. She loved it here, and she cared for Isaac a lot, but it wasn't going to work. He didn't feel the same.

The bay breeze was cool, the sun sparkling brightly on the water. She looked out across it and then turned to face Isaac. "Thank you for everything," she said. "That was a great project to do."

"It was," he said. "But Gemma..." He reached out and pushed back a lock of her hair.

He was going to kiss her goodbye. Just like he had before. It had rocked her teenage world and she'd never gotten over it.

"I wish you wouldn't go," he said.

She turned away and set Fang down into his little dog seat on the passenger side of the car. She had to avoid Isaac's kiss. Maybe then, she wouldn't be so sad.

"Gemma." He said her name forcefully, so forcefully that she turned back to face him. He was so handsome, and his eyes were so warm.

She felt like she couldn't breathe. "Yeah?" she managed to say.

"Gemma, I mean it. Don't go. Stay and let's see if we can make something of this."

His words soothed a sore, aching part of her heart, but she still felt insecure. "Your aunt said it. I'm not your kind. I won't fit in."

"You fit in perfectly. You *fit* perfectly." And then he was pulling her close and tucking her against him, and they *did* fit perfectly together.

He lowered his mouth to hers.

The kiss was epic. Of course, because it was the last.

After a moment, she pulled away. "I can't stand it," she said. Tears pressed at her eyes, but she wouldn't cry. Wouldn't let herself cry.

"You can't stand…what?" He looked puzzled, hurt.

"I can't stand for you to kiss me and leave me feeling so much when it's never going to work."

Fang barked behind her. She needed to get on with her drive, with her life. The trouble was, the life she was going back to seemed cold and desolate.

Isaac took her hands and held them firmly. "I just want you to explain," he said. "Okay, you're going to leave, but why? What is it? You don't like it here? You don't want to get involved with a man who's middle of the road in looks and success and income?"

He thought *he* was middle of the road? "Don't you see, Isaac, that I'm an outcast?"

He tilted his head and studied her, so closely that she felt self-conscious and looked away.

He touched her face, let his hand tangle in her hair. "No. I don't see that."

"Then you're not looking."

"I *am* looking. I see a woman who's stronger in the broken places. A woman who's gone through things and has scars, sure, but who's more beautiful for all she's been through. A woman who's creative and funny and yeah, different, but different is good."

She gulped in a breath. "I *want* to believe you, but…" But she'd heard the reverse for most of her life, first from her family, and then from the husband they'd picked for her.

"I can make you believe if you'll stay and try," he said. "Stay and try." He held out his arms, but he didn't come closer. It was up to Gemma to decide.

She hesitated. There would be adjustments to make, efforts to fit in that might or might not work. A business to start.

A relationship to try, to take a chance on.

Back home there was... Familiarity? The comfort of knowing where she fit in, even if it wasn't a good place?

She looked at Isaac's strong, open face, his warm eyes. *Yes*, everything inside her said all at once, and she stepped forward.

Fang barked as they kissed again, and then Bisky and Sunny came out of the house. "You're still here!" Bisky sounded happy.

"I think..." Gemma said. "I think I'm going to stay in Pleasant Shores for a while."

"You are?" Bisky opened her arms wide. "I'm so glad. Let go of her, Isaac. I want to hug her, too."

"Yes!" Sunny pumped her fist. "You can keep Mom company."

Fang whined from his dog seat, and Isaac reached into the car and picked him up. "What do you think, dude? Stay awhile and get to know me better?"

Fang barked, and they all laughed, and hugged, and Gemma cried a little, happy tears.

She'd never felt a part of things, not really. But now...

She leaned against Isaac's chest, and he put a strong arm around her.

This, her heart said, and it came to her: this was

what home felt like. This place and these people, and most of all, this man.

Finally, after a lifetime of longing for it, she was home.

* * * * *

Will Bisky find romance at long last?
Don't miss the next full-length book in
Lee Tobin McClain's The Off Season series,
Home to the Harbor,
available May 2021!

Read on for a sneak peek!

Chapter 1

"That's a wrap on oyster season." Bisky Castleman tied her skiff to the dock, fingers numb in the March morning chill, then turned toward the wooden shed that connected the dock to the land. She hung up her coverall on the outside hook, tossed her gloves in the bin and sat down on the bench to tug off her boots. "You coming?" she asked her sixteen-year-old daughter, Sunny.

"I'm coming, I'm just dragging." Sunny hung her coverall beside Bisky's and then flopped down on the bench beside her, letting her head sink into her hands. "*Some* kids get to chill out during teacher work days."

"I appreciate your coming out dredging and culling when most of your friends were sleeping in." Bisky slung an arm around her daughter and tugged her close for a quick side-hug. "Come on, I'll make pancakes and then you can take a nap."

Sunny frowned. "No pancakes, thanks."

"You sure? You've been working hard. Too hard." Bisky paused, thought about it. "Maybe I'll see if we can hire some of the teenagers from around here to work the traps with us, come crab season. Heard Tanner Dylan dropped out of school."

"He's not going to want to work with us, Mom." Sunny's face flushed a deep red. "Please don't ask him."

If Tanner was one of the boys who'd been teasing Sunny about her height and size, Bisky would tan him herself. She lifted her hands. "I said maybe. We need to find some help. If you have better ideas, tell me, because I'm not keeping you out of school."

She paused to look out over the Chesapeake Bay and a feeling of peace settled over her heart. The bay was the love of her life. Which was fortunate, since no man had ever stuck around long enough to fit that bill. Not that she minded. Bisky was too independent, she'd been told, but it had always served her well.

Usually. Not always.

She shook off a stab of melancholy. Now that they were done oystering, the second half of March would give them a rare break. Mostly, they'd spend the next couple of weeks scraping down and repainting the hull of their boat and trading out the dredging rig for the simpler setup they'd use for crabbing season.

It was increasingly hard to find a crew to work the water, and Bisky worried about her family business. Worried about a lot of things.

At the outdoor sink, she and Sunny washed their

hands, and then they both pulled their hair out of ponytails, shook it out. Bisky ran a hand over Sunny's brunette hair, removing a piece of oyster shell. "Don't worry, I won't ask Tanner if it embarrasses you. But if you think of anybody else who needs a job, send 'em my way."

If she could help out a needy teen in the process of hiring, she would. The community of Pleasant Shores had taken care of her and helped her out since she was a kid, and she tried to pay it forward.

"I'd know you as mother and daughter if I'd never met the pair of you before." The voice behind them came from Mary Rhoades, the energetic seventy-year-old philanthropist and bookstore owner who was one of Bisky's closest friends. She approached with her dog, Coco, a young chocolate-colored goldendoodle who was as tall as Mary's waist, but lanky. Coco let out a bark, but remained at Mary's side. Clearly, her training was coming along.

"Hey, Mary." Sunny turned and smiled at the older woman. "No, don't hug me, I need a shower. And Mom needs one too," she added, wrinkling her nose at Bisky. Then she knelt down to pet Coco. The big dog promptly rolled onto her back, offering her belly for Sunny to rub.

Bisky pulled a plastic lawn chair forward for Mary and then flopped back down on the bench. "Have a seat. I'm too tired to stand up talking."

"I will, just for a few minutes," Mary said. "I'm supposed to meet the new Victory Cottage resident this morning. Hoping he'll take on the therapy dog program. If not, I'll have to advertise for someone." As one of Pleasant Shores's major benefactors, Mary had started many useful programs in town, including her latest, a respite cottage for victims of violent crimes and their families. Victory Cottage was a place for them to heal, volunteer in the community and find new hope.

"Don't advertise for someone," Sunny said with more energy than she'd shown all day. "I can do it. I can start the therapy dog program."

Mary raised her eyebrows, frowned and then patted Sunny's hand. "You're good with dogs, for sure. Just look how Coco loves you. But I need an adult for this."

"But—"

Mary cut off Sunny's protest. "There are legal requirements and regulations. And anyway, you need to be a kid, not take on more work."

"She's never had the chance to be a kid," Bisky said, sighing. "And it's my fault." Money had always been tight, and Bisky had the business to look after. Sunny had started early with cooking, cleaning, doing laundry and serving as Bisky's assistant on the boat. No wonder she was strong and assertive, just like Bisky was.

"It's not like you have people pounding down your door to work in Pleasant Shores," Sunny argued now.

"I have connections, if the Victory Cottage resident doesn't work out," Mary said.

"When he doesn't, and you can't get an adult to take the job, you know where to find me," Sunny said, just on the edge of disrespect. She gave Mary's dog a final ear rub and then headed across the street and toward the house.

"Sorry she's sassy," Bisky said. "Getting up at the crack of dawn puts her in a mood."

"*Aaanddd* the apple doesn't fall far from the tree," Mary observed, watching Sunny depart. "She got her sassiness from you, and it's a useful trait in a woman."

"It can be. I'm glad she's not afraid of her shadow like some kids."

Mary nodded. "You've raised her well. No doubt she *could* start a therapy dog program. She could probably run the high school or Salty's Seafood Company if she wanted to."

"You're right, she could." Bisky watched Sunny walk toward the house, holding her phone to her ear as she jabbered with one of her friends, and a wave of mother-love nearly overwhelmed her. "Raising her is the best thing I ever did."

"Of course it is." Mary's voice was a little pensive, and it made Bisky remember that Mary had had a daughter and lost her.

"So tell me about this new guy who's coming to Victory Cottage," Bisky said, trying to change the subject.

Mary ran a hand over Coco's furry head, and the dog sat down, leaning against Mary. "He's from here, actually. And he has a sad story, but that's his to tell." She frowned. "I just hope that the support system we've put into place will work. He's set up with counseling, and the cottage is a dream, but I'm still unsure about what volunteer gig he'll be best suited for." Volunteering was an integral part of the Victory Cottage program, just as it was in Mary's other program, the Healing Heroes project.

At the dock beside them, an old skiff putted in, and eighty-year-old Rooker Smits gave a nod as he threw a rope to his five-year-old great-grandson, who'd been waiting to tie up the boat. Rooker waved to the boy's mom, who was dressed in a waitress uniform, obviously headed for work now that Rooker was back to help with childcare.

Like many watermen from these parts, Rooker didn't talk much, but he'd give the coat off his back to her or Sunny or any neighbor. Now, he and his great-grandson tossed scraps from the oysters he'd culled into the bay. Gulls swooped and cawed around them, drawn by the remnants of a day's fishing.

The smell of brackish water and fish mingled with that of the newly fertile March soil. Spring was coming, Bisky's favorite season. Maybe she'd plant some flowers later today, if she could find the energy to get to the hardware store for seeds.

She stretched and yawned. "Boy, that change to daylight savings is a tough one," she said. "I'm like Sunny, probably going to need a nap today."

"You work too hard," Mary said. "And speaking of work, I should be on my way. Lots to do." She stood and hugged Bisky against her protests—Sunny had been right, Bisky needed a shower—and then she and Coco walked off toward town.

Bisky stood and stretched her back. At thirty-seven, she was starting to feel the aches and pains of a lifetime's physical work. She loved what she did, loved the water, but it took its toll.

She spent a few minutes wiping down her rig, did the minimum she could get away with and then called it a job done. Not well done, but done. As she crossed the road, heading for her house, she glanced in the direction Mary had gone.

A tall figure walked slowly down the middle of

the road. So tall and broad-shouldered that she had to look twice at him, because it wasn't anyone from around here.

Or rather...

She stared, then took an involuntary step toward the man, unable to believe what she was seeing. It looked like her beloved childhood friend William Gross, only that wasn't possible. After the sudden way he'd left, she'd never expected him to come back to Pleasant Shores.

As William walked the familiar and yet strange road toward the home he'd successfully escaped almost twenty years ago, he heard a man's shout. "Look out, boy! I told you not to play by those..."

William cringed, an instant flashback to his childhood here: his father's yelling and the likely painful aftermath. He snapped back to the present and turned in time to see a huge pile of crab traps teetering near a boy of five or six, who was poking at a small crayfish on the dock. The child didn't even glance up.

William bolted toward the child and swept him up just as the big wire boxes crashed to the ground.

A couple of the traps bounced against William's back, and he tightened his hands on the boy's waist, holding him high and safe. As the clatter died away, William blinked, studied the startled-looking boy to ensure he wasn't injured, and then deposited the child in front of the old man who'd shouted. "Is he yours?"

"He's my great-grandson, and he's not to be playin' around this close to the docks or the water. And that's why." He gestured at the cluttered heap of crab traps.

"Come on, boy, you can help me clean up the mess you made."

Fair enough. William was just glad the kid wasn't going to get a beating. "Need any help?"

The old man looked at him. "No, the boy needs to learn. Sure do appreciate your pulling him out of harm's way." He cocked his head, studying William. "You look like a kid used to live here, name of Gross."

William held out a hand. "That's me, William Gross." He tilted his head to one side. "And you're… Mr. Smits?"

"Guess you're old enough to call me Rooker." The old man shook hands and studied William, curiosity in his sharp blue eyes. "Been awhile." He limped over to the cluttered traps, ushering the boy in front of him.

"You sure I can't help you straighten out these traps?"

"We got it. Get to work, boy," he told his great-grandson, and then turned back to William. "Heard you're living in the city."

"Uh-huh," William said. "Nice talking to you." He wove his way through the fallen crab traps before the man could ask any more questions.

When he got back to the street, he stood a minute, processing what had just happened. Three college degrees and twenty years had changed him a lot, but the local people would still think of him as the big, gawky kid from a bad family. He'd have to figure out how to deal with that.

The sun was at its peak now, casting a surprisingly warm light that made William slide out of his sports jacket and sling it over his shoulder. Just being here made him think he shouldn't wear a sports jacket, anyway. He felt pretentious, dressed up, here on the docks.

He wasn't even sure why he'd come. The docks were like a magnet, even though the memories they evoked were anything but pleasant.

"William?" came a soft voice behind him. A voice that brought him back to laughter on sparkling water, and catching crayfish, and good meals around the table of a family that actually liked each other.

He turned and studied the tall brunette who stood before him. She wore work clothes, and she was older than the last time he'd seen her, but he'd never forget the eyes and the smile of his childhood best friend. "Bisky Castleman?"

"It *is* you!" She flung herself at him and hugged him fiercely.

She was tall for a woman, and more muscular than she'd been in school. Still, she was the first woman he'd held in two years and the hug felt good. Having a friend felt good, and was something he needed to try to cultivate, now that he'd sworn off love.

They let each other go, finally, and stepped back.

"Where have you been, and what are you doing back?" Bisky asked. "I heard you were teaching in a college."

"I was." The casual way she asked the question told him she didn't know what had happened. "Life's dealt a few blows, and I'm here for an R&R break." He tried to keep the words light.

She didn't buy it. "Come over here and sit down," she said, taking his hand and drawing him toward the same old fishing shack her family had always had. There was the same bench outside it, a little more weathered than he remembered. "Tell me what's going on, because I know it would take a lot to bring you back to Pleasant Shores."

"I appreciated your note when Mama died," he said instead of starting up the story of where he'd been and what all he'd been doing, what had transpired.

"I'm glad my note found you. No one seemed to have a recent address."

"I've lost touch." He looked out over the bay, watched a pelican dip, snag a fish, and carry it away.

"Heard you had a daughter. Couple of years older than my Sunny, so she must be, what, eighteen?"

She definitely didn't know. He glanced at her and then shook his head. "Not anymore," he said through a tight throat.

It had been two years, and he still couldn't talk about it. Still hadn't really processed it, and that was why his department head at the college had teamed up with someone from HR to find this program for him. It was his last chance to heal before he'd lose his job that he'd gotten worse and worse at.

He'd agreed to do the program despite its location, because Mama was gone and his father had moved away. He wanted to heal for the sake of his students, who'd come to be his whole world.

But those of his students who'd gotten too close had seen the ugly, damaged side of him, had scraped his emotions raw. He couldn't let that happen again. Couldn't let anyone get too close.

He had to make sure that these people who'd known him in younger days didn't worm their way into his heart.

"What happened to her?" Bisky asked quietly.

He'd dodged that question a million times, but for some reason, he couldn't dodge it when it came from Bisky. He cleared his throat, hard. "She was shot by an intruder who broke in to steal a TV. She was taking a nap and surprised him, from what the police could figure out."

Bisky's face contorted with horror she didn't try to hide. "You poor, poor man," she said, tears in her voice and eyes.

"Don't feel for me, feel for her." He didn't deserve the sympathy of Bisky or anyone.

She ignored that. "As a mother, I can only imagine...oh, William." She leaned close and hugged him again.

Maybe it was because of the familiar, salty smell of her, or the fact that she knew him from childhood, but something broke off inside William then, a tiny piece of his grief. His throat ached and tears rose to his eyes, even though he tensed all his muscles trying to hold them back.

"You can cry in front of me," she said, patting his back as if *he* were the child. "It wouldn't be the first time."

She was right about that. He remembered, then, the rabbit he'd kept as a pet, what his father had done to it, and how he'd beaten William for crying. William must have been seven or eight, and he'd run to his best friend for comfort. She'd hugged him and cried with him then, just like now.

He pulled out his bandanna, wiped his eyes and blew his nose. Then he smiled at her, a real if watery smile. "Thanks. I guess I needed that," he said.

"You're here for the Victory Cottage program." It wasn't a question.

He nodded. "The woman who runs it wanted to seek out people who had a connection with this place. I'm the perfect candidate according to her." He quirked his mouth to show Bisky he didn't think he was perfect at anything.

"You are," she said thoughtfully. "There are plenty of people who'll be glad to see you."

"That I doubt," he said. "My family wasn't the most popular."

"No, but most folks knew you were cut from a different cloth. Come inside." She gestured toward the house across the road, where her family had always lived. "I'll make pancakes and coffee. Sunny could use a meal, and I could, too."

The thought of sitting around the table with Bisky and her daughter—her alive and healthy daughter— tightened a vise around William's insides. "Thanks for the invitation," he said, "but I won't be able to. I need to get going." He ignored the puzzlement in Bisky's eyes as he turned and strode away.

He couldn't let himself get that close, feel that much.

Don't miss Home to the Harbor,
the next book in Lee Tobin McClain's
The Off Season series!